MIRACLE

OF THE

TALKING

STICK

Also by Felix F. Giordano

Montana Harvest

Mystery at Little Bitterroot

The Killing Zone

Missing in Montana

For more information go to:

jbnovels.com

Miracle
of the
Talking Stick

A Novel in

The Jim Buchanan Series

Felix F. Giordano

Red Road Publishers

Ashford, Connecticut

RRP

Published in the United States by Red Road Publishers, PO Box 460 Ashford, CT—www.redroadpublishers.com

Copyright © 2021 by Felix F. Giordano

http://jbnovels.com

First Edition 2021,
All Rights Reserved

Miracle of the Talking Stick, a Jim Buchanan Novel

Front and back cover art: plbmdesign.com
ISBN: 978-0-990568-44-5

Registration Number, U.S. Copyright Office: TXu002235900
U.S. Copyright Office Case #: 1-9628893501
Library of Congress Control Number: 2020921637

Printed in the United States of America
Available from Amazon.com and other retailers

10 9 8 7 6 5 4 3 2 1

"They are not dead who live in the hearts they leave behind"

– Tuscarora proverb

"We will be known forever by the tracks we leave"

– Dakota Indian proverb

"There is no death,
Only a change of worlds"

-- Chief Seattle (Seath),
Duwamish-Suquamish, 1785-1866

Readers can find supporting information for the locations and characters in my novels by going to my website:

jbnovels.com

There you will find two individual web pages with the headings:

<u>FICTIONAL CEDAR COUNTY</u> –

- Maps of fictional Cedar County
- a list of community organizations, businesses, and facilities
- a diagram of the Cedar County Sheriff's Office

<u>CHARACTERS OF THE JIM BUCHANAN NOVELS</u> –

- Photos & bios of the fictional main characters in my novels

Miracle of the Talking Stick is dedicated to:

Martin "Marty" Friedberg - husband, father, WWII vet & war hero

1926-2018

Through sheer willpower, Marty's thirst for knowledge and his leadership skills were evident when he became a blueprint interpreter at the age of 16 at Electric Boat in 1942. There he taught other employees that were much older to read blueprints and apply that knowledge to submarine construction. That innate drive was accentuated by his fearlessness in 1944 when, at the tender age of 18, he rejected a draft waiver for building submarines for the war effort and instead enlisted in the U.S. Army. Marty then demanded a poor eyesight waiver to become an infantryman. His less than 20/20 vision did not deter him from qualifying as a sharpshooter and becoming a Grenadier. Marty served in the European Theater during WWII and captured three Nazi officers singlehanded. After the war, Marty was assigned to an artillery division where he was responsible for coordinating radio communication. In civilian life, Marty became an expert in photography and electronics and constructed his own darkroom. He also established his own refrigeration business and then went on to begin a more than thirty-year career at Pratt & Whitney Aircraft. There, Marty was renowned for his accuracy, work ethic, and loyalty. He quickly rose up the corporate ladder to become a supervisor and then was promoted to Foreman of an Instrumentation Lab. During Marty's retirement years he and I became quite close. He took a serious interest in my writing and helped me with technical questions related to my novels regarding weaponry, ballistics, aircraft, mechanics, and radio communication among others. I can say with heartfelt gratitude that as my father-in-law, Marty was my best friend.

Marty is the inspiration for a character in this novel:
Detective Martin "Marty" Aronowitz

MALLORY MONTANA –

WHERE MISSING PERSONS GO TO DIE

·1·

When people began disappearing from Mallory Montana, it turned a once vibrant town into a pit of despair. Mind you, it wasn't just the disappearances that frightened the populace but the circumstances surrounding those disappearances. It pierced the hearts of the townspeople and caused some to not venture out alone at night. The once proud town of more than six-thousand was reduced to just over four-thousand citizens.

People with the resources were able to move to other towns such as Taylor, the governing seat of Cedar County. The toll of the human exodus from Mallory resulted in an impoverished populace, shuttered businesses, and a town in a downward spiral.

To explain the vanishings, many local citizens adopted a centuries-old, local Native American legend. Moon Man or *Saka'am Skaltamiax* as the Flathead Indians called him. He was a malevolent entity that dwelled in the deep hidden caverns of Great Northern Mountain. His lair existed within the vast and dense Kootenai National Forest near Howard Lake. According to the legend, *Saka'am Skaltamiax* would hunt tribal members at night for their flesh and bones. He would devour them except for their eyes and display them in his cave so that his victims would forever see *Saka'am Skaltamiax's* new trophies. Or so the elders would tell the little ones to keep them from wandering outside after dark.

Others believed it was the work of Hamilton Jackson, a Canadian doctor arrested a few years earlier for murder and procuring body parts. But it was neither.

On Sunday, June 29, 1997, a few minutes before midnight under clear, moonlit skies, beneath the cover of an aspen tree at the far end of a parking lot in an apartment complex, was a dark colored panel van. With glass only on the driver's and passenger doors and front windshield, the lack of side and rear windows offered a concealed environment for the van's occupant to work. Inside the vehicle, a man in a black balaclava and a pair of black work coveralls sat in the driver's seat. He raised a pair of binoculars to his face and kept his eyes peeled on apartment number 9. On his left chest pocket was imprinted the scripted nametag, *Charlie.*

He put down the binoculars and then mumbled under his breath, "I hate this fucking town, and I hate the fucking people...especially the damn Indians. Why don't they goddamn stay on their own reservations and stop mingling with us?"

Then he noticed the front door to apartment number 9 open. He again raised the binoculars to his face. A man with long black hair tied into a ponytail stepped outside.

The man in the van said, "Goddamn unemployed Gary Driver, lazy good-for-nothing Indian. And his stupid Indian wife, Janice thinks she's going to amount to something...a nurse, my ass."

The man spied Gary Driver as he climbed into the only car the Drivers owned, an old Chevrolet Vega that somehow hadn't yet rusted through and through. Gary backed out of his assigned parking spot and drove out of the parking lot.

The man sensed the car would be gone for a few hours just as it had nearly every week for the past six months. He knew that Gary waited at home every Sunday night until Janice returned from a day spent studying at the Taylor University Library. He even sometimes followed a comfortable distance behind the Vega on Janice's half-hour ride from Taylor to Mallory. The man noticed that because the Drivers had only one car, Gary would leave the house after Janice arrived. He assumed that was because Gary was cooped up inside all day.

The man scanned the other apartments. All was quiet since most residents had since gone to sleep. The Drivers' apartment still had its lights on. He was certain that Janice was alone and preparing for bed.

When the downstairs lights from the Drivers' apartment went out, the man stepped toward the back of the darkened van. Using a small flashlight to guide his way, he walked past

2

the 32-gallon plastic trash bin, and opened a large wooden ammo box with the words <u>U.S. Army</u> imprinted on the lid. The man reached inside and pulled on a pair of black disposable latex gloves and slip-on booties. Next, he used industrial tape to seal off the airflow for added protection of his wrists and ankles.

On a separate shelf, the man unzipped a U.S. Army WW2 parachute cargo bag. He grabbed an industrial-strength garbage can liner, shook it open, and then placed it into the trash can.

Then he pulled out a zippered body bag and a 21-inch Bowie Knife with its solid brass guard and pommel. A wandering beam from the waning crescent moon's faint light that penetrated the van's windshield reflected off the full tang, 15-inch, razor-sharp, carbon steel blade.

The man got out of the van with the knife and body bag and sped toward the building. He slithered along the outer wall and when he reached the front door of apartment number 9, he simply knocked on the door.

A voice from inside the apartment said, "Gary, what have you forgotten now?"

When the door opened the man thrust a foot against the bottom of the door and then pushed the door open the rest of the way. He used a firm, two-handed grasp and swung the Bowie knife upward like a sword across Janice's neck as she tried to back away. The diamond-sharpened blade caused a deep incised wound as it sliced through Janice's larynx and rendered her unable to speak or scream. As blood spurted from her throat, she reached for her neck, staggered, and then fell backwards onto the floor. As Janice shook and rolled in pain, she descended into a state of shock from the hemorrhaged blood. Janice entered a stage of no return when she began to asphyxiate from her own aspirated blood.

The man closed the door and was on top of her in an instant. He pulled her onto her back and drove the Bowie knife's blade deep into her chest and penetrated her left lung. When it struck bone, he pulled it out and then plunged it deeper into Janice's body with such force that the tip of the knife struck the hardwood floor. He then jerked it out and thrust the long, sharp knife into her abdomen and ripped it upward, spilling her bowels onto the floor. He then turned Janice over and repeatedly stabbed her back. Blood sprayed into the air and spattered onto the floor, walls, and furniture.

Felix F. Giordano

When Janice's body went limp, the man laid flat the zippered body bag. After the life had left Janice and with the body bag next to her corpse, the man shoved her into the bag, scooped up her entrails, and plopped them onto the open wound in her abdomen. He gazed at her face and glared at her open eyes that stared at the ceiling. The man then picked up the Bowie knife, carved out both of Janice's eyes, and set them onto the coffee table in the living room. Then he zippered shut the body bag, grabbed for the custom hook toward the head of the bag, and hauled it out of the house.

He dragged the body bag toward the van, opened the back doors, and lifted it inside. Then the man climbed into the van, closed the doors, and removed the booties and coveralls. He dropped the bloody garments into the open trash bin, pulled off the gloves, tossed them into the bin, and closed the lid. With the balaclava still on, he climbed into the driver's seat and drove off.

*****

Early that Monday morning around 12:30 a.m., a dark van turned into a parking lot at the entrance to the Howard Lake Recreation Area. It continued past the black and white sign that read, <u>Park Closed From Sunset To Sunrise</u> and drove deep into the campground and then up to campsite number 9. A man by the name of Mac Drew opened the door and stood on the running board with his left arm leaned against the driver's door and his right arm draped over the van's roof. In his right hand was a bloodstained Bowie knife.

Amid an eerie silence in the van and with a smile on his face, Mac gazed inside toward the back of the darkened vehicle and said, "Stay put girly girl. I ain't done having my way with you. The fun is just about to begin."

Mac laughed hard and long, slammed the door shut, and walked toward his yellow tent.

4

·2·

Early that same Monday morning, Alma Rose Two Elk popped up in bed. Startled from a deep sleep, she sat with the sheet held under her chin and shivered. Although it was late June, there was a clammy feeling to the air in the darkened bedroom. After she rubbed the sand from her eyes, she surveyed the space and felt a strange uneasiness. She glanced at her nightstand and stared at the greenlit display on her alarm clock. It read 2:37 a.m.

It took her a few seconds to remember where she was. The reality of reservation life and its sense of hardship on the high plains of the Crow Reservation in south central Montana were in her rear-view mirror. It was replaced by the pervasive awareness of her father's affluent and comfortable lifestyle in the western Montana town of Taylor, deep in the Rockies near the Idaho border.

That sense of privilege was provided partly by the financial security from her father's former landmark career in the NFL and his noteworthy status as Cedar County Sheriff.

Alma Rose collected her thoughts and remembered that she had heard an unfamiliar voice call to her during her dreams. She got up and shut the window. As she turned back toward the bed, she noticed a glimmer of light from the hallway peek out from under the closed bedroom door.

She rushed toward the door and opened it. An eerie silence enveloped the house. She stared down the hallway at her father and stepmother's bedroom. Their door was closed. Then Alma Rose noticed a flicker of light from downstairs.

She made her way to the staircase and that's when she saw it. A four-foot by four-foot jagged sheet of pure white light hovered four feet off the ground and one-foot from the ceiling. It seemed to consist of an impenetrable dense light but at the same time it was wafer-thin. There was no noise, no sound, just silence. Alma Rose gazed at it and sensed that it returned her stare. Then it sped away from her in an instant.

She ran down the last few steps and then scanned the great room toward the back door. A wisp of light streaked past a side table and through a brown pot designed in the Mandan style of pottery of the Great Plains Indians. The pot teetered and then fell to the floor where it shattered into more than a dozen pieces. Then the light slipped through the screen of an open window and was gone.

Alma Rose stood in the threshold between the great room and kitchen and wondered what she had just witnessed. Then she felt a hand on her shoulder, and it made her jump. She turned and came face-to-face with her father, Sheriff Jim Buchanan.

"Alma Rose, what are you doing up this early?"

"I saw something."

He looked past her and asked, "Is someone outside?"

"No dad. It was in the house, but it's gone now."

"Who was in the house?"

"No one, it was a spirit."

"Oh, Alma Rose." Jim walked over to the living room couch and sat down. "You just got home from the hospital on Saturday. You had a concussion. Your mind is playing tricks on you." He glanced around the room. "There's nothing here."

"There was, dad. Look at the bowl on the ground."

Jim glanced at the floor and the pottery fragments. "That was handed down to Sarah Whispers by your grandmother. You must have bumped into it while you were half-awake."

"No dad. I was at the bottom of the stairs when I saw the light knock it off the table."

"What light?" Jim asked.

"The light in the house…Dad, a spirit visited us."

"What spirit?"

Alma Rose sat next to him on the couch. She looked up at him and said, "It was a Native woman."

"Who?"

Alma Rose spoke in a slow and deliberate voice. "That's what we have to find out." Then she said, "I have to grab my journal."

·3·

At 4:10 a.m., Alma Rose adjusted her crisp, newly ironed Khaki shirt and olive-green trousers of her Cedar County Sheriff's Department uniform. She couldn't go back to sleep after her early morning encounter with an ethereal specter. Instead, she showered and dressed for her big day. As she lifted the gold-shaded nametag off the bureau, she stared at the embossed last name.

It read, TWO ELK. She pinned it to the right side of her shirt just above the pocket. Across from that nametag, over her left pocket was the gold badge of the Cedar County Sheriff's Office with its seven-pointed star.

Alma Rose was a tall, slim nineteen-year old with waist-length black hair braided into a ponytail. Her hazel eyes with their combination of green, gold, and brown colors hinted at her mixed-blood Crow Indian heritage. Fresh out of high school, she was anxious to jumpstart her college career. She insisted to her father that she continue with the plan to spend the summer working as an intern in the sheriff's office.

It had only been four days since her encounter with the Screaming Skulls, an outlaw biker gang. A severe beating she endured from the gang's leader, Videl Tanas in the Yaak Wilderness, left her bloodied and with a slight concussion.

After she was released from Taylor University Medical Center, Alma Rose spurned the medication prescribed by the hospital emergency room doctor. Instead she relied on her own medicine bag to maintain the harmony and balance in the three worlds that she perceived around her.

Sleep deprivation overwhelmed her but it was a difficult night at her dad's house. It was bad enough she experienced an encounter with an otherworldly visitor. However, she also faced the uncertainty and stress of her upcoming first day as a junior officer in the Cedar County Sheriff's Office.

Her thoughts drifted to something her father said a few days ago while she was still in the hospital. He argued that as an incoming freshman at the University of Montana she would have numerous opportunities to serve the internship. Taking this summer off would allow her a smooth transition to college life.

But Alma Rose would have none of that. She rationalized that her father's objection was the result of him finding out about the summer internship on short notice. Alma Rose explained to him that she was obligated to the terms of her full scholarship in the Criminal Justice Studies program. If she did not serve the internship prior to the upcoming fall semester she would lose the advanced credits the program provided.

She adjusted her brown necktie and then put on her Stratton brown felt campaign hat. Gazing into the mirror, she nodded approval. She lifted one foot onto a wooden stool to polish her steel-toed, Gore-Tex blacktop boot with a facecloth. She then did the same with the other boot.

Alma Rose grabbed her journal and walked downstairs. At the bottom of the staircase, she was accosted by the family pet. Angel was a four-year old female German Shorthaired Pointer who'd been a member of Jim and Kate's family since she was a puppy. When Alma Rose stooped to pet Angel, she felt a cold wet nose nudge her hand from behind. The nose belonged to Shadow, a two-year old male German Shepherd. He was rescued from Videl Tanas' biker gang earlier this year. When Alma Rose petted both dogs, they overwhelmed her with kisses.

"Angel…Shadow, here!" Jim yelled from the kitchen. The two dogs ran to him.

When Alma Rose entered the kitchen, she noticed Jim and his wife Kate seated at the table. Beyond them was the wraparound picture window in the corner of the expansive kitchen with its panoramic views of mountain vistas. On the table, a pile of scrambled eggs dominated one serving dish while a stack of French toast occupied another.

"Coffee?" Kate asked with a smile.

"Sure," Alma Rose said and then took a seat. She noticed her father's stare. "What?" she asked.

"You should take off those dangly earrings."

8

"Why?" Alma Rose asked. "Cousin Becca made them and I bought them from her with my own money."

Jim said, "They're inappropriate for the job. I got the mayor's office to agree to a uniform concession on your braided hair, earrings would be pushing the department regs."

Alma Rose stared at her father's shoulder-length hair gathered into a ponytail. "You have long hair."

Jim smiled and took a cup of coffee from Kate and placed it in front of Alma Rose. "I do have long hair but trust me I wouldn't look good in earrings."

Alma Rose said with a wink, "Well, maybe just one earring?"

Her comment drew laughter from Jim and Kate. Alma Rose removed the sterling silver earrings and then stared at them in her hands. Each earring had two large sterling silver clamshell disks with strands of smaller dangling clamshell disks. She stuck the earrings in her fringed leather purse. When everyone's plates and mugs were full, Jim reached out and clasped hands with Kate and Alma Rose.

Jim recited, "Dear Creator, thank You for the gracious blessings of this nourishment and our good health to enjoy it. Also, thank You for the opportunity for us to experience this as a family. Amen."

"Are you ready for some real police work?" Kate asked.

Alma Rose swallowed a sip of coffee. "I'm really looking forward to it." Glancing at her father she said, "I'm just so grateful for the chance to spend this summer with my dad."

"Kate starts something new as well," Jim said.

Alma Rose turned to Kate and asked, "What's that?"

Kate smiled. "I'm teaching music at the university."

"At Taylor University?" Alma Rose asked.

"No, the University of Montana." Kate said.

Jim added. "Kate's driving there today. What did you say today is?"

"It's a summer school class. Classical Guitar 101, the Basics of Finger Picking," Kate said with a smile. "It's just a one-time, ninety-minute class. I'll be back home later this afternoon."

"That's great! I'm so happy for you," Alma Rose said. Then she asked, "Can you get a campus map for me? I can use one when I start school this fall."

Kate smiled. "Of course I can."

"If it wasn't for you, Kate would never have seen this day," Jim said.

Alma Rose replied, "I just wish that I could have also…"

Jim interrupted her, "Please Alma Rose. We don't speak his name in this house. He's buried in the eastern side of our mountain. His body feels the sunrise warm the earth around him every day."

Alma Rose reached out to Kate and touched her hand. "I'm so sorry."

Kate wiped away a tear. "God has different plans for us all. Maybe He doesn't have plans for me to be a parent."

Alma Rose said, "But you would be such a great parent. I know that I couldn't ask for a better stepmother than you."

Kate put her head down and covered her eyes with her right hand. She began to openly weep.

Alma Rose got up from her seat and stepped over to Kate. She placed her arm on Kate's shoulder and said, "I'm sorry. I didn't mean to make you cry."

Kate reached back with her right hand and touched Alma Rose's arm. She sniffed and then said, "It's…it's all right. It's not your fault. It's me." Kate glanced at Jim. "Maybe I should see that therapist again?"

Jim said, "Kate, let's not harbor on what could have been and instead concentrate on what could be."

As Kate nodded, Alma Rose went back to her seat.

Then Jim turned to Alma Rose and asked, "You're still in training to be the Crow Tribe's Shaman, correct?"

"*Akbaalia* dad, *Akbaalia*. We *Apsáalooke* don't use the word shaman."

Jim nodded, "I'm sorry. I'll remember to say *Akbaalia*."

"Dad, do you even remember your *Apsáalooke* name, *Issaxchí-Káata*?" Alma Rose felt Jim stare straight into her hazel eyes.

Jim said, "I'm afraid there isn't much Crow left in me. Not many refer to me by my Native name, much less its English equivalent, Little Hawk."

Alma Rose grasped her father's hand and squeezed it. "Dad, you have been away from the Rez for far too long."

Kate grounded the conversation and remarked, "Alma Rose, all I know is that you saved my life."

"I had to do it. I felt compelled to do something." A blush overtook Alma Rose's cheeks. "The elders don't look kindly at what I did."

"Why not?" asked Kate.

"It was outside the sanction of the tribe."

Kate remarked, "You worked a miracle. I would have died in that hospital two years ago if not for your healing. Willie Otaktay was dead in the Yaak last week and you revived him."

"It wasn't me."

"Pfft," Kate scoffed. "If not, then who?"

Alma Rose confessed, "I get a feeling…a voice telling me what to do and how to do it."

Kate adjusted her posture in the chair. "I just got chills up my spine."

Alma Rose asked Kate, "Did dad tell you what happened last night?"

Kate stared at Jim. "What happened?"

Jim shrugged. "Nothing. Alma Rose heard something."

Kate turned to Alma Rose. "What did you hear?"

Alma Rose said, "I woke up around 2:30 and…"

Jim broke into the conversation. "Alma Rose, when you were in the hospital, you said that Grandma Jenny Nightstar gave you a new copy of that book, *Chakras of the American Indians*."

"She did," Alma Rose said.

"How is that possible?" Kate asked.

Alma Rose put down her coffee cup. "She came to me."

Jim took a deep breath. "Grandma Jenny Nightstar Two Elk has passed on to the long quiet. However, I have no doubt that she visited you when you were in the hospital. What I don't understand is how could someone from the other side bring you an actual physical book?"

Alma Rose smiled. "Because it's bound to her spirit."

"How can something like a book come into our world from somewhere else?" he asked.

"Dad, we live in the midst of three worlds and they are interconnected."

Jim stared at Kate who shrugged her shoulders. "What three worlds are you talking about?" he asked.

"There's the physical world, the spiritual world, and then there's the supernatural world. There are three worlds, dad."

Jim shook his head. "I don't understand."

11

"Dad, I know you don't." Alma Rose took a bite of her scrambled eggs. The silence was deafening and then she stared at her father. "Don't worry dad, someday you will."

After they finished their breakfast, Alma Rose got up from the table, grabbed her journal, and walked toward the front door.

·4·

Clouds that would soon burn off from the heat of the rising sun marred the eastern vistas over the Cabinet Mountain Range. It was now 5:25 a.m. and Jim intended to get an early start. He was a strapping, six-foot-five, thirty-five-year-old with penetrating green eyes and shoulder-length brown hair tied into a ponytail.

He was a former professional football defensive end who chose to retire in 1986 after a devastating knee injury. A subsequent four-year hitch in the U.S. Air Force as a military policeman introduced Jim to law enforcement.

Upon his honorable discharge, Jim began a two-year service with the Montana Highway Patrol and was assigned the Fort Benton to Havre patrol route.

In 1993, upon Cedar County Sheriff Dan McCoy's retirement, Jim ran for the open vacancy. He won a close election that many say was influenced by ballots cast on the Flathead Indian Reservation by his fellow Native Americans.

Today, Jim's plan was to provide Alma Rose a quick tour of the sheriff's office and then assign Undersheriff Rocky Salentino to her day's orientation. Standing on the front porch, Jim turned to Alma Rose and said, "I have a 6 a.m. meeting with agents Costa and Killian. You met them last week in the Yaak."

"You mean the bald guy and the biker with the long hair? Yeah, I remember them," Alma Rose said.

Jim shook his head in an almost imperceptible manner and then continued, "Good, I'll drop you off at the sheriff's office and get you squared away with your schedule before I leave. I'll be back in the afternoon."

Alma Rose asked, "Your meeting with the FBI will last all morning?"

"Only for an hour or two at Lucy's Luncheonette, then I'm attending a 10 a.m. funeral for the fallen officer from the Taylor Police Department."

Alma Rose asked, "Was he the officer that Videl Tanas murdered outside Jia Li's apartment?"

Jim nodded. "He was parked outside Billy's Bar to provide security for Jia Li. Tanas shot him point blank in the face."

Alma Rose asked, "Will he pay for what he did...he killed others too, right?"

Jim raised his eyebrows and again nodded. "Yes. He's a violent sociopath. He almost killed you. Tanas is in the county jail. We're waiting for paperwork to process so he can be transferred to Helena for trial."

"When will that happen?" Alma Rose asked.

"It may take a few weeks...maybe up to a month. He left a trail of murdered victims across the state so every jurisdiction wants a piece of him. That's why they'll hold the trial at the state capital."

"Where's the officer's funeral?" Alma Rose asked.

"The services are at Mount Olive Lutheran Church. We've got nine different departments represented."

"I feel that I should go."

Jim shook his head. "No. The last thing I want is for a new officer to attend a funeral for a slain fellow officer. I want you to go to work today." Jim walked over to his county-issued SUV with Angel and Shadow. He opened the back hatch and said, "Kennel-up."

The two dogs leaped into the back cargo area which was separated from the rest of the SUV by a steel-mesh barrier. Jim shut the hatch, walked over to the driver's side, climbed inside, belted himself in, and started the engine. Alma Rose got in and adjusted her passenger side seat belt.

"Dad, about your meeting today with a..."

Jim laughed. "You mean with the bald guy and the biker dude?"

Alma Rose smiled. "Yes, doesn't the FBI meet other law enforcement officers in clandestine places?"

Jim held back a smirk and then glanced at her. "Where do you expect us to meet?"

Alma Rose titled her head as if in thought. "Well...like in some dark abandoned warehouse or in a basement garage, or maybe on a park bench. Not in a public and not in a luncheonette."

Jim laughed. "Alma Rose, you must be watching those secret agent movies."

"Really dad, aren't you putting yourself or the agents in danger meeting in public?"

Jim shook his head and stared at her. "Alma Rose, this is Taylor Montana, not New York City. Besides, the undercover agent is closing his case and he'll be leaving the area later today. As far as the luncheonette, someday I'll introduce you to Lucy Brown who runs the joint. No one goes into her establishment unless she knows exactly who they are and what's their business."

"I don't understand."

"Alma Rose listen, Lucy Brown used to be the police chief in town. Everyone in the county knows that plus she has only one rule. What is seen and spoken in her establishment stays in her establishment unless she deems otherwise. She doesn't take lightly to people spreading gossip especially if it's something that took place inside her luncheonette or was overheard in there. The county folk mostly bring concerns of goings-on to her and she passes them on to me or to the police department. But no one ever dares repeat something they heard in there to another citizen because it might get back to Lucy."

Alma Rose asked, "Besides her being a former police chief, what could she do now if something got back to her?"

Jim stared at Alma Rose square in the eye. "Lucy's a tough customer. She's participated in the past three Olympics as a powerlifter."

"Really, wow! Has she won anything?"

Jim said, "Bronze medal last year in Atlanta. Lucy Brown is 6-1 and a solid 210 pounds."

Alma Rose laughed. "Dad, that sounds like an excerpt from your NFL scouting report."

"How would you know about that sort of thing?" Jim asked.

"Dad, it's the age of the Internet. The 1984 NFL Scouting Combine in New Orleans. You ran a 4.68 forty at 6-5 ½ and 280 pounds. The guide said, limitless upside, perennial Pro-bowler, once in a lifetime player."

"Is that what they said?"

"Yeah dad, I memorized it. It went on to say, can have a lengthy pro career as long as he avoids major injury."

Jim took a deep breath and wiped the sweat from his face. "Yeah, well I guess they were right about that one."

Alma Rose turned to face him. "I'm…I'm sorry dad. Now I've gotten both Kate and you upset today. This is an awful start to my first day on the job. I didn't mean to…"

Jim interrupted her apology. "That's okay. Kate's coming to terms with what happened. I know she's thrilled to have you stay with us this summer." Then he stared deep into her eyes. "Kate loves you."

Alma Rose smiled. "I love you and Kate too."

As Jim started the engine, he said, "As for me, it was three seasons and out. My line coach for the Bears is trying to get a few other teams to give me a tryout. A washed up thirty-five-year-old defensive end with a bum knee isn't going to get a decent looksee from any teams."

Alma Rose smiled. "Dad, one door closes and another opens. Think about the lives you've saved as sheriff."

Jim didn't say a word but instead backed the SUV away from the house. As they drove down the driveway, Jim asked, "Why did you begin to tell Kate about what you saw in the middle of the night?"

"Why not, shouldn't Kate know?"

"Alma Rose, Kate is still recuperating from her illness. She doesn't need the added stress of what you saw."

"Her illness is gone."

Jim said, "Kate has to regain her strength."

"Dad, you can't protect her forever."

Jim gripped the steering wheel a bit tighter and spoke in a stern voice, "Alma Rose, I'm not protecting her. I'm just trying to make sure that she's strong enough to resume doing the things that she loves. Teaching music is one of those things."

"Dad, she'll be all right."

Jim glanced at Alma Rose. "You still didn't explain why you started to tell her about last night."

Alma Rose said, "She needs to know there was an entity in our house."

"Why do you think it would help her to know something like that?"

Alma Rose said, "So that she won't be fearful if she encounters it when she's alone."

·5·

Monday started out like any other early summer's day in Taylor Montana, a town with the civic infrastructure to support more than thirteen thousand residents. Settled in the late 19th century, Taylor was a jewel of a town in northwestern Montana. The hallmark of this town, besides being the government seat of Cedar County, was Taylor University. Situated on 634 mostly wooded acres on the southwest bank of the Clark Fork River, the school's coed student body comprised of 3,949 undergrads and a few hundred graduate students.

Access to town from all points was Taylor International Airport which served most major airlines. The building consisted of two concourses and one terminal. Attached at one end of the building was the Greyhound Bus Terminal with a few car rental agencies nearby.

At the other end was Union Station. A private railroad passenger service operated out of that station, the Western Montana Railway Company, or better known as WMRC. It connected Missoula with the greater Libby area. The tracks wound their way north through the scenic Bull River Valley and eventually connected with Amtrak service up on the highline just west of the town of Libby in the vast Burlington Northern Santa Fe freight yard in Troy Montana.

Taylor was indeed a travel hub. It witnessed significant business for those commuting to and from other neighboring towns like Missoula, Kalispell, Whitefish, and Columbia Falls. Taylor was dissected from southeast to northwest by U.S. 200 and the Clark Fork River which flowed parallel to the highway on its long westward journey to the Columbia River in eastern Washington State. Because of Taylor's significant location in northwestern Montana and its connections to the Idaho towns of

Sandpoint and Coeur d'Alene and also Spokane Washington, Taylor was bestowed with the unofficial title, "Gateway to all Points West".

Law enforcement in Cedar County consisted of the Cedar County Office of the State Crime Lab, the IX District Office of the Montana Highway Patrol, and of course the Cedar County Sheriff's Office. Supporting those agencies in Cedar County were local police departments in the towns of Taylor, Mallory, Spaulding, and Trout Hollow.

At the Cedar County Sheriff's Office most incoming calls to the dispatch desk consisted of coyote sightings, a few stray livestock, even a wildfire, or two that would pop up overnight in the heavily forested mountains on either side of the Clark Fork River.

However, the recent events that occurred at a certain apartment complex in Mallory would have a multitude of far-reaching ramifications not only for all of Cedar County but the entire state of Montana and beyond.

There were a few other cars in the Cedar County Sheriff's Office parking lot as Jim backed into his assigned spot. Cedar County dispatcher Sergeant Martha Wilson's car was parked in her reserved spot while Undersheriff Salentino's patrol car was next to the door, ready to hit the pavement upon receipt of a 911 call.

Jim asked Alma Rose, "Are you ready for your first day?"

She glanced at her father and then responded, "Ready as I ever will be."

Jim shut off the engine and faced his daughter. "With all the craziness that went on in the Yaak and the short lead time provided by the University of Montana regarding your internship, I haven't reviewed with you what your schedule will look like."

Alma Rose smiled. "Oh dad, I'm just happy to be involved in something that I've dreamed about my entire life."

Jim said, "I want you to take it slow. The doctor said your concussion was very mild and by tomorrow you should be able to resume normal activities. Today, no running or jumping and don't fall. Now, your orientation schedule will consist of two days of patrol ride-alongs."

"I'm eager for it."

Jim stared at her for a moment and then continued. "Undersheriff Salentino will be your training supervisor. You'll report to him and he'll be responsible for evaluating your performance."

"I thought I'd be shadowing you?"

"Alma Rose, the University of Montana requires that a nonrelative conduct your supervision. You and I are not allowed any professional interaction."

Alma Rose was at first silent and then said, "I guess that's okay. I know Rocky so we'll get along well."

"That's another thing. You should get used to calling him Undersheriff Rocco Salentino."

"But dad, I've always known him as Rocky. He's like an uncle to me."

"When you're alone in a vehicle you can still call him Rocky but in the office, in the presence of other officers, or on radio calls, you need to at least refer to him as Undersheriff Salentino."

After a few seconds of silence, Alma Rose winked. "All right, Sheriff Buchanan."

Jim let out a muffled chuckle and Alma Rose burst out laughing with a huge grin across her face.

Jim continued, "You'll also be assigned to spend one day with administration services, court services, youth services, and animal control. Also, one day each of community policing, criminal and traffic court, media relations, evidence training and criminal investigation, dispatch, and self-defense training."

Alma Rose turned to him and said, "Dad, that's ten whole days of training. When does the real police work begin?"

"That's a two-week schedule that will be repeated throughout the summer until your eight-week internship is completed." The silence gnawed at Jim until he glanced at Alma Rose and noticed her furrowed brow. "Are you okay with that schedule?" Jim asked.

The words slowly escaped from Alma Rose's lips and in a hushed voice she said, "Yeah...I'm...I'm okay. It's just that..."

Jim interrupted, "Just what?"

Alma Rose faced him. "I thought I'd be doing more hands-on stuff, that's all."

Jim laughed. "Let's hope there's more training and less hands-on stuff."

The pitch of Alma Rose's voice increased. "But dad, training can be boring. What's the point of training if I can't use what I've been trained to do?"

Jim spoke with a sense of authority. "Alma Rose, this training will be useful for your entire life."

"Then when will I get firearm training?"

Jim stared at her. "No firearm training."

"Why not?"

"You're an intern. There's no reason to carry."

Then the radio crackled. "CC-1, this is CC Dispatch. Are you clear to copy?"

Jim grabbed at the radio. "CC Dispatch, clear to copy. Sergeant Wilson, what's going on?"

"We have a ten-seven-niner, code 4 on U.S. 228 twenty-four miles west of Mallory near Howard Lake, driver foot-bailed. Can you respond?"

Jim said, "That's the Mallory Police Department's jurisdiction."

Sergeant Martha Wilson responded, "They've got their hands full with a possible abduction that occurred last night. They asked us for assistance on this accident."

Jim said, "Then send one of the deputies."

"We can't. Deputy McDale is the only one on duty. Deputy Blair and Sergeant MacAskill are assigned to Officer Hoffmann's funeral detail. Deputies Haggerty, Griffin, Holden, and Coleman are due in at oh-seven-hundred. I figured since your home is halfway between Taylor and Howard Lake, it'd be best that you respond."

"Martha, I'm right outside the office."

"Then don't bother coming in and go directly to the accident scene. You'll be the first responder."

"I'm on my way. Dispatch Griffin and Coleman when they arrive and have them meet me there."

"Will do," Martha said.

"Oh, and Martha, contact Agent Costa and tell him that I'll be unable to meet them at Lucy's because of this call. Ask him if we can meet at the sheriff's office at 1 p.m. after the funeral."

"You got it," Martha said.

Jim flicked on his strobe lights, sounded his siren, and drove his SUV at a high rate of speed toward Howard Lake. He glanced at Alma Rose. "Just hold tight. It looks like you've got your wish for hands-on training sooner than you expected."

·6·

The early morning sunrise danced across the mirrored surface of Howard Lake as Jim pulled up alongside an accident on U.S. Highway 228. He logged the time of arrival, 06:20 Monday, June 30, 1997.

While Angel whined and Shadow barked, Jim got out of his SUV and surveyed the scene. He spotted a yellow Mustang hardtop with a smashed-in windshield and a partially collapsed roof. The car's passenger side tires were mired in the mud of a ditch off the south side of the road.

Splayed on the pavement in front of the Mustang was an elk, brown with its distinctive yellowish rump patch. It bellowed a weak and mournful sigh. A wide trail of blood tracked from the car's hood and across the eastbound lane. One of the elk's legs was severed and the other three legs were visibly distorted. A grounded eagle flapped its left wing next to the elk.

A semi-tractor trailer cab was parked in the other lane, its driver's door wide-open. Two witnesses leaned against a pickup truck parked in the westbound lane behind the accident scene. The men kept a safe distance from the traumatized raptor and the dying animal.

Jim asked, "Anyone injured?"

Both men spoke at once. "No."

"What're your names…what happened here?" Jim asked.

One man stepped forward. "My name's Mike Templeton. I saw everything. The kid in the Mustang was pushing…maybe a hundred when he flew by my pickup. Then he slammed on his brakes but broadsided the elk."

Jim hurriedly took out his notebook and began transcribing the man's words. Then he asked, "What occurred next?"

"It all happened so fast, but I saw the Mustang take out the animal's legs. The elk flew onto the hood, smashed its head into the windshield, and then crashed onto the roof. When the car came to a stop, the elk tumbled back down in front of the car. By then the Mustang was off the eastbound lane and in the drainage channel. It looks like the airbags didn't deploy so the kid scrambles out of his car, all bloody and whatnot, and takes off into the brush."

Jim flipped the page in his notebook. "How'd the eagle get involved?"

"Well, not more than a few minutes after the accident this eagle swoops down onto the elk and started picking on the animal. Then this guy's semi comes along and..."

The trucker interrupted the conversation. "Name's Wyatt Dodge...I couldn't help it. I braked hard up the road but I'm carrying a full load of timber. Took me a good stretch to come to a stop...I avoided the elk but clipped the bird when it flew right in front of my rig. Now I don't want any trouble with State Wildlife. I didn't cause this shit."

Jim stopped transcribing. "Don't worry. It's the driver of the Mustang that I want to speak with." Jim walked over to the car, took down the Mustang's plate number, grabbed his hand-held radio and called it in. "Martha, please check out Montana plate number five-seven, three-one-six-eight-Papa. Send backup as soon as possible."

Jim stepped toward the bird with the brown head that he assumed was a Golden Eagle. Then from a distance he spied the white mottling on the breast and belly and back and the magnificent heavy white mottling on the underwings when the eagle spread its left wing. He then realized it was a second-year juvenile Bald Eagle screeching and hopping unabated.

While both Angel and Shadow barked, Alma Rose got out of the SUV and ran toward her father. Jim took another step toward the eagle and drew his Colt Python revolver. He yelled, "Alma Rose, no running. Remember? Stay put."

Alma Rose stopped in place. "Dad, don't kill it."

Jim set his eyes on the bird and said, "I'm not going to shoot unless it poses a threat. Alma Rose, get back on the radio and call Fish, Wildlife, and Parks."

While the raptor hobbled, screeched and continued to flap its left wing, Jim kept himself between the injured bird and the accident scene.

Alma Rose walked back to Jim's SUV and then spotted someone sitting in the passenger seat. It was a Native woman with blood covering her face. Alma Rose stepped around to the passenger side but when she looked inside the SUV, the seat was empty.

Amid the whining antics of Angel and Shadow, Alma Rose walked back to the driver's side and settled into the seat. A tingling sensation enveloped her entire being, but she dismissed it in the heat of the moment. As she had seen her father do countless times before, Alma Rose picked up the radio's hand mic, depressed the push-to-talk button, and spoke loud and clear, "CC-1 to CC-Dispatch, do you copy?"

Following a burst of crackling, a voice erupted on the other end. "CC-1 this is CC-Dispatch. Is that you Alma Rose?"

"Yes."

"This is Martha. Where's your father?"

"He's got his hands full."

"I thought it was just a 61-12-401 and the driver bailed," Martha said.

"What's that?" Alma Rose asked.

"Abandoned Vehicle."

Alma Rose stuttered, "Well…there's probably a whole bunch of other codes out here that you can also assign."

"Like what?"

"There's an injured bald eagle. We need a wrecker, someone from Fish, Wildlife & Parks, and can you send the ACO out here too? We have an injured elk blocking one lane."

Alma Rose ended the call, turned to Angel, and asked, "You saw her in the front seat too didn't you?" Then Alma Rose jumped out of the SUV, and stepped toward the elk. She stared at the animal as it breathed its last breath and spoke the Lord's Prayer in *Apsáalooke*. She ended the prayer with, "*Kótak.*"

Jim walked over to her. "Alma Rose, get back to the SUV."

"I will dad. The elk will need the help of the Great Spirit. I prayed to *Iichihbaalia* and recited the Lord's Prayer for the elk in *Apsáalooke*. The elk didn't understand what happened to her or what words these men were speaking but she understands our language. It's seated in her memories handed down to her kind from a time when the animals could speak and shared the same language as our elders. Now her spirit can move on."

23

·7·

A patrol car with deputies Griffin and Coleman arrived on the scene just before 7:30 a.m. Jim instructed them to hunt for the suspect while he secured the accident scene. After a search that lasted nearly all of ten minutes and a few warning shots, the deputies emerged from the brush with a bloody suspect in handcuffs. The deputies found his wallet in which was a driver's license that identified him as twenty-year old Louis Miller. A student ID indicated that he's a matriculating student at Taylor University, future graduating class of 1998.

Jim asked, "Did you read him the Miranda Warning?"

One of the deputies said, "Sure did sheriff and he didn't like it one bit."

Jim took a good look at the boy. He was thin and nerdy, with blood-soaked blond hair on the left side of his head. His tattered powder blue, button-down, short-sleeve shirt, and his soiled white jeans bore signs of his futile escapade into the brush.

Jim asked, "Are you hurt son?"

"I only banged my head on the steering wheel when that animal jumped in front of me."

"We'll see to it they take a good look at you at Cedar County Hospital."

"Thanks," said the boy.

Jim asked, "Well son, what do you have to say for yourself?"

Louis stared at him. "What do you mean?" Louis cocked his head toward the elk lying on the road and yelled, "That animal ran right in front of my car. I had no chance to avoid it."

"You think that dead elk should have known better?"

25

Louis replied, "Well…yeah."

Jim said, "That elk was minding its own business crossing the road. It seems to me it was the elk that stood no chance."

Louis responded, "Well, it wasn't my fault. That animal should have kept off the road. It should have stayed where it's supposed to be."

Jim glanced at his deputies who collectively rolled their eyes. Jim struck a serious tone. "That elk was where it was supposed to be. You see son, I see this every June. That was an old cow scouting a summer trail for a herd of cows, calves, and yearling bulls. Once she knew the trail wasn't flooded or that predators weren't lurking, she would have gone back for the others and led them up into the hills. They winter in the lowlands and summer up in the mountains. She was only looking out for her own kind." Jim sensed that he temporarily disarmed the boy about the elk, so he then asked, "What do you suggest we do about all this?"

Louis said, "Well, the Mustang's totaled but I had my eyes on a new Corvette anyway."

Jim felt his patience wear thin at the ignorance of the boy. He stared at Louis and blurted out, "I don't give a damn about your fancy cars. There's a dead elk in the road and in trying to avoid the mess you caused, a trucker accidently injured an innocent eagle."

Louis countered, "Hey, I'm sorry about that animal but I didn't cause any property damage, no one got killed, so I didn't do anything wrong. Just remove these handcuffs, tell me what it costs to take care of the animal, and send me a bill. I'll pay whatever the fine is and be done with it."

Jim asked, "Son, do you think money solves everything?"

Louis grinned. "Doesn't it? And you can stop calling me son. I don't look like you and I'm certainly not your son."

Jim continued, "Son, that may be how things are done in New York but in Montana, we do things here a bit differently."

Jim noticed the boy's face transform into a frantic stare and then his head swiveled at each of Jim's deputies.

"What do you mean and how do you know I'm from New York?" Louis asked. "Oh I know. You saw my New York drivers' license."

"Not quite son." Jim pushed up the brim of his Stetson and asked, "Aren't you the son of Thomas and Barbara Miller?"

Louis asked, "You know my parents?"

Jim said, "Sure do, I hear your dad made his billions on Wall Street. Then they moved out here back in '94 from New York City when you had just graduated high school. They built that five-thousand square foot mansion high up in the Cabinet Mountains."

Louis rolled his eyes. "Yeah, well I hate that house. I wish I was back in the City instead of this godforsaken place."

Deputy Griffin laughed. "Well, he sure ain't a roughneck."

Deputy Coleman joined in the laughter. "He's not a roustabout either."

Louis glanced at Jim. "What are they talking about?"

Jim ignored Louis' question and instead said, "You should follow your parents' example. They volunteer on several civic boards, raised a lot of money for the homeless shelter, a number of churches, youth organizations, the battered women's shelter, and the wildlife sanctuary. Many people say they're outstanding members of our community."

Louis let out a sarcastic laugh. "Yeah, that's a joke. They do that model citizen shit so no one knows what goes on up at the house. You ought to live with them and see what I get to see...it's gross."

Jim said, "I'm sure that you tax their patience. I haven't met them yet, we run in different social circles. But I've seen you. You're always out and about, busy racing cars, getting into fights with a few of our local boys, and breaking the hearts of some of our young women. Mind you, nothing that would have gotten you in serious trouble with the law up until now. It's just a whole lot of bad behavior on your part."

Louis said, "I apologize for hitting the animal and I'm sorry for everything that happened here...even the eagle though that really wasn't my fault. Like I said, just send me a bill."

Jim slowly shook his head and then said in a gruff voice, "No, I think we'll settle this down at the office. Speeding, reckless driving, and evading responsibility should suffice for starters. What do you boys think?" Jim said as he glanced at his deputies.

Deputy Griffin nodded and then Deputy Coleman said, "Sounds about right to me."

Louis raised his voice. "Now wait a minute, I've never been arrested before in my life, and this isn't going to be the first time. Now just tell me how I can..."

Jim interrupted Louis. "And we'll contact your parents."

27

Louis' eyes widened. "What, my parents? Oh no, no. My parents are NOT to find out about this."

Jim placed his hand on Louis' right shoulder. "You see son, we're not going to arrest you despite good cause. To us you're just another spoiled rich kid from back east who will most likely get a dismissed sentence or maybe just some community service. You won't learn any lessons from this and go on to do things like this again...or even worse."

Louis shook his head from side to side. "I won't...I mean I understand I did wrong so I won't do it again."

Jim released his grip on Louis' shoulder. "I doubt it. Oh, maybe right now you mean it but in 24 hours, a week, a month from now, you'll be doing the same damn things you've always been doing."

"No sir, I..."

Jim interrupted him. "Listen to me. In your case, you'll be in enough trouble already with the university and its zero-tolerance community policy. Then your parents will find out that you triggered the death of an elk. And it led to severe injuries to a juvenile eagle when a trucker swerved his rig trying to avoid your accident. Now all that won't look good for your parent's reputation, them being on the conservation board and their fundraising efforts for the new Thomas and Barbara Miller Wildlife Sanctuary along the Clark Fork River." Jim noticed tears well up in the boy's eyelids and then he continued. "Now it's sad that an elk had to lose its life and an eagle may never be the same. However, if this occurrence prevents you from causing harm in the future to an animal or even worse, to a human being, then this lesson is well served."

The boy began to openly cry, and his body trembled. He slowly shook his head. "I won't ever do something like this again."

"I hope you won't." Jim continued, "I want you to see what happens to that elk. Stay here with me until the ACO arrives. You'll accompany him to Taylor Vet. Cedar County Medical Center is right across the street. We'll have them check out your head wound."

Louis smiled. "Thanks."

Jim said, "Maybe they'll find something in there after all."

Louis cocked his head. "Hey..."

Jim continued. "The ACO has a Wildlife Salvage Permit which he'll use at the Vet and once the animal is processed, someone from my office will give you a ride home. Then arrive at my office tomorrow morning at 9 a.m. sharp, I'll have a project for you. Then you're square with the law. The damage to your car and any repercussions with the university or with your family is something that you'll have to deal with on your own accord...agreed?"

The boy nodded. "Yes, I understand. Well, thank you for not arresting me."

Jim shook hands with the boy. "Remember, be at my office at 9 a.m. tomorrow. If you're even one minute late, I'll draw up a citation, and you'll sit in one of my cells until your parents decide if and when to bail you out."

Angel and Shadow uttered welcoming barks in unison as Jim walked back to his SUV. He opened the driver's door and climbed inside. As he started the engine, he sensed Alma Rose's puzzled question. He turned and stared at her.

"Aren't you going to arrest him for what he did?" she asked.

Jim turned away. "No."

Alma Rose swiveled in her seat to face her father. "Isn't he going to be held responsible for what he did?" she asked.

Jim explained, "There are better lessons to be learned than placing someone behind bars. If we arrest him, he could build a grudge and then blame us for the consequences."

"But he did wrong. Why should he get away with it?" Alma Rose asked.

Jim pulled the SUV back onto the road, headed toward Mallory, and said, "Let him sort this out between the university and his family. It may have a more lasting effect than if we simply threw the book at him. Besides, I've got plans for him."

Jim drove up to a building with signage that read, Mallory Public Works Department. Jim told Alma Rose to stay in the SUV with Angel and Shadow. He went inside to meet with the director of public works.

Jim looked around the mostly empty office and asked, "Is Lyndon Bell in today?"

A seasoned employee stood up from behind a desk. "I'm Jenny, his assistant. What do you want, sheriff?"

"I've got a favor to ask of him."

Jenny responded, "Well, he won't be back for a couple three hours. He's with a crew up at Howard Lake reviewing a repaving job with John Sheppard."

Jim said, "I just came back from Howard Lake. A kid hit an elk on U.S. 228. I didn't see Mister Bell or a work crew in the area."

The woman scoffed. "No disrespect sheriff but I'm sure you know we don't have active jobs on state highways. There are so many back roads around Howard Lake I doubt you'd run into them. The mayor has this hunch that paving the perimeter roads around the lake just might draw seasonal folks back to Mallory. Quite a few lakefront rentals have been unoccupied going on a couple three summers now."

Jim nodded. "I know that things have been tough around Mallory the past few years…"

Jenny interrupted Jim. "No sheriff, you don't know. People around here don't feel safe anymore cause of that Moon Man crap. The ones who can afford to leave did. The ones who can't leave, because their job disappeared when the business they worked at closed, struggle just to put food on the table. I'm one of the lucky ones, I still got a job. But I was supposed to retire two years ago and move to California. The housing market is off kilter and I can't sell my house even if I tried to auction it off."

Jim replied, "I'm sorry but…"

Jenny again interrupted Jim. "Early this morning I heard on the scanner there was another disappearance. You'll do all of us who's left in this town a big favor if you put an end to the disappearances and just find the killer."

Jim said, "I didn't hear anything from dispatch."

Jenny smirked. "Yeah, well that's cause the powers that be in Mallory don't want anyone else finding out what's going on. They moved some emergency calls to a different channel."

Jim asked, "Why is it that I haven't been informed? We have county-mandated consolidation of 911 calls."

Jenny said, "I know and it pisses me off that they run separate channels depending upon the level of emergency and what the emergency is. My dear husband, God rest his soul, was a deputy in Lake County back in the day and he did the job like it was supposed to be done. Nowadays, I sometimes often wonder who's running the show."

Jim nodded and then as he headed toward the door he told Jenny, "Please tell Mister Bell that I'll be back either today or tomorrow."

Jim climbed into the driver's seat and glanced at Alma Rose. "Well, that was a waste of time that I'll never get back. I have to return later."

Alma Rose said, "Dad, there's a reason for everything. When we think that things don't work out the way we planned it's only because they follow a higher plan."

·8·

Jim and Alma Rose returned to the scene of the accident. Jake Hunter, the town of Mallory's Animal Control Officer arrived within minutes driving a flatbed truck and took charge of the elk carcass. Later, a Mallory Public Works payloader arrived and lifted the elk onto the bed of the ACO's truck. Louis Miller climbed into the passenger side of the flatbed truck as Jake got in the cab and drove off.

It took much longer for the Montana Fish, Wildlife & Parks Warden Arnie Simmons to reach the scene of the accident. His gray Ford F250 pickup truck came to a stop, its strobe lights still flashing. Jim held out his hand and when Arnie got out of his truck, the men clasped hands. "Arnie, what can you do for this injured eagle?" Jim asked.

Arnie stared at the raptor for a long moment, and then shook his head. "I don't think it'll make it. At least not in the wild even if it survives. It shows signs of an inability to stand, convulsions, head tremors, and difficulty breathing. It's in bad shape. It might be best to put it out of its misery and report it to the state."

Jim whispered to Arnie, "It's my daughter's first day of summer internship with the Cedar County Sheriff's Office. I don't want to make today tougher on her than it already is. She would like to see the bird's life saved."

Jim watched Arnie glance over at Alma Rose in the SUV. Jim spotted Alma Rose wipe her eyes dry.

Arnie turned back to Jim. "I'll see what I can do. The highway department's foreman with the Mallory Public Works Department is a raptor rehabilitator."

Jim asked, "You're talking about John Sheppard?"

33

Felix F. Giordano

"Yeah, but you can call him Easy, everyone does. You ever meet him?" Arnie asked.

"No, I've only spoken with his boss Lyndon Bell on the phone during civil emergencies. I haven't had the opportunity to meet John. How long has he been involved with wildlife rehab?"

Arnie said, "Practically his whole life but you better get used to calling him Easy. He'll be glad to get the raptor. I heard he's got a few other birds that he's rehabbing."

Jim said, "I plan to ask his boss, Lyndon Bell if he could hire the boy who caused this accident. A summer job would be a way to keep the kid out of jail and also teach him a lesson."

Arnie nodded. "That'll work especially if the county pays the boy's salary."

"It will." Then Jim said, "I had a conversation a while back with Medical Examiner Hank Kelly when we were working on a separate case. We were looking into the background of Lyndon Bell. Something struck me hard when I heard about what he went through. I know that you know Mister Bell. What can you tell me about him, his parents?"

Arnie took a deep breath and then exhaled. "That's a tough one. My dad went to school with him. Lyndon was fourteen when his mom died. It hit him pretty hard. His father waited until Lyndon was done with high school and then he hightailed it out of Mallory. Later that same year, Lyndon volunteered with the Marines. He never married and work is everything to him as he says." Arnie laughed. "He's sixty-six now. He said he plans to retire next year."

Jim asked, "Can you tell me about Lyndon's father...what was his name?"

Arnie said, "His name was Charles Bell. He once worked for a local electrical supply outfit that's now out of business. A few people swear they've seen him in town from time to time but if he's still alive he'd be in his mid-eighties now. I even thought I saw him once down by Howard Lake at dusk one night wearing his old mechanic's overalls. I called to him but he didn't answer. I went to follow him down a trail but it stopped at the water's edge and he was gone, just vanished. Kind of like a ghost if you ask me. Sent shivers down my spine that night. Even to this day, I won't go to Howard Lake after sundown."

Jim asked, "How did Charles' wife die?"

Arnie explained, "Well here's the long and short of it. Lyndon's parents never got along. They fought constantly. One

34

day after work Charles Bell picks up Lyndon at school, drops him off outside their home, and then heads to work. When Lyndon goes inside, he calls the police because of what he found at the house. His mom was missing but there was blood all over the house."

Jim asked, "When was that?"

"My parents told me Lyndon's mom died in 1947. Hell…that was before I was born."

Then Jim asked, "Did they ever find out who killed her?"

"Well, they never arrested anyone. During an ongoing investigation, rumors floated that Charles Bell staged his wife's disappearance and that she's at the bottom of Howard Lake. He was harassed at work. Some townspeople began throwing rocks through his windows. Someone even set fire to his garage. A few years later, like I said, after Lyndon was done with high school, Charles takes off and abandons his son. After Charles left, the rumors that he killed his wife pretty much became fact for most people. I guess we'll never know for sure."

Jim probed deeper, "Did Lyndon receive professional counseling for the loss of his mother and father?"

Arnie said, "As I mentioned, after his father took off, Lyndon sold everything he had and volunteered with the Marines. When he got out of the service, he went backpacking first in the Yaak wilderness and then in the Crazy Mountains to clear his mind. He was only twenty-two then. That was back in '53, and he didn't return to Mallory until ten years later in the winter of '62-63. Crawled in like a wounded dog."

"How's he doing now?"

Arnie laughed. "I'm amazed that he's recovered so well. Hell, if that was my life, I probably would have shot ma' damn brains out. I drop in on him a couple weekends a month. We go hunting, fishing, and backpacking."

Jim said, "I'll see if I can get this kid a summer job elsewhere. I don't want to put too much on Lyndon's plate."

"I can't say that he'll hire the kid but I think you can speak with him. He's got the time. Lyndon's such a good guy. Besides, now's your chance to ask before he retires."

Jim nodded. "Okay, then I'll ask Lyndon for that favor."

"Sounds like a great idea. I'll check with Easy and find out if he's got room for one more raptor. I can't guarantee anything."

"I understand." Jim nodded.

Arnie took a deep breath. "I got that funeral to attend for Officer Hoffmann this morning."

Jim said, "I'll be at the funeral too. Damn shame what happened."

Arnie asked, "That biker guy's gonna fry, right sheriff?"

Jim took a deep breath. "If I'm summoned to testify I'll make sure the jury hears the truth. If somehow Tanas doesn't get convicted of capital murder, he should end up a lifer."

Arnie nodded and then said, "Well, let's see if we can do something for the bird."

"Whatever you can do for the eagle would be much obliged," Jim said.

Arnie pulled on a pair of heavy-duty utility gloves and safety goggles from his truck's glovebox and snatched a blanket off the passenger seat. He instructed Jim to grab the plastic dog carrier from his truck bed. Then the two men approached the fallen raptor with caution.

Arnie warned, "Watch out for the beak and talons."

Arnie first covered the raptor from behind with the blanket to reduce its visual stimulation. Then he gently placed his gloved hands on the blanket and folded the bird's wings onto its body. Finally, he lifted the eagle into the carrier which was slightly larger than the bird. During the entire procedure the raptor was relatively calm except for a bit of jostling when Arnie expertly removed and then maneuvered the blanket onto the carrier thus again restricting the bird's visual field. When the eagle was secured, he brought the carrier to the back of the pickup truck and latched it onto the truck bed.

Jim said, "Much obliged."

Arnie closed and latched the tailgate. "After I call Easy, I'll let you know if he's willing to take the bird. If not, I'll bring it to Taylor Vet."

"Let's hope things go well." Jim offered his hand to Arnie. "Thanks for going the extra yard. I appreciate it." Jim gestured toward his SUV and his daughter.

Jim watched Arnie turn and stare at Alma Rose. When he turned back to face Jim, Arnie said, "If we can save this eagle, maybe it'll return the favor and capture some of those pesky white-tailed jackrabbits that seem to have invaded my farm."

The men nodded and returned to their trucks. When Jim climbed into the driver's seat, he saw Alma Rose turn to him.

"What's going to happen to the eagle?"

Jim started the engine and checked the road through his side mirror. "The eagle's going to a raptor rehabilitator."

Alma Rose asked, "What does that mean?"

Jim stared at her as he began to pull onto the road. "It means that they will do their best to heal any injuries the bird may have and then when it's ready, reintroduce it into the wild." Jim began to drive away from the accident scene."

She asked, "What if they can't?"

As Jim left the scene and drove toward the sheriff's office in Taylor he turned and said to her, "Let's only think of positive outcomes."

·9·

When Jim and Alma Rose reached the sheriff's office just before 9 a.m., Jim leashed Angel and Shadow and let them jump from the SUV. He asked Alma Rose to wait for him in the lobby and went toward the back of the property. Jim used his security passcard and entered the gated, expansive lot that abutted the county garage behind the sheriff's office.

He entered the garage and walked toward a back-room kennel belonging to the county sheriff's office canine unit. It housed three German Shepherds, Bullet, Scout, and Caesar, and one young Bloodhound named Beauregard.

Jim placed Angel and Shadow in separate metal crates. He then told the on-duty kennel worker that he would be back in the afternoon. Until then Jim instructed the kennel worker to provide the dogs with their usual exercise.

Jim then walked through the back entrance to the building, beyond the holding cells, through the office, and past the dispatch center. Inside and behind the bulletproof glass, Jim spotted Martha wave him over.

Jim met her at the window on the office side and asked, "What's up?"

Martha said, "All hell seems to have broken loose in Mallory."

"Explain," Jim asked.

"The Mallory Police received an early morning call about a home invasion...blood all over the apartment. The husband's spouse is missing."

Jim glanced into the lobby and caught Alma Rose staring through the bulletproof glass. Then he asked, "Did Mallory request assistance?"

39

Martha shook her head, "Not yet but from the description of the inside of the apartment, they'll be calling on Hank soon enough."

"Thanks Martha, keep me informed if anything changes."

"Will do," Martha said.

Jim nodded and then opened the door to the office lobby. He let Alma Rose in and led her to his office.

"Have a seat," Jim said to her as he maneuvered around to the back of his desk and sat down. "And keep what you heard from the dispatcher to yourself."

"I will." Then she said, "This morning I saw something."

Jim asked, "You saw what?"

"I saw a Native woman in your car at the accident scene."

Jim stood up. "What do you mean...where's she now?"

Alma Rose rolled her eyes. "Dad, you don't understand. She's not of this world."

"What do you mean, not of this world?"

Alma Rose sat forward in her seat. "She's of the spirit world. She may be the one who visited us in your house last night."

Jim took a deep breath. "Alma Rose, your preoccupation with these sightings..."

Alma Rose interrupted, "Dad, it's not a preoccupation."

Jim sat back down and said, "We'll discuss this later."

He then dropped a spiral-bound book on the desk in front of her. The title on the cover read:

<u>Department Rules, Regulations, Policies, and Procedures</u>
<u>Cedar County Sheriff's Office 1994-97</u>

Jim noticed Alma Rose stare at the 464-page book without saying a word. Then he said, "This is your copy. It's not allowed to leave your sight. Study it in the office, take it on patrol with you, and read it on break, during lunch, or dinner but you cannot take it home with you nor can you photocopy it. It's the sole property of the Cedar County Sheriff's Office, got it?"

"Dad, I understand."

"That's another thing."

"What?"

"When we were at the accident scene you addressed me as dad. You are not to ever do that again as long as we are both in uniform and in public."

"I'm sorry but under the circumstances, I had the privilege to suspend professional courtesy."

A confused expression stretched across Jim's face. "What...what do you mean by that?"

Alma Rose explained, "Undersheriff Salentino told me that since we are a small office that when we are under duress in public whether it's at an accident scene, a wildlife call, a domestic disturbance, or even a crime scene we can dispense with the usual regimented courtesy formalities."

"Rocky told you that...when?"

"Last week."

"How did you speak with him last week?"

"I called him on the phone."

"Why?"

"Because I knew I'd be working with him."

"How did you know?"

"Dad, do I have to explain to you how the entire Universe works? It would be such a waste of time. Just have faith and trust and accept it for what it is."

"Well, then who said you could call him?"

"Who said I couldn't?"

Jim shook his head. "Alma Rose, sometimes I have a great deal of trouble understanding you."

"Junior Deputy Two Elk."

"What?"

"Under the current circumstances, here in the Cedar County Sheriff's Office, Junior Deputy Two Elk is how you should refer to me under the generally accepted regimented courtesy formalities, Sheriff Buchanan."

Jim felt his cheeks grow warm and then he noticed Alma Rose wink at him.

"Miss Two Elk, I..."

Alma Rose interrupted him. "Dad, I'm just kidding. I'm good however you wish to refer to me. Know that I love you not just because you're my father but because of how you go about doing your job protecting the people of this county."

Jim took a deep breath and then smiled. "I love you too, Junior Deputy Two Elk. Let me show you to your desk."

41

·10·

After he sat a few minutes with Alma Rose and reviewed with her the weekly schedule that she would adhere to, Jim called into the office Undersheriff Rocky Salentino who was a stocky second-generation Italian-American. Once Rocky took a seat, Jim explained to him how he expected him to work together with Alma Rose during her summer internship.

"Rocky, it's important that you work closely with Alma Rose so that you can provide the university with an accurate report on her performance."

Rocky turned to look at Alma Rose who returned his stare. Rocky said, "Jim, we'll be fine together, just like a team."

Alma Rose faced her father. "Sheriff Buchanan, I have complete confidence in Cedar County Undersheriff Rocco Salentino's use of unbiased and excellent judgement."

When Rocky turned to Jim and stared at him, Jim said, "Alma Rose and I had a previous discussion about professional protocol."

Rocky stifled a laugh and nodded. "I understand."

"Great," Jim said.

They reviewed Alma Rose's schedule and developed a weekly reporting plan that would fulfill the requirements for the university.

Once they finished, Jim got up and said to Alma Rose, "In a few minutes, Rocky and I will be leaving to attend Officer Hoffmann's funeral. Then we're having lunch with a few other officers at noon. We'll be back by 1 p.m. because, as you know, I have a meeting with two FBI agents at that time."

Alma Rose asked, "What should I do until you get back?"

Jim smiled. "I've arranged for a tour of the Cedar County Office of the State Crime Lab. Chief Medical Examiner Hank Kelly is waiting in the conference room. Are you ready to meet him?"

Alma Rose said, "Cool." Once she saw Jim and Rocky stare at her, she continued, "I mean, yes I'm ready. I appreciate the opportunity."

"Good let's go." Jim turned to Rocky. "I'll meet you outside in five. Are you driving?"

Rocky nodded. "Yes, but I'd rather not have to go. I wish this never happened."

"That's why we need to prosecute Videl Tanas and make sure that he's put away for good." Jim walked to the hat rack and grabbed his Stetson. Then he turned to Alma Rose. "I'm sorry I brought up his name."

Alma Rose said, "That's all right. He hurt me, but he can't hurt me anymore."

With that last comment, Rocky left the office and Jim and Alma Rose headed for the conference room. Inside, Chief Medical Examiner Hank Kelly got up and extended his hand to Alma Rose.

"Young lady, we finally meet under normal circumstances. Your father has told me so much about you that I feel I already know you very well." Hank shook Alma Rose's hand.

Hank was of average height. His white hair had begun that slow progression of male-pattern baldness. Hank Kelly was impeccably dressed, and you could even say that he was overdressed by Montana standards.

Alma Rose smiled. "And I've heard a lot about you as well. How's your wife Mary? My stepmother thinks the world of her."

Hank laughed and glanced at Jim. "Kate and Mary have much more than just a niece and aunt relationship. When Mary and I lived in New York, Kate visited us every summer during high school vacations."

Jim gave Alma Rose a kiss on her cheek. "Take care, I'll meet you back here at one." He turned to Hank. "See that Alma Rose has all her questions answered."

Hank smiled. "I'll do my best."

Jim left the room and then Hank extended his arm with his palm outstretched and pointed toward the door.

While they walked down the hallway, Alma Rose asked, "How long have you been working as a medical examiner?"

Hank laughed. "It seems like it's been for my entire life." Hank explained. "Four years ago, in 1993 on my sixtieth birthday, I retired from the New York City Office of Chief Medical Examiner. Your stepmother, my niece Kate had been trying to get Mary and me to move to Montana for the past twenty years. We finally decided to relocate here and spend our retirement years basking in the peace and solitude of this magnificent landscape. However, the previous chief medical examiner submitted his letter of retirement. When your father learned of that he contacted me and suggested that I apply for the open position. The rest is history and I was hired as Montana's Chief Medical Examiner."

Alma Rose said, "It would be an honor to learn even a fraction of what you have experienced during your long career."

Hank turned to her. "I'll do whatever I can to help advance your career aspirations while you serve your summer internship. Your father has helped me succeed both professionally and personally in this position. I want to give back to someone like you. I can see the enthusiasm you have for your vocation and I can tell that you have the right stuff to make a positive influence on both those who you will work with and those whom you will serve in your profession."

Alma Rose and Hank crossed the parking lot toward his car. They got in and Hank drove to the state crime lab. They went inside and Hank gave her the VIP tour. Then they took the elevator to Hank's office on the third floor. Once inside, Alma Rose noticed the panoramic window. She stepped over to it and gazed below at the rushing waters of the Clark Fork River. As it continued its westward journey toward Idaho, the river ran parallel to State Highway 200. Then Alma Rose noticed a framed quote on the wall behind Hank's desk. It read:

"When a man comes to die, no matter what his talents and influence and genius, if he dies unloved his life must be a failure to him and his dying a cold horror...we should remember our dying and try so to live that our death brings no pleasure to the world."
— John Steinbeck, East of Eden

"That's an interesting quote," Alma Rose said to Hank as she stared at the frame

Hank turned to look and then harrumphed. "That old dust collector? Mary bought it for me at a flea market. She thought it would help keep me grounded. So I do my best to try and take those words to heart each day."

Alma Rose said, "There's something sinful about that statement."

Hank glanced back at her and then asked, "Steinbeck wrote those famous words, you disagree with him?"

Alma Rose stepped over to the frame and pointed to the last few words. "I understand that we must live a good life so that people are saddened that we have died. But if a man has led a bad life, when he dies why would the world take pleasure in his death? Isn't there also something very wrong with those who are rejoicing? All life should be exalted no matter who or what it is."

Hank hesitated and then a smile broadened across his face. "Touché young lady, you are wise beyond your years."

Alma Rose said, "All life has value. Unless we embrace all living things with whom we share this world, then we are devalued to just simply empty souls."

Hank asked, "Where did you learn that philosophy?"

Alma Rose explained, "It's an extension of the Red Road."

"I've heard your father talk about the Red Road. Is that a metaphor for something?"

Alma Rose explained, "It's more than that. It's a way of life for my people. We must all be honest with ourselves and follow the Red Road."

Hank said, "As we age we learn that maturity is the one virtue that allows us to view the world for what it really is, a wonderful, unique experiment with abundant choices for love, understanding, and brotherhood. It's a shame that young people don't experience it sooner and tragic that some never do. I think however, young lady that you have experienced it."

They stared silent at one another for a long moment and then the phone on his desk rang. Hank answered the call.

"Hello…yes…where…in Mallory, when did that happen…I see, well where's the body…really…what, with that amount of blood it certainly sounds like a homicide…have they begun the criminal investigation…waiting for me…good, then tell them to *hold off until I get there and my department will begin the forensic investigation…it's almost ten now, I can be there in about thirty minutes…good, call Leon and tell him to gather the team and meet me there…thanks, goodbye."*

"What happened?" Alma Rose asked.

Hank turned to her. "It appears there may have been a murder in Mallory. Would you like to accompany me?"

"Can I?" she asked.

Hank smiled. "I don't see why not. You're on the county payroll and you've been assigned to me by the sheriff's office until 1 p.m. If you don't contaminate the crime scene, don't speak with anyone else but me unless I tell you otherwise, agree to follow my orders to the letter and not share any conversations or information with the media, then I'll take full responsibility for your attendance."

"Yes sir, I'd like to attend."

·11·

Sandwiched between Libby Creek and Fisher River along U.S. Highway 228, Mallory was Cedar County's second largest city. A community known for its proximity to the mirrored surface of Howard Lake, Mallory had its own police department and was supported by the county sheriff's office.

The citizens of Mallory were proud of their town's frontier character. Mallory Is What Montanans Are All About was etched in painted gold lettering against a green patina backdrop on a massive ornate copper sign that hung over the entrance to the town hall. It was Mallory's adopted slogan, a targeted message meant to attract new residents to the community. That is, attract potential residents who were unaware of the Moon Man legend.

Alma Rose and Hank Kelly arrived at an apartment complex in Mallory. Hank looked for a spot to park, but two police cars blocked the entrance to the lot. Hank finally pulled his car onto the lawn, got out, and asked Alma Rose to stay inside. He walked up to one officer and asked, "I'm Chief Medical Examiner Henry Kelly. Can you tell me what happened here?"

The officer pointed to a man who stood next to an unmarked police car. The man wore a gray sport jacket and held a pair of blue latex gloves in his hand. The police officer said to Hank, "Talk to Detective Aronowitz over there."

Hank walked up to the detective who stood next to an eyewitness and prodded her for answers. Hank overheard the conversation.

The woman said, "I told you, it was dark. All I know was that it was some kind of a van."

49

Detective Aronowitz pressed on. "Ma'am, did you get the license plate?"

"How many times have I told you? It was dark."

Aronowitz wouldn't let up. "Ma'am, you said that from your living room window, you saw a vehicle…uh van, drive away at a high rate of speed. What time did you say that was again?"

"I don't know…after midnight, about twelve-thirty. Maybe earlier, I didn't look at the clock until I went back to bed."

Aronowitz asked, "Are you always gazing out your living room window after midnight?"

"When I can't sleep, I stare out the window."

Aronowitz continued, "Ma'am, how long have you had this insomnia problem?"

"Are you for real?" The woman rolled her eyes. "Ever since seventh grade."

Aronowitz persisted, "Are you sure it was a van? Maybe you were taking something to help you sleep and thought you saw a van?"

The woman raised her voice, "What the hell…if I took something, then I'd be asleep, don'tcha think?"

Hank saw his opportunity to interrupt and introduced himself. "Detective, I haven't had the opportunity to meet you. I'm Chief Medical Examiner Henry Kelly."

The detective turned, glanced at Hank, and then said to the eyewitness, "Ma'am, thanks for the information. Don't go away. One of my officers would like to ask you some additional questions."

The woman replied, "Yeah, well I got nothing else to tell him. It was darker than shit."

Aronowitz turned back to Hank and held out his hand. "I'm pleased to meet you Doctor Kelly. I've heard a lot of good things about you. I'm Detective Martin Aronowitz but you can call me Marty."

Hank shook the detective's hand and then asked, "Have you finished processing the crime scene?"

"Unfortunately, Doctor Kelly, this isn't New York City. It's Montana, Big Sky Country. I apologize that we don't have the resources that you're accustomed to back east."

"Well Marty, you can call me Hank. So if there's still work to do, I'm available if you need me…and any resources that I can contribute."

Detective Aronowitz replied, "And I'm here to assist you."

Hank said, "I received a call from Mallory Police Chief Joseph Delaney. He requested that the State Crime Lab get involved. Who will be coordinating the investigation?"

"I've been out here since around 1 a.m. so I guess I will. If I had my way, I would have contacted you sooner."

"Then why did I receive a call almost twelve hours after you responded?"

Marty said, "Ask Delaney. I've got both of my forensic investigators working the crime scene. However, we have no body. Can you help me figure that one out?"

Just then the Cedar County Corner's van pulled up to the crime scene. Coroner Leon Madison climbed out along with two members from his team of death investigators.

Leon asked, "Hank, who's in charge?"

Marty raised his hand. "Detective Aronowitz here. My investigators have secured the crime scene, took detailed measurements, sketched and diagramed the scene, took photographs, documented evidence taken from the scene, and packaged and labeled evidence for transfer to the lab."

Hank stood shoulder to shoulder next to Leon and replied to Marty, "Tell us what you've found."

Marty said, "Come with me to my car and we'll talk."

Hank and Leon followed Marty to his car. They climbed inside with Hank in the passenger seat and Leon in the back.

"I have an intern in my car and we have to return to the Cedar County Sheriff's Office by one," Hank replied. "Leon will handle the remainder of the investigation for my office."

Marty said, "Don't worry, this won't take long to explain. What I'm going to tell you is strictly confidential."

"You can trust Leon and me to adhere to protocol. Tell us what happened."

Marty continued, "We received a call from a neighbor around midnight. She reported a disturbance in the apartment complex. Two of our uniformed officers arrived within twenty minutes and they found one apartment's front door wide-open."

Hank asked, "Which apartment?"

"Number nine," Marty said.

Leon asked, "And."

Marty explained, "And they found blood everywhere."

"What do you mean by everywhere?" Hank asked.

51

"I mean everywhere...floors, walls, furniture, windows, everywhere."

Hank asked, "Did you examine the scene?"

Marty said, "We did as much as we could. Hank, I know that your department has greater resources."

Hank nodded. "We'll shut off all the room lights and comb the entire apartment."

Marty asked, "Do you plan to use luminol?"

Hank shook his head. "If the apartment is awash with as much blood as you say, we'll take samples but luminol won't reveal much more. However, using one of our UV lamps will expose seminal fluid, saliva, urine stains, and bone and teeth fragments. If we can find any of those substances, then we can collect them and submit them for DNA analysis."

"I'd appreciate any assistance you can provide." Marty then cautioned, "There are body parts in that apartment."

Hank had a puzzled look on his face. "You said there was no body."

"Yes, there's no body. They're checking the blood type on the body parts to see if it indicates that it came from one person or more than one. Regardless, it seems that we have at least one homicide on our hands."

"Explain?" Hank asked.

Marty took a deep breath and then exhaled. "We found a pair of eyes on the coffee table."

Hank asked, "What...Marty, tell me who lives there."

"A Native American couple by the name of Driver."

Leon asked, "Do we know who the victim may be?"

Marty turned to Leon in the backseat. "We think it may be the wife. The husband returned home around 3 a.m. He had blood on his shirt, blood in his car, and a possible defensive wound on his hand."

Hank asked, "Where is he now?"

Marty stared at Hank. "We brought him to the station, arrested him on suspicion of murder, and booked him."

Hank winced. "Murder?"

Marty said, "With all due respect Hank, with two severed eyeballs and the blood evidence we found in the apartment, you don't have to be a forensic pathologist to determine a murder was committed. Even the judge was convinced and denied him bail."

"Why?"

Marty replied, "I told the judge since he's a member of the Blackfoot Nation, we were concerned that if he jumped bail he'd split for the reservation. If he did that and decided not to show up in court, the reservation could refuse our warrant. Then we'd never be able to get our hands on him again."

Hank asked, "Has he ever been in trouble with the law before?"

"No but I don't fool around when there's a murder investigation."

Hank pleaded, "Would it be all right if I speak with him?"

"We took his shirt for evidence and we impounded the car. He refuses to talk." Marty sat silent for a moment and then added, "I doubt he'll speak with you, but you're welcome to try. I know that you said you need to be back in Taylor by one. I can arrange for you to sit in on an interrogation later this afternoon. Can you meet me at the Mallory Police Station by 4 p.m.?"

"Yes, I would appreciate that."

Marty asked, "I know that an interrogation is a bit out of your field but it may assist in your end of the investigation."

"I may be able to help you out as well."

"How so?" Marty asked.

"Optography," Hank said.

Marty had a quizzical look on his face. "What's that?"

Hank explained, "If the victim's last thing she saw was her killer, it's possible the image may be imprinted on her retina."

"What? That sounds a bit hokey to me."

Hank smiled. "Perhaps, but I'd just like to see for myself. I'll have Leon preserve the eyes as best as we can. Then I'll have a looksee."

Marty asked, "Do you think it has merit?"

"Probably not, but I may have an Ace in the Hole," Hank said with a smile.

·12·

Hank Kelly and Alma Rose drove back to the Cedar County Sheriff's Office in Taylor. After Hank parked the car, they walked into the lobby and Martha buzzed them inside the office. They returned to the conference room and Hank took a seat at the long, oval table.

Hank said, "Please sit, Deputy Two Elk."

Alma Rose accepted the invitation and sat across from Hank. "What else would you like to discuss?" she asked.

Hank spoke with deliberation in his voice. "As you know, we just returned from a possible crime scene."

"It's not like what I expected."

Hank asked, "What do you mean?"

Alma Rose folded her hands. "I expected more officers and more witness interviews."

Hank said, "First of all, Mallory is a small town. Also, my experience has been that most people who see or hear a crime committed, usually don't want to get involved."

"Why? Isn't it their duty to report what they saw?"

Hank nodded. "You're completely correct but there are so many reasons why people won't step up and reveal what they know."

"Like what?"

"Like..." Hank seemed deep in thought for a moment and then leaned forward in his seat and continued, "Retaliation, publicity, the safety of their family, the risk of losing their livelihood by participating in the criminal justice process or..."

Alma Rose portrayed a puzzled expression on her face. "Or what?"

Hank continued, "Or the fact that they may not want to expose their own criminal background."

Alma Rose sighed. "I didn't realize that."

Hank said, "It's true." Then he sat back in his chair. "I'm returning to Mallory for a 4 p.m. interrogation of the suspect with Detective Aronowitz. Would you like to accompany me?"

"Could I?"

Hank asked, "Is that a yes?"

Alma Rose blushed with excitement. "Yes...yes."

"I know that you have an appointment with Undersheriff Salentino. Can you be back by 3 p.m.?"

Alma Rose said, "I'll check with him and if I can't be back by then I'll let you know."

"Good, that will give us enough time to get to Mallory." Hank then shifted gears. "Would you like to join Mary and me for dinner this week?"

"Me?"

Hank's eyes surveyed the conference room. "I don't see anyone else here."

Alma Rose smiled. "I'd love to. What about my dad and Kate?"

Hank laughed. "They've been over our house many times. I've got a forensic collection that would make your eyes pop out. Would Friday evening work for you?"

A smile erupted across Alma Rose's face. "All right, I'll tell my dad."

Hank nodded and shook her hand. She felt a sting when their hands touched and, in her mind, she saw blood spatter onto steps. Although she winced, she knew that Hank didn't notice. She thought it better not to reveal the vision unless she knew more about whom, why, where, and when.

When Hank left the sheriff's office, Alma Rose walked to her desk in the corner of the nearly empty staff room of the office. She sat down and opened the book of department regs that her father had left for her. She leaned her head over it for more than a half-hour and tried to absorb as much detail as she possibly could. Then Undersheriff Rocky Salentino approached her desk.

When she heard his steel-toed boots resonate across the floor, she raised her head. Then she asked, "Rocky, where's my dad?" Alma Rose caught herself and rephrased her question, "I mean, Undersheriff Salentino, where's Sheriff Buchanan? I thought he'd be with you."

Rocky laughed. "Let's dispense with the formalities, it's just us."

Alma Rose exhaled. "Thanks."

Rocky continued, "Your dad is attending funeral services for Taylor Police Officer Carl Hoffmann."

"I know but why aren't you there? I thought you left with him?"

"I did but I returned once the funeral procession entered the church. Your father needed five people to manage the sheriff's office while the rest of the staff attended the funeral. I've only been on the job for two years and I never got to meet Officer Hoffmann. That fact plus I had a work detail to attend to in the evidence locker downstairs were the deciding factors in your father asking me to return to the sheriff's office." Rocky glanced at his wristwatch. "They should be back any time now. Your father has a meeting in fifteen minutes."

Alma Rose said, "Yeah, I know...with the FBI."

"You know about that?" Rocky asked.

Alma Rose nodded. "Of course, it's those two agents that I met in the Yaak. One's an undercover biker and the other's his boss."

Rocky said, "You're right. Axe Killian rescued you from the Screaming Skulls biker gang and Special Agent Costa apprehended its leader, Videl Tanas."

Alma Rose exhaled. "If it wasn't for them, I'd probably be dead right now."

"Don't be so modest. You saved Willie Otaktay from certain death. Tanas would have finished him off if you hadn't intervened. I also heard that you revived Willie in the Yaak Wilderness."

Alma Rose felt her cheeks grow warm all over. "I keep telling people that it wasn't me. I'm only a conduit. My purpose is only to help along what's supposed to happen anyway."

Rocky shook his head. "Well, whatever it is, wherever it comes from, you're special." Rocky sat silent for a moment and then said, "Well, I have news too. Taylor Police Captain Linda Stevens and I have begun dating."

Alma Rose smiled. "That's great. I'm so happy for you both. I've always known you two would make a great couple."

"Whoa, hold on. We're only dating...that's all," Rocky said. Then he continued, "We found out that we have a lot in

57

common. She and I both love music. We've been practicing as a duet."

"You mean a band?"

Rocky said, "Linda plays electric guitar and I'm on bass guitar."

"What type of music do you play?"

"Classic rock and country, British Invasion, blues, doo-wop, and a cappella."

"What do you call yourselves?"

A smile grew across Rocky's face. "The Rocky Blues."

"Awesome."

Rocky added, "We've been trying to convince your stepmom to join our band for the past four months. She can play guitar, banjo, mandolin, piano, and even the drums. With her musical background she'd be a good fit and I think it would help in her recovery."

Alma Rose's eyes lit up. "I think you're right. What's the hold up?"

Rocky explained, "Your dad. He's very protective of her."

Alma Rose snickered. "You can say that again. Want me to see what I can do?"

"Would you?"

"You got it."

Then Rocky looked at his wristwatch. "We're due to run a patrol north on Route 56. Are you ready to hit the road?"

Alma Rose nodded. "Yeah but I need to be back by three. Mister Kelly offered to have me sit in on an interrogation."

Rocky asked, "Did you check with your father?"

"No."

He smiled. "Don't worry. I'm second in charge and responsible for your training. Hank Kelly will clear the necessary hurdles for you to attend. It'll look good on your resume. Let's go on that ride-along."

Alma Rose and Rocky got up, left the office, and stepped into the lobby. They came face-to-face with a man dressed in a black suit and tie and another man, sporting a black leather outfit, a doo rag, and a full blond beard.

Rocky extended his hand to the man in the suit. "Agent Costa, how are you? I'm Undersheriff Salentino." A former amateur boxer, Rocky's athletic physique was on full display pushing the department regs and uniform codes to their limit.

FBI Special Agent in Charge Manny Costa returned the handshake. "We worked together last year on the Bitterroot Killer murders, right?"

"Yes sir."

Costa said, "Undersheriff Salentino this is my associate, Special Agent Axe Killian. He's a former military man just like you."

Rocky nodded and offered his hand to Killian. "Rocco Salentino, Airman First Class, U.S. Air Force, Security Police. I was stationed in Kuwait after the Gulf War. That's where I met Sheriff Buchanan. He was a Military dog handler. We had a few scrapes with the locals there."

Killian shook Rocky's hand. "Staff Sergeant Alex Killian, 3rd Battalion, 75th Ranger Regiment, Fort Benning, Georgia. I commanded a Ranger strike force in Somalia during '93."

Alma Rose exhaled long and hard as if to disperse the testosterone-saturated air.

Costa asked, "And this is Sheriff Buchanan's daughter?"

Alma Rose stepped out from behind Rocky's shadow. Black, braided hair flowed from under her oversized department issued chocolate brown hat. Its traditional center crease was a distinct departure from the Campaign four-dent style hat of the same color that the full-time sheriff deputies and her father wore.

Her bronze-tinted cheeks framed a smile that preceded her response. "Yes, I'm a summer intern. I start college this fall."

A sly laugh erupted from Manny. "Don't be so modest young lady. I remember what you did in the Yaak, saving people's lives...putting your own at risk. Not everyone gets the privilege to be selected as a law enforcement intern."

Rocky said, "We were just leaving for a patrol ride-along. It was nice to see you again Agent Costa."

Manny nodded. "Same here," he then turned to Alma Rose, "Miss Buchanan..."

"Two Elk, Alma Rose Two Elk."

"Well, Miss Two Elk. I know that you have this gift of yours."

"It's more of a curse," she admitted.

"Well whatever it is that you have, you were chosen for a reason. I hope that we have the pleasure of meeting again and perhaps working together."

"I'm know we will…I mean, I'm sure that we will," Alma Rose said and took a few steps toward the door, then stopped, turned, and stared at Manny. "I have to tell you about that man you caught whose name has the same letters as Satan."

Manny said, "You mean Videl Tanas?"

Alma Rose said, "Yes."

Undercover Agent Axe Killian pushed his long blond hair away from his face and asked, "What about him?"

Alma Rose stared at Manny and replied in a deliberate voice, "One whom you have forgotten will deal with him."

Manny laughed. "Tanas is safe in jail, where he ought to be."

"Agent Costa, many are the fools who do not recognize who their friends are."

Manny said, "Miss Two Elk, I don't understand."

Alma Rose continued, "A star from the north will make amends and deliver that man Tanas to you."

Manny said, "Tanas will never see the light of day."

"When help comes, just accept it," Alma Rose said.

"And when will that help arrive?" Manny asked.

"Not for many moons as they travel across the sky." She then glanced at her wristwatch. "Hey, look what time it is. I've got to go."

Alma Rose said goodbye to Costa and Killian, then turned and left with Rocky.

Outside the sheriff's office, Rocky questioned Alma Rose. "What are you…a modern-day Nostradamus, speaking in quatrains?"

"Pardon me?"

"Those words in there, where'd they come from?"

"I see them typed right before my eyes, like the credits on a movie screen."

How does that happen?"

As they got into the squad car, Alma Rose glanced at Rocky. "I never question the why, how, or when. I only accept it for what it is."

Rocky asked, "And what is that what?"

Alma Rose stared at Rocky. "That what starts and ends with our Creator."

·13·

Undersheriff Rocco "Rocky" Salentino climbed behind the wheel of his 1995 Chevrolet Caprice black & white patrol car. At Rocky's request, the Cedar County Sheriff's Department motor pool equipped the vehicle with an LT1 engine rated at 350 horsepower. Rocky insisted that he needed it to keep up with the newest generation of gearheads and their souped-up muscle cars.

Junior Deputy Alma Rose Two Elk stared at the Chevy. She had never seen a car like this, so shiny and so new. Nothing on the Crow Reservation even approached the beauty of Rocky's car. Alma Rose opened the passenger door, slid into the passenger seat, and buckled her seatbelt. The inside of the patrol car was just as amazing to her as the outside. The only word that came to mind for Alma Rose was immaculate.

They pulled out of the parking lot and began their ride-along. Rocky headed west on U.S. Highway 200 and only traveled two blocks down Main Street when he glanced at Alma Rose.

"Sheriff Buchanan wanted me to stop by Taylor Veterinary Clinic. He said to check on that young man who hit the elk up on U.S. 228 this morning."

Alma Rose replied, "Louis Miller…is he still there?"

"Your father asked Doc Larson to keep him there until we arrived."

"Why?"

Rocky said, "We have to give him a ride home. I also need to remind him about tomorrow's meeting with your father."

They continued west about a mile past Route 56, turned onto Bitterroot Avenue, and then pulled into the parking lot of the Taylor Veterinary Clinic. Louis Miller was sitting on a bench

61

outside the front of the building. When Rocky got out of the patrol car, Louis Miller stood up.

"Finally, it's about time someone showed up," Louis said.

Rocky stared at the boy and said, "I'm Undersheriff Salentino. Sheriff Buchanan warned me about you."

With defiance in his voice Louis asked, "And what do you mean by that?"

"Sheriff said you have no manners." Rocky stood his ground. "Do you want a ride home or not?"

Louis shrugged his shoulders. "Yeah, I guess. As long as you drop me off before my parents get home from work."

"How did you make out at the ER? Sheriff wants to know."

Louis scoffed. "Yeah, I'm fine...no concussion."

"What's that bandage on the side of your head?"

Louis raised his hand to his head. "I got cut when my head hit the steering wheel during the accident. It stopped bleeding but the doc said he wanted to close it up so it doesn't get infected."

Rocky said, "I need the ER report."

Louis handed a curled up paper to Rocky. "Here you go." Then Louis said, "You should have seen the hot nurse that took my blood pressure."

"Get in the car," Rocky ordered. "I have business inside."

They walked over to the patrol car, Rocky opened the door to the backseat, and Louis got in. Rocky closed the car door and then headed into the veterinary clinic. Junior Deputy Alma Rose Two Elk turned to Louis from behind the half-inch thick polycarbonate, steel divider between the front and back seats.

"You're that boy from the accident this morning," Alma Rose said through the latticed, six-inch square metal insert partition, positioned just below the roof of the vehicle in the middle of the divider.

Louis leaned back, extended his arms across the top of the bench seat, and said, "Listen sweetheart, I'm no boy."

Alma Rose turned away, shook her head, and then said, "It seems like you haven't learned your lesson."

Louis leaned forward. "What lesson is that?"

"That all life is precious."

62

Louis rolled his eyes. "What do you know anyway? You probably lived on the reservation your whole life." He laughed and then leaned back in the seat. "You work in the casino?"

"We don't have casinos on the Crow Reservation."

"No, well you probably should. You could become rich like the other tribes."

Alma Rose hung her head. "I don't know any tribes that are rich. I do know that how we treat others, including animals in this life will have a bearing on how our Creator judges us."

That dumb elk had it coming walking in the road like that."

"That elk was one of Creator's creatures."

Louis' mouth was agape. "You believe that crap?"

"I do."

Louis laughed. "Hey, I have news for you. When we die, it's like turning off a light switch. Nothing happens. That's why you've got to take everything you can in this life regardless of who or what gets in your damn way."

"*Ahóoh*," Alma Rose said.

"What was that?" Louis leaned forward again.

Alma Rose stared out the window and then spoke in a hushed voice, "*Baaiisdúukualitdeete.*"

Louis said, "Now what was that? It's not fair for you to be speaking in a language that I don't understand."

Alma Rose turned to him. "First, I said thank you."

Louis looked around and then smiled. "Thanks."

Alma Rose shook her head. "I was being sarcastic."

Louis' brow furrowed. "Really...what was that other thing that you said?"

"*Baaiisdúukualitdeete*?"

"Yeah, what's that mean?"

Alma Rose turned, faced forward, and said, "It means you have no respect."

Louis leaned back and was silent for a long moment. Then he leaned forward again. "Hey, look...I'm sorry."

Alma Rose answered without looking back. "Yeah, right."

Louis replied, "No, I am. I'm really sorry. I know that sometimes I can be a real jerk. In New York, if you're not a wiseass you get picked on."

Alma Rose turned to him. "In Montana we treat strangers the same as friends. You don't have to be a wiseass with us."

63

Louis took a deep breath. "Can I make it up to you?"

"No." Alma Rose faced forward again.

Louis persisted. "Oh come on now. I'm truly sorry for the things I said. I was out of line, stupid, and selfish too. What can I do to apologize?"

"Tell Creator that you're sorry for killing that elk today."

"That dumb elk? I don't think so." They were both silent for a long moment and then Louis said, "At least tell me your name."

"Junior Deputy Two Elk."

Louis fidgeted in the back seat and then said, "I'm...I'm sorry. Your last name is Elk?"

"Two Elk."

"Geez, I'm so sorry. What's your first name?"

"Alma Rose."

Louis said, "Look, I'm real sorry about the elk. Yeah, I'll ask God for forgiveness. But Alma Rose...yeah, I kind of like that name."

Alma Rose asked, "What's your name?"

"Louis Miller but my friends just call me Lou."

Alma Rose turned her head toward Louis. "You have a lot to learn about how we live in Montana."

Louis nodded. "I'm starting to realize that but I'm willing to learn."

Alma Rose said, "Just take things slowly and let your ears speak to you." She turned back in her seat and faced forward.

Louis smiled. "Hmm, let my ears speak to me...yeah." Louis then leaned forward and said, "I'll have to remember that advice. Can I take you out to dinner? Maybe you can help me adjust?"

Alma Rose blushed, turned back to him, and responded, "Are you serious?"

Louis shrugged his shoulders and smiled again. "Yeah, I am."

"Why should I go out with you?"

"Why not...you got a boyfriend?"

"We broke up earlier this summer. Are you dating anyone?"

Louis stated, "Not anyone serious. What do you say, wanna go out with me?"

Alma Rose faced forward again and shook her head. "My father would kill you."

Louis laughed. "I know but like I said, I'm just waiting for the light switch to go off. Whatdaya say?"

Alma Rose turned to face Louis. "It's not a good idea sneaking around behind my father's back."

Louis leaned back in the seat once again and grinned. "Why does he have to know?"

Alma Rose thought for a moment. "Friday evening I've been invited to dinner with the Chief Medical Examiner and his wife. Maybe I can ask if it's all right to bring a friend. My dad won't be there."

Louis said, "Great, I can enjoy my last moments on this earth with a beautiful girl before her dad finds out about us."

Alma Rose shook her head. "I'm not beautiful."

"Well I think you are. You're beautiful and...mysterious."

Alma Rose replied, "You have no idea."

·14·

R ocky exited the veterinary clinic and returned to the patrol car. He climbed into the driver's seat and then looked in the backseat. Louis Miller sat still and silent. Rocky turned to Alma Rose and stared at her but said nothing.

She sensed the tension between Louis and Rocky like a mountain lion stalking its prey. She just wasn't sure when that big cat would pounce, or in Louis' case, when he would say or do something inappropriate. She felt it important to keep tabs on this young man.

"Have you been sociable?" Rocky asked. He glanced in the rearview mirror and noticed a smile on Louis' face.

Alma Rose said, "We've had a few discussions. It's been civil."

Rocky smiled. "I'm glad everyone's getting along."

"What happened with the elk?" Alma Rose asked.

Rocky replied, "They'll process the carcass and it'll be donated to the Taylor University Department of Ecology for research. The staff taxidermist will fix the damage from the accident. Then he'll mount the hide in the university's Frontiersman's Museum."

Louis asked, "Then some good will come out of what happened, right?"

"I suppose you can say that," Rocky admitted.

"Good," Louis added.

"What about the bald eagle?" Alma Rose asked.

Rocky said, "The vet told me that he heard from Fish & Wildlife. They found a raptor rehabilitator and so far, the eagle's doing well."

Alma Rose asked, "Would it be all right if I visit the eagle from time to time? I'd like to see its progress."

Rocky said, "I don't see why not. Then he leaned to the right and stared between the front seats and into the backseat.

Louis asked, "What?"

"Don't forget about tomorrow's 9 a.m. meeting with the sheriff." Then Rocky's voice grew stern. "Be on time if you know what's good for you."

"Yeah, what's that all about?" Louis asked.

"Sheriff's got a special job for you."

"Like what?"

"That's between you and the sheriff." Rocky started the patrol car and left the veterinary center.

They drove east on U.S. 200 until they reached Montana Highway 56. Rocky turned left and headed north. About two-thousand feet north of the lower end of Bull Lake, Rocky turned right onto Mountain View Drive into the Cabinet Mountains. He followed the switchback road until it abruptly ended at a more than one-hundred-acre parcel with a five-thousand square foot log home as its centerpiece.

Rocky pulled his patrol car onto the red brick driveway, parked in front of the house, and then got out. While he walked behind the patrol car, Louis Miller got out and Alma Rose hit the passenger door power window switch and handed Louis a folded piece of paper.

She whispered, "It's my cellphone number. Call me."

Louis smiled, took the paper from her, and stuck it in his pocket.

When Rocky stood next to Louis, he reminded the boy, "Remember, tomorrow…9 a.m. sharp."

"I'll be there. Don't worry." Louis turned to Alma Rose. "Nice to meet you…Deputy Two Elk. Hope to see you again."

Alma Rose said, "Stay out of trouble Mister Miller."

While Louis Miller walked toward the front door, Rocky climbed into his patrol car. As he drove back toward Route 56, Rocky asked, "What's going on between you and that kid?"

Alma Rose stared at Rocky. "What makes you think something's going on?"

Rocky laughed. "Trained officers can sense things like that. Now tell me what's going on."

"He asked me for a date."

Rocky glanced at her. "What did you say to him?"

Alma Rose stared out the passenger window. "Yes."

Rocky shook his head. "That won't go over well with your father."

Alma Rose swiveled her head back toward Rocky and snapped, "I'm nineteen-years-old."

"Yeah, I know but still, Jim's going to be concerned. This Miller kid may be bad news."

Alma Rose asked, "What better way to keep tabs on him than by staying in touch with him?"

Rocky let out a brief laugh. "Are you going undercover?"

Alma Rose looked straight ahead. "I'll tell my father I'm dating him."

Rocky was silent for a moment and then said, "If you don't tell your father, then I'm not allowed to keep that fact from him. For me to do otherwise would go against protocol."

Alma Rose turned to face Rocky. "Why?"

Rocky spoke in a deliberate voice. "Mister Miller may be subject to criminal charges."

Alma Rose turned forward in her seat. "He's not charged yet so there's no conflict of interest. Besides, I can date who I want and I think there's more to be learned here."

Rocky didn't say a word for a long moment. Then he briefly shook his head and turned to Alma Rose. "All right, we better start that self-defense training first thing tomorrow."

·15·

After the funeral at Mount Olive Lutheran Church and a graveside service and burial at Saint John's Cemetery, Jim returned to the sheriff's office. He took the elevator down to the basement and made a beeline for the men's locker room. Jim removed his dress uniform and placed it onto the hanger in his locker. He showered as if in a futile attempt to sanitize himself from the abstract visage of death. He then put on his everyday uniform.

As Jim went to close the door to his locker, he noticed the yellowed, tattered handwritten note that was taped to the inside of the door. His grandfather, Cecil Gordon Two Elk or better known among the Crow people as Red Hawk, mailed Jim that note in the fall of 1995 after Jim had paid Red Hawk a visit during the annual Crow Fair.

On the note was a drawing of his grandfather's talking stick. It was a simple branch, thirteen inches long, made of cedar wood with an eagle feather on one end and rabbit fur on the other. Jim knew that cedar wood represents the properties of cleansing, protection, prosperity, and healing. Jim stared at the drawing and read the note to himself.

Issaxchí-Káata, as I told you on the day that you visited me, the talking stick's eagle feather is for courage and wisdom to speak truthfully and wisely and the rabbit fur is to remind you that your words must come from your heart. The talking stick has the power of words and it binds our earthly world with the spirit world. One day, from our tribe a spirit woman will appear. The talking stick will guide her to change our world as we know it today. This has been foretold in the Apsáalooke oral tradition

71

Felix F. Giordano

handed down to my father from his father, and from his father before him.

A shiver ran down Jim's spine and he closed his locker door. Jim put on his Stetson and took the elevator up to the first floor. He reached his office, shut the door, and sat at his desk. He corralled the black rotary telephone, which he steadfast refused to relinquish throughout the sheriff's office remodeling phase. Jim dialed a familiar number. A soft voice that brought a smile to Jim's face answered his call on the other end of the line.

Jim said, *"Hi Sarah Whispers...yes, it's Little Hawk...I know it's been a while...yes, Alma Rose is doing well. Is Becca taking good care of you...Bobby too? Good, how's your recovery going...don't worry, a liver transplant takes time...I'm glad to hear that. A little step forward every day is good...I need to ask you for a favor...thank-you, can Bobby take time off from managing the grocery store and bring grandfather Red Hawk to Taylor...I know it's the only store on the Rez but Bobby's son has been the assistant manager for a few years now. Can't he run the store himself...good, please ask Bobby because it's very important that grandfather come to Taylor. It has to do with Alma Rose, she saw something...no, nothing's wrong, she's all right. Alma Rose just needs grandfather's guidance...good, call me tonight at my house, and then let me know when Bobby can leave. Tell them I'll pay for the flight. They can stay at my house...good...love you too sis, goodbye."*

Jim hung up the phone and leaned his elbows on his desk. He raised his hands to his face and cupped his head in his palms. A knock on his office door made him look up. Through the glass of the door, Jim noticed Dan McCoy standing in the hallway. Jim waved him in.

Jim asked, "What brings you down from Whitefish?"

"I smell trouble."

Dan McCoy was a seventy-two-year old, balding man with wisps of white hair that danced across the back of his collar. He was Jim's predecessor in the Cedar County Sheriff's Office and was nearly as tall as Jim with a rugged face carved from years of exposure to the unforgiving Montana weather. A recently grown short white beard gave Dan an aura of intellectuality. However, Jim was keen on the fact that based upon Dan's four-year military hitch in Vietnam and his more than forty years of law enforcement experience, Dan's language

72

could be fragrantly flowery if he was pressured or challenged on a vast array of fronts. Jim knew that Dan liked to stay abreast of any criminal activity in the area. Dan always liked to remind Jim that he was willing to assist the Cedar County Sheriff's Office in any capacity, anytime, anywhere.

Jim asked, "What kind of trouble?"

Dan took a seat in front of Jim's desk and leaned forward. "I heard what happened in Mallory."

Jim cupped his chin in his hand. "Tell me."

Dan shifted his weight in the chair. "I heard they've got the husband at the station. They plan to question him later today."

"How did you hear that?"

Dan took a deep breath. "I not only sleep with the scanner to my ear, and my .38 under the pillow, but the car keys are on my nightstand."

Jim nodded. "Dan, law enforcement's in your blood."

Dan crossed his legs and folded his arms behind his head. "I was going to say that I also sleep with my old duty boots on, but I don't think you'd believe that."

Jim held back a laugh. "I wouldn't be surprised by anything you tell me."

Dan deadpanned, "Well, let me tell you this, I used to complain about old farts but sadly now I find that I'm one of them myself."

Jim laughed and then his voice conveyed a serious tone. "I can use your help on this one. Are they treating the husband as a suspect?"

Dan stood up. "What do you think?" Then he motioned with his head toward the door. "What say you and I get a coffee in your newfangled cafeteria and then you show me how they bastardized this lovely lady of a building? Then I'll know whether or not to accept your request for help."

Jim got up from behind his desk. "Coffee's a good idea. Then we'll discuss compensation."

Dan laid his hand on Jim's shoulder. "If Mallory asks for help, you and I will get to the bottom of this."

They made their way to the cafeteria, grabbed a couple of coffees, and sat at a table. Jim sipped his coffee, placed the cup down on the table, and looked straight at Dan who took several gulps of his coffee.

Jim said, "I want you to spend a few days in Mallory. Talk to some locals who remember you when you were sheriff. They may be more open to telling you what they saw or heard last night. Report back to me on everything you can find out about the disappearance of Mister Driver's wife."

Dan shook his head. "Jim, I've been in law enforcement and the military for more than forty-eight years. You don't need to be a forensic pathologist with framed scraps of paper on the freaking wall to prove that young woman got her goddamn guts carved up and someone carted her away."

Jim put down his coffee cup. "And that Dan, is what I want you to find out."

Dan asked, "Ain't the officers in Mallory up to the task of finding out what happened?"

"Come on Dan, you know that the police department in Mallory is a fraction of the size of Taylor's."

Dan lifted the cup to his mouth and slugged down the remainder of his coffee. Then he slid sidesaddle in his chair, dangled his coffee cup between his thumb and index finger, and stared at Jim.

"Back in the day I did twice the work with half the crew these yokels got today. Aw hell, I'll go to Mallory. I'll see what I can learn. Then Dan asked, "What're ya paying, the usual twenty?"

Jim said, "Thirty an hour plus expenses."

Dan snickered. "Thirty…when did my services become so expensive?"

Jim got up from his seat. "When Governor Robert Ross increased my expense budget."

"And why did that happen?"

Jim waved his hand for Dan to follow. "Ross says a state-of-the-art facility requires a 21st century budget. Come on. Let's start that tour of the building."

They began their jaunt outside. Jim first pointed the kennel to Dan. It was a small addition to the new state-of-the-art Cedar County Sheriff's Office companion building that was just completed this past spring. The funding for the renovation and addition was initiated by Governor Ross, the former mayor of Libby Montana whose daughter, Peta went missing in 1992.

The old part of the sheriff's office that housed the first-floor jailcells in the rear of the building was rededicated to new locker rooms and an evidence locker. The basement remained mostly a storage area. A staff cafeteria was constructed by enlarging the former first floor lunchroom. Many of the rooms in the state-of-the-art facility allowed conversion of the second and third floor rooms in the old sheriff's office into training facilities and conference rooms.

However, Sheriff Jim Buchanan was a stubborn man. He insisted that his office and the old conference room remain on the first floor. His rationale and convincing argument was what better way to engage the community. He thought that if they needed to speak with him or huddle with staff then let them walk the fewest steps possible.

The multi-level basement gym included a regulation size basketball court with retractable wooden bleachers on each side of the long end of the court on the lower level. The intended purpose for the court was recreation for both staff and inmates and community events. Also on the lower level were several storage rooms and a ground floor exit door. On one end of the basement's upper level was a weight room complete with a Nautilus circuit and male and female locker rooms. At the other end of the basement was a handgun firing range and an evidence locker.

Above the gym, the building's first floor contained a new booking facility, a general holding cell, inmate cafeteria/library, a three-bay Sally Port, and the garage and motor pool. Rounding out the first floor besides Jim's office was the dispatch center and a number of conference rooms.

The second floor included a series of administration offices, more conference rooms, a training center, three rooms dedicated to inmate legal representation, and two interrogation rooms with an observation room between them.

The third and last floor was dedicated to inmate housing. Twenty brand-new jailcells were installed along with a central observation station.

When they were done, Jim turned to Dan. "Okay, Dan head over to Mallory. See what you can find out. I want a list of people who say they saw or heard something...and statements from witnesses. Someone's got to know what happened."

·16·

Rocky and Alma Rose spent a few hours together and patrolled the northern and southern areas of Cedar County. They drove north on Route 56 to where it intersects with U.S. Highway 6 and stopped in Libby for a quick bite to eat at a burger joint. Then back down Route 56 into the town of Taylor and south along Route 200 to the border with Sanders County. When they returned to the Cedar County Sheriff's Office, Hank Kelly was waiting for them in the conference room. He was seated at the oval table. An open briefcase and numerous piles of papers were scattered on the table in front of him.

Hank said, "Undersheriff Salentino, it's about time you returned. Deputy Two Elk and I have a 4 p.m. interrogation in Mallory."

Rocky glanced at his wristwatch. "I heard about that. You'll have plenty of time to get there."

Alma Rose said, "Thank you, Undersheriff Salentino. I really enjoyed the ride-along."

Rocky reminded her, "Don't forget, self-defense training tomorrow. Bring a pair of sneakers. We've got department issued sweats for you to wear."

Once Alma Rose nodded, Rocky tipped his Stetson and left the office. She turned to Hank who was gathering his paperwork and stuffing them inside his briefcase.

"Doctor Kelly?" she asked.

"Yes?"

"Is that Friday dinner invitation still open?"

Hank smiled. "Of course, why do you ask?"

"I'd like to accept your invite, but I was wondering if it would be all right if I brought someone with me?"

Hank nodded. "Of course...is it that boy Acaraho?"

"No we broke up and besides, he's back home on the Rez in Crow Agency."

"Then who...a boy from around here?"

"Yes."

"Do I know him?"

"Maybe." Alma Rose sat down and remained silent.

Hank sat next to her. "Is anything wrong?" he asked.

Alma Rose put her head down. "I...uh, it's that boy from the accident in Mallory."

Hank winced. "Does your father know about this?"

Alma Rose turned to Hank and pleaded, "Not yet. Can we keep this between us until I have a chance to tell my father?"

"Well, I..."

Alma Rose interrupted him, "Please, Doctor Kelly. There's something about to happen but I can't pinpoint it yet. I think it may involve this boy but if my father gets involved the consequences may become much worse. I can sense it."

Hank sighed. "It goes against my better judgement but knowing your gift, I'll give you some rope. Just don't trip over it."

"Thank you, Doctor Kelly. You won't regret this."

Hank stared at her. "You better be right young lady." He then shifted gears. "Are you about ready to leave for that interrogation?"

Alma Rose said, "Ready as I'll ever be."

·17·

It was late in the afternoon when Hank Kelly and Alma Rose drove to the Mallory Police Station next to the town hall. The police station was a two-story building with a cornerstone inscribed with the 1917 construction year. Offices, meeting rooms, and storage occupied the first and second floors, and a small number of jailcells were situated in the basement.

Hank got out of his car and charged up the granite steps to the heavy wooden door. Alma Rose followed a few steps behind. They walked inside and up to the security glass window in the lobby.

"I'm here to meet with Detective Martin Aronowitz," Hank said to the female officer on duty.

"Are you Medical Examiner Henry Kelly?" she asked.

"Yes."

"Who's the recruit?"

"This is Sheriff Buchanan's daughter. She's a Junior Deputy with the Cedar County Sheriff's Office."

The officer first glanced at Alma Rose and then at Hank. "How'd she get that gig?"

Hank replied, "She's serving a summer internship."

Alma Rose piped up, "I was accepted into the Forensic Studies Program at the University of Montana."

"Congratulations," the officer said in a sarcastic tone and with a furrowed brow. She then pointed at the metal door leading to the office proper. "Go in that way, Detective Aronowitz is waiting." She buzzed Hank and Alma Rose inside.

The main responsibility of the Mallory Police Department is to serve the local community by investigating all crimes within the city limits. Hank also knew that those crimes could range from classic misdemeanors to serious felony charges of the highest degree. He noticed that Detective Aronowitz waited outside his office.

Aronowitz said, "Hank, right on time. And I see you brought your guest just like you explained over the phone."

Hank smiled and offered his hand. "Marty, I always keep my appointments and my promises."

"Good, come inside and have a seat."

Aronowitz settled into the chair behind his desk. Hank and Alma Rose sat in the two side chairs that faced Aronowitz' pine desk.

"Marty, earlier today you invited me to an interrogation."

"I did Hank but before we begin, I wanted to brief you on what my department is up against." Marty turned to Alma Rose. "Listen to what I'm going to tell you because they won't teach you this in school."

Alma Rose pulled a notebook from her left breast pocket and a pen from the other pocket. "We're ready," she said.

Marty explained, "The Mallory Police Department has eighteen sworn officers covering three shifts, one sergeant, a captain, two forensic technicians, and a support staff of two civilian employees, Police Chief Joseph Delaney, and yours truly. That's it for a community of more than four-thousand people."

Alma Rose jotted the data in her notebook, glanced at Hank and then looked at Marty. "I understand."

"Good, I just want you to realize that investigations here may take longer to get completed than elsewhere where there are more resources."

Alma Rose nodded. "I understand."

Marty continued, "Before we begin the interrogation, I want to fill you in on the details of what happened today."

Hank said, "You told me that you received a call around midnight of a disturbance at an apartment complex and that you found the front door of unit number nine wide-open and blood everywhere."

"That's right. We found pools of blood and blood spatters. You don't need to be a professional criminologist to determine that a homicide occurred. The husband, Gary Driver arrived home around 3 a.m. We found blood in his car, blood on his shirt, and what appeared to be a defensive wound on his hand. We're assuming his wife was the victim."

Hank asked, "Do you have any idea how the suspect may have suffered his injury?"

"As I said, it appears to be a defensive knife wound. Perhaps his victim wielded her own knife in self-defense, or she temporarily took the weapon away from him and there was a struggle."

"Did you find a weapon?" Hank asked.

"No."

"Then without a body or confession this is all conjecture that a murder happened, correct?"

Marty said, "Of course but as you know we found a pair of human eyeballs on the coffee table. The eye color matches that of the suspect's wife. Further forensic analysis will determine if the eyes belong to the victim. If they do, then there'll be conclusive evidence that we have a murder victim."

Hank asked, "You keep saying victim but there's still no body, correct?"

Marty said, "Yes but we start with a blank canvas and then populate it with whatever evidence presents itself to us. Shall we go to the interrogation room?"

Marty led Hank and Alma Rose from his office and down the hallway. On the left was a 10x12 foot interrogation room. Next to it was a larger room. Marty opened the door to that adjacent room and prompted Hank and Alma Rose to enter. The room was dimly lit with one-way glass offering a wide view of the interrogation room. Marty offered Hank and Alma Rose a seat at a conference table.

"I thought we'd be in the room with the suspect," Alma Rose said.

"No, no," Marty said. "I'll conduct the interrogative and other than a telephone connection with Mister Kelly, from time to time, I'll return to this room and speak with the two of you to get your take on the progress."

Alma Rose glanced at Hank who gave her a nod.

Hank said, "Tell us what happened when you first spoke with the suspect."

Marty replied, "When the suspect arrived at the scene, we approached him, but he acted as if he knew nothing. He even pretended that he thought we were there simply to evict him and his wife from their apartment. He identified himself as the victim's husband."

Hank said, "I'm sorry but I have to bring this up again. You keep saying victim but there's no body."

"Hank, we know the husband and wife were the only ones living in that apartment, the wife is missing, there's blood all over the floors and walls, human eyeballs in the living room, and the husband was covered in blood."

Hank shook his head. "I don't like to pull rank but I've been investigating mob murders and serial killers in New York since the 1960s. We never arrested anyone for suspicion of murder until we either found a body, a murder weapon tied to a suspect, or the suspect's confession."

Marty's voice grew louder. "Body or no body, we know this is a clear-cut homicide investigation. All we're looking for is a confession and a tip to where the husband dumped the body."

"So, you're sticking with the husband as your suspect?" Hank asked.

Marty nodded. "Yes."

"Has he confessed?"

"He isn't cooperating."

"He's Native American, correct?"

"Yes, why do you ask?"

Hank glanced at Alma Rose. "Because Deputy Two Elk here is our Ace in the Hole."

·18·

The prison holding cell felt cold and oppressive to Gary Driver. The nearly ten hours of imprisonment since he had been apprehended was beginning to drive him to the precipice of madness. It wasn't just the isolation but the fact that the police wouldn't tell him what happened to his wife. All he knew was that something terrible occurred at the apartment and that his wife was no longer there. The sole fact that Janice Driver's spirit was completely intertwined with his was the only thing that kept him from losing it altogether.

A member of the Blackfeet Nation, Gary paced back and forth in his holding cell mumbling random words and phrases. "I wish I had a gun. I wish I had a goddamn gun."

Gary clenched his fist and pounded it on the cinder block wall. The pain seared through the nerves in his arm, then into his shoulder, migrated up his neck, and then swept behind his ear and across his cheek. The shock waves agitated the beaded perspiration on his forehead and caused them to cascade down his face and onto his orange jumpsuit.

An officer rushed up to Gary's cell. "What's going on in there, Driver?"

Gary craned his neck at the metal cell door. "Nothing," he said.

He collapsed onto his bunk and rested the back of his head against the dark spot on the gray wall. The heaviness of the atmosphere in the 6x8-foot holding cell pressed against his wounded spirit with a vengeance

If Janice is hurt, I'll kill whoever harmed her, Gary said to himself.

He leaned forward on the bunk and held his head in his hands. A fleeting moment of clarity enveloped him.

How many times had he relived what happened last night? He came home to find the apartment complex awash in police cars. The ongoing torture was his only hope that, in some way, he could make sense of it all. What he thought he experienced and what others were telling him was a never-ending chess game that played out in his mind. At times he even wondered if perhaps everyone else was right and his account of what happened was simply a wishful version of events.

Random thoughts ran through his mind. Damn Mallory. Why did I ever listen to Janice and move here with her? It was the biggest mistake of our lives. Then he thought back to a stranger who harassed him one day at the lumberyard where he worked. The man confronted Gary and blurted out that he loved Janice more than Gary ever would and that if Gary left her, everyone's lives would be better off. Harsh words between the men led to profanity and then tempers escalated into a fistfight. Gary ended up with a bloodied nose and got fired from his job. He began to wonder if that stranger had something to do with his wife's death.

The telephone in the cellblock proper rang and the officer on guard duty answered it. After a brief phone conversation, the officer said, "Driver, Detective Aronowitz wants to see you."

Gary swiveled his head and saw the officer outside through the peep hole of the holding cell door. "I have nothing to say," Gary said.

The officer responded, "He knows that. He wants to see you anyway. He said he's got coffee and doughnuts."

Gary got up, stepped over to the holding cell door, and shoved his arms into the tray slot. The officer affixed a pair of handcuffs to Gary and then ordered him to back away from the door. The officer opened the holding cell door and with the help of two other officers, they placed a belly chain around Gary and replaced the handcuffs with a set of cuffs that kept Gary's hands at waist level attached to the belly chain. Finally, they affixed a pair of leg irons and connected them to the belly chain by a long connector chain. Gary Driver was in full harness combination that restricted most of his movement.

The officers brought Gary into the interrogation room where Detective Aronowitz sat at a table.

"Have a seat," Aronowitz said. "Call me Marty. Do you want an attorney present?"

Gary stared into Marty's eyes and said, "There's no need for an attorney. I didn't do anything wrong."

Gary sat down across the table from Marty. One officer stayed in the room while the other two left.

"Here's coffee." Marty slid a Styrofoam cup toward Gary. Marty then opened a box of doughnuts. "Do you prefer crullers or jelly?"

"What?" Gary asked.

"Doughnuts, do you prefer crullers or jelly doughnuts?" Marty smiled. "You're allowed to say both."

"Just coffee," Gary answered. He reached for the cup with his handcuffed hands, bent his head downward toward the tabletop, and took a sip. Then he looked up. "Am I being charged with something?"

Marty said, "Mister Driver, you're being held on a five-hundred thousand dollar bond for one count of suspicion of kidnapping and two counts of obstruction of justice charges in relation to the disappearance of your wife, Janice Driver. There may be more charges coming. You'll be arraigned in a few days."

Gary then said, "I didn't do anything wrong. Let me go. I'll find Janice." Gary bowed his head and then perked up in an instant. "There's a guy, he stopped by work a few weeks ago."

"What guy?" Marty asked, "The guy that you got into a fight with at the lumberyard?"

"Yeah, him, I didn't know him. He wouldn't' tell me his name but I noticed an odd tattoo on his neck. I never met him before. He took off before the police showed up."

"We can show you a few mug shots. Maybe you can identify him?"

Gary said, "Yeah sure." Then he thought for a moment and added, "There was another guy."

"What guy?"

Gary replied, "Last winter, this guy rang the bell at the apartment, I answered the door and he asked for Janice."

"Did he say why he was there?"

Gary nodded "He said he was conducting a survey for the Cedar County Ledger on prejudice against Native Americans."

"What did you tell him?"

"Janice is Flathead and I'm Blackfeet, so prejudice against our people is something we're both concerned with. I told him that I could answer his questions but he persisted to ask where Janice was. I told him she was at school."

"What did he say next?"

"He asked when it would be good for him to return and speak with Miss Jenny in private. That's what he called her. Then he said, I'd like to give her something."

"What did you tell him?"

"I told him that he better leave and not show up here again or else."

"What did he say to that?" Marty asked.

"He stared at me for the longest time and then he just laughed and left."

"Did he show up again?"

Gary shook his head. "No sir."

"Can you describe him?" Marty asked.

"Yeah, I think so." Gary's eyes searched the ceiling for a face. Then he said, "He wore dark glasses and what looked like one of those…uh, black ski masks but it didn't cover his whole head, only up to his eyes. He also had like…like, I dunno, a brown fur hat with ear flaps, like you see the Russian military wear."

Marty asked, "So you didn't get a good look at his face?"

"No sir. The mask and the sunglasses covered his whole face."

"How about hair color…length?"

"No sir. The hat blocked everything. He even had the ear flaps down. I couldn't make out anything."

"Clothes?"

"A heavy coat, knee-length."

"How about shoes?"

"I think he had boots on but I couldn't tell you what brand or even the color but they were probably black…oh, he did have mechanic coveralls on under the coat."

Then, Marty's cell phone rang. He answered it with a hello but then remained silent. "I see, all right." Marty jotted down words in a spiral notebook. After more than a minute, he ended the call. He read to Gary from the notebook, "*All over the earth the faces of living things are all alike. With tenderness have these come up out of the ground. Look upon these faces of children without number and with children in their arms, that*

86

they may face the wind and walk the good road to the day of quiet."

"You speak of Black Elk?" Gary asked.

"What's a black elk?" Marty asked

Gary replied, "He was a *Wičháša wakȟáŋ*, a holy man of the Oglala Lakota. They're his words." Gary then turned and stared at the expansive black mirror on the wall. Then he stared back at Marty. "Who's in there, what game are you playing?"

Marty said, "This is no game."

Then the door to the interrogation room burst open and Alma Rose rushed in followed by an officer trying to grab her.

"Gary, follow the Red Road," Alma Rose pleaded. "No harm shall come to you if you are truthful."

Gary stared at Marty. "Who's this?"

Marty sighed, "Gary Driver, meet Junior Deputy Alma Rose Two Elk, Sheriff Buchanan's daughter."

Hank Kelly entered the room and with a series of heavy breaths explained, "I tried to restrain her, but she had the strength of a superhuman."

Marty looked up at the second officer. "Bring in two more chairs, will you Rex?"

"Yes sir," the officer responded and then left the room.

Gary first bowed his head, then looked up and stared at Alma Rose. "I've heard of ones like you. Many call people like you, The Ones Who Know. A few say they are *midewikwe*."

"What's that?" Marty asked.

Gary turned to him and said, "A member of the *Midewiwin*, they are like the white man's Masons. Only unlike the white man, they follow The Way of the Heart and are of pure spirit."

Alma Rose said, "I am not a *midewikwe*. I am who I am. I'm just a woman who's a conduit."

"A conduit for the Great Spirit?" Gary asked.

Alma Rose said, "I'm not really sure."

Gary stared at Alma Rose in her uniform. "I know who you are. You're a holy woman. You're Crow, aren't you?"

Alma Rose simply said to Gary, "I think I saw your wife."

"Where?" Gary asked and then hung his head down to his chest and began to cry.

Alma Rose continued, "I can't be sure if it was her but please tell me what happened so that I can speak with her."

Gary looked up, raised his arms as far as the belly chain would allow, then put his head down and used the sleeves of his jumpsuit to absorb the tears from his eyes.

He turned to Marty and spoke in a trembling voice, "When a Native holy woman tells you they've seen someone it's not the same meaning when a white man says it. I'm no longer afraid for my wife. I know that she's in the spirit world now. I want to find her killer." Gary wiped away more tears. "All right, I'll tell you what happened."

·19·

Marty sat at the table in the interrogation room with Hank Kelly by his side. Alma Rose Two Elk sat at one end of the table while Gary Driver sat at the other. One officer remained in the room and stood guard at the door. Marty set a tape recorder onto the table and pressed the record button.

"It's Monday, June thirtieth, nineteen ninety-seven. We're at the Mallory Police Station in Mallory Montana. My name is Detective Martin Aronowitz of the Mallory Police Department. I'm now interviewing kidnapping suspect Gary Driver regarding the disappearance of his wife Janice Driver. In attendance is Montana Chief Medical Examiner Henry Kelly, Junior Deputy Alma Rose Two Elk of the Cedar County Sheriff's Office, and Officer David Jordan of the Mallory Police Department."

Marty signaled for Gary to begin speaking. Gary's memories transported him back to the previous evening and as he spoke, he saw the events unfold right before his eyes as if they were occurring in real time.

*****

Gary had waited for his wife, Janice to return home in her Chevy Vega from studying at Taylor University. He stared through the front window of their apartment. He watched Janice turn off the engine and step out of her car. Their first six months of marriage had been burdened with financial problems. Gary's firing, two months overdue on the rent, and a telephone disconnect were just too much to bear. When Janice opened the apartment door, Gary confronted her.

89

"Where were you? I was worried when you didn't get home by dinnertime."

"I was at the university."

"It's almost nine o'clock, what were you doing there?"

Janice dropped her books onto the kitchen table with a thud and then placed her keys on top of them. "I was studying at the university library until it closed. Then I went to a classmate's house to study."

"What classmate?"

"You don't know her."

"You were late coming home on Friday too. You knew we had to drive to Browning that night. What's going on? Was it that guy that started a fight and got me fired from work?"

"What guy?"

Gary said, "I never asked him his name."

"Was it Lester?"

"Who's Lester?" Gary asked.

Janice shook her head and rolled her eyes. "He's some middle-aged guy who used to follow my mom and me around at the powwows before you and I met."

"Is he the guy that popped me at work and got me fired?"

Janice said, "Probably."

Gary took a step toward Janice. "So are you seeing him?"

"NO!" Janice yelled. "I stopped by the emergency clinic."

"Why, is there something wrong?"

"I haven't been feeling well for about a week." Then Janice smiled. "I'm pregnant."

"What?"

"I've missed my last two periods. That's why I went to the clinic."

Gary hugged her. "That's great."

Then Gary pulled back and his elation manifested itself into a pained and weary stare.

"Is anything wrong?" Janice asked.

"We shouldn't be so self-centered. How can we care for a child when we can't even take care of ourselves?"

Janice said, "That's why I'm taking summer classes."

Gary turned away. "Janice, you know I got fired at the lumber mill. Now I can't even support us. With only one car between us, that limits where I can work. Maybe we should go back to the Rez. Maybe I can get my old job back in the school's kitchen? On the Rez, it's only a five-mile walk to the school from your cousin's house."

Janice threw her arms around Gary and rested her head against his back. "Slow down. We're not moving back in with my cousin. I can take the fall semester off and ask Mister Bailey at the Mallory Pharmacy if I can work double shifts."

Gary turned around and returned the hug. "A full-time job plus college classes are already too much. And now with a baby on the way you can't keep up that schedule. You have to take time off."

Janice said, "The baby's not due until January. I can skip the spring semester and make up the classes next fall and graduate. I have to finish school."

Gary held Janice in his arms. "I'll call Sheriff Buchanan. My friend used to serve with him in the sheriff's office. Maybe I can do odd jobs, sweep up, or file paperwork. Then I can earn enough to get my own car."

Janice smiled and kissed Gary. "Good, then in the morning we'll come up with a plan. Now it's time for me to shower and go to bed. I'm exhausted. I need all day tomorrow to study. Finals for the first summer session are next week."

"Janice, I need to use the car to get to the post office."

"When?"

"Now."

"Why?"

"I heard about a job opening."

"What job?"

Gary explained, "It's a job position with the Burlington Northern Railroad. They just extended tracks to the coal mines in the Powder River Basin south of here. They're hiring for five-day shifts. I picked up a blank application the other night when I borrowed the car to go grocery shopping."

"That's great."

"Yeah, I filled out the application today and need to get it in the mail as soon as possible. I can drop it off at the post office tonight. I'll only be gone a half-hour."

"Can't you do that in the morning?" Janice asked.

Gary said, "You know I can only borrow the car at night. Plus this way, my application will be in the mail pickup first thing in the morning. Don't worry, I'll drive safely."

Janice kissed Gary again. Then she said, "Well I guess I can't stop you. I'm going into the shower. I'll see you when you get back."

"All right, I won't be long."

Gary remembered snatching the keys off Janice's textbooks and left. Reliving his past actions in the apartment transported Gary to another state of consciousness and the experience overwhelmed him.

·20·

Gary Driver sat still. He hung his head and began to cry. Marty stood up and pushed his chair aside. He motioned to the officer and telegraphed a special signal. The officer shifted his stance toward the door, opened it, and then stepped outside the room.

"Don't worry son. You're doing well. Just let it all out," Marty said.

"I didn't kill Janice." Gary wiped his tears onto the upper sleeves of his jumpsuit.

Marty glanced down at the tape recorder to ensure it was still recording. Then he said, "Just tell us what you recall."

The officer returned and placed a can of ginger ale on the table in front of Gary.

Hank turned his head to glance at Alma Rose. When he saw her weep, he offered her the handkerchief from the breast pocket of his sports jacket. She took it and dabbed her eyes.

Gary took the soda can in his hands, popped the top, bent over, and took a sip. "You want me to continue?"

Marty said, "Yes, you were leaving the apartment."

Gary continued, "I remember leaving the apartment, driving to the Town Pump gas station and filling up the tank. Then I drove to the post office in Mallory, walked into the lobby, and slipped my application into the outgoing mail drop."

Gary continued to speak and related what transpired as if in a trance that he couldn't pull himself out of.

*****

Gary remembered standing outside the post office after he mailed his job application. He returned to his car and sat for a moment in the silent beauty of the night sky. He recalled how things seemed to be looking up. Janice would work in a doctor's office, he would get a job with the railroad or the sheriff's office, and they would start a family. He recollected slapping his hand across his face to make sure it wasn't just a dream. Last night he had never felt this elated in his entire life.

On the way home, he recalled that he noticed the signpost for Howard Lake and spotted a familiar Dodge van pull into the parking lot. He had to announce the news to an old friend. Gary stopped his car at the entrance to the campground and watched the van pull into campsite number nine. He spotted Mac Drew climb out of the van, then laugh, and head toward his tent. Gary pulled into the main parking lot and walked toward campsite number nine. He stepped past the van and toward the tent. A solitary glow brightened the inside of the tent. Gary recalled the conversation.

"Hey, Mister Drew. Any luck?"

A few seconds elapsed and then a man with long, white hair poked his head out from the tent. "Who's there? I can't see you in the dark," Mac Drew said.

"Mister Drew, have you been drinking? It smells like an old brewery in there." Gary chuckled.

"Maybe it does. So what's it to you, you gonna arrest me for drinking while fishing?"

Gary laughed. "No I'm not, Mister Drew. I'm not a cop, not just yet anyway."

On bended knees, Mac's head bobbed. "My damn eyes ain't rightly focusing. How do you know me?"

Gary explained, "You're the only one in Mallory that I know who owns a van and a yellow tent. Most campers drive pickups and use green tents in the summer and white tents in the winter to conceal themselves from their prey during the hunt. I never did understand why you use yellow."

Mac raised his voice. "I ain't a hunter, I'm a fishin'. The trout don't matter what color my goddamn tent is."

Gary laughed. "Right. Well, I have something to tell you."

"This better be good, bothering me after midnight. I got to get back to my van. I got pressing needs." Mac squinted, and then stared at Gary. "Shit, you're Gary Driver...ain't ya?"

"I am, Mister Drew."

"Call me Mac. Come on inside. We might as well down a few beers together." A smile crept across Mac's face.

Gary suggested, "Why don't we sit in your van? It's awfully small in this tent of yours."

"My van?" Mac raised his voice, "My van...no we'd be better off right here."

Gary stepped toward the van. "Come on Mac, let's sit in the van and stretch out."

Mac raised his voice. "Get the hell away from my van."

Gary stopped in his tracks, nodded, and muttered, "Okay, okay. I'll sit in your cramped tent."

"What did you say?" Mac asked.

Gary responded, "I said, I wish I paid the rent."

"You got money problems?"

"Don't we all," Gary said.

Mac laughed. "That's why I drink and fish...mostly drink or drink like a fish."

Gary stepped into the shelter and shared a few minutes of conversation with the man who had been his foreman at the lumber mill. The scent of stale beer pervaded the air inside the tent. Gary remembered that it was a stark contrast to the scent of the wild in and around Howard Lake.

Gary asked, "How long you been retired now?"

"Next month it'll be a year. Damn, I didn't want to retire but that rich Miller guy comes down from New York, buys out the lumber mill, and then decides that he can make more money by forcing some of us old-timers to retire. Those fuckers don't understand that sometimes it's those jobs that keeps our tickers going." Then Mac took a deep breath. "Hell, it'll also be five years ago on this 4th of July that my daughter, Kat went missing."

"I'm sorry to hear that Mister Drew. People say it was *Saka'am Skaltamiax* who's responsible."

"English, speak English damn boy."

"Moon Man, it's that Flathead tribe's legend," Gary said.

Mac squinted. "Moon Man...Moon Man, now that's stupid shit. I don't believe goddamn crap like that."

Gary said, "Some people say it's that cult up in the Yaak, the Children of the Big Sky. They kidnapped Governor Ross' daughter the same day your daughter went missing."

Mac shook his head and let out a cry. "That Peta Ross they kidnapped was just a child. My daughter was thirty-four years old." Mac wiped away a tear from his cheek. "It's goddamn cruel

95

that people say it was the same people. That just makes it more difficult for the police to find out who really stole my daughter."

"The police will find her, don't worry," Gary said.

Mac raised his voice. "Bullshit, your mother-in-law went missing too. There's been a lot of that shit going on in these parts. I don't trust the government or the law anymore. There's that mayor of Taylor a few years back cutting people up and sending their body parts to hospitals. Then there was also that white supremacist undersheriff who was killing those people to hide his bootlegging business. I tell ya now, it ain't goddamn safe in these parts anymore. The people who are paid to protect us are the ones who are killing us."

Gary nodded. "I know what you're saying. It's true, my wife's mother disappeared in '88, I think."

"Yeah, I knew her," Mac said.

Gary explained, "Janice told me that she was Bitterroot Salish. They lived on the Flathead Reservation. Her name was Beth Astride a Horse. When she married, she took Roger's last name...Weatherwax."

"Well, we ain't gonna solve a bunch of disappearances tonight, are we?" Mac said. "Hey, I got to get back to that van."

Gary asked with a laugh, "Why? Who or what are you hiding in there?" Gary got up to head to the van.

Mac stood up and blocked Gary's path outside. "You ain't fucking going nowhere."

Gary faced his palms to Mac. "Okay, okay. Forget about going to your van. We'll just sit right here."

Mac said, "Well I've still got to go to the van. You stay right here."

Mac left the tent and ran to the van. He climbed inside, slammed the door shut, and the audible sound of the door locks engage resonated in the still night air.

About ten minutes later Mac returned and said, "How are you doing Gary Driver? I heard you got fired a few months ago because some guy came to the mill and popped you one for no good reason. Fucking new management at the lumber mill don't know how to treat people. If I was still your boss there you wouldn't have gotten fired. I blame that rich Miller guy again. He'd squeeze a penny through a keyhole if he could."

Gary said, "I'm doing okay. But I don't know where or when I'll find work. I just dropped off an application for a railroad job."

"Railroad work's okay. In Montana the only steady jobs are working for the railroad, in timber, or the goddamn law. You ever consider submittin' an application with the Cedar County Sheriff's Office? Maybe you'd be the one to make things right with the law?"

Gary snickered. "Actually, I had a conversation with Janice about that tonight. Maybe I'll be doing some custodial work in Taylor?"

"Bullshit, I ain't talking about no broom pusher. A lawman's job. Deputy to Sheriff Jim Buchanan...I guess you Indians call him Little Hawk, right?" Mac asked.

"His name is *Issaxchí-Káata*. That means Little Hawk in the *Apsáalooke* language," Gary said.

"Apsa-what?"

Gary repeated, "*Apsáalooke...Apsáalooke*. That's the tribe's name. It's the white man that calls them Crow Indians."

"Whatever his name is or wherever he comes from, that ain't the point I'm trying to make. I'm talking about a real job with the sheriff's office. A deputy's job."

Gary laughed. "Naw. I don't know nothing about the law."

"You told me once that you got a friend who works there. He'd clue you in on what to do," Mac suggested.

Gary shook his head. "He doesn't work there anymore."

Mac pivoted his head. "Why not?"

"He moved his family to California and got a job with the FBI. Maybe California's where I should take Janice."

"Janice? Yeah. Janice. You and her, I tell ya, the salt of the Earth you both are, the salt of the Earth. I never met better people. But don't move. Then I'd have no chance to see her from time to time. So, Janice...yeah, how's that sweet wife o'yours?"

"That's what I wanted to tell you." Gary smiled. "We're gonna have a baby."

Mac stood up and based on Gary's recollection, the old man seemed to ponder for a moment. Then a smile erupted across his face, then widened, and he bellowed a hearty laugh. "Well, congratulations. You got the makings of a fine family there. How about we fry us up that trout I caught today?" Mac asked. "It'll be a celebration for the grandchild."

Gary said, "Grandchild? Janice's parents are both dead."

"Right, uh, I mean a grandchild for your parents."

"I don't see my parents anymore. They still live on the reservation up north. I stay in touch with an uncle of mine though."

Mac continued, "Yeah, well, anyways, let me give you my blessings. This is an occasion to rejoice."

Gary took a step toward the front of the tent. "I promised Janice I'd be right back after the post office."

"Well, you tell that lovely wife of yours that if she has any problems with you getting' home late to just give old Mac Drew a call. I'd love to hear her sweet voice again."

Gary distinctly remembered that he noticed a tear escape from Mac's right eyelid. Then Gary said, "Deal."

Mac then put down his beer and said, "You clean the fish. I'll get the propane grill started."

Gary cleaned and filleted the trout. When he was nearly done, the knife slipped, and Gary sliced his left index finger. The deep cut nearly went to the bone.

Gary screamed, shook his hand, and then sucked on the wound. "Man, that really hurts. Dammit, how sharp do you keep these knives?" Gary wiped blood across his shirt and rubbed his blood-smeared face onto his sleeve.

Mac smiled. "Sharp enough. A dull knife ain't gonna do a good job cuttin' flesh." Then he tossed a white handkerchief to Gary. "Take this and press it onto the wound or else your blood'll attract a shark or two."

Gary grabbed the handkerchief, and spotted Mac laughing at his own humor. "It's not funny," Gary said. He brushed his hand across his shirt, took the handkerchief, and then wrapped it tightly around his hand. Blood from his wound oozed and spread throughout the handkerchief turning it from white to red in a matter of seconds. "Damn, this thing won't stop bleeding."

"Take this." Mac reached into his first aid kit and pulled out a gauze bandage and a bottle of hydrogen peroxide.

Gary first unfolded the handkerchief and then stuck it in his pocket. In an alcohol-induced stupor, Mac poured peroxide onto the wound, spilling some of the bloody residue onto Gary's shirt. Mac dried off Gary's wound with a clean towel and then bound Gary's finger in the sanitary dressing. Mac took a healthy strip of tape and used it to keep the gauze in place.

Gary said, "Man, it still hurts."

Mac reached into his cooler, pulled out a can of beer, and offered it to Gary. "A few of these and you ain't gonna feel any pain. I had six already…I think it was six. Anyway, it sure feels like a six-beer buzz."

Gary explained, "I've got to drive home. My wife expects me back soon."

Mac laughed. "With that open wound you ain't leaving for a couple three hours. Otherwise it'll open up the minute you turn the steering wheel. Sit and relax with me. Let's enjoy the trout and have a few beers. Tell that wife of yours you spent a few hours humoring an old man on Howard Lake. She'll know who you mean. I knew the Weatherwax family before you two met. Roger and Beth were friends of mine."

Gary cocked his head. "Janice never told me that."

Mac continued, "That's cause the bad blood between her dad and the town kept her mom from telling Janice about the true friends her dad had. Truth is, I got Roger jobs at the lumber mill three separate times."

"Really?"

"Sure enough, but each time he seemed to get himself fired. That got me in some damn trouble with the manager. I could have wrung Roger's goddamn fucking neck."

"But Mac, Janice told me he was killed."

Mac contorted his face. "Uh, yeah...I guess. Aw, some folks who don't like your kind tend to say that he ran off. Left his wife and kids and either found some pretty young Indian girl or hopped a freight train for the west coast...maybe even both."

Gary shook his head. "That's not what I heard. Talk around town was that he was murdered."

Mac stood up. "How can they say he was murdered? There was no body." He tossed his empty beer can toward the back of the tent. "Aw fuck, don't believe everything you hear, especially from those drunkards down at the Chuck Wagon Bar & Grill. Besides, if Roger Weatherwax was murdered, he damn well deserved it. And I hope he suffered a slow and painful death."

Gary asked, "How can you say that?"

Mac pointed his finger at Gary and his voice crackled. "I helped Beth and the kids stay in their apartment. Paid the goddamn rent and the fucking bills too. That's something that bastard Roger never fucking did. Hell, Janice was way too young to really know everything about her mom's shithole husband. I even minded the kids for Beth while she had things to do. Truth is, I, uh, I had a fancy toward Beth, so to speak. At least we didn't let on to the kids about us. I really loved that woman. Yeah, it was 1988 when she disappeared, a year after Roger disappeared. Geeze, I'm talking too much now. Saying things that oughtn't be said. Must be the beer. How's that saying go, best to let sleeping dogs lie? Hey, I got to get back to my van."

By now, Gary's mouth was agape, and he stared straight ahead. When he regained his composure from hearing a possible confession that only a man in a half-drunken stupor would utter, Gary nodded. "Sleeping dogs, yeah...something like that. I guess."

*****

And with that, Gary offered to Detective Martin Aronowitz his explanation on why he didn't return home earlier on Sunday evening.

·21·

Marty shook his head and then exhaled. He turned to Hank Kelly and the two men shared a look that spoke volumes. Their combined experience told them that the mysterious disappearance of Janice Driver may not be the only crime that needed to be solved.

Marty said, "Driver stay put. I'll have more questions for you later." Then he turned to Hank. "What do you say; wanna go for a walk?"

Hank nodded and whispered to Alma Rose. "Join us."

Marty turned to the officer in the room, "See to it that Mister Driver gets something else to eat. Nothing that would require silverware, mind you, a cheeseburger, fries, and a pop would do it." He glanced at Gary. "How's that sound to you?"

Gary nodded. "I haven't eaten since Mister Drew's trout last night. Doughnuts ain't real food."

Marty, Hank, and Alma Rose stepped outside the room and walked down the hallway.

Marty suggested, "Let's get some food from the cafeteria. I'll buy."

Hank and Alma Rose agreed and the three grabbed a table and ordered fast food. After they had eaten they got down to business.

Marty said, "It seems we have a number of unsolved crimes on our hands."

Hank responded, "Driver's wife, both of his in-laws, Mister Drew's daughter, and this Peta Ross girl."

"Peta Ross…yes, she's the governor's daughter."

"What happened to her?" Alma Rose asked.

Marty said, "Disappeared in Troy Montana on the 4th of July five years ago. She'd be about your age now, Deputy Two Elk."

Hank asked, "Anyone looking into these disappearances?"

Marty said, "The Peta Ross case is being handled up in Lincoln County. The authorities are sure a cult up in the Yaak Wilderness has her but every time they receive a tip and go to investigate their compound, she's nowhere to be found."

Hank then asked, "How's Governor Ross holding up with the disappearance of his daughter?"

Marty shook his head. "Not well. He gets meaner each month that goes by. This week will make five years since Peta's been missing."

Hank asked, "What about the others?"

Marty rubbed his eyes. "Well, except for Mac Drew's daughter who disappeared the same day as Peta Ross, Gary Driver's in-laws were adults. There's no evidence of foul play or what happened to them. It's as if they walked off the face of this earth. Someone in town started a rumor that Roger and Beth Weatherwax were abducted by aliens."

Hank pressed Marty on. "You do realize that Driver's wife, his in-laws, Drew's daughter, and Peta Ross are all Indigenous people?"

Marty stared at Hank. "I investigate murders and missing persons on a one by one basis. I don't have the time or resources to delve into conspiracy theories like you people do back east. We're a small department and can barely keep up with the drunks, the meth users, drug dealers, prostitutes, and the wife beaters around here. Many of the working class families left Mallory when the disappearances began. Now what's mostly left is lower income and destitute people some with substance abuse issues and others with emotional problems."

Hank asked, "Tell me about Drew's daughter. You said she went missing the same day that Peta Ross went missing?"

"Yeah but they were different circumstances and in different places."

Hank asked, "Can you explain?"

Marty said, "Sure, like I said Peta Ross went missing in Troy but Kat Drew…now that was really different."

"How so?" Hank asked.

Marty was about to speak, glanced at Alma Rose and then said to Hank, "Peta Ross was only a twelve-year-old sweet kid when she disappeared on the 4th in '92 but Kat Drew, now she…she was a thirty-four-year-old prostitute."

"Did you investigate?" Hank asked.

"No sir, she had moved to Billings, got herself involved with the wrong crowd, did drugs, ended up living on the street, and supported herself by selling her body." Marty turned to Alma Rose, "Pardon me for being so blunt, Deputy Two Elk."

Alma Rose spoke up, "Detective Aronowitz, no apology is necessary. Growing up on the Rez I've experienced more than you realize. Is that where she disappeared, in Billings?"

Marty turned to her. "The Billings Police said she got a john to rent her an overnight room in a motel just outside the city. Then her friends spread the news where she was holed-up and a series of customers were sent her way."

Alma Rose asked, "How did she disappear?"

Marty replied, "The motel housekeeper had had enough of the Do Not Disturb sign that had hung on the doorknob for almost a full week, unlocked the door, and entered the room. She called the police and they found blood everywhere but no body. Interestingly enough, there were two disembodied eyeballs in the bathroom sink."

Hank said, "I assume they belonged to the victim."

Marty nodded. "They were unable to make a concrete conclusion. You see, the eyeballs were in an advanced state of decomposition."

Hank said, "Well now, that's the same M.O. in this Janice Driver case. You need to contact the Billings Police."

Marty nodded. "I placed a call early this morning. Someone from their department will arrive tomorrow. The FBI is also interested. They're sending an agent by the name of Paul Harris. He'll arrive on Saturday."

Hank said, "I know Agent Harris. We worked together before. Do you have more questions for Mister Driver?"

Marty answered, "I sure do, let's get back to the room. But let me do the talking this time."

·22·

Marty, Hank and Alma Rose returned to the interrogation room. Gary Driver was seated at the table but with his head resting on the mahogany laminate-surface. The officer in the room stepped toward Gary and nudged him. Gary awoke with a startle and rubbed his eyes.

As Hank, Marty, and Alma Rose sat at the table, Marty restarted the tape recorder and asked, "Mister Driver, how was the burger?"

"Good."

Marty then said, "Mister Driver...may I call you Gary?"

"Of course," Gary said.

"Good, I'd like to ask you a series of questions. Is that all right with you, do you want an attorney?"

"No, I didn't do anything wrong. I don't need a lawyer."

"Then tell us about what time it was that you recall leaving Mac Drew's tent."

Gary stared at Marty. "It was well after midnight."

Marty continued. "And can you explain the blood on your shirt, and in your car, and that wound on your hand?"

"I told you, I cut myself cleaning the trout that Mac caught. I wiped my hand on my shirt, but it wouldn't stop bleeding. Mac bandaged me up pretty good, but the bandage came loose while I was driving. It bled all over the dash and the front seat."

"And Gary, what happened when you returned home?"

"I looked for a parking space, but a bunch of police cars blocked the lot. I got out of my car and asked the officers what happened. The door to my apartment was wide open and police were coming and going. I thought we were getting evicted from our apartment."

105

Marty said, "Go on."

Gary rolled his eyes. "You know the rest, you were there."

"Humor me. We need your response for the record. If you're innocent of your wife's disappearance, we'll see to it that this transcript gets to the prosecutor."

Gary continued, "You walked up to me and asked if I was Janice's husband."

"Please identify the name of the person who asked you if you were Janice's husband."

"It was you, Detective Aronowitz."

"Then what?"

"An officer asked if I showered recently."

"And your response?"

"I told him I showered Sunday morning."

"And it was early Monday morning when you spoke with that officer, is that correct?"

"Yes."

"Then what happened?"

"When I tried to push past him to look for my wife, one officer grabbed me from behind and looped his arms around my chest. Detective Aronowitz asked the officer to ease up and then said to me that he was hoping I could tell him where my wife was."

"And...?"

"Then he asked me if the Vega was my car. I told him yes and then he said they were impounding it."

Marty asked, "What happened next?"

"He said when did I last saw my wife and if I had been drinking."

"Were you?"

"I told him I had a beer or two. And then he said my wife was missing and if I knew where she was. I tried to get free and yelled for Janice but this big officer behind me pulled my arms together and handcuffed me."

Marty asked, "What happened next?"

"I screamed and tried to wriggle free. Then you read me my rights and told your officers to bring me downtown."

Marty said, "For the record, please identify who read you your rights."

"It was you...uh, Detective Aronowitz."

"What else?"

"They impounded my car." Gary yawned and then began to rub his eyes. "Can I go back to my cell now? I haven't slept since I woke up Sunday morning."

Marty stared at Gary. "Where were you last weekend?"

Gary replied, "On Friday, I...I mean Janice and me drove to Browning. We visited my cousin's family. They live on the Blackfeet Reservation. We stayed overnight. Then we drove back home late Saturday."

Marty asked, "Do you have witnesses who can attest to where you were during the day on Saturday?"

"Yes."

"The entire day?" Marty asked.

"Uh...until about 9 p.m."

"What about later Saturday night and on Sunday?"

"No, Janice and I returned to our apartment around 2 a.m. Sunday. Janice got up at dawn and drove to the Taylor University Library. I don't know how she does what she does with so little sleep."

"Were you with anyone else on Sunday?"

Gary pleaded, "What does this have to do with Janice being missing?"

"Just answer the question," Marty said.

Gary Driver exhaled and then continued his response. "After driving more than four hours, I was tired. I slept in until sometime after 10 a.m. I didn't leave the apartment again until Sunday night after Janice returned home."

"No one witnessed you at your residence on Saturday or Sunday or Monday?"

Gary said, "I told you, I was alone most of the day on Sunday. Janice saw me before she left and then again once she got home."

Marty persisted in the questioning. "So, you could have killed her when she returned Sunday evening, dumped her body, and then doubled back to visit Mac Drew on Howard Lake after midnight, isn't that correct?"

"No sir," Gary said.

"Don't lie to me."

"I'm not lying. I went to the post office, then visited Mister Drew, and then came home right after that."

Marty asked, "Can anyone vouch for you?"

"Mister Drew can."

Marty shut off the tape recorder.

·23·

The interrogation was not over. It was now nearly six-thirty in the evening and Detective Aronowitz wanted to dig deeper into Gary's alibi with Mac Drew and cull any information that he could corroborate with the former lumber mill foreman. Aronowitz wanted to get to the bottom of things. He restarted the recorder.

Marty asked, "Are you certain you don't want an attorney?"

"No, I didn't do nothing wrong. Where's my wife?"

Marty walked over to a banker box on the floor, opened the lid, and removed a sealed plastic bag. "Is this your shirt in the bag?"

"Yes."

"Whose blood is this?"

"Mine."

"How'd you get all that blood on this shirt?"

"I said, where's my wife?"

Marty replied, "That's what we're trying to find out. Now explain to me about this blood."

"I cut myself filleting a fish, see?" Gary raised his index finger still sporting the bandage.

Marty stood up and paced the room. Then he asked, "You said that you were drinking?"

"Yeah, like I said, I had a few beers with Mac Drew."

"Tell me where again."

"What does that have to do with my wife?"

Marty raised his voice. "Just answer the question."

"Howard Lake. Mac was fishing."

"What time did you get there?"

"We went through all this before."

"Tell me what time."

"I dunno, about midnight."

Marty turned to the officer. "Send Brown and Cooper to Howard Lake. See if Drew's still there. If he is, have them bring him in."

"You got it," said the officer who then left the room.

Marty got up, opened the door, and shouted down the hallway, "And tell them not to take no for an answer." Then he turned back to Gary. "Now tell me what you were doing down on Howard Lake."

"Like I said, I mailed my railroad application at the post office and on the way home, I saw Mac, I mean Mister Drew's van parked at Howard Lake, so I thought I'd give him the news."

"What news?"

"Uh, that Janice was pregnant."

"Was pregnant? Did you say she was pregnant?"

"No, I mean she is pregnant.

The uniformed police officer returned to the interrogation room. Marty looked up and then nodded to Hank and Alma Rose.

Marty stared at Gary and said, "Sit there and don't move. We'll be right outside." Marty turned to Hank Kelly and Alma Rose and waved them toward the door. "Let's go, we gotta talk." Marty then turned to the officer in the room. "Make sure our guest doesn't harm himself and secure that recorder until I get back."

Marty, Hank, and Alma Rose stepped toward the door and then left.

When they were outside the room Hank turned to Marty. "I got a call from Leon. They were able to perform an optography on the eyes found in the apartment."

Marty seemed interested. "What did he find?"

Hank hesitated for a moment as the suspense built. Then he responded, "Nothing."

·24·

Gary gazed about the interrogation room. There were no pictures, clocks, curtains, drapes, or shades and no furniture other than the table and the chairs. Vertical bars on the solitary window helped focus Gary's view on a municipal building across the street with an illuminated billboard on its rooftop that read <u>Howard Lake Brewery</u>.

Gary's thoughts wandered to when Janice told him how her family was forcefully relocated off the Flathead Reservation under the Federal Government's Indian Relocation Act of 1956. When Janice was only four years old, her parents Roger and Beth Weatherwax, were sent to live in the town of Mallory in a third floor apartment. It was common knowledge among the Plains Indians that the assimilation of Native Americans into the European immigrant way of life was a disaster.

Gary sat in the room for what seemed to him like several hours. During that time, he ignored the officer's periodic yawning. Gary simply rested his head on the table and whimpered himself to sleep. After a few minutes, commotion outside the door prompted Gary to raise his head and look up. Detective Aronowitz opened the door and stepped inside. Gary noticed that the white-haired man and the holy Native woman they called Two Elk were not with him. It would just be Detective Aronowitz, the officer, and Gary.

The officer handed the recorder back to Marty who pushed the record button. Then he said to Gary, "I sent a couple of patrolmen to Howard Lake, but Mac Drew wasn't there. I told them to wait and about an hour later Drew shows up. He says he had to make a beer run to his house. When we did speak with him, he confirmed your story about visiting him. However, he says that he can't say what day or time you were there. He said the two of you were drinking but he doesn't remember you cutting your finger. When I mentioned to him that we were investigating your wife's disappearance, at that point he clammed up. Now why do you suppose he did that?"

"I don't know," Gary said.

Marty's voice grew louder. "We've got Drew in another room. I can have him come in here right now. Then we can get to the bottom of this."

Gary's brow furrowed. "The bottom of what?"

"Did you ask Mac Drew to provide you with an alibi?"

Gary took a deep breath. "Of course not, he was half-drunk. He wouldn't know what I'd be talking about anyway."

"So, you didn't ask him to cover for you?"

"No...NO--I mean, there was nothing for him to cover for me. I didn't do anything."

Marty leaned his arms on the table and continued, "Then let's talk about Janice's family."

Gary's voiced elevated. "What about her family...what does that have to do with anything?"

Marty sat down and removed a pad and pencil from his inside sports jacket. "I need to understand your relationship with your in-laws."

Gary shook his head. "I dunno, Janice's dad died long before I met her."

Marty smiled. "I understand that Roger was a wrangler on the Flathead Reservation. When I was a teenager, I even saw him bronc riding at the Bozeman Roundup Ranch Rodeo. They say he won a few trophies in his day."

Gary shrugged his shoulders. "So what, I told you I never met him."

Marty continued, "Let's put things into perspective. It's a fact that after Roger left the reservation, he couldn't hold a job in Mallory. The idle time lured him toward alcoholism. He began stealing to support his demons and numerous barroom fights led to frequent jail time. In fact, you could say that he had his own private jailcell right here in this building."

"I don't know what you're getting at."

"You don't? Well then Gary, let me explain. Roger became less and less of a provider until his supposedly fatal beating outside the Chuck Wagon Bar & Grill in town. Now I know they never discovered Roger's body but the amount of blood we found by the dumpsters in the back alley tells me that he didn't just walk away from that fight."

Gary rolled his eyes. "I still don't know what your point is."

Marty said, "When Roger Weatherwax disappeared, Beth became the sole supporter of what was left of the family. And tell me if this is right, Janice was just a young girl, correct?"

"Yeah, that's right. We already said that."

Marty smiled. "Just making sure the facts aren't changing. At least we agree on something. So, after Janice's father either died or disappeared, she would make Native American jewelry and regalia with her mother Beth in their home, correct?"

"Yeah, that's right."

"And for the next year before Beth died, they'd travel to powwows throughout Montana selling their jewelry, sage, dream catchers, and talking sticks, right?"

Gary nodded. "Right."

Marty's unrelenting questions continued. "I understand that when her mother disappeared when Janice was only thirteen, she and her siblings went to live with relatives on the Flathead Reservation. Then a few years later, on a trip to a powwow, up near Browning, on the Blackfeet Reservation, she met you."

"That's right."

"Gary, do you know that my wife and I have three beautiful daughters. Just like Janice's parents had?"

"No, I didn't know that. You must love your children. Janice and I were going to start a family."

Marty said, "I would do anything to protect them. Don't you think that Janice's parents would have done anything to protect their daughters too?"

"I guess."

"You guess?"

Gary said, "I mean, yes. I suppose. I never met Janice's parents but I'm sure they would have."

Marty continued, "And because you were estranged from your own parents, you soon moved to the Flathead Reservation to live with Janice. She was only sixteen at the time. Then you got a job at the lumber mill. Also, after she graduated from high school Janice began taking college classes at Taylor University. Then, the two of you got married and moved to Mallory so that you could be closer to work, and she could be closer to the university, right?"

Gary took a deep breath and sighed. "Yep."

Marty continued, "So, Janice was just two semesters shy of becoming a member of the first graduating class of physician assistants at Taylor University. I understand that she told her professors it was her way to honor her parents' memory. She wanted to help those who suffered from physical and mental illnesses."

Gary asked, "Why aren't you telling me where Janice is?"

"Mister Driver, we don't know what happened to your wife. She's missing and there was blood throughout your apartment. Did you kill Janice in a fit of rage?"

"No, I didn't kill her."

"Before you told me that Sheriff Buchanan's daughter convinced you that your wife is dead."

"Yes, she did, but I don't know."

"What do you mean you don't know?"

"I mean...I dunno, maybe Janice is still alive." Gary wiped his eye on the sleeve of his jumpsuit. "Maybe the sheriff's daughter was wrong. Ain't she allowed to be wrong just once?" Gary started to cry and hung his head.

"Look Gary, I'm sorry about your wife's disappearance. I need to be blunt with you right now. Your life seems to be a mirror image of Janice's father's life. Perhaps she saw that you were becoming just like her father. You're unable to hold a job, like her father and she was becoming the sole supporter of her family, like her mother. Did she complain to you that she didn't want to relive her parents' failed marriage? The community may believe that in a fit of anger, fueled by alcohol, before or after you met with Mac Drew, you killed her and disposed of her body. If you confess to that I can try to convince the prosecutor to go easy on you."

When Gary looked up, the tracks of his tears glistened in the glow of the florescent overhead lights. "No, none of that is true."

"Gary, if you did something to your wife, are you willing to confess to me right now? I can guarantee that a huge weight will be lifted off your chest."

Gary continued to weep. "I have nothing to confess, I didn't do anything wrong."

Marty stood up. "Look, I'm going to assume the role of a prosecutor. If you end up facing a murder charge in court, the following questions will be asked of you. Are you willing to play along with me?"

Gary took a deep breath. "Go ahead."

Marty asked, "Could your wife be lying at the bottom of Howard Lake right now as we speak? Did Mac Drew help you dump her body?" Marty placed his palms onto the table and stared into Gary's eyes. "Her body, the body you made love to when the two of you conceived your unborn child, that's now beginning to decompose...no, rot in her womb, is that what you really want? Tell us where you dumped her body and we'll make sure your wife and unborn child are treated with respect and receive a decent burial."

With tears flooding his eyes, Gary looked up at Marty. "What are you trying to do to me? I loved her."

Marty smiled. "I know you did, son. I know you did. If we don't get to the bottom of what happened to your wife, the county prosecutor will drill you just like that or even worse."

"But I didn't kill anyone."

Marty straightened up and stepped away from the table. "Gary, we received an anonymous tip from a neighbor about yelling and screaming coming from your apartment. When my officers arrived, they found the door wide open, the place ransacked as if there was a struggle, and blood all over the walls, the furniture, and the floors. There were no signs of forced entry, no sign of your wife, and no sign of you either. But you arrived a few hours later all alone, all bloodied up, blood on your shirt, blood in your car, a defensive wound on your hand, and a bloody handkerchief in your pocket. How do you explain that?"

"It was my blood."

Marty shook his head. "Gary, I want to help you but I can't if you don't help me."

·25·

Hank Kelly left the Mallory Police Station with Junior Deputy Alma Rose Two Elk. They climbed into Hank's county-issued maroon Crown Vic. It was so huge inside that Alma Rose simply couldn't believe it. She stretched her legs in the passenger seat, something that was impossible to do in her mother's red 1956 Ford pickup truck with the black driver's door. On the drive down U.S. 228 to Taylor, Alma Rose's stomach began to growl. It was nearly 8 p.m.

Hank turned to her. "Hungry?"

Alma Rose felt her cheeks grow warm. "You heard that?"

He nodded. "I know we had fast food in Mallory but let's stop for a better meal at Lucy's Luncheonette. It's on the way home."

Alma Rose said, "I don't want to get back to my dad's house too late."

"I called your father while you visited the ladies' room at the police station. He said not to rush home. He also said he had a surprise for you at the house."

"A surprise, did he say what it is?"

Hank turned to her. "No and it wasn't my privy to ask."

Hank pulled into the parking lot of Lucy's Luncheonette and parked next to a couple of Taylor Police Department patrol cars. Hank and Alma Rose got out and stepped inside the restaurant. It was spacious, hinting that its name, luncheonette was a clear misnomer.

At Lucy's everything was on the menu. It was busy in the morning, crowded at lunch, and intimate at dinner. Lucy Brown designed the space to accommodate a counter and booths for breakfast and lunch. She opened a back room for dinner guests

117

and special occasions such as graduations, retirement parties, and birthdays. Lucy's Luncheonette was the only eatery in Taylor for good home-cooked meals.

The first thing Alma Rose noticed was the walls that sported framed awards and newspaper articles. They boasted how great the meals were at Lucy's.

"Nice place. It's so big, why is it called a luncheonette?" Alma Rose asked.

Hank said, "Jim told me that when Lucy Brown opened this place back in 1989 all she had was a 20x30 hole in the wall with a lunch counter and three booths. After four years she bought out the business next door, knocked down the wall, and expanded the dining area by tripling the seating capacity. Then last year she remodeled the place and built an addition in back for the banquet room and began serving dinner."

"Then why isn't it called Lucy's Restaurant?" Alma Rose asked.

Hank laughed. "Jim told me that Lucy kept the name luncheonette because she wanted a reminder of what this place was when she first started and the hard work she's put into it to become what it is today. He said she told him it was her way of staying grounded and not becoming jaded."

A hostess walked up to them and asked. "Do you have a reservation?"

Alma Rose stared at the woman and felt a sense of anger at the double meaning of that word that apparently only she picked up on.

Hank replied, "Uh, no we don't."

Alma Rose stepped forward toward the reception desk and channeled her anger into a sense of assertiveness. "This is State's Chief Medical Examiner Doctor Henry Kelly."

Alma Rose noticed the hostess first glance at Hank and then at the Cedar County Sheriff's Office badge pinned to Alma Rose's uniform.

The hostess said, "A party of two? Right this way."

Following the hostess, Hank and Alma Rose made their way toward the banquet room in back. Twenty tables populated the space, but the hostess led then to a table against the back wall. At the table next to theirs sat three Taylor Police Officers. Alma Rose didn't know the two male uniformed officers but immediately recognized Captain Linda Stevens.

Alma Rose asked, "How are you, Captain Stevens?"

Linda was on the fair side of thirty, with short, sassy blond hair, tall and athletic. She knew Jim and Kate since high school. Linda turned to look, and then smiled. "Looking good, Deputy Two Elk...your father told me about your internship."

Alma Rose removed her Stratton brown felt campaign hat and sat down. "It's my first day. I have a lot to learn."

Linda glanced at Hank and then said to Alma Rose, "You can't find a better teacher than this old man."

Hank said, "Oh, come on now. I don't feel old."

"I heard you're working on that missing person case in Mallory," Linda said. "That case in Mallory seems to be open and shut. I heard they got a suspect in custody, a guy by the name of Gary Driver. He's the husband, isn't he?"

Alma Rose piped up, "Yes but he didn't do it."

Linda asked, "What do you mean, didn't do it?"

"He didn't kill his wife."

Linda asked, "How do you know?"

"I just know it," Alma Rose said. "I have a feeling."

One of the officers sitting at the table with Captain Stevens scoffed. "Husbands are always the prime suspect."

Linda turned to the officer. "Andrews, Sheriff Buchanan's daughter may be right."

"You're Buchanan's daughter?" Andrews asked and then continued, "I didn't know. I apologize if I offended you ma'am."

Linda tipped her head toward Alma Rose and said, "Andrews, get used to referring to her as Deputy Two Elk."

Just then a person approached the table and a voice boomed, "Well I heard an awful lot about you but never got to meet you."

Wearing her blue and yellow apron and her auburn hair pinned back in a mass of bobby pins, Lucy Brown's six-foot one-inch frame, complete with sinewy biceps, sauntered over to Alma Rose.

Alma Rose offered her hand. "You must be Lucy Brown."

"Yep, the renowned old Lucy Brown." Lucy took Alma Rose's hand and pulled her up out of her chair. She then grabbed Alma Rose and gave her a bearhug. Then she pulled away, held Alma Rose's shoulders at arms-length and said, "I'm awfully pleased to meet you. Any kinfolk of Jim and Kate is like kin to me."

Alma Rose said, "I heard a lot about you too. My father told me that you're an Olympic weightlifter and was a Taylor Police Chief."

Lucy laughed, "Don't believe everything your father tells you but...yeah, that stuff's true. I also used to be a bouncer in my prime up in the Yaak but that's neither here nor there. Now I'm fifty-four years old and tired as all freakin' hell." When laughter erupted from customers at a few tables, Lucy turned to them. "Hey you good for nothin' rowdies, tone it down, we got decent customers over here." She stared at Alma Rose. "What'll have sweetheart?"

"Oh, I'll have the turkey dinner, salad, and a Coca-Cola."

Lucy noted it down on her server order pad and then announced, "Your meal's on me sweetheart."

Hank then said, "In that case, I'll have the blackened bourbon salmon with mashed potatoes, mixed vegetables, the crab cakes as an appetizer, and a tall lemonade."

Lucy stared at Hank. "Yours is not on the house. You already got your freebie when Jim introduced me to you."

Hank put the menu down on the table. "In that case strike the appetizer."

Alma Rose winked at Hank and then asked, "Can I have the crab cake appetizer?"

Lucy turned to her. "Of course you can sweetie, on the house too."

When the meals arrived, Alma Rose checked to see if any wait staff were in close proximity. When she saw none, she slid the appetizer to Hank's side of the table.

Hank and Alma Rose settled in, had their meals, and spoke about what had transpired during the long day. Linda and her fellow officers left Lucy's Luncheonette before Hank and Alma Rose had finished their meals. When it was time for Hank to pay his bill, Lucy came over to their table.

"Where's the bill?" Hank asked.

"It's on the house," Lucy replied.

"I thought you said..."

Lucy shook her head. "I couldn't very well let Captain Stevens and her officers believe that I was giving out free meals to everyone, now could I?"

"I suppose not," Hank said.

Lucy settled her hands on her hips and asked, "By the way Hank, how was that crab cake appetizer?"

Alma Rose laughed while Hank cleared his throat and then said, "It was great."

Lucy sat down at their table and whispered, "I'll keep my eyes and ears open about that poor kid in Mallory. I'll let you and Jim know if I hear anything."

"Thanks," Hank said.

"Damn shame shit like that has to happen. Things like this make me remember why I left the police force." She turned to Alma Rose. "Honey, you keep doing what yer doing. I just kept getting tired of seeing the same old shit happening to innocent people. It just broke my heart. I had to get out...for my own damn sanity. You're a youngin and you got your daddy's genes. I think you'll be okay. I just hope to God Almighty you guys catch whoever's responsible."

Alma Rose asked, "Have you seen either Gary Driver or Mac Drew in your place?"

Lucy got up out of her seat. "Aw sweetie, I know those folk but people like Gary and Mac don't come in here that often. They live in Mallory and usually hang out up that way. But come to think of it, I do remember Janice Driver coming in here a few times. It was when she was attending Taylor University and would sometimes stop by for a quick lunch between classes."

Alma Rose asked, "Is there anything that you can remember...anything unusual?"

Lucy touched her chin. "Not really. But wait...there was this English fella though, never seen him before or since. One day last fall he comes in around lunchtime and sits at the counter next to Janice. They strike up a cordial conversation, then something was said, I don't know what, and Janice gets up and leaves without finishing her sandwich."

"Would you recognize that man if you saw him again?" Alma Rose asked.

"I sure would." Lucy said. "I do remember his first name. Janice called him Lester."

After saying goodbye, Lucy left for the kitchen leaving Hank and Alma Rose to contemplate the recent conversation.

"What do you think?" Alma Rose asked.

Hank said, "We'll have to look at all the evidence. But your technique, it's in your blood."

"What is?"

"The way you interviewed Lucy."

Alma Rose stood up and put on her hat. "I only asked her a few logical questions."

Hank got up. "I can see your father in you."

·26·

Hank and Alma Rose made their way toward the front door of Lucy's Luncheonette. They stepped outside and approached Hank's car. Alma Rose walked with slow and measured steps. She fell behind Hank's steady stride and when she saw him stop and look back, she quickened her pace. When they reached the car and got inside, Hank didn't say a word but started at Alma Rose.

Alma Rose felt Hank's eyes upon her, turned to him, and asked, "What?"

Hank pursed his lips. "I know something's up, what is it?"

Alma Rose asked, "Doctor Kelly, do you know how that eagle is doing?"

Hank shook his head. "No I don't."

Then she asked, "Can we visit it?"

"Now? It's almost ten p.m."

Alma Rose shifted her position in the passenger seat. "Why not?"

Hank hesitated and then said, "Well, I'll have to call the rehabilitator. I don't know who he is."

"My dad does, call him."

Hank smiled. "You are one persuasive young lady."

Alma Rose listened in as Hank put in a radio call to Jim and got the rehabilitator's information. Hank then called John Sheppard who agreed to allow Hank and Alma Rose to visit the eagle for an hour.

When they reached the front door of John Sheppard's home, Hank introduced himself. "Mister Sheppard, pleased to meet you. I'm Doctor Hank Kelly."

John Sheppard was a sixty-six year-old man nearing retirement. Sheppard extended his hand. "Nice to meet you doctor. Then he stared at Alma Rose. "Who's this?"

"Mister Sheppard, I'm Junior Deputy Alma Rose Two Elk. My father is Sheriff Buchanan."

Sheppard nodded. "Yes, I know who your father is. But don't call me Mister Sheppard, call me Easy, everyone does."

Alma Rose's eyes scanned the inside of Easy's home. "Where's the eagle?"

Easy said, "We named him Ralph. Come with me." Easy then waved them inside and grabbed a flashlight off a nesting table. As they walked down the stairs to his basement, Easy commented, "The bald eagle is not nocturnal so he may be sleeping but I'll let you spy in on him anyway. Ralph is doing great, the little fella." Then Easy turned to Alma Rose. "I heard that you prevented your dad from putting him down."

Alma Rose nodded. "I guess so."

Easy said, "That was a good decision. I think he's going to pull through. Then we'll decide when and if he's ready to be released into the wild."

Toward the walk-out side of the basement were a series of cages built into the basement wall that allowed the birds to move freely from inside to outside within their cages.

Alma Rose noticed the bald eagle in one cage, a broad-winged hawk in another, and finally a great horned owl in the last cage.

"They're beautiful," Alma Rose said.

"Aren't they?" Easy smiled and then said, "They're God's creatures and I love them all."

Alma Rose walked up to the bald eagle's cage and watched as the raptor turned its head and followed her every move.

Alma Rose smiled. "He does look better."

Easy asked, "I rehydrated him intravenously. He's begun eating solid food. Would you like to offer him some food?"

Alma Rose smiled broader. "Can I?"

Hank displayed a sense of caution. "Alma Rose, I'm not sure." He turned to Easy. "Is it safe? I don't want her to get bitten or clawed."

Easy pulled a pair of raptor handling gloves off a desk and handed them to Alma Rose. "Use these."

Alma Rose pulled on the gloves and then Easy opened a refrigerator and grabbed a bait bag. Alma Rose's nostrils were infiltrated by the distinct odor of herring.

"Wow, I didn't expect such a strong smell," she said.

Easy laughed. "Believe me, you may not like the smell of these, but Ralph loves them just fine."

Alma Rose took a couple of herrings from the bait bag and then stuck her gloved hand into the cage. Ralph gently took one herring in his beak and swallowed it. Then Alma Rose offered the other herring to him and he snatched it with more assertiveness.

Alma Rose laughed. "I like him."

Easy then smiled. "Yeah, he's a lucky bird. He's gonna make it. You did a great thing and I admire you for it."

"I was just trying to do the right thing."

Easy said, "Deputy Two Elk, we need more people like you to do the right thing."

Hank interrupted their conversation. "Alma Rose, let's get you home before Jim sends out a BOLO."

Alma Rose nodded, thanked Easy, and then left with Hank who pulled out of the driveway and drove into the foothills of the Cabinet Mountains toward Jim and Kate's home.

As they approached the house, Hank said, "I see there's a visitor."

Alma Rose stared at the familiar car in the driveway and was in utter disbelief. As Alma Rose felt her anger grow, she clenched her teeth, curled her fingers into a balled fist, closed her eyes, and then everything else went blank.

When they pulled up to the front door Hank turned to her. "I'm not coming in. I have to get home to Mary. Now don't forget about Friday. Bring along that new boyfriend of yours but be sure to tell your father about him before you come."

Alma Rose opened her eyes and glanced at Hank. She didn't say a word, turned, and got out of the car. When her thoughts returned to the present, she heard Hank call to her. She turned and asked, "Yes, what is it?"

"Didn't you hear me, I said don't forget about Friday. Dinner at my house and bring your friend."

Alma Rose nodded. "I'm sorry. Yes, I'll be there. Thank you."

Hank left and Alma Rose trudged up the steps onto her father's' front porch, all the while she stared at the car in the driveway. She got up to the door, stood there and took a deep breath as if preparing herself for what was about to happen. She reached for the doorknob and felt a burst of static electricity surge through her fingertips.

Alma Rose opened the door and immediately heard the tinny sounds of inaudible conversation and felt as if she were in a tunnel. When she met Kate at the threshold, she received a hug and a kiss on the cheek. Then she saw her father step into the foyer from the great room with a big smile on his face. Alma Rose's hearing returned to normal and she heard her father's words loud and clear.

"Alma Rose, we're so glad you're home. We have a big surprise for you." Jim continued, "I guess you know who's here because of the car in the driveway."

Kate added, "Your father insisted that he stay with us so that we can keep an eye on him."

Alma Rose's eyes swelled up with tears but as she wiped her cheeks dry, more tears saturated them. From the side of the great room's shadows a boy came into view.

Jim said, "Alma Rose, aren't you going to say something? He wanted to see you and he said he's sorry for everything that happened and hoped that you could forgive him. We thought it best that he stays with us this summer so that he has a chance to finally get his head on straight."

Alma Rose stood frozen in the foyer with tears flooding her eyes. The boy stared at her, but all Alma Rose could do was tremble at the sight of him in her father's house. How he could be there after all that had happened mystified her. How could her father and stepmother have given in to him and allowed him to stay, she thought.

"Hello Alma Rose. It's nice to see you again," Acaraho Otaktay said.

Alma Rose ran past them, rushed up the stairs to her room, and slammed the door shut. Angel ran up the steps and scratched on the door. Alma Rose's bedroom door opened, Angel slipped inside, and the door slammed shut again.

·27·

The town of Spaulding, population 2,852, situated north of Bull Lake on Route 56 had a police department that consisted of Chief Ben Kettering, Sergeant Anders Larsen, three officers, and two staff employees. Spaulding was an old town settled in the late 19th century and built around The Church of Jesus Christ of Latter-day Saints. Needless to say, Spaulding was a tight-knit and closed community.

That is, it was that way until earlier this year when two members of the Screaming Skulls Motorcycle Club (SSMC) robbed BJ Liquors, the only liquor store in town and shot dead two employees. They were the first murders in Spaulding since 1901 when a crazed miner hacked his foreman and two fellow employees to death.

These latest murders caused the Spaulding Town Council to enact a law prohibiting liquor sales in stores and restaurants, and close down all package stores and bars from operating within the town boundaries. Just like that, Spaulding had become a dry town literally overnight and the citizens, most of whom were descendants of the original settlers, welcomed it.

To understand the town of Spaulding you must go back to 1894. Thirty-five Mormon pioneers on their journey from New Bedford Massachusetts to Utah's Valley of the Great Salt Lake stopped to rest in the valley north of Bull Lake about ten miles south of the newly registered town of Troy.

With a few in the group suffering from malnutrition and others weary of the long trek westward, the group's leader, Jeremiah Churchill Spaulding, in an act of mercy, decided to settle in Montana. Because of the strong religious influence on the town, Spaulding became a model community of peace and tranquility, love, neighborly attitudes, and low crime. However, all of that was about to change in 1997 and in a most shocking and violent manner.

On a remote homestead, a retired school teacher named Louise Leonard lived a quiet life of reading, cooking and baking for the community, and growing both vegetable and flower gardens. Louise did not grow up in Spaulding. In fact, she was born and raised in Mallory. However, she left the town of her birthplace in an attempt to escape the deteriorating conditions and the heavy shroud of horror that hovered over Mallory.

Living in a safe community such as Spaulding convinced people to drop their guards. Louise fell into that trap and slept with at least one window open each night because she enjoyed the crisp night air. Tuesday evening, a few minutes past 11 p.m., a dark van, with its headlights off, slowly pulled up at the end of Louise's 900-foot long driveway.

It took the driver nearly fifteen minutes to prepare for his beastly undertaking. Finally, he opened the back door to the van and stepped out dressed in black mechanics coveralls, black gloves, black booties, and a black balaclava. A black body bag was in one hand and a 21-inch Bowie Knife in the other.

The man reached the front door and then walked around the house and peered inside each window to ensure there was no one else inside the residence. The man stared at Louise Leonard's 1988 Ford Bronco parked in the driveway.

Along the back porch, he found one of the kitchen windows open about five inches above the sill. He slowly raised it a few inches more. A left to right downward slash with the Bowie knife and then a right to left downward slash left an X-sliced opening in the window screen. He climbed inside, placed one foot in the kitchen sink then the other, and then stepped onto the kitchen floor.

He placed the body bag on the kitchen table and then crept through the house along the walls. He held his Bowie at his side and then flipped the handle so that he was ready to deploy a downward strike. He raised it shoulder height as he approached the bedroom.

The man stepped into the bedroom and spotted Louise Leonard flat on her back, asleep in her bed, the covers tucked up to her neck. The man focused on that neck. He then flipped the knife in his fingers so that he could swing it in a sweeping motion. He edged his way to the bed, stealthy climbed onto the mattress and knelt with one leg on either side of Louise. Just as

Louise stirred in bed, the man raised his right arm above his head and as Louise opened her eyes, with a swift and violent downward stroke, he nearly decapitated her. His forceful and extreme upstroke embedded the point of the knife in the wall next to the bed.

Blood spurted everywhere as Louise tried to scream. No sound emanated from her lips. He ripped the bedcovers off Louise as his legs kept the flailing woman's body in place. He yanked the knife out of the wall and flipped the handle in his hand. He then drove the knife deep into her torso. The handle quivered with each heave of Louise's chest. Her mouth gaped open and the sudden whoosh of air escaped from the wound in her throat. It was no more than a few seconds for her body to go limp and her head slid to one side.

He took the handle of the Bowie knife in both hands and struggled to rip it through tissue and bone, down the chest to the abdomen, splaying the corpse in two. Then he took his knife and buried it to the guard for safekeeping in the corpse's right thigh. As he reached inside the body, he yanked out the internal organs one-by-one and tossed them onto the hardwood floor. The white bedsheets, drenched in bodily fluids, turned a crimson red.

The man then pulled his Bowie knife out of the corpse's leg, climbed off it and stood next to the bed. He bent over, placed his lips to the corpse's ear, and whispered, "Darling, you're coming home with me to Mallory."

Then he straddled the hollowed out corpse, raised the Bowie knife to its face, and carved out the eyes from the head. He grabbed the eyeballs in his gloved hands and climbed off the blood-soaked bed. He stepped to a bureau that stood between two windows that faced the driveway. He placed one eyeball facing one window and the other eyeball facing the other window.

He laughed to himself and then stepped into the kitchen. The man gathered the body bag off the table and returned to the bedroom. He laid the body bag on the floor next to the disembodied bowels. When the man lifted the body off the bed, he noticed that the hollowed out corpse seemed remarkably lighter. He placed the Bowie knife in a holster on his belt and then shoved the corpse into the body bag. He zipped it shut and slung it over his shoulder.

Once outside, he walked down the driveway to his van. The man opened the back doors, just above the blacked out license plate, and dropped the body bag inside. When he stepped away from the back doors, he noticed the far away nighttime running lights from a slow patrolling Spaulding black and white Chevy Impala.

The man ran to the back of the van. He swung open a folded, heavy metal bar and unhitched it from under the van's bumper. He let its full twelve foot length drop across the road with a clank. He then climbed inside the van, revved the engine and peeled away at a high rate of speed.

He looked in his side mirror and saw the police car's flashing lights and heard the blaring siren.

When the police car ran over the homemade stop stick, the angled, grade 5 titanium spikes penetrated all four tires and ripped them to shreds. The car skidded to a stop off the side of the road and crashed into a ditch. When it came to a stop, the driver's side was two feet off the ground.

As the man in the van drove away, he slapped the steering wheel and laughed.

·28·

Alma Rose got up at 5 a.m., showered, and dressed in her uniform. She lugged a gym bag downstairs as Angel followed her. Alma Rose spied Kate at the stove minding pancakes on the griddle and a pan of fried eggs on a second burner. Jim sat at the table with his head buried in last evening's newspaper. Angel walked over to Shadow and the two dogs welcomed one another the only way dogs can with licks and indiscernible doggie whining.

Kate spoke first. "Good morning, Alma Rose. How'd you sleep?"

Alma Rose walked past her and dropped her gym bag on the floor next to her chair. She sat at the kitchen table and stared through the picture window at the mountain vistas. Alma Rose turned to Kate and asked, "Is your guest awake yet?"

Kate said, "No, but he should be up soon. He's going to the sheriff's office with you and your father."

Alma Rose said, "I'll drive in myself. I don't want to see Acaraho. So, if you don't mind, I'll take my breakfast to go."

Kate glanced at Jim who put down the newspaper and nodded. Kate said, "Of course, how does an egg sandwich and a coffee to go sound?"

Alma Rose said, "That's great."

Jim sliced a hard roll and buttered it. He handed it to Kate who slid two fried eggs into it along with a slice of cheddar cheese. Kate wrapped it in tin foil and placed it on the table. Jim walked over to Alma Rose and handed her a covered Styrofoam cup.

"You take it black, right?"

Alma Rose nodded. "Thanks dad." When she saw Kate leave the kitchen, she turned to her father. "Dad, you seem preoccupied today."

Jim took a deep breath. "It looks like there was a murder in Spaulding last night. Today will not be a good day."

"Tell me about it."

Jim put down the paper. "Not now. I don't have all the facts…but you also seem preoccupied about something."

Alma Rose said, "About last night. You have to understand what Acaraho did to me. He demanded that I not go to college and stay on the reservation with him. Then he met that girl and was with her on the Rimrocks when he got hurt. I can't be his girlfriend anymore."

"Alma Rose, Acaraho is enrolled in summer classes. He applied for and received a two-year, tuition-free scholarship in Native American Studies at Taylor University. He's more than 500 miles from his home in Crow Agency and he needs to figure out where in Taylor he'll live and how he'll afford it. I suggested that he stay with us until he finds an apartment and a job."

Alma Rose wiped away a tear. "I hope he finds a place soon or else I'll have to..."

Jim interrupted her, "Alma Rose!"

She got up from the table, slung her gym bag over her shoulder, took her sandwich and coffee. "Dad, I need to concentrate on my internship and my studies. I don't have the time, effort, or energy to salvage a casual teenage relationship that never had a future."

"You don't?" Acaraho asked as he stood in the doorway to the kitchen.

Alma Rose spotted Kate walk back into the kitchen and she thought to herself how Kate seemed stunned by the stand-off. Alma Rose first stared at Acaraho and then glanced at Jim and Kate. "I have to leave. I'll drive my mom's truck to the sheriff's office."

She walked out the front door, climbed into her mother's red 1956 Ford pickup truck with its black driver's door, and started the engine. Alma Rose arrived at the sheriff's office at 6 a.m. and drove into the back parking lot. She found a parking spot near the garage and kennel.

Alma Rose swiped her cardkey and entered the new part of the building. She proceeded down a long hallway toward the common elevator that now served both the new and old sections of the building. She avoided her father's office, even though she knew he hadn't yet arrived. The emotions from the interrogation of Gary Driver and the interaction with the entity were a bundle of raw energy that Alma Rose needed to contain. Putting her father as far away from her consciousness as possible was her initial way of coping.

She stepped into the elevator and pushed the button for the basement. Once in the expansive multi-level basement, the smell of fresh paint and construction materials permeated the entire area.

Alma Rose heard the sharp squeaks of sneakers on the hardwood as two deputies played a game of one-on-one at one end of the court. She walked up to the women's locker room and once inside, changed from her uniform into a pair of sweatpants, a tee-shirt, sweatshirt, and sneakers.

She made her way into the gym and spotted a lonely basketball in the corner next to the bleachers. She jogged over, picked it up, and dribbled along the baseline at the other end of the court away from the two deputies.

Alma Rose shot a few layups to warmup and then dribbled to the top of the key and sunk nothing but net. She then dribbled into the corner and hit a deep two-hand jump shot. She ran over and plucked the ball from under the net, and then threw up a reverse layup, then dribbled to the corner of the foul line and lofted a blind hook shot that made the net hum and flip over onto itself. Alma Rose scooped up the ball and noticed that the squeaking in the gym had stopped. She glanced at the other end of the court and spied the deputies staring at her.

"What?" she asked them.

One of the deputies said, "You haven't missed yet."

Alma Rose let out a brief laugh, dribbled to half court, sunk another two-hand jump shot, turned to them, and asked, "Yeah, so what else is new?"

The deputy said, "You're damn good. Have you played somewhere?"

Alma Rose said, "This past season I was captain of my team. We were undefeated, twenty-two wins. Then we finished second in the state finals."

The other deputy asked, "Where have you played before? I know you're not from Taylor."

"Rezball at Father Ravalli Missionary School," Alma Rose said.

The first deputy asked, "Tell me about it."

Alma Rose sped toward the basketball and spoke as she dribbled and ran. "I played with the boys until my junior year when they started a women's team." She drove toward the basket and shot a layup that teetered on the rim. She jumped and with the tip of her fingers tapped the ball on the rim and let it fall through the basket.

The other deputy said, "I never saw a girl jump that high."

Alma Rose smiled. "I averaged 11 a game against the boys but that shot up to 21 when I was on the women's team."

"You averaged 21 points a game?" The deputy asked.

Alma Rose laughed as she picked up the basketball and again dribbled. "No silly. Rebounds, I averaged 21 rebounds a game."

"How many points did you average?" the second deputy asked.

Alma Rose sunk another hook shot. "Against the boys or the women?"

"Both," the first deputy asked.

"I averaged 16 a game against the boys and 34 against the women."

"What was your best game?" the second deputy asked.

Alma Rose scooped up the basketball, dribbled toward the top of the key, and sunk another jump shot. "Last season against Busby on the Northern Cheyenne Rez, I scored 67 points with 32 rebounds."

The first deputy asked, "Which reservation are you from?"

"The Crow Reservation."

"Oh, are you Sheriff Buchanan's daughter?" the second deputy asked.

"Yes."

The two deputies walked over to Alma Rose but before they reached her, they were distracted by a piercing whistle. The deputies and Alma Rose each turned to the sound and spotted Undersheriff Rocky Salentino walk onto the court in sweats, sneakers, and a towel draped around his neck with a whistle between his lips.

Rocky let the whistle drop from his mouth. "Shouldn't you third-shift deputies be heading home now?"

"Yes, Sir," one of them said.

The other deputy said, "We were just getting ready to pack up. Had to blow off a little steam on the court after what we saw at that woman's house in Spaulding."

"Good, now get a move on. Deputy Two Elk and I have a self-defense training session here in the gym."

When the deputies left, Alma Rose stared at Rocky and then asked, "What happened in Spaulding? My dad wouldn't tell me."

Rocky explained, "We received a call for assistance from the Spaulding Police around 3 a.m. An officer on patrol noticed a van drive away at a high rate of speed. Apparently the driver used a custom stop stick to disable the patrol car and got away. The officer called it in and then checked on the occupant of the house. There was blood everywhere. That's about all I can say. I'll let your father tell you about it. Those deputies were dispatched and just got back about an hour ago when their shift ended. We sent replacement deputies out there to help secure the crime scene. Hank and Leon arrived around 4 a.m. and they'll probably be there for a few more hours."

Alma Rose shook her head. "That's terrible."

Rocky took a step toward Alma Rose. "Get used to it. We never know what's coming, when it's coming, and where's it's coming." Then he changed the subject. "Let's get back to you. I watched you on the court. You have the athletic abilities of your father and then some."

"Yeah, well I hope I have more common sense than him."

Rocky took a step back. "Whoa, what brought that on?"

Alma Rose gritted her teeth. "I'm not feeling like myself today. Something happened last night."

"Was it another premonition?"

"No, a flesh and blood visitor."

"Where…at your father's house?"

"Yes…an old boyfriend I have to deal with."

"Are you all right?"

"I will be one way or another." Then she stared at Rocky. "You have more concern and compassion for me than my own dad."

"I'm sorry. My intent wasn't to pry into your private life. Help me with the gym mats. We'll need six."

Alma Rose assisted Rocky haul the mats out of storage and then set them down on the gym floor in two rows of three.

135

Rocky instructed Alma Rose to sit cross-legged on the mats facing him.

"Do you know what Aikido is?" Rocky asked.

"I heard my dad talk about it a couple of times. Wasn't that what the mayor was trained on?"

"Yeah, the one who killed people for body parts." Rocky continued, "Aikido is a way of life. It should never be used in anger, only to deflect aggression from others without harming them."

Rocky began the session with hand exercises to develop flexibility. That evolved into stretches and agility skill training.

Then Rocky showed her how to redirect a punch. "Go ahead try to hit me."

Alma Rose swung at him and Rocky stepped to one side and used his forearm to push her fist away.

"See how it's done? Now watch this. Do it again."

"Okay." Alma Rose lunged at him. Rocky grabbed her forearm and pulled her forward and away from him. When she reached out and latched onto his arm, she saw him freeze and stare at her. Then she kicked his leg out from under him, yanked him facedown onto the mat, pulled his arm behind him, and sunk her knee into the small of his back.

Rocky yelled, "What are you doing? That's not part of the lesson."

Alma Rose released her grip on Rocky's arm, stood up and backed away. "I'm sorry. I didn't mean to knock you on the ground."

Rocky turned over onto his back. "I could end your internship right now based upon what you just did. Where'd you learn that training?"

"The elders on the Rez make sure that the children learn how to protect themselves, especially the young girls. We have a program that draws on the spirits of our ancestors. We channel their energy to help keep us safe."

Rocky got up and fixed his rumpled tee-shirt. "Well, I didn't see that coming."

Alma Rose asked, "You're not mad at me?"

Rocky shrugged his shoulders. "My bad."

She smiled. "Sorry, but part of the Rez training was using the element of surprise."

Rocky shook his head. "Why don't you show me what you know? You may be able to teach me a few tips."

They spent the next hour sharing defensive techniques. They ended the training session at 7:30 and each went into their respective locker rooms. They showered, dressed into their uniforms, and went upstairs to the first-floor offices.

·29·

Jim arrived at the sheriff's office at 8:30 a.m. and headed toward the cafeteria. He noticed Rocky holding a steaming cup of coffee and eying a single Danish pastry in the glass case. Jim walked up behind him and grabbed a coffee cup.

"Rock, how did the self-defense training go this morning?"

When Rocky turned to face him, Jim noticed a rose-colored bruise across Rocky's left cheek.

"We both learned a lesson," Rocky said.

Jim poured decaf from the carafe into his coffee cup and then laughed. "Is that how you got that mark on your face?"

Rocky touched his cheek, glanced at the cashier, and then whispered, "Why didn't you tell me about the reservation's self-defense program?"

Jim said, "I'm not aware of what they're teaching over there. Don't forget, I got kicked off the Rez when I was sixteen. A lot has changed since then."

Rocky took a deep breath and exhaled. "Next time give me a clue what might happen. Your daughter's athletically gifted and seems very strong for her age."

Jim said, "I've seen a dramatic change in her over just the past couple of years. She did tell me that she's been using a weight room they have at the reservation community building and she's grown at least two inches. She's nearly six-feet tall now." Jim shook his head. "Sometimes Alma Rose surprises me."

Rocky said, "Surprise is a good way to explain things but something else seems to be going on."

Jim cleared his throat. "Like what?"

Rocky said, "I don't know. She seems on edge, almost like something's been bugging her."

"Let's grab a seat, we need to talk," Jim said.

They went through the cashier line, found a table near the back of the cafeteria, and sat facing each other.

"What's up boss?" Rocky asked. "You're a bit late this morning."

"I dropped off Acaraho in Mallory. He's my daughter's ex-boyfriend. I got him a summer job working in the office with the public works department. He'll be reporting to John Sheppard."

Rocky asked, "You mean Easy, the foreman of the highway department in Mallory?"

"Yeah, that's right. He told me that Acaraho's summer job could lead to a permanent position while he attends school at Taylor University."

Rocky asked, "How's that working out, them being under the same roof?"

Jim sipped his coffee and then said, "At best, it's a work in progress. I just want to warn you that Alma Rose can be difficult at times."

"What do you mean?"

"She has a mind of her own and when she goes down that road there's no stopping her."

Rocky smiled. "Yeah, like they say, the apple doesn't fall far from the tree."

Jim cringed. "You mean, I'm like that too?"

Rocky nodded. "Sorry to say boss, but yeah."

Jim shrugged. "I'll have to work on that. But getting back to Alma Rose, don't let her influence the training that you have planned for her."

Rocky said, "I won't. We had the self-defense training this morning and after that I sent her to the evidence locker with Sergeant MacAskill. They'll be there the rest of the day."

Jim said, "Good. I want her to see what transpires on a day-to-day basis. If a DUI or domestic occurs today, then she can see how we gather, categorize, and file the evidence."

Rocky nodded. "You'll like this...we can go one better."

"What's that?" Jim asked.

Rocky said, "Detective Aronowitz called around 8:30 and said that Hank Kelly requested the evidence collected in the Janice Driver case be transferred as soon as possible from the Mallory Police Department to the State Medical Examiner's Office."

Jim asked, "Why? We have no body, no real proof of a homicide. What does Hank know that we don't?"

Rocky explained, "It has to do with the Louise Leonard case up in Spaulding. Leon Madison collected the evidence for Hank on that one since Spaulding has no evidence locker."

"And…"

"Because that happened on the heels of the Driver case and both cases seem similar, Hank's considering them related."

Jim asked, "How did Aronowitz take it?"

Rocky shook his head. "He was pissed-off for sure. I don't think he wanted to lose control of the investigation. Do you think the same person is responsible for what happened in Mallory and Spaulding?"

Jim responded, "It's worth looking into. Early this morning I sent Sergeant MacAskill over to Spaulding to supervise the investigation. When you get a chance, see if you can determine if other disappearances having the same circumstances occurred in our county going back about fifty years."

"Sure boss."

Jim added, "Because what happened in Mallory and Spaulding occurred within days of each other and they seem to be related, perhaps our person of interest is someone on a rampage. Also see if you can recognize a pattern, any pattern at all. Until we get a clearer picture, we won't know what we're up against." Then Jim asked, "When will Mallory transfer the evidence?"

Rocky said, "Sometime this afternoon."

Jim breathed a heavy sigh. "I wish Hank didn't go down that road."

Rocky asked, "Why?"

Jim shook his head. "Because, once the evidence is under county control, they'll soon be transferring Gary Driver too."

"Don't worry, boss. Governor Ross appropriated the funds for that new wing of the jail, so why not utilize it? At least Driver will have a dozen or so other prisoners to talk with instead of the one or two in the Mallory jail."

Jim breathed another heavy sigh. "I know and that's what I'm worried about."

·30·

Jim left the cafeteria around 8:50 a.m., his second cup of coffee firmly in his hand. He made his way down the hallway to his office. Placing his cup on his coffee-stained desk blotter, he then rummaged through his daily mail. Just when he noticed a large envelope from the State Medical Examiner's Office, his telephone rang.

"*Buchanan here…uh-huh.*" Jim then looked at his wristwatch. "*He's a few minutes early…good, send him in.*"

Jim sat down and took a sip of coffee. He stared at Louis Miller in the hallway outside his door.

"Sheriff, am I too early?"

Jim waved him in. "Not at all. Have a seat. I'm glad you're punctual."

Louis stepped inside and sat down. "Uh, how long will this take? I have an appointment this morning at the car dealership. I'm buying that Corvette I spoke about."

Jim ignored him. "Mister Miller, I have a resolution that will keep you out of jail."

"Yeah, I'm all for that. What is it sheriff?"

Jim slid a Town of Mallory street map across his desk and presented it to Louis. "The Town of Mallory has an opening for a seasonal employee."

Louis furrowed his brow. "What's that got to do with me?"

Jim folded his hands. "You'll be working this summer for the Town of Mallory Public Works Department."

Louis' mouth was agape for a split second and then he asked, "Are you serious?"

Jim nodded. "I am, I spoke with John Sheppard."

"Who's he?"

"He's foreman of the highway department."

Louis spoke up right away, "Oh no, no, no."

143

Jim's voice grew louder. "You do this, or face charges."

"What charges?" Louis asked.

"Speeding, reckless driving, evading responsibility."

Louis Miller stood up. "Listen Sheriff, I…"

"Sit down!" Jim barked.

Louis Miller sat right back down. "Sheriff I'm really sorry for what happened and I'm willing to make restitution. But it's the summer and I have plans."

Jim held his ground. "Then you should alter your plans."

"Sheriff, you don't understand. I have reservations with this special girl for two weeks in Bermuda. We're leaving next month. Then when I get back, me and two buddies are leaving for a road trip to Las Vegas. I don't have time to hang around Mallory all summer."

Jim stood up. "Then you'll hang around in my jail."

"I doubt it," Louis said.

Jim glowered at Louis and had just about had it. "Come with me. I want to show you something."

Louis took the map and followed Jim down the hallway to the elevator. They stepped inside and Jim hit the button for Floor 3. When the elevator reached the third floor, the door opened, and they stepped outside. The entire 8,400 square foot area of the third floor consisted of twenty jailcells, half of them populated with inmates, and a central observation area where three deputies monitored the facility.

From inside each jailcell, prisoners had the privilege of viewing outside their windows, a series of six-foot long, reinforced steel bars. They were set into the side of the building three feet below the cell windows. The steel bars jutted up and outward at a forty-five-degree angle. Barbed wire looped from bar to bar through holes set six inches apart in the bars. Every bar consisted of twelve strands of barbed wire. If a cellmate happened to escape through a jailcell window, they would find themselves caught in a spider web of flesh-ripping barbed wire.

The design firm hired by Governor Ross even thought through a scenario where if inmates got through the barbed wire and escaped onto the roof, they would come face-to-face with a formidable barrier of triple concertina wire.

This newly constructed jail at the Cedar County Sheriff's Office had already gained a legendary reputation as a secure and inhospitable facility to any potential breakout intentions by its occupants.

The inmate in cell number four, a hulking prisoner with shoulder-length brown hair and a brown beard leaned against the back wall and stared at Louis.

"What the hell is wrong with you?" Louis asked.

"Yeah, well fuck you. I've killed more than ten people. I'll squash you like a fly," the inmate answered.

Louis glanced at Jim for an answer.

Jim responded, "That's Videl Tanas. He was the leader of an outlaw biker gang. He's facing multiple murder charges including killing a police officer."

"What's going to happen to him?" Louis asked.

Jim said, "He was arrested last month. The State Attorney General is processing a case against him and they plan to have him extradited to Helena for trial. It'll take a month or two before we move him."

"So he'll be here all summer?" Louis asked.

Videl said, "That's right you candy-ass punk. When I break out of here, I'll be on the lookout for your sorry ass. You little shithead, goddamn rich kid, you piss me right the fuck off."

Jim stared at Louis and said, "Welcome to the Cedar County Jail. Let's go back downstairs. Tanas will get what's coming to him."

Videl Tanas shouted, "I heard that you fucked-up sheriff. How's your damn daughter? All I needed was a few more minutes with her up in the Yaak and you'd be burying her today."

Jim said, "Shut up Tanas. You're lucky I don't have the keys to your cell."

Videl Tanas rushed to the cell door and gripped the bars. "Well go get 'em. I'd be happy to knock you on your ass again."

Jim and Louis descended the stairs and Jim continued, "Governor Robert Ross secured funding and helped the county construct this new addition to the sheriff's office. If you don't accept that job in Mallory, this is where you'll be for the next thirty days."

Louis stared at the map in his hands. "I don't want to spend one day in here with that crazy biker guy. How long is this job for?"

"You start next Monday...the job ends Friday, August 29th."

"What do I have to do?"

145

Jim said, "It's an office job...strictly inside work. You won't get your hands dirty. Filing, processing invoices, timesheets, and things like that."

"What does it pay?" Louis asked.

"It's strictly minimum wage. You'll get paid $4.75 an hour with opportunities for overtime."

Louis stopped on the second floor landing. "Four-seventy-five an hour? That's slave labor."

Jim turned and stared at him. "Take it or spend up to 120 days in this jail if the judge thinks 30 days is too lenient."

Louis said, "I'll have to think about it."

"You have until we get back to my office."

"What?"

Jim bluntly stated, "Look at it this way. If you take the job, you're still free every night and weekends. If you don't take the job, you'll spend days, nights, and weekends in jail."

"All right, I'll take it." Louis looked down at his wristwatch. "Hey, I've got to go to that appointment at the car dealership. How do I get to this job in Mallory?"

Jim said, "Show up at my office next Monday at 6 a.m. I'll give you a ride to Mallory and pick you up at the end of the day. Then next Tuesday, you're on your own."

·31·

After Louis left the building, Jim made his way to the dispatch office. He pressed the red button on the counter. When a buzzer sounded, Martha Wilson, who doubled as the desk sergeant and chief dispatcher, got up from her console and stepped over to the service window.

"What's up Jimmy Boy?"

"Did you set up that appointment for me with Lyndon Bell in Mallory? I also wanted to meet with his foreman, John Sheppard."

Martha replied, "Yes sir. Mister Bell agreed to the 2 p.m. meeting time that you suggested. He said he'll be waiting in his office at the town hall. But Sheppard is in the field today. By the way, you better refer to Sheppard by his nickname, Easy if you know what's good for you. He sometimes gets madder than a grizzly in a barren huckleberry patch when someone calls him John."

"Thanks Martha. Tell my daughter where I went. If our schedules overlap and we don't happen to end the workday together, tell her I'll figure out a way to get her a ride home tonight."

"Will do…call in if you need us."

"I will."

Jim occupied himself for the next couple of hours with required paperwork. After lunch, he headed for the rear of the sheriff's office. He picked up Angel and Shadow from the service dog kennel and secured them inside his SUV. Jim pulled out of the parking lot, onto Main Street, and then turned east onto U.S. 228 headed for Mallory.

He pulled into the Mallory Town Hall parking lot, a few minutes before 2 p.m. He noticed a man sitting on the building's

147

concrete front steps. Jim got out of his SUV and as soon as he shut the driver's door, he heard the man call out to him.

"Sheriff Buchanan?"

"Yes, are you Lyndon Bell?"

"Yes."

"I heard that John…I mean Easy's out of the office today."

Lyndon held out his right hand and laughed. "Well, it's not easy when Easy's not around. I depend upon him for a lot around here." Then he said, "It's a pleasure to make your acquaintance, Sheriff Buchanan. I've heard a lot about you. Finally I get to meet the man behind the badge."

Jim and Lyndon shook hands and entered the town hall. They walked down a long corridor toward a backroom office. Inside the office, Jim noticed a town employee who stood at a six-foot long table with his palms down on a set of blueprints. Two other employees were seated at their desks typing away at their keyboards and eying their computer screens. Lyndon then led Jim to a glass partitioned space at the rear of the office.

"Please have a seat," Lyndon said. "I'm sorry that I can't invite your two dogs inside, town policy."

Jim replied, "I understand. They'll be all right out there. The windows are down and they have fresh water in back."

"Good, can I get you a cup of coffee?"

"No thank you. I've had enough today already." Jim pulled up a chair in front of a cluttered desk and sat down. "Where's Easy?"

Lyndon settled behind his desk. "He's up at Howard Lake supervising a paving project. What did you wish to speak with me about, Sheriff? Sergeant Martha Wilson said it was a matter of urgency."

Jim removed his Stetson, placed it on his lap, and nodded. "It is. We're investigating the missing person case of Janice Driver. I was hoping to ask you and Easy a few questions."

Lyndon folded his hands on his desk. "That's a terrible thing to have happened to such a young couple. I saw on the news they said she was pregnant and they have her husband in custody."

Jim shook his head. "As far as I know that information that she was pregnant was not released to the press. But yes, that's right. We also have another incident up in Spaulding where a retired schoolteacher is missing, and the crime scenes seem identical."

"How can I help, sheriff?"

Jim ran his cupped palm down his face until he rested his chin on his hand. "I apologize if I'm opening up old wounds, but I need to know if what happened to your parents in any way appears similar to what happened to these two women."

Lyndon's brow furrowed and his cheeks flushed red. "You want to know about my parents?"

"If you don't mind my asking."

Lyndon got up and walked to the door of his partitioned space. He peered at a couple of employees who stared at him. Lyndon closed the door and turned to Jim. "I'm sure that you can research the evidence by searching the Mallory Police archives."

Jim nodded. "I'm sure that I can but I wanted to ask you personally. Do you know of anything that the police may have overlooked in their investigations?"

Lyndon said, "I'm sorry, but I have nothing."

"Okay, then let's talk about what happened in Mallory."

"What about that?"

Jim asked, "You live in the same apartment complex as the Drivers?"

"I do."

"Then I need to know if you saw or heard the attack as it occurred, spotted a suspect, or noticed anything that looked suspicious in the vicinity. Any information that you can provide would be helpful."

Lyndon shook his head. "I wasn't home. I was on a mutual aid assignment to assist Lake County. They had tree damage near Flathead Lake and their road crews were shorthanded. Easy was in charge here in the office while I was away. In fact, a few weeks ago Mister Driver stopped by looking for work. Walked the entire couple three miles down here from their apartment...can you believe that?"

"Did he seem out of sorts?"

Lyndon replied, "No, no. He was so polite. He impressed me as such a nice young fella. I would've hired him but we have no openings."

"Well, seeing that it was such a violent attack do you have suspicions as to who may be responsible? Do you know if the Drivers had any enemies?"

"No, I don't know."

Jim asked, "What about your father?"

"What about him?"

"Do you know what happened to him?"

"No and I don't care. He treated my mother like shit. If he didn't run off, if someone killed him I'd like to meet that person and pin a medal on their chest."

"Do you think your father killed your mother?"

"I doubt it. Oh he'd beat her up pretty good at times but he was such a coward. I don't think he had it in him to commit murder."

Jim then asked, "Do you know if the Drivers received any threats? Were there any grudges or bad blood between them and anyone else?"

"No sir, no one. I never met the wife. I only saw them in passing. Seemed like a nice enough couple." Lyndon continued, "I did hear some people in town talking about that Indian legend, the one where they say a spirit rose from the dead, stalked people, and killed them. I think they said every few years he comes down from Great Northern Mountain when there's a full moon. Like a Beowulf monster. They uh, they call him Moon Man, something like that."

"*Saka'am Skaltamiax*," Jim said.

Lyndon stood up from his desk. "Yeah that's it. I remember now. I could never pronounce those words. Do you think there's any truth to that legend?"

Jim got up. "My job is to look for the person or persons responsible for the crimes."

Lyndon asked, "The crimes that have been committed can't be done by a rational human being, now can they? Maybe whoever's responsible for that poor unfortunate young Indian woman's disappearance is the same person who did that to my mother?"

Jim put on his Stetson, faced Lyndon, and said, "My job is to find that out."

·32·

Sergeant Bonnie MacAskill was a third generation Scottish-American. Her noticeable attributes were a thin build, fair complexion, and blond hair rolled into a bun. Her fellow employees knew that beneath that porcelain exterior laid hidden a rock-solid personality sworn to honor and duty. It was that sense of responsibility Alma Rose picked up on as they both worked inside the evidence locker in the upper basement level that afternoon.

Bonnie glanced at the wall clock. "The evidence for the Janice Driver case will be here any minute. Are you almost done with the supply inventory?"

Looking up from her desk, Alma Rose said, "Just a few minutes and I'll be all set."

Bonnie smiled. "Good work, Deputy Two Elk. I'll show you how to secure the evidence as it comes in, catalog it, and then file it in the locker."

Alma Rose finished the inventory and glanced at Bonnie. "I'm done." Then Alma Rose said, "Am I allowed to ask you a question that doesn't have to do with my job?"

"Sure, what is it?" Bonnie asked.

"What happened in Spaulding?"

Bonnie spoke right away, "I can't speak about that. You better ask your father if you want to know."

Alma Rose nodded. "Then I need advice on something else."

"What's that?" Bonnie asked.

"Dating."

"What about dating?"

Alma Rose stood up. "Well see, I never dated a white guy before. I've only dated boys from the Rez. I don't know what to expect."

"I can't help you there," Bonnie said.

Alma Rose asked, "Why not?"

Bonnie glanced around the empty evidence locker and then said, "I live with my partner."

Alma Rose nodded. "So you haven't dated in a while?"

Bonnie laughed. "It's not that. I live with my girlfriend."

Alma Rose was silent for a moment and then said, "I'm cool with that."

Bonnie turned to face Alma Rose. "Yeah, your father is too." Then she leaned forward. "Not a lot of people know, so let's keep this just between us."

Alma Rose nodded. "Sure, okay." Then she asked, "Who's your partner?"

Bonnie smiled. "She works at Lucy's Luncheonette. Her name is Thea Bond."

"How'd you guys meet?"

Bonnie shook her head and looked at the ceiling. Then she stared at Alma Rose. "Back in '89, before your father became sheriff, two white guys from back east were on a hunting trip. Thea served them a late dinner. She said they seemed high on something. They were waiting outside when her shift ended that night. They jumped her, manhandled her, and then threw her in their crew cab. They drove to the alleyway of the Frontier Hotel in Mallory."

"I'm so sorry," Alma Rose said. Then she asked, "Was one of them named Lester?"

Bonnie replied, "No, why do you ask?"

Alma Rose said, "Maybe it's nothing but Lucy Brown said some guy named Lester may have been harassing Janice Driver while she was at Lucy's."

"That may be but it's not anyone on our radar." Bonnie continued, "Taylor Police Chief John Peters was in Mallory overnight and heard screams coming from an alley. Thea was getting raped by those men. They called her a whore, slut, and even the "N" word among other things. Chief Peters caught them, called it in, and hauled their asses to jail in Mallory. Chief Peters personally brought Thea to Cedar County Hospital. Because I was the only female officer on duty at the time in both the Taylor and Mallory police departments and the sheriff's office, Chief Peters requested I follow-up with Thea once they released her from the hospital. I began helping her with daily tasks. One thing led to another and we've been together ever since."

"Wow, she's fortunate Chief Peters was there."

Bonnie hung her head as a tear fell from her eye. "Thea came to Taylor to escape the drugs and violence from back east, but it followed her here."

"Was she injured badly?"

Bonnie wiped the tears from her eyes. "Thea suffered a broken wrist and bruises on her arms. She even received a knife wound to her neck where one of them pressed his Bowie knife against her throat. She still has a scar under her chin from that attack." Bonnie wiped another tear from her cheek.

Alma Rose's eyes widened. "My gosh, Thea could have experienced the same fate that those women suffered in those recent disappearances in Mallory and Spaulding."

Bonnie nodded. "Don'tcha think I've asked myself that question when I heard what happened to Gary Driver's wife?"

Alma Rose asked, "Has anyone looked back to compare what happened to Thea in relation to what occurred in Mallory and Spaulding?"

Bonnie shook her head. "The two men who raped Thea were arrested, tried, and sentenced to prison in Deer Lodge."

"Do we know if they're still there?"

Bonnie replied, "The trial dragged on a bit but in '91 they each received ten-year sentences. I'll check to see if they're still serving their time."

Alma Rose then asked, "I read that rape offenders often serve about half their sentences?"

Bonnie agreed. "Sadly, it's true."

Alma Rose tilted her head. "Then if they got out after serving half their ten-year sentences, they would have been released..."

Bonnie interrupted her. "Last year."

Alma Rose took a deep breath and then exhaled. "We need to look into this. If they're responsible for what happened in Mallory and Spaulding, it could happen again."

"I'll mention it to Rocky and your father." Bonnie wiped away another tear. "Enough about me, now about you and this boy you're dating. Look, women have a certain instinct about these things. Let your senses dictate what you should do. All I can say is don't get yourself into a situation where you have no escape route."

"I'll try."

"Don't say you'll try. Stay close to other people. Whoever this guy is, don't let him corner you."

Alma Rose nodded. "I'll try not to. I was invited to Doctor Kelly's house for dinner on Friday and..."

Bonnie interrupted her. "On the 4th of July?"

Alma Rose smiled. "Yes, and I got permission to bring my friend."

Bonnie winked at her. "Dinner with Mary and Henry Kelly is a privilege that not many of us will ever see. You should consider yourself fortunate. I imagine he's got a lot of forensic information to share with you."

Alma Rose smiled. "That's what I'm looking forward to."

"Then use your best judgement about this guy. I'm sure he'll be on his best behavior in front of Doctor Kelly."

Alma Rose said, "I hope so."

Then Bonnie's cellphone rang. She picked it up the call on the second ring and repeated the word okay quite a few times. Then just before she hung up she said, "We'll be right there, give us a few minutes." Bonnie turned to Alma Rose. "The evidence is here. Grab the cart and follow me upstairs."

Alma Rose took the cart and followed Bonnie to the elevator. They went up one floor, through one secure passage desk and beyond the holding cell. Alma Rose looked through the holding cell's ballistic glass and noticed two men in handcuffs sitting on a bench with a deputy who stood guard over them. Bonnie and Alma Rose stepped through a second secure passage desk that led to the sally port.

Outside the building, a van drove up. Deputy Jared Pollard, who was assigned to the secure passage desk, responded to the entry request and opened the outside sally port garage door. Once the van drove inside, Pollard first closed the garage door and then opened the inside sally port door. Then he waved Bonnie and Alma Rose forward.

Alma Rose wheeled the cart to the side of the van and stood behind Bonnie. The driver's door of the van flung open. A uniformed officer climbed out.

"Hey Charles, how's it going?"

An officer with more than twenty-three years of service in the Mallory Police Department, Charles Ginalta was a little bit overweight and quite a bit balding.

"Doing well Bonnie...how's by you?"

"Can't complain."

"Who's the trainee?"

Bonnie glanced behind her and then stepped aside. "This is Junior Deputy Alma Rose Two Elk."

"Native huh?"

"She's Buchanan's daughter."

Charles nodded and with a smile that preceded his statement he said with folded arms, "Oh, I see. Well, Cedar County Sheriff Jim Buchanan's daughter, I wish you the best." Then he offered his hand and continued, "You'll learn right by Bonnie. She used to boss us around in Mallory. We thought for sure the department would fall apart after she left."

Alma Rose shook Charles hand as Bonnie laughed. "That was more than fifteen years ago," Bonnie said. A lot has changed since then."

Charles nodded. "Yes it has, yes it has." Then his tone turned darker. "And not for the better I might add. Folks are all bent out of shape and jittery as all hell about the ongoing disappearances."

He went around to the back of the van and opened the doors. Inside sat two lone banker boxes labeled, <u>Janice Driver 6/30/1997</u>.

Bonnie slapped labels onto the boxes and wrote 97-CF-011 in the blank case number section on the label. Then she turned to Alma Rose. "Place them on the cart."

"Yes, Sergeant MacAskill. What does the CF stand for?"

The words flew matter-of-factly from Bonnie lips in a uniform, regimented manner. "Criminal Felony."

Alma Rose took the first box and placed it on the brushed steel cart. When she reached inside the van for the second box, she felt faint and stumbled against the rear gate of the van. Bonnie grabbed her as Alma Rose collapsed and fell to the ground.

Alma Rose said with weariness in her voice, "Oh, I'm…"

"Are you all right?" Bonnie held Alma Rose by the arm.

Alma Rose got up and replied, "I'm fine."

Then she reached again for the box. When she touched it the second time, she felt a spark though her hand. She stepped away, bent over, and then regurgitated onto the floor.

"Whoa, we better get you to the women's room and then the cafeteria." Bonnie used her cellphone to call Rocky and inform him of what happened. When Bonnie and Alma Rose exited the women's room, Rocky was waiting outside. Bonnie said to him, "Can you take her to the cafeteria? I'll bring the boxes down to the evidence locker."

Rocky entered the cafeteria with Alma Rose leaning onto his arm. Rocky turned to one of the three cafeteria employees, "Deputy Two Elk's not feeling well. Do you have something that will calm her stomach?"

One of the cafeteria workers stepped toward them. "I'll make her a cup of peppermint ginger tea."

Rocky helped Alma Rose sit at one of the cafeteria tables. He sat across from her as they waited for the tea.

"What happened in the sally port?" Rocky asked.

"I'm not sure. Something tried to get inside of me."

"What do you mean?" Rocky asked.

Alma Rose leaned forward and whispered, "I felt the spirit of the woman who was murdered."

Rocky sat back in his seat. "Janice Driver?"

Alma Rose asked, "Is that her name?"

Rocky replied, "Yes, tell me what you felt."

Alma Rose whispered even lower. "She was trying to tell me something."

The cafeteria worker brought Alma Rose her cup of peppermint ginger tea and provided Rocky with his usual cup of hazelnut decaf coffee. While they sat together they discussed tomorrow's schedule. When they were finished, Alma Rose straightened up.

"I'm feeling fine. I can go back to work."

Rocky shook his head. "Oh no, you can't. You're taking the rest of the day off. Can you drive home?"

Alma Rose nodded. "I'm fine to drive."

"I'll follow you home."

Alma Rose asserted herself. "I'm all right. There's no good reason why you have to babysit me."

Rocky stood up. "Section 45-19-10 of the Cedar County Sheriff Office Regulations states that no officer injured on the job that is deemed unfit for duty shall be permitted to operate a motor vehicle unless accompanied by a superior officer."

"I'm not unfit for duty."

"I just declared you unfit for duty."

"Wait a minute, I…"

Rocky interrupted Alma Rose. "You're lucky I'm letting you drive as long as I follow you home."

·33·

Alma Rose left the sheriff's office, climbed into her pickup truck, and drove off the sheriff's office parking lot. Rocky followed in his patrol car. A few seconds later, a shiny, brand new, yellow corvette convertible slowly pulled out from a side street and kept a safe distance behind Alma Rose and Rocky.

Alma Rose pulled up to her father's house and then got out of her pickup truck. As she walked up the front steps, Rocky drove up the driveway and parked behind her truck. Alma Rose stumbled and fell at the front door. As she pushed herself up, Rocky threw the driver's door wide-open, sprang from his car, and rushed toward Alma Rose. Before she could open the front door of the house, Rocky reached out and grabbed her by the arm.

"Are you sure you're all right?" Rocky asked. He then released his grip on Alma Rose's arm.

She turned to him, took a deep breath, shivered, coughed a few times, and then stared into his eyes. "I'm fine," she said.

Rocky shook his head. "Let's make a quick stop at the Cedar County Hospital and have you evaluated. You could be suffering a relapse from Tanas' beating in the Yaak."

"I told you, I'm fine. I'm going inside to take a nap."

Rocky then said, "Look, it's almost two-thirty now. Your father told me that Acaraho's staying here and that he found him a job in Mallory. Jim has to pick up Acaraho after work, so they won't be home for a few hours. It's not a good idea for you to be alone."

Alma Rose said, "That's okay, Kate will be home soon."

Rocky grimaced. "I know that Kate is teaching at the University of Montana in Missoula, but I don't know when her classes end. It's more than an hour's drive from Missoula to Taylor. Are you sure that you'll be all right if I leave?"

"I told you, I'm fine. I'm going to take a nap."

Rocky persisted, "Will you be all right when Acaraho gets home?"

Alma Rose nodded. "I can handle Acaraho."

Rocky handed her his official business card from the sheriff's office. "If you feel in danger or need to contact me, my cell phone number is on this card. I'll be at the office the rest of the afternoon. I can be here in ten minutes. If you feel better tomorrow, be at the sheriff's office by 7 a.m. If you need a ride in and want to avoid Acaraho, just give me a call."

Alma Rose smiled. "Thanks, Rocky. You're a kind man."

Rocky said, "Maybe someday you'd like to have dinner with me and Linda."

Alma Rose nodded. "That would be nice."

Rocky said, "Hey, don't forget, you said you'd attend my do-wop gig in September at Greta's Place in Missoula."

Alma Rose offered a quizzical look on her face. "What's do-wop again? That's way before my time."

Rocky explained, "Do-wop singers like the Big Bopper, the Tokens, and Dion & the Belmonts."

In an instant, Alma Rose sensed a repertoire of songs that Rocky had sung and that she had never heard of before. Songs like "The Lion Sleeps Tonight" and "Up on the Roof". She said to Rocky, "I've never heard songs by those people so I'm looking forward to it. We don't have a lot of music choices from the radio station on the Rez. One day a woman donated a bunch of Beatles records after her husband died so that's mostly what they play. If I have to hear "The Long and Winding Road" one more time, I'm going to scream."

Rocky laughed. "There'll also be another singer there who's going to perform standards by Sinatra, Bennett, Vale, and some others."

As Alma Rose unlocked the door, she waved goodbye to Rocky and went inside. She connected her cellphone to the charger on the kitchen island and then went upstairs to her room. Alma Rose stripped down to her bra and panties, climbed into bed, and wrapped the comforter around her. Within five minutes she was fast asleep.

Less than a half-hour later, a song floated into Alma Rose's subconscious. It was a song she had never heard but she knew it was the Bobby Darin song, "Dream Lover" and the lyrics resonated with her. While the song played, she saw scattered images of both Acaraho and Louis.

Then an image of an older man who carried a Bowie knife barreled into her awareness. She saw his head covered by a mask and then saw the man sink his knife into her right thigh. Then a female voice in the background of her dream shouted to her. *Get out! Get out!*

Alma Rose awakened from a deep sleep, covered in sweat, and unable to move. She noticed that her right leg was numb.

When she heard the sound of a vehicle pull up the gravel driveway, it gave her a shudder that raced up her spine. The vehicle's door closed and she heard the footfalls of boots on the front porch. Alma Rose swung her left leg over the side of the bed but still couldn't move her right leg and was stuck in a contorted position.

A downstairs window shattered, glass crashed onto the oak floor, followed by a loud thud. Alma Rose used her elbows and dragged herself toward the edge of the mattress. She threw the comforter onto the floor, rolled off the bed, and fell onto the comforter. The piled fabric blunted the sound and impact of her fall. She crawled toward the door, reached up, and threw the latch shut.

When she heard footsteps in the hallway, Alma Rose rolled her body in the comforter. She slid away from the door and huddled on the floor. For the longest time there was no sound. Then the footfalls resumed and she heard them stop outside her bedroom door.

Alma Rose rested her cheek on the comforter and gazed through the crack in the space between the door and the floor. She spotted black boots in the hallway positioned right in front of the bedroom door. When the doorknob turned, she buried her head in the comforter and covered her mouth.

Alma Rose shook with each thump of pounding fists on the door. Then as quickly as the banging on the door began, it subsided. She then heard a vehicle's engine start and then head away from the house down the gravel driveway.

Alma Rose remained on the floor in a heap. Tears welled up in her eyes as she fell back to sleep in the comforter.

·34·

Alma Rose remained asleep on the floor, next to her bed. It was a cool day, 62 degrees, but under the comforter, her body warmth caressed her in a shroud of wellbeing.

After a few hours, Alma Rose awakened to the familiar sound of Kate's Volkswagen Samba Bus. Alma Rose pulled the comforter closer to herself when she heard the sound of the front door open. A few seconds later, Kate's screams resonated throughout the house.

Alma Rose heard Kate call to her and then the sound of footsteps up the stairway toward her bedroom. Kate shouted, "Alma Rose, Alma Rose!"

When the doorknob jingled, Alma Rose pulled herself closer to the door, let the comforter slide off her, and then struggled to reach up and unlock the door. Then she fell back onto the comforter, exhausted.

When the door opened, Alma Rose noticed that Kate held a Glock 26 semi-automatic pistol in her hands and aimed it into the room. Kate waved it around and when Alma Rose told her that no one was in the room, Kate tucked it into her side holster.

Kate asked, "Alma Rose, are you all right?"

"My leg is numb."

"Let me see." Kate threw back the comforter and saw a bruise the size of a clenched fist on her thigh. "Who did this to you?"

Alma Rose looked at her leg. "No one, it just hurts."

Kate said, "I'll take you to the hospital right now. Can you get up?"

Alma Rose nodded. "I think so." She reached for Kate's arm.

As Kate helped Alma Rose onto her feet she asked, "I saw your pickup truck outside. The downstairs window's broken. What happened?"

Alma Rose took a deep breath. "I got sick at the office. Rocky sent me home. I took a nap and then someone broke into the house. They came up to my bedroom door and tried to get inside."

"Do you know who it was?"

"No."

"Where are they now?"

"I heard him leave."

"You know that it was a man?"

"Yes, an old man. I felt it."

"We'll tell your father about this."

Alma Rose said, "I wish Angel or Shadow were home with me."

Kate helped Alma Rose sit on the edge of the bed. Then she grabbed a bathrobe from the closet and helped Alma Rose put it on.

Alma Rose turned to Kate. "I have to do something."

"What is it?"

Alma Rose said, "Please help me to the bureau."

After Kate obliged, Alma Rose leaned on the bureau and opened the top drawer. She pulled out a smudge stick with a blackened tip. Alma Rose took out a box of kitchen matches, lit the smudge stick, and used her hand to disperse the smoke.

Kate asked, "I see your father do that at the beginning of every season. Why are you doing that now?"

As Alma Rose walked around the second floor of the house with Kate's help she said, "An evil presence entered the house. The smoke will chase away the negative and stagnant energy. It followed that man inside and collected in the corners, the windows, and behind the doors."

Kate said, "Be careful. Let me help you down the stairs." Alma Rose leaned on Kate's shoulder as she continued to smudge the entire first floor.

Alma Rose pressed the smudge stick into a white sand dish on the coffee table in the great room. Jim kept it there for the sole purpose of extinguishing smudge sticks. Then Alma Rose said, "Let me grab my cellphone."

Kate nodded. "I'll get it for you." She led Alma Rose to the great room couch and helped her sit. "Where is it?" Kate asked.

"I left it on the kitchen island."

After a long moment, Kate returned. "It's not there."

"It's there, connected to the charger."

Kate shook her head. "There's no phone or charger anywhere in the kitchen."

"Are you sure?"

Kate said, "Yes, I looked all over. You must have left it at the sheriff's office."

"No, I brought it home with me."

Kate suggested, "Let's get you to the hospital. Then we'll return and make a renewed effort to find your cellphone."

Kate guided Alma Rose into the Samba Bus and then drove to Cedar County Hospital.

After an hour of testing in the emergency room, the staff doctor could find nothing wrong. Alma Rose's vitals were stable and except for the bruise on her leg, she was fine. The doctor diagnosed her injury as a contusion limited to the soft tissue of her thigh. He administered Extra-Strength Tylenol, gave Kate a script for an anti-inflammatory, and told her that it would be best if Alma Rose stayed off her feet for twenty-four hours.

The doctor asked Alma Rose, "Do you know how you received that injury? Did someone punch you very hard?"

"No."

The doctor continued, "I've seen battered women come here with injuries like this. They tend to be of a domestic nature. Are you married? Do you have a boyfriend?"

"No I don't...well, not really."

"Then you must have gotten hit very hard by someone."

"I was fine before I got home. I got hurt during a dream."

"You said a dream?" The doctor's brow furrowed. "Did you participate in any physical activity today?"

"I had a self-defense class this morning."

The doctor said, "Well now, that's how you got injured. In the moment you didn't notice it and it manifested itself later in the day."

Alma Rose's voice crackled with anger. "I didn't get hit in the class. I can take care of myself."

The doctor smiled. "All right...all right young lady. That's okay. You'll feel better with rest and the meds I prescribed."

"I need to find my cellphone. When can I get out of this place?"

The doctor said, "I'm sorry Miss Two Elk. We need to keep you under observation for the next few hours."

·35·

It was 4:37 p.m. Tuesday, one day after the interrogation that seemed to go downhill at a rapid pace. It was also a few hours after Gary Driver's initial appearance in court where he heard the charges levied against him. Now Gary's thoughts returned to the present. He wiped perspiration from his brow and then rubbed his eyes. A succession of taps on the jailcell door made him raise his head. He stared at the door as a voice called to him.

"Gary Driver, you have a visitor."

Gary stood up and said to Officer Dewey who was on guard duty, "Who is it?"

"A lawyer."

"Whose lawyer?"

"Your lawyer."

"I don't have a lawyer."

"You do now."

"What the hell does he want?"

"Are you going to accept the visitor?"

"No." Gary then reconsidered. A spark of reason and logic enveloped Gary. It convinced him that a visit would at least get him out of his cell for a few minutes, an hour if he was lucky. "All right...all right. I'll see him."

Gary backed up against the door. Officer Dewey cuffed him, and then asked him to step away. Officer Dewey opened the door and two other officers grabbed Gary from behind and led him out of his cell and down the hall.

The narrowness of the hallway made Gary vaguely recall early Monday morning at the apartment complex. There he was led by a few law enforcement officers through a gauntlet of vengeful people. He couldn't get their shouts out of his mind.

Now the barren green walls of the local jail seemed to speak to Gary. Disembodied cries of BORN LOSER, LIAR, DIRTY FELON, WIFE BEATER, BUTCHER, MURDERER, and BABY KILLER echoed throughout his head like a philharmonic orchestra tuning up before a concert. Gary shifted his head to the left and then to the right to avoid the ghost-like shouts that haunted his mind. He sensed that what little was left of his sanity had begun to slip away.

·36·

Inside a blue-walled interview room at the Mallory Police Station, Attorney Jeremy Bowers sat at a dark walnut stained, pine table. He opened his appointment calendar and then thumbed to the page that referred to today's date, Tuesday July 1, 1997. He noticed movement from the corner of his eye, glanced upward, and stared through the glass panel of the security door. In the hallway that connected to the police station cellblock, Bowers spotted the staggered approach of an inmate and his police guard.

A buzzer sounded and then the heavy door swung open. Bowers crooked his neck as the shackled prisoner shuffled into the room. An overpowering odor of Clorox invaded the room as it sought pedestrian nostrils to invade. It masked the faint whiff of musty deodorant along with a slight stench of urine that wafted in from the cellblocks. The officer held onto the inmate's upper left arm and led him to the table.

Bowers gazed upward at the twelve-foot ceiling and then rolled his eyes. He sighed and then glanced back down at the table. Bowers methodically opened his briefcase and pulled out a binder. It contained numerous manila folders composed of state letterhead copies, coffee-stained handwritten notes, and police reports adorned with yellow, green, and blue sticky notes that displayed unrecognizable annotations.

Bowers stood up and held out his hand. "Mister Driver, I'm glad to meet you. My name is Attorney Jeremy Bowers. I'm obliged to inform you that the state has assigned me as your court appointed counsel."

Gary Driver raised his handcuffed wrists as far as his belly chain would allow, shook his long hair away from his clean-shaven face, and stared at the attorney.

"I didn't ask for you," Gary said.

Officer Dewey gestured to the chair anchored to the concrete floor. "Take a seat, Driver." Dewey chained Gary Driver's leg irons to the eyebolt in the floor and then glanced at Attorney Bowers. "I'll be outside the door. If you need anything, just holler. I'll be watching through the glass."

Once Officer Dewey left the room, Attorney Bowers turned to Gary. "Mister Driver, I'm here to help you. They are planning to transfer you to county jail by the end of this week. You're being arraigned next Monday for the murder of your wife."

Gary slowly raised his head. "If it's true she's dead, can't you find her killer?"

Attorney Bowers first rested his forehead on his right palm and then looked up at Gary. "Mister Driver, the evidence points to a violent homicide. I'm only trying to save your life."

Gary took a deep breath and exhaled. "I have no life. My entire existence has been a huge mistake."

"Mister Driver, may I call you Gary?"

"What does it matter?"

Attorney Bowers spoke louder, "Mister Driver…"

"Yes, yes...call me whatever you want."

"Gary…I believe that you're innocent. Let me prove that the blood found on your clothes and in your car was your blood and not your wife's. I'll make sure that they share the DNA evidence with us."

"I told them it was my blood when they arrested me. I would never hurt my wife."

Attorney Bowers closed the folder. "Then let me help you. I can gather resources, assemble a team."

Gary stared at Attorney Bowers and then said, "On one condition. Get me *Issaxchí-Káata*."

"What gibberish is that?" Jeremy asked.

"It's a name."

Attorney Bowers sighed. "Who is that?"

"Little Hawk."

"I'm sorry Mister Driver, but if you don't explain yourself, I have no clue who you're speaking about."

Gary Driver stood up and slammed his handcuffed palms onto the table. "Get Sheriff Jim Buchanan and his daughter. He's the county sheriff and she's the only one who can find my wife's killer."

·37·

Jim received a phone call from Kate. She explained what had happened at their home while Alma Rose was alone. Kate told him that she brought Alma Rose to the ER for treatment and that she would stay with her until they discharged her. Kate said the doctor was hinting that by late afternoon Alma Rose may be ready to leave. When Jim said that he would stop by the hospital to visit, Kate suggested that it might be best he let Alma Rose rest until she got home. Kate reasoned with Jim that the less stress placed upon on Alma Rose the better. Kate also recommended that Jim ensure the house was safe before Alma Rose's return that evening.

Jim and a couple of deputies arrived at his house to see what evidence they could obtain. The deputies spent more than two hours dusting for fingerprints both inside and outside the home. They secured the broken glass as evidence and then checked the driveway for tire tracks and footprints.

While they did that, Jim armed himself with his Colt Python service revolver and his personal Marlin 1895 Cowboy Lever-Action rifle. He surveyed the perimeter of his property for any evidence of the intruder.

Unfortunately, the deputies didn't find much in the way of evidence other than the broken glass and neither did Jim. The number of vehicles at Jim and Kate's house over the past few days had masked any potential intruder's tracks or footprints. No collected fingerprints outside or inside the home suggested to the deputies that the suspect most likely wore gloves.

Jim asked an employee from Taylor Hardware to drop by and repair the broken window. However, Jim knew that it would be more difficult to mend the rift between him and his daughter.

Jim realized the physical and emotional trauma that Alma Rose had experienced would take much longer to heal.

He left the house around 6 p.m. after the investigation was completed. Jim promised to give Acaraho a ride home at the end of his workday at the Mallory Public Works Department. When Jim pulled into the parking lot of the Mallory Town Hall he noticed Acaraho hunched over on the building's front steps. Jim got the boy's attention and nodded to him. He walked over to Jim's SUV and climbed inside.

Acaraho said, "Thanks for calling and letting me know you'd be late. Easy let me work a couple hours overtime."

Jim glanced at him. "You like the job so far?"

Acaraho shrugged. "It's okay. If I didn't get hurt this summer, maybe I could be working outside with Easy. Working all day in the office gets really boring. It sucks big time."

Jim pulled out of the parking lot and doubled back onto U.S. 228. He turned to Acaraho. "You suffered a concussion from that fall off the Rimrocks. You dislocated your kneecap, tore your meniscus, and strained the ligaments in your knee. You're lucky you didn't tear any ligaments. I tore my ACL playing football. That was the end of my career. Have you been rehabbing?"

Acaraho replied, "The doctor in Billings said I should be able to ride a horse again in the fall. He gave me exercises to do and said I'm making good progress, no crutches, no cane. I just have to be careful with stairs and no kneeling or running."

Then Jim asked, "What's going on with you and Alma Rose?"

Acaraho stared out the passenger window. "I don't know. I guess she's mad at me for seeing that girl up on the Rims. I didn't know that girl was an FBI agent. I think it was all a scam. She used me to drive her up onto the Rimrocks to investigate that biker gang." Then Acaraho turned to Jim. "But you heard what Alma Rose said. She broke up with me when you saw Johntall and me outside Shield's Supermarket in Billings. That was before I met that FBI woman."

Jim glanced at Acaraho. "I know but if Alma Rose is mad then she may still have feelings for you."

Acaraho looked forward and smiled. "Do you think so?"

Jim replied, "That's not what I'm getting at."

Acaraho turned his head and faced Jim. "Then what are you trying to tell me?"

Jim had trouble getting out what he truly meant and instead suggested, "I think it's best to get you settled in a place of your own. That way you and Alma Rose aren't bumping into one another every day in my house."

Acaraho nodded. "That would be helpful. Maybe the less she sees of me the more she'll be thinking about me?"

"Could be," Jim said. Then he glanced back at Acaraho. "I need to tell you what happened at my house today."

Acaraho stared at Jim. "What do you mean?"

Jim looked back at the road. "Today, Alma Rose got sick at work and Undersheriff Salentino followed her home. He said that she was all right when he left her but then..."

Acaraho asked, "Then what?"

Jim continued, "She was napping in her room and someone broke into the house."

Acaraho shouted, "What...did they hurt Alma Rose?"

Jim replied, "No, but she was startled. We need to find out who the intruder was. We don't know if they were after Alma Rose or if it was a simple home invasion."

"Was anything stolen?"

"No."

"Has that sort of thing happened before?"

Jim glanced back at Acaraho. "No, but we want to make sure it doesn't happen again."

·38·

Jim parked his SUV when they arrived at the house and Acaraho jumped from the vehicle. He raced toward the front door and then went inside. Acaraho ran up the steps to the second floor and burst into Alma Rose's bedroom. Alma Rose was lying on the bed with her head propped up by three pillows. Kate was by her side seated in a wooden chair. The look on their faces convinced Acaraho to pump his brakes.

Acaraho swallowed hard. "Alma Rose, are you all right?"

When Alma Rose turned to look at Acaraho, he felt her gaze penetrate his soul. Then it seemed as if an eternity passed before she spoke.

Alma Rose looked away from him. "I'm fine. Please let me rest."

Acaraho felt the double-edged dagger sink deep into his heart. He nodded and was about to tell her that he would wait downstairs but then clammed up. Instead, he simply sulked away.

When he reached the bottom of the stairs, Jim came in through the front door. Acaraho caught up with him.

"Why is she in bed?" Acaraho asked.

Jim said, "Let's talk in the rec room."

Acaraho followed Jim downstairs into the basement. A tiled and carpeted recreation room floor greeted them. Acaraho stared at the many mounted animal heads that adorned the paneled walls. A fireplace dominated the far wall. A TV sat in one corner while a computer station bookended the other corner. Two recliners populated the middle of the room. An expansive bookcase lined the left wall along with a locked gun safe and a glass display case of Bowie knives. Across from it on the right wall was an extra-long recliner sleeper sofa. It was large enough to accommodate Jim's six-foot, five-inch frame.

Jim said, "Have a seat."

Acaraho sat in one of the two recliners while Jim settled in the other. The room was silent for an inordinate amount of time. Acaraho felt the tension elevate to an uncomfortable level and then asked, "Mister Buchanan, what did you want to speak with me about?"

Acaraho stared at Jim and when he heard words that he had hoped he would never hear, they echoed throughout his mind.

"I think it's best that you no longer see Alma Rose."

Acaraho grew a pained expression on his face. Then tears welled in his eyes. "What did I do wrong?" he asked.

Jim got up from the recliner and turned to face the wall away from Acaraho. "You didn't do anything wrong." Then he pivoted and confronted Acaraho. "Alma Rose needs to complete her training this summer with the sheriff's department. She can't if you and she live under the same roof."

Acaraho wiped away a tear. "But you...you and me just spoke a few minutes ago about me getting a place of my own."

With a raised voice, Jim blurted, "I'm not talking about that. I'm suggesting that you and Alma Rose never see one another again."

"Why?"

"Because it would put a lot of stress on what she's trying to accomplish."

Acaraho wiped away another tear. "But what about what I'm trying to accomplish?"

"What are you trying to accomplish?"

Acaraho stared at the carpeted floor and then looked up at Jim. "I'm trying to earn enough money so that when I attend classes at Taylor University, I'll have an apartment to live in."

Jim shook his head. "You won't have enough saved to live on your own. What's your end game?"

Acaraho stood up. "There's nothing for me on the Rez anymore. Alma Rose is doing something with her life. I want to prove to her that I can do something with mine. That way, when we're both done with school, we can..." Acaraho took a deep breath. "We can get married."

Jim shouted, "Didn't you just hear what I told you?"

174

Acaraho sat back down. "Yes sir. You said that you didn't want me living in this house with Alma Rose."

Jim continued in a loud voice. "That's not what I said. I told you that I don't want you to ever see Alma Rose again."

Acaraho sat with his mouth agape. "Do you mean like, forever?"

Jim nodded. "Yes, if that's what it takes for Alma Rose to realize her dreams."

Acaraho thought of a few hurtful things that he could say to Jim. Things like, *you're not Apsáalooke like me, you're only a half-breed. You think just like a white man. You don't really understand what love's all about. When Alma Rose was just a baby you abandoned her mother Shoshanna. I've shown Alma Rose more love and attention than you've ever given her since the day she was born.*

But Acaraho thought better and simply said, "I'll do what you want because I love her."

·39·

Jim went upstairs leaving Acaraho in the basement rec room to contemplate what they had just discussed. Jim made his way up the second-floor staircase toward the bedrooms but before he reached the landing, he noticed Kate's stare from the top steps. Jim took the last few steps and attempted to walk past Kate to Alma Rose's bedroom, but Kate grabbed him by the upper arm.

"Why did you yell at that poor boy? What did you say?"

Jim whispered, "I told Acaraho I didn't want him to see Alma Rose anymore."

Jim felt Kate's grip tighten.

"You can't expect him to do that."

"Why not, I'm her father. I can tell him anything I want."

Kate released her grip on Jim's arm and shook her head. "Don't become like your own father. Don't you remember what he did to you?"

Jim covered his face in his hands and then sat down in one of the chairs in the sitting area on the second floor. He looked up at Kate. "That's not fair. This is different."

Kate said, "The circumstances may be different but the hurtfulness that's felt by the victim is just as painful."

Jim shook his head. "I don't want to happen to them what happened to me and Shoshanna."

Kate took Jim by his hands. "It won't…it can't if you treat them as adults and not like children."

Jim asked, "How can you be sure?"

Kate smiled. "Give them space. If it's meant to be, let it happen. If it's not meant to be, they'll discover that too. Don't force them to regret something that didn't happen just because of your influence on them."

Jim rubbed his eyes, exhaled, and got up. "I guess you're right. I'll go speak with Acaraho and repair the damage I caused. Then I'll sit down with Alma Rose."

Kate patted Jim on his shoulder. "You do that."

Jim went back downstairs into the rec room. He noticed Acaraho in front of the display case of Bowie knives.

Jim asked, "Acaraho, are you okay?"

Acaraho turned to face Jim. One of the Bowie knives was in his hands.

Acaraho said, "For a minute I thought about using one of these knives to slice my own wrists." Acaraho placed the knife down on the display case. "Then I thought, if I did that, I might cause pain to those I loved." He turned to Jim. "I wouldn't want to do that to them."

Jim said, "Doing harm to oneself never solves anything."

Jim stepped over to Acaraho and picked up the knife. He opened the display case and placed the knife back into its spot. Then Jim noticed an open spot next to the Bowie knife. A twelve-inch, wooden handled Bowie knife with an almost eight-inch stainless steel blade with a saw back was missing. Jim simply stood there and stared into the display case.

Acaraho asked, "What's wrong?"

"One of my Bowie knives is missing. Did you remove another knife from the case?"

"The one I held was the only one I touched."

Jim grabbed his cell phone and called the sheriff's office. *"Martha, tell Rocky that I think one of my Bowie knives was stolen during today's break-in at my house...Good...Photo of the knife? Yeah, I can bring in tomorrow...Thanks."* Jim hung up the phone.

Acaraho asked, "Am I in trouble?"

Jim clasped both his hands on Acaraho's shoulders. "Remember that conversation we had earlier?"

Acaraho glared at Jim's large hands and winced. "Yes?"

Jim released his hands and then put his arm around Acaraho's shoulder. He started to lead Acaraho toward the stairs. "I was wrong to speak to you like that. Whatever you and Alma Rose have together is between you and her and only the two of you can sort that out. I shouldn't be trying to intervene in your lives."

Acaraho stopped and stared at Jim. "Are you serious?"

"Yes. I'm here if either of you've got questions. As far as the two of you, that's something that you and Alma Rose have to sort out yourselves. I won't interfere."

Acaraho smiled. "Thank you, *Issaxchí-Káata*. I think that your suggestion of me getting an apartment is a good idea."

Jim said, "I have an idea on how to make this work, at least for the summer anyway. Let me see if I can pull the pieces together before we make any commitments."

"Thank you, sir. About Alma Rose, I won't disappoint you if she decides to give me another chance."

With Jim's relationship with Acaraho now renewed, he focused on mending his paternal bond with Alma Rose. Up the stairs he went again. Kate was not on the landing or in the sitting area near the bedrooms. Jim approached Alma Rose's bedroom and knocked on the door.

Alma Rose answered, "Who's there?"

"It's your father."

"Come in."

When Jim opened the door he saw Kate in the chair next to the bed. She got up without a word. She smiled at Jim and he stared at her as she walked toward the door. Kate shut the door and left father and daughter alone in the bedroom.

Alma Rose asked, "What's up, dad?"

"May I sit on the bed?"

Alma Rose tilted her head and then giggled. "I guess. It'll be a first for you so I'm going to let this moment soak in."

Jim sat on the edge of the bed near Alma Rose's feet. He said, "Listen to what I'm going to say."

"Okay." Alma Rose propped herself up in bed.

"First of all, I'm having a company come to the house tomorrow and install a security system."

Alma Rose gave him a quizzical look. "Is that it?"

"No, I want to talk about Acaraho."

Alma Rose rolled her eyes. "What about him?"

Jim took Alma Rose by the hand. "He cares about you a great deal."

"Is that what he told you to tell me?"

"Not exactly."

"Then what?"

Jim grimaced. "He said he's in love with you."

Alma Rose rolled her eyes again. "Doesn't he mean he was in love with me?"

"No, he told me tonight that he loves you."

Alma Rose raised her upper lip, wrinkled her nose, and pulled her hand back from Jim. "Did Acaraho love me when he was with that girl on the Rimrocks?"

Jim said, "I can't answer that, only Acaraho can."

Alma Rose leaned to one side and rested her head on the pillow. "Dad, I don't know what to do. Can you help me?"

"If it's about Acaraho, I'm going to try and get him settled for the summer. It'll uncomplicate things if he lived elsewhere while you serve your internship."

"It's not about Acaraho."

Jim asked, "Then what, what do you need from me?"

"Advice."

"Go ahead, ask me."

"Well, I got invited to the Kelly's for dinner on Friday."

Jim smiled. "That's great."

Alma Rose sat up again. "Doctor Kelly gave me permission to bring someone."

"Acaraho?"

"No."

"Then who?"

"Louis Miller."

Jim froze for a split second and then said in a loud voice, "Louis Miller?"

"Dad, yes."

"Why?"

"Because, I think something bad will happen if I don't."

"Alma Rose, something bad might happen if you do."

"Well, I'm going with him anyway."

"Alma Rose, he's not the type of kid that..." Jim stopped in his tracks and thought of what Kate had told him earlier. He then continued, "What are you sensing about him?"

Alma Rose leaned over and grabbed her journal from the nightstand. She thumbed through a few pages, and then said, "I'm not sure. I do know that if I don't go with him a series of events will unfold that will make things much worse."

"Alma Rose, I may be busy with another case up in Troy through the holiday weekend. I'm going to compartmentalize things here. That will allow me to address that other case, what happened today in this house, the issues with the Louis Miller boy and the disappearances of those women in Mallory and

Spaulding. Do you think you'll be well enough to return to work tomorrow in the evidence locker?"

"If I rest up tonight, I think I'll be good tomorrow."

"How's the leg?"

"The bruise is still there but I can move it now. It'll be fine by tomorrow."

Jim asked, "Are you hungry?"

Alma Rose shouted, "No, my stomach is tied up in knots. I have my water bottle here. That's all I need."

Jim replied, "Good. Then report to Sergeant MacAskill at 8 a.m. Tell her that I assigned you that reporting time. I've got a family to visit in the morning. I should be back by noon."

Alma Rose asked, "What family?"

"Thomas and Barbara Miller."

Before Jim could leave, Alma Rose called to him. "Dad, there's something I have to tell you."

"What is it?"

She said, "Today I saw a flesh and blood man. That's the killer we're looking for."

Jim was silent for a long moment. Then he nodded to Alma Rose. "Rest up...we've got work ahead of us."

Jim left the room and went downstairs to the great room. Kate had gone to bed leaving Jim to stare at Angel and Shadow's sleepy eyes. The two canines shared an oversized dog bed. Each dog had their head on the back of the other in either a sort of reciprocal kindness or a sense of mutual vigilance. Then the telephone rang.

"*Jim speaking...oh hello mayor...yes, I'm going there tomorrow...what, I don't understand...what do you mean by that...but...yes, I know that...are you sure...but...all right, I will...yes...goodnight mayor.*" Jim hung up.

Kate entered the great room. "I heard the phone ring. Who was that? I'm so on edge. Did it have anything to do with what happened today?"

Jim sat on the great room couch and looked up at Kate. "No, it was Mayor Dayton."

"What did he want?"

Jim sighed. "As you know, he's a hands-on mayor and reviews the sheriff's daily logs every evening. He reviewed my log and I always list my schedule for the next day."

Kate asked, "What did he see?"

"He saw that I made reference to the Miller's."

"What did you say about them?"

Jim replied, "My schedule lists a planned visit with them tomorrow. I noted that I wanted to speak with them about their son and the accident up on U.S. 228."

"What did the mayor say?"

Jim reached out his arms to Kate. "Come here."

Kate shook her head. "Uh-oh, this is bad."

Kate sat on the great room couch as Jim cradled his arms around her. She leaned into him to get comfortable and rested her head against his.

"The mayor said to not give the Millers any trouble. He said they're pillars of this community. Much of the progress that the town of Taylor and Cedar County have seen over the past three years can be attributed to their involvement...so he says. Plus their generosity and the connections they have."

"Like Governor Ross?"

Jim confirmed, "Yes, like Governor Ross."

Kate whispered, "You're always doing the right thing. I know you will this time."

Jim replied, "This time it's not a question of me doing the right thing. It's a question of doing what I'm told."

Kate asked, "Does that mean not doing what's right?"

"Not really. It's more about looking the other way. Not judging how these people live their lives."

Kate asked, "What does that mean?"

"I asked him that same question. He said that I'll know what he means when I get to the Miller's home."

"Do you expect trouble with the parents or their son?"

"I don't think so." Then Jim paused. "The only thing that stuck in my craw was when the mayor said the Millers are good friends with Governor Ross."

"Jim, are you concerned about that?"

"Kate, the mayor said that if I want to run again for sheriff in the fall election then I better keep my hands off the Millers. Otherwise the governor will have something to say about it." Then Jim stared straight into Kate's eyes. "I'm leaning toward taking my name off the ballot."

·40·

It was 9:07 a.m. on Wednesday July 2nd when Jim drove up Mountain View Drive toward the Miller's homestead. Once Jim pulled into the driveway, he was astonished at the size of the home. Various ornate appointments marked the two-story, five-thousand two-hundred square foot log and timber home set on one-hundred and thirty-four acres.

To Jim, the home reminded him of the estates that dotted the eastern shore of Flathead Lake. It was unlike the modest neighboring homes that inhabited the pine and cedar forests along the perimeter of the Cabinet Mountains just outside Taylor.

Jim got out of his SUV and put on his Stetson. Then one of the six garage doors opened. When the door was high enough for Jim to see inside, he spotted Louis Miller sitting behind the wheel of his brand-new canary yellow Corvette. Louis revved the engine as Jim walked toward him.

When the Corvette sprang forward, Jim had to leap out of the way. Louis slammed on the brakes and the car came to a halt with Jim positioned next to the driver's door.

Louis snickered and said, "Hey man, sorry. New car, you know? I'm not used to the gas pedal. Boy, this baby howls and just wants to lurch and run."

Jim put his hands on the top of the driver's door and leaned over the car. "It seems that you haven't changed."

"Hey, hey…get off my car, watch the finish."

Jim straightened up and then turned to gaze at the house. "Are your parents inside?"

Louis emitted a series of loud laughs. Then he regained his composure. "Yeah, they're um…" Louis waved his hand in the air. "Somewhere in there."

Jim nodded. "Good." Then he stared at Louis. "Be nice to our young women in Taylor."

Louis stared at Jim, hesitated, and then replied, "Yeah, well, I gotta go. See ya."

Louis revved his Corvette and threw it into gear. He laid a strip of rubber on the cement pavement as he raced down the switchback driveway.

Jim shook his head as he watched the car roar toward Route 56. Jim turned and walked toward the front door. He climbed the mahogany steps and rapped the heavy brass knocker on the ornate, eight-foot tall oak door.

The door opened a crack and a large Hispanic woman wearing a housecoat held open the door. "*¿Me vas a arrestar?*" (Are you going to arrest me?).

Jim removed his Stetson, held it in his hands, and gazed past her. "Is Thomas Miller home?"

"*Señor, sí Señor Miller está en casa,*" the woman said. (Sir, yes Mister Miller is home).

"I'd like to speak with Thomas Miller."

The woman smiled and opened the door. "*Entrar, se puede hablar con las Señora Miller.*" (Come in, you can talk to Mrs. Miller).

Although Jim did not speak Spanish, he sensed that the woman invited him inside. When he stepped past her, the woman called out, "*Señora Miller, un policía está aquí. ¿Estoy en problemas?*" (Mrs. Miller, a cop is here. Am I in trouble?).

Jim noticed movement from the corner of his eye. On a staircase that connected the first floor with a lower level in the home, a lean, tan, and toned barefoot woman in her mid-thirties climbed to the upper level. She strode up to Jim as if she were a fashion model strutting down a runway. Her shoulder-length black hair had streaks of pink and she wore a sheer black cover-up over a black slingshot bikini which revealed an ample amount of cleavage. Her body was arrayed with an assortment of tattoos and she held a martini glass that contained a tooth-picked Spanish olive submerged in an amber liquid. She exhibited a sly smile, exchanged the drink from her right hand to her left, and then extended her free hand to Jim.

"I'm Barbara Miller. You must be Sheriff Buchanan. I'm pleased to meet you my dear." Then she turned to the Hispanic woman and spoke in a flourish of Spanish-accented language. "*Margarita, sé que te preocupa que te arresten y te deporten a*

Honduras pero no dejaremos que eso suceda. ¿Por qué no vas a tu cuarto y me dejas encargarme del sheriff?" (Margarita, I know you are worried that you'll be arrested and deported to Honduras but we won't let that happen. Why don't you go to your room and let me handle the sheriff?).

The Hispanic woman's glance shifted from Barbara and settled on Jim. For a moment, she seemed frozen in place. Then she turned back to Barbara Miller and said, *"Sí, gracias. Señora Miller"* (Yes, thanks. Mrs. Miller). She then turned and hurried away.

Jim felt Barbara Miller's roaming eyes as she appeared to size him up. She took a step closer to him, smiled, and placed her right hand on Jim's forearm. "I've heard so much about you Sheriff Buchanan. The word is that you're a tough, courageous, and daring lawman. I just didn't realize how tall you would be and...just how handsome you are. What can I do for you...my dear?"

Jim said matter-of-factly, "I'd like to speak with you and your husband about your stepson, Louis."

Barbara leaned forward and whispered into Jim's ear. "What would you say if I offered an invite to our poolside cabana where you and I could discuss Louis in private? I can assure you that no one would bother us. You and I could get to the bottom of whatever you've come to discuss."

Jim stood his ground. "I'm sorry ma'am but I need to discuss this with both you and your husband."

Barbara wheeled around and curled her finger. "Fine, please come with me. My husband is downstairs." Then she turned back to Jim. "Sheriff, my private invitation will remain open and I will expect nothing less than your gracious etiquette in accepting my offer. And I promise I will not disappoint you."

Jim didn't respond and instead followed Barbara and descended the steps. Through the floor to ceiling windows on the lower level, he noticed the expansive deck, swimming pool, cabana, and hot tub. Beyond, in the distance, Jim spotted a traditional Mongolian yurt next to a private lake. But Jim's eyes quickly focused on the hot tub and the allover tanned bare back of a twentysomething woman with long blond hair. The woman's broad shoulders and thin waist accentuated her lean figure. The woman pressed her body against another person in the hot tub, blocking Jim's view of the individual.

Barbara walked up to the sliding doors and opened them. "Thomas, it's time to get out."

Jim heard a male voice call out from behind the young woman's body. "Barbara, what's the rush? Anna's just getting into the mood. Barbara darling, aren't you coming back to join us?"

"Thomas, the sheriff is here, and he wants to speak with us about Louis."

From behind and beneath the young woman, a fiftyish, overweight man with a trimmed white beard and full head of gray hair that reached his shoulders raised himself out of the hot tub. He reached for a bathrobe off a deck chair and wrapped it around his nude body.

As he cinched his robe, he said to the young woman who was still in the tub, "Anna, I have business with this gentleman. It should be brief. Barbara and I will rendezvous with you in the sauna."

Anna turned and stared at Jim. He felt her eyes linger on his. As they looked intently at one another, and as Jim's eyes tracked hers, Anna dropped her chin. When Jim's eyes reached her bosom, he returned his gaze to her face.

Anna giggled, smiled, winked at Jim, and then emitted a devilish laugh. As she climbed out of the hot tub, Jim noticed the water droplets cascade down her naked back, then onto her bare backside, and finally down her long legs. She strutted across the deck and toward the spa building next to the in-ground swimming pool.

Thomas Miller walked up to Jim and Barbara and asked, "What can we do for you, sheriff...Sheriff Buchanan, I presume, correct?"

"Correct. I'm here to speak with you about your son."

"What about my son...has he misbehaved?"

Jim asked, "Did you know that he hit an elk on U.S. 228 which caused a rig to hit a scavenging bald eagle?"

Thomas nodded. "Yes, we know all about that incident. It's a damn shame that Louis totaled his car but isn't it a miracle that he didn't get hurt?" Thomas pointed to a patio set. "Please sit with us."

Jim walked toward the table and sat in one of the stack chairs. Thomas and Barbara each took a seat on either side of him at the table.

Jim placed his arms on the table. "Your son's conduct was reckless. He killed an animal and endangered another. I could have arrested him but chose not to."

Barbara touched Jim's left arm. "Thank you sheriff. I'm sure that Louis will be more responsible with his actions going forward."

Jim withdrew his left arm. "From what I've seen of his behavior since the accident, it seems that he hasn't learned any lessons. As a more effective alternative to incarceration, I've secured a summer job for him in Mallory. He'll be working at the town's public works highway department. All I need is his family's approval."

Barbara laughed. "Sheriff, that's not necessary. We will handle him in our own way."

Jim shook his head. "I'm sorry but that's not acceptable. If he doesn't participate in this summer job, then I have no alternative but to insist that the county press charges. I have paperwork drawn up at my office for reckless driving and evading responsibility."

Barbara put her hand on Jim's right forearm. "Please sheriff, I think you and I can reach an agreement." She ran her hands up and down Jim's forearm and stared into his eyes. "Sheriff, I would be delighted to provide you with whatever actions are necessary on my part to keep Louis out of jail." Jim pulled his right arm away and folded his hands on his lap.

Thomas interjected, "Well, I'm pleased to hear that one way or another we'll come to terms on some type of agreement that will satisfy everyone. Sheriff, you don't know how difficult it is to…I guess how would you say out here, to corral him." Thomas laughed at his own joke.

Barbara asked, "If we go along with this…this summer job, what will he be doing?"

Jim replied, "That's up to the director of public works, Lyndon Bell and his foreman, John Sheppard."

Barbara asked, "Sheriff, who is this John Sheppard?"

"They call him Easy. He supervises the road paving crews for the Mallory Public Works Department. I've been told that he'd be a good role model for Louis. He's a raptor rehabilitator."

Barbara shivered. "That's horrid. It sounds absolutely dreadful."

Thomas turned to Barbara. "Actually darling, that sounds wonderful for the boy. It'll shield him from harm's way and instill in him a certain measure of responsibility."

Jim noticed Barbara glance toward the spa building where Anna retreated to. Then he spotted a grin grow over her face.

Barbara turned to her husband. "Thomas, if Louis did have a summer job to occupy his time, it would provide us with additional privacy to spend with our guest."

Thomas shook his head. "That's true however I'm not entirely swayed over this new proposition." Thomas glanced at Jim. "Will we be assured that Louis earns a fair salary if he performs this employment? Or is this a volunteer assignment?"

Jim leaned back in his seat. "It's not a volunteer project. I can assure you that if you and your wife agree that he should do this, then he will get paid the going rate for a new hire."

Barbara asked, "Does Louis have a voice in any of this?"

Jim nodded. "He does but if he decides not to participate in this summer job, then the offenses I spoke of will be subject to enforcement. He will face the full extent of the law."

Thomas clapped his hands once and then stood up. "See Barbara, Louis has no alternative unless he desires to fritter away his young life incarcerated in a dirty county jail."

Jim noticed Barbara stare at him. Then she said, "Sheriff, we're going to think about this proposition. We'll contact our family attorney, Miles Boothe. He can arrive in a matter of days and represent Louis."

Thomas slapped his hand on his forehead. "Barbara don't be absurd. It will cost us more to defend Louis than what it's worth. Plus, the lessons Louis will absorb may finally transform him into the young man that he should have become long ago."

Barbara rested her elbow onto the table and leaned her head on her palm. "Thomas, do whatever delights your intellect. I simply implore that you recognize what you're undertaking."

Thomas glanced at Barbara and then said to her, "Do you mind if the sheriff and I converse in my study?"

Barbara replied, "Go ahead. I'll entertain Anna in the sauna." She then added, "Thomas, if you have the desire, please join us once you're done with the nice sheriff." She smiled at Jim and then got up from the table.

Barbara left for the spa building while Jim followed Thomas into the house and down a hallway to the study hidden deep in the bowels of the massive home's lower level.

"Have a seat, sheriff." Thomas walked over to a solid wood credenza desk and sat in a leather banker's chair. "Let's have a truly old-fashioned, man-to-man repartee where status, rank, and decorum are devoid of importance. What do you say to that?"

Jim sat in a leather recliner facing Thomas and said, "This is your house. We can speak in however a manner that you wish this conversation to proceed." Jim then gazed at the Bowie knife collection on one entire wall.

"Good." Thomas then asked, "Would you like to indulge in a libation with me…something to drink, sheriff?"

Jim was occupied with Thomas' knife collection and didn't hear the invitation. He counted nearly thirty knifes, some with wooden handles, others with leather handles, most with 9-inch blades and a few blades nearly a foot long. Jim wondered to himself if the Millers move to Taylor coincided with the several bloody disappearances that have stricken the county. Before Thomas again asked him if he wanted a drink, Jim stared at him, processed Thomas' previous question, and then said, "No thank you, Mister Miller."

"Please, call me Thomas or Tomás as Margarita refers to me." Then he asked, "Would you mind if I pamper myself with a drink?"

Jim shook his head. "Not at all, go right ahead."

Thomas smiled. "Thank you. A lengthier interval in that hot tub and I swear I'd have morphed into a well-wrinkled prune." Thomas laughed. "And Anna would not have articulated any well-earned adoration over that."

Jim ignored Thomas' statement and asked, "I noticed that you have an empty spot in your Bowie collection."

Thomas laughed. "Oh that, my son Louis always seems to be borrowing a different knife every day. He finds many uses for them. Sometimes, he's tossing them at tree trunks, other times he's skinning some wildlife. Why one day he was putting sticky notes with messages on them and throwing them at the wood-hewn posts on the patio. He calls them Kmails." Thomas whispered, "I know he's a bit immature but he always brings back the knives one way or another…bloody or whatnot." He gave out a deep belly laugh.

189

Jim said, "I don't find that amusing, sir."

Thomas snorted and then got up and walked over to the wet bar in his study. He grabbed a bottle of eighty-proof, Gosling's Family Reserve Old Rum. Thomas then opened an overhead cabinet door and extracted a shot glass. He poured himself a full serving.

Jim asked, "When did you first move to Taylor?"

"Why in 1994, that's when we relocated to this gorgeous abode. I believe that's when you decided to make your career choice of becoming sheriff, unless I stand corrected?"

"Yes, that's when I was sworn in as sheriff. Who helped you with the design and construction of this house and when was that?"

Thomas asked, "Explain exactly what your inference is when you say, when?"

"I mean when were the design and construction phases for this house begun and completed and were you living here in Montana during that time?"

Thomas hesitated, then stuttered, "I, uh...I..." He stared at Jim. "I would have to research that in my files."

Jim asked, "Surely you can provide me with a general idea of the years when you first spoke to realtors, had an architect draw up the blueprints, first met with the contractors, closed on the sale of the land, conducted site reviews, and monitored the construction progress?"

Thomas' voice cracked. "Well...I"

Jim continued, "Would you say it's a safe bet that you visited Montana in the late '80s and that site construction began around 1991?"

Thomas' hand shook and he spilled a few drops of rum from his shot glass. "I...uh, I can arrange for that information to be available the next time that we meet. Why do you inquire?"

Jim's earlier analysis into the backgrounds of the Millers began to lend support to his newfound suspicions that perhaps Thomas Miller lived or had visited Montana when a few of the disappearances occurred. However, Jim wanted to sidetrack Thomas' thoughts away from the disappearances and instead decided to utilize a more convenient diversion.

Jim answered, "We checked the town land records and saw that your date of occupancy conflicts with the date your son established residency for matriculation with Taylor University."

Thomas asked, "That seems to be a vastly trivial point. Why is that of any great substance?"

Jim replied, "You see sir, the university has a zero-tolerance policy regarding student behavior. When I complete my report, if your son is arrested, I'll have to provide that information to the university. Within that report is a box that indicates how long your son was a resident of Taylor. Now if he falsified his residency status to save money on his tuition as a five-year or longer resident of Taylor, then that would be apparent to the university when they compare their records to my report. It could get him expelled. Of course that would be up to the university's administration department."

Thomas nodded and took a gulp of rum. "Thank you for the heads-up. I will verify the exact date when we travelled to Montana in response to any preconstruction meetings. My son did accompany me numerous times, to uh, explore the female population. You know how young men are. I'll speak with the university administration to ascertain if his time spent here merits the criteria to satisfy his residency requirements. My son and I did spend considerable time in Taylor prior to the construction phase as I went over logistics and contractor hiring. If we were in violation of any university matriculation policies, I can assure you that I'll adhere to a policy of strict compliance so that my son doesn't get expelled."

Jim responded, "Good, you do that."

Thomas exhaled deeply and then said, "Well now, let's transcend to a more titillating discussion. What's your opinion of our friend, Anna Jónsdóttir?" Thomas asked.

Jim said, "I don't know her so I can't provide you with an answer."

Thomas laughed. "Oh come now, none whatsoever?" "My Lord, Have you not acquired an indelible first impression?" Thomas guzzled the rest of the rum from his shot glass.

Jim squeezed the brim of his Stetson. "I'd rather not continue this conversation."

Thomas laughed and poured himself another shot of rum. "Sheriff, do I suspect a hint of repressed fantasy or perhaps a faint measure of intimidation? Well, then let me relate to you her charismatic charm and primeval magnetism."

Jim stood up. "Mister Miller this conversation has ended.

Thomas Miller ignored him and took a sip of rum. "Sheriff, please sit back down and let me explain. It may fill in some gaps regarding my son."

Jim sat down. "All right, I'll listen."

Thomas continued, "Anna was born and raised in northern Iceland. We met her family in the late 80's when she was just an innocent child although her allure was quite apparent even then. Her father owned a hotel near Mývatn, and we lodged there for several years. When Anna turned eighteen, she decided that she wanted to see the USA and asked if she could visit with us. New York with its fast-paced night life appealed to her but after her first visit to Montana three years ago, she eschewed all other locales. She spoke of western Montana as if it were Iceland without the glaciers and volcanos. For the last five years, she's been our summer and winter guest. She returns to Iceland twice every year, in the spring and fall."

Jim asked, "So, she'll be leaving soon?"

Thomas took another sip of rum. "Yes, just for a scant few months. Her brother, Einar Jónsson owns a bookstore in the port city of Akureyri. Anna helps him every year during this time with wholesale book orders for the winter season. She's usually done in October and then returns to Montana to live with us throughout the winter. As you may know, winters are rather bleak in Iceland, all that darkness, cold, ice, and snow." Then Thomas asked, "Does she arouse your libido?"

Jim replied, "Sir, I have no opinion."

Thomas laughed. "Liar...It's impossible for any male of normal vigor not to be distracted by that Nordic goddess and her exquisite innate, feminine endowments, her raw, fascinating inhibitions, and her enchanting methods of seduction." Thomas winced, smiled, and then said, "That is unless your sexual curiosities aren't grounded within the female gender. Hell, mine isn't always for that matter."

In less than a second, Jim answered with frankness, "I'm happily married to a wonderful woman."

Thomas laughed, "A young, virile fellow like you? When I was your age, I was dispersing my wild oats near and far with whomever I wished." Thomas took another sip of rum and then explained, "A while back, Barbara and I made the opportunistic decision to participate in an open marriage. We share and share alike."

Jim stated, "Sir, I don't judge your personal values. Please get to what you wanted to tell me about your son."

Again, Thomas laughed. "Well, poppycock. I'm waiting for the day when he's out on his own. I wouldn't even care if I never saw him again for the rest of my life. Hell, I'm not even sure that Louis is my son. My first wife fucked around a lot."

That provided Jim with an excuse for additional questions. "Mister Miller, tell me a little bit about your first wife."

"My first wife, you mean Louis' mother?"

Jim nodded. "Yes, Gretchen Miller. You were married to her for more than twenty years. I understand she was murdered while you two lived in New York City."

Thomas harrumphed. "Uh, not really sheriff...we were staying at our summer home in Montauk when that happened."

Jim asked, "Tell me about it."

Thomas wiped away a tear that seemingly came out of nowhere and then said, "It's so hard. Gretchen was murdered more than nine years ago but it still seems like yesterday."

Jim continued, "I'd like to corroborate some facts with you so that we both agree on the findings."

Thomas sighed. "How does what happened to my first wife have anything to do with my life here in Montana?"

Jim inched forward in his seat. "We have a killer on the loose in Cedar County and I need to investigate all historical homicides that involve people currently residing in our county. The killer could have followed someone to Montana."

Thomas nodded. "All right, what you need from me?"

Jim pulled out the notebook from his shirt pocket and flipped past a few pages. "I understand at the time the coroner concluded that a perpetrator attacked your wife at the front door. He believes that she turned to run back into the house and that's when she was struck from behind with a blunt object to her head, maybe a hammer, and then to her back. Then she fell to the floor and was repeatedly struck with the blunt object to her ribs and then stabbed with a long blade."

"Yes, that's what I was told at the inquest."

Jim asked, "Where were you when your wife was murdered?"

"What are you inferring? Are you suggesting that I had something to do with my wife's murder?"

Jim replied, "No sir, I'm not accusing you of anything. I just need to know of your whereabouts."

Thomas stood up and spilled some of his rum. I was working in the City, goddamn-it."

Jim said, "All right. I just needed to ask you that for the record. That way if our chief medical examiner suggests that we bring you in for questioning based upon your first wife's murder then I can provide him with your answer. It may save you a trip downtown."

Thomas Miller sighed, gulped down the rest of his rum, and then leaned his forearms on his desk. "Why am I divulging so much about myself?" He looked down at his empty shot glass. "I have had an uncommon too many of these today." Then he shifted gears. "Hey, did Barbara engineer a pass at you today?" Thomas waved his hand, "Never mind, you needn't respond."

Jim replied, "Sir, I'm here on business."

"What's with this sir crap, I told you to call me Thomas."

Jim nodded. "Sure, now getting back to your son. I'm trying to keep him from getting into more trouble than he's already gotten himself into. I believe this summer job will keep him busy and provide him with a sense of responsibility."

Thomas' face lit up. "Sheriff, are you postulating we're not parenting well?"

"No sir, I'm just…"

Thomas slammed his empty shot glass down onto the desk and interrupted Jim. "Now just cut the fucking goddamn shit. You call me sir once more and this conversation is over, you hear?"

"Yes," Jim said.

Thomas poured himself another shot of rum. "All right, now let's get back to Louis. Good parenting or not so good parenting, I think Barbara and I will go along with this job idea of yours. As you say, it should keep Louis out of trouble…" Thomas then laughed. "And I'll have fewer worries about Louis attempting to seduce Anna."

Jim got up. "There's one other thing that I wanted to speak with you about."

"What's that?"

Jim said, "My daughter just graduated high school and is involved in an internship at the sheriff's office for college credit. She was invited to dinner at Doctor Henry Kelly's house this Friday."

"On the 4th of July?"

"Yes."

"And?"

"And she invited your son to accompany her."

"Did he accept?"

"He hasn't told you?"

Thomas laughed. "I'm fortunate if he and I communicate two words between ourselves each day. I told you about the knives, remember?"

"Right, well he did accept her invitation," Jim said.

Thomas smiled, got up, and slugged down his rum. "Well, really now? I'm astonished. Louis is usually captivated by women older than himself. I'm sure he'll treat your daughter with the utmost respect."

Jim stepped toward Thomas until they stood face-to-face. "Mister Miller, I don't know what my daughter sees in your son, but I trust her judgement. However, if any harm at all comes to my daughter, I will hold your son fully responsible. Nothing comes between me and my daughter."

Thomas again slammed the shot glass down onto the desk. "Is that a goddamn fucking threat, sheriff?"

Jim put on his Stetson. "You heard what I said...now, good day."

As Jim walked past him, Thomas said, "And sheriff..."

Jim turned toward him. "Yes, Mister Miller?"

"Not many people have witnessed what you've observed today. Barbara and I, and Anna as well, would like to preserve a certain veil of discretion over our private lives. Please employ explicit acumen and keep to yourself what you've witnessed here today. Barbara and I have a particular persona to uphold in this community. There are distinct elements in our lives that we would prefer not become exposed to the general fuckin' curious public."

Jim said, "Sir, I have no judgement on your private life."

"Good, because it would be detrimental to the financial wellbeing of the town of Taylor and it's many civic and volunteer organizations. If Barbara and I were compelled to relocate due to embarrassing press or hearsay gossip from a few inquiring, little-minded people who have no fucking business snooping into our private lives, then..." Thomas poured himself another shot of rum which emptied the bottle and then continued, "You see SIR, there would be hell to pay. I have many acquaintances in government that could have the people responsible for spreading that vile gossip forfeit their fucking precious jobs..." Thomas gulped the last shot of rum and then asked, "Do you understand me, son?"

Jim gritted his teeth and then said as he walked away, "I understand, sir." After Jim exited the front door, he whispered to himself under his breath, "Damn Thomas Miller...Mayor Dayton and Governor Ross too."

·41·

Later that morning, at the sheriff's office, a few minutes past 11 a.m. a man approached the main desk in the lobby. Dressed in a casual suit and carrying a briefcase, he stopped at the ballistic glass window and waited. After what seemed to him like an inordinate amount of time, the man placed his briefcase on the floor and harrumphed.

Sergeant Martha Wilson, seated at the dispatcher's desk, pulled off her headset and asked, "Can I help you?"

"May I see Sheriff Jim Buchanan?"

Martha got up from her console and walked over to the front desk. "Show me ID."

As the man slipped a business card and his driver's license into the seamless quarter-inch stainless steel integrated cash tray, he said, "My name is Attorney Jeremy Bowers. I'm from the Office of the State Public Defender."

Martha first examined the business card and then the driver's license. After she compared them she asked, "What business do you have with Sheriff Buchanan?"

"I was assigned as public defender for a Mister Gary Driver. He requested that I get in touch with the sheriff. My client would like the sheriff's assistance with his ongoing case."

Martha nodded. "Attorney Bowers, please have a seat. I'll let Sheriff Buchanan know you're here."

Bowers thanked her, picked up his briefcase, turned, and sat on the bench seat in the lobby. He waited for what seemed to him like a half-hour. Then the door to the office proper opened and a tall man in a sheriff's uniform, with shoulder-length hair tied into a ponytail, approached him and held out his hand.

197

"Attorney Bowers...it's nice to meet you, I'm Sheriff Jim Buchanan. I understand you're representing Gary Driver."

Bowers, not expecting such an intimidating man, stood upon shaky knees, shook the sheriff's meat hook hand and asked, "How did you know that I'm Mister Driver's court appointed attorney?"

Jim reached out with his arm to Bowers, gestured toward the main door and said, "Let's talk inside."

They made their way down the first floor hallway and into Jim's office. "Have a seat," Jim said. He settled into the swivel office chair behind his desk. "Excuse me if I seem rude, I'm having a rough day."

Bowers shook his head. "Not as tough as my client's." Bowers sat facing Jim's desk and set his briefcase on his lap. "Sheriff Buchanan, now please tell me how you know that I'm representing Gary Driver."

Jim folded his hands and rested his forearms on the desk. "Attorney Bowers, State Chief Medical Examiner Henry Kelly sat in on an interrogation of Gary Driver at the Mallory Police Station and was informed that a court-appointed attorney would be provided to represent him." Jim added, "I also understand that Mister Driver's arraignment was rescheduled until Monday, July 7th due to the 4th of July holiday this week."

Bowers nodded. "Yes, that's correct."

Jim said, "Good, I plan to be at that arrangement. As you know, the jail at the Mallory Police Department only consists of two holding cells. According to county law, they'll transfer custody of Mister Driver to the Cedar County Sheriff's Office for processing and incarceration in the county jail prior to and throughout the trial phase. Now, what else can I do for you?"

Bowers placed his briefcase on the floor. "I had a conversation with Mister Driver early this morning. I believe that he's innocent."

Jim moved a few pieces of mail to the side of his desk blotter. "Attorney Bowers, I can understand your concern but how could you reach that conclusion? Besides Gary Driver's missing wife, they say there's another missing person case in Spaulding. There's a slim possibility that Mister Driver had the opportunity to be at both locations on early Monday morning. He also has no alibi for either case other than the words of a lone drunk camping on Howard Lake."

198

Bowers leaned forward. "Sheriff Buchanan, with all due respect, my client was being held at the Mallory Police Station when a patrolling officer from the Spaulding Police Department observed a suspicious vehicle on Tuesday evening. The operator of that suspicious vehicle engaged the officer and caused the officer's patrol car to become disabled. When the officer visited a nearby home, he discovered that a probable homicide had taken place. It was a crime scene nearly identical to my client's apartment." Bowers then raised his voice, "Now how do you suppose my client was able to presumably murder Louise Leonard in the exact same manner as his own wife when Mister Driver was incarcerated in a jailcell at the Mallory Police Station?"

Jim closed his eyes and then exhaled deeply. "We still aren't sure of the exact timing. If Hank determines the forensic evidence points to Louise Leonard's apparent murder on Monday evening then Gary Driver's culpability is in play. However, if you're correct that the apparent murder happened on Tuesday when the officer was on scene then yes, Gary Driver can be eliminated from the Louise Leonard case. It's pure speculation at this point. The forensic crew is still onsite."

Bowers then said, "I understand that severed eyeballs were found in Louise Leonard's bedroom along with human entrails on the floor."

Jim faced Bowers. "How did you learn about that? That information has not been released to the media."

Bowers said, "Sheriff, I can't reveal my sources. I do have a hunch though. Even if Mister Driver did kill his wife Sunday night or Monday morning, and I believe that he didn't, we have a literal monster on the loose who murdered Louise Leonard."

Jim titled his head as if in a quizzical way. "We're still processing the information."

An exasperated Bowers slapped his forehead with his left palm and then offered both upturned palms to Jim and shook them. "The crime scenes are identical. Blood spatters on the floors, walls, and furniture…plus no bodies other than a pair of eyes. It points to one killer and Gary Driver isn't your suspect."

Jim asked, "Are you saying that because Gary Driver says he didn't kill his wife that you believe him simply based upon his word?"

Felix F. Giordano

Bowers answered, "Sheriff Buchanan, look...Mister Driver went out that evening to drop off a job application at the post office. I seriously doubt that someone would plan to kill their spouse and then casually mail a job application."

Jim shook his head. "I know people who have done much stranger things when committing murder."

"Sheriff Buchanan, listen..."

Jim folded his arms. "Listen...did you say listen?"

Bowers clasped his hands and shook them. "I'm sorry sheriff. My passion is overriding my patience. But please hear me out."

Jim nodded. "All right...I'm listening."

Bowers continued, "If we can obtain that job application, we'll have proof of a portion of Mister Driver's alibi. We'll have the postmark date, Mister Driver's fingerprints, and if he had killed his wife before he mailed that job application, the cut on his hand would have bled onto the envelope. If indeed the postmark is from Monday morning, then his fingerprints are present, and if the envelope has no blood on it, then we have reason to believe the rest of his alibi and that he killed no one."

Jim said, "He could have mailed the job application before he killed his wife."

"Sheriff Buchanan, I understand the post office has a 24/7 security camera installed in the lobby."

Jim said, "I wasn't aware of that."

Bowers nodded. "I was told it was installed this past spring after a number of homeless people made a habit of sleeping there every night last winter."

Jim nodded. "All right then, I'll see to it that we intercept the envelope before it arrives at the railroad corporate offices. I'll ensure that the post office cooperates with the investigation and allows us to view the video from that security camera."

"One more thing, sheriff."

"What's that?" Jim asked.

"Mister Driver called you something. He referred to you by the word, is-he-a-cheetah."

Jim corrected the pronunciation. "*Issaxchí-Káata.*"

"Why yes, what does it mean?" Bowers asked.

"It's my Native name, it means Little Hawk."

Bowers asked, "Is there significance to it?"

Jim took a deep breath. "When I was thirteen, my half-brother Bobby was like a father to me. He was twenty-six and

200

dropped me off in the wilderness of Waterton Lakes National Park in Canada."

"What for?" asked Bowers.

Jim stood up, walked behind Attorney Jeremy Bowers, and explained, "My tribe's elders said it was time for me to go on a vision quest and learn to become a warrior. I was to find Old Man Coyote. We call him *Isáahkawuattee*."

Bowers turned around in his seat and faced Jim. "Who is Old Man Coyote?"

Jim said, "Some call him the Creator God but others say he's the Trickster. He's a beast, a shapeshifter. I believe he's not a benevolent spirit. He's the temptation of lust, the lure of greed, the enticement of envy. He's the whisper you hear when all else is silent."

"So he's a myth." Bowers smirked.

Jim raised his voice. "He's not a myth. I've come across his deeds many times in this job. He invades the bodies of many people turning them into lawbreakers."

Bowers asked, "Do you really believe that?"

Jim shook his head. "How else can you explain pure evil?"

Bowers asked, "Now you're talking about Satan?"

Jim said, "You can call him what you wish. He's not of this Earth."

"Did you find him on your vision quest?"

Jim replied, "I searched seven days for *Isáahkawuattee*. I didn't find him, but I learned everything I needed to be a warrior. When I returned to the reservation, I told our medicine man, Runs with Wind how one day a juvenile Red-tailed Hawk had swooped down nearby during the vision quest, he told me that *Issaxchí-Káata* would become my name for the rest of my life."

"Well Sheriff Buchanan, that's an interesting story about evil spirits and such. But back on Earth here we're talking about the life of a flesh and blood man. We need to find the flesh and blood person that may have killed this man's wife."

Jim leaned over Attorney Bowers, rested his hands on the back of the chair, and then said, "It's not flesh and blood that commits crimes."

Attorney Bowers turned to stare at Jim and then asked, "What do you mean by that?"

Jim said, "It's not our outward appearance of flesh and blood that makes us who we are. It's what is inside of us, our incarnate soul. For some of us, it's the malicious spirit within the flesh and blood that consumes and drives the craving to commit evil."

·42·

Back at the Mallory Police Station, Detective Martin Aronowitz had a chance to sober up Mac Drew. A full day in custody plus plenty of coffee, breakfast, and lunch not only settled Mac's empty stomach but also apparently cleared the cobwebs from his brain. One of the officers on duty handcuffed Mac Drew and led him into the interrogation room and onto a chair. A second officer was in the room along with Detective Martin Aronowitz. Marty turned on the tape recorder.

Mac asked, "What in the hell am I doing here?"

Marty, who sat across from him replied, "We're holding you on a public intoxication charge and a DUI citation. However, if we determine that it's warranted to charge you with accessory to murder then you'll stay a whole lot longer."

Mac screamed, "Whose murder? This is bullshit and you know it."

Marty asked straightforward, "What were you doing on Howard Lake Sunday evening?"

"I was fishing. There a law against that?"

"Were you in Spaulding over the weekend or anytime on Monday or Tuesday of this week?"

Mac laughed. "Now why would I go to such a godforsaken place as Spaulding? There ain't nothing to do there no more. No bars, no liquor stores, it's a goddamn dry town ever since that biker gang robbed BJ Liquors over near Bull Lake earlier this year and killed two employees. Those holier than thou Mormons made the whole town go nuts and shuttered everything that's worth a damn."

Marty asked, "Who can vouch for you that you weren't in Spaulding?"

Mac shook his head. "Aw, come on now. I packed up my van, hauled my boat, and went to Howard Lake on Friday. I was all alone all weekend until Gary Driver stopped by to visit Sunday night. I didn't leave the lake until one of your officers grabbed me yesterday."

"You know that's not true. You left the lake on Monday to get more beer."

Mac rolled his eyes. "Is there a law against buying beer after the liquor stores reopen on a Monday morning?"

Marty replied, "No...that is if that's all that you did while away from Howard Lake."

"I didn't do nothing wrong."

Marty persisted. "Do you know Louise Leonard?"

"Who's she?"

"Answer the question."

"No, never heard of the name."

"I'll provide a clue. Louise Leonard was a retired schoolteacher...lived alone in Spaulding...kept to herself. She was a good person, so I've been told."

"What does Louise Leonard have to do with me?"

Marty stood up, rested his hands on the table, leaned forward, and spoke pointblank to Mac, "We suspect she was murdered."

Mac rolled his eyes. "Well don't you go thinking I had anything to do with that...oh, sorry to hear the lady died. Like her, I also keep to myself. Fishin', huntin', having a good drink or two...them things keep me in spades. I don't bother no one."

Marty sat back down and then provided a revelation to Mac. "The crime scene was identical to Janice Driver's house."

Mac's eyes widened. "What do you mean by that?"

"Janice Driver is missing."

"What?"

"Did you help Gary Driver dispose of the body of Janice Driver?"

Mac asked, "What...what did you say about Janice?"

"We think Janice Driver may be dead."

Tears welled up in Mac's eyes. "Janice is dead?"

Marty reiterated, "We believe that she is and because the crime scenes are identical, Louise Leonard may be dead as well. Since there's a less than 24-hour window of opportunity, we have reason to believe that the crimes are connected. What do you know about this?"

"I don't know...I don't...." Mac Drew then bent over at the waist and sobbed.

Marty said, "We'll stay in this room all night until you tell us what you know about the disappearances and possible murders of Janice Driver and Louise Leonard. Do you understand?"

Mac Drew straightened up and cried. "Janice's not dead, she can't be dead."

Marty said, "The Driver's apartment was covered in blood and so was Gary Driver."

Mac confessed, "Gary Driver had no blood on him...uh, that is until he left. He cut himself fileting a trout."

"Are you covering for him?"

"Covering for him? No sir."

Marty said, "Well now, if you're not covering for him then perhaps he's covering for you. Maybe now we're getting somewhere."

Mac yelled, "I told you I didn't do nothing to any woman. Uh...no sir, I didn't do nothing." Then Mac hung his head and sobbed. "I did see a girl but..." Then he looked up at Marty. "No, I didn't do nothing at all."

Marty asked, "What girl?"

Mac said, "Nothing. There ain't...look I got a girlfriend."

Marty asked, "Who?"

"I, uh...I don't know her name."

"A girlfriend and you don't know her name?"

Mac yelled again, "She's a girl who comes by a few times a month. She told me she doesn't want anyone to know her name. Look, I didn't break any laws. She came on to me."

Marty leaned back in his chair. "Describe her for me."

Mac shrugged his shoulders. "I dunno...maybe five feet tall, long black hair, brown eyes, Native too...yeah definitely Native...purdy too...and a body that won't quit."

Marty asked, "Is she a hooker?"

"No...oh no. I think she lives around Howard Lake. I dunno, maybe she's a squatter?"

"But you give her money for sex?"

"No, I give her money but not for sex. I feel sorry for her living out there all by herself. She said she uses the money for food." Mac stared at Marty. "Hey, I'm doing a good deed. You should give me a medal."

205

Marty shook his head. He nodded to one officer in the room. "Send someone to Howard Lake and look for the girl." The officer nodded and left. Then Marty turned his attention back to Mac Drew. "Now let's concentrate on Janice. Do you know where she is? Do you have her hidden somewhere? If you cooperate, tell us where she is, and who else is involved, we'll see to it that the D.A. goes easy on you." Marty turned to the other policeman in the room. "Get Officer Erickson in case we have a confession to transcribe."

"Yes sir," the officer said and left the room.

"I can't help you," Mac said through a series of sobs with his head down.

"And why not?"

Mac looked up. "Because I didn't do nothing to Janice. I couldn't hurt her."

"Why not?"

"Because Janice..." Mac hung his head and bawled. Then he looked up and stared into Marty's eyes. "I can't tell you."

"Why not?"

"Because I promised."

"Promised who, the kidnapper of Janice Driver? What did you promise, not to reveal where she is or what happened to her?"

"No sir, no."

"Then tell me about Louise Leonard first, and then we can talk about Janice. Tell me what you know before it's too late."

Mac stared at Marty again and with sorrowful eyes said, "I told you before, I don't know a goddamn thing about no Louise Leonard. But Janice...Janice Driver's my flesh and blood. She was my daughter." He hung his head. "I loved her."

Marty's eyes widened. He stood up and yelled, "What?" Then he turned off the tape recorder.

Mac Drew looked up at Marty. "Me and Janice's mother had this thing. It started quite a few years ago, way before Roger Weatherwax disappeared. I loved Beth and she loved me. We had a child, Janice. I couldn't do nothing about it because of Roger. After he was gone, Beth and I talked about getting married but then Beth disappeared."

Marty shook his head. "You do know they never found Roger's body."

Mac said, "I know,"

"Then did you have anything to do with Roger and Beth's disappearances?"

"Hell no. To be honest, I wasn't sad that Roger died. But I didn't kill him. Geez, I was glad because I thought Beth and I could finally have a life together and then we could raise our own daughter ourselves. Then when Beth disappeared, I lost it and started drinking." Mac wiped his eyes. "It made the pain go away, ya know what I mean? For chrissakes, I lost the love of my life."

Marty stared at Mac for a long moment and then a subtle realization came to his mind. He sighed and then said, "Mac, I believe you. Who else knows about this?"

"No one. We never told Janice and even after Beth disappeared, I didn't want any shame coming to Janice. She's a good kid, a lot of smarts. You know what I mean?"

Marty said, "You better hope she's still alive." Then he thought for a moment and asked, "Can you keep this just between you and me? If you're truly innocent then I'd like to see if you can help me fish out the real killer."

"All right," Mac said. "Anything for Janice."

"Good."

Mac said, "You don't know what I've been through all these years, keeping a secret I promised to Beth. It actually takes a huge weight off my shoulders finally telling this to someone."

Marty asked, "Are you sure? You had no responsibilities, no concern for Janice's welfare while she was growing up."

As if changing masks, Mac's forlorn face morphed into an image of pure rage. He then said, "Janice is full of spirit. I told you, she's my flesh and blood. I'd kill anyone who harmed her."

When the officer on duty returned to the room along with Officer Erickson, Marty said to them, "We won't need a transcript of any confession." Marty stared at Mac. "Mister Drew decided not to cooperate. Take him back to his holding cell."

"Hey, wait a minute," Mac said. "I did cooperate."

Marty said, "Mister Drew, what we charged you with still applies. Until we receive more conclusive information on Gary Driver's activities, whether or not you were involved, we have to keep you here, if for no other reason, just for your own safety."

As Mac Drew was being led from the interrogation room, Marty opened the door to the tape recorder, pulled out the cassette, ripped the tape from the cartridge, and shoved both into his pocket.

·43·

Early that afternoon, Alma Rose was still in the evidence locker assisting Sergeant Bonnie MacAskill cataloging evidence. Alma Rose was feeling much better and hadn't had any additional episodes of sickness. It had been a busy morning and other than a quick coffee break in the staff cafeteria with Bonnie, she hadn't had anything to eat.

Alma Rose said to Bonnie, "I think I better go to lunch."

Bonnie looked at her wristwatch and gasped. "Alma Rose, I'm so sorry. You should have gone to lunch an hour ago. I get so wrapped up in work that I forget all about the time. I've got to run an errand. Would you like to go with me and grab a bite to eat at Lucy's?"

Alma Rose shook her head. "No, that's okay. I'll grab something from the cafeteria."

"Are you sure?"

"Yeah, go ahead. I'm fine here."

Bonnie nodded and left. Alma Rose went upstairs to the first-floor cafeteria and purchased a tuna salad sandwich and a ginger ale. After only twenty minutes, she was done eating and returned to the basement evidence locker. No one was in the gymnasium, or the Nautilus exercise room. No one was even inside the indoor handgun firing range. It was as quiet as could be. Alma Rose used her cardkey to gain entrance to the evidence locker. That's when she heard the crying.

Alma Rose asked, "Who's in here?"

No one answered but the crying continued. Alma Rose looked around the evidence locker but saw no one, yet the crying lingered unabated.

She again asked, "Who's in here?"

The crying subsided into intermittent sobs. Then Alma Rose felt a hand on her forearm. She didn't jump away but instead called out to the entity.

"Are you the one who visited me the other night at my father's home?"

A disembodied voice replied in a whisper, "Yes."

Alma Rose asked, "What's wrong, why do you cry? What can I do to help?"

The voice simply said, "Gary."

"Gary who?"

"Help Gary."

Alma Rose heard the evidence locker door open and a whooshing sound followed by a sudden breeze of short duration flowed past her.

Bonnie stepped into the evidence locker and asked, "How's everything? I hope you had lunch."

Alma Rose nodded. "Yes, I ate upstairs.

Bonnie said, "Good, let's get back to work, finish up, and get out of this hellhole. This is the original basement of the repurposed sheriff's office and it gives me the willies."

Alma Rose said, "It's just a basement."

Bonnie leaned over to her and explained, "Do you know that prisoners died down here during an escape in the 1930s? I think their ghosts are still hanging around. Often I hear funny noises so I try to do my work and get out as soon as I can."

Alma Rose said, "It's not the ghosts that you have to be afraid of."

·44·

Wensday evening after dinner, Jim stepped onto the front porch and sat on the bench seat under the picture window. He faced the western sky and observed the sun begin its slow descent behind Government Mountain. Jim heard the front door open and his eyes followed Alma Rose's entrance onto the porch. He turned to look and see if Acaraho was with her, but saw no one. Alma Rose shut the front door and joined her father on the bench.

Jim asked, "Where's Acaraho?"

"He's inside."

"Have you spoken with him since you got home?"

Alma Rose shook her head with a sarcastic smirk on her face. "Nnnnnope."

Jim turned and faced Alma Rose. He said, "Tomorrow, I plan to speak with Rocky and see if he's willing to let Acaraho rent a room in his house. Of course, until Acaraho finds his own apartment."

Alma Rose asked with an uplifted spirit, "Do you think he'll be willing to let Acaraho stay with him?"

Jim said, "Rocky was just telling me how big his house is and that he was considering advertising for a roommate."

Alma Rose nodded. "Good, Acaraho and I have been trying to avoid each other over the past few days."

Jim asked, "So tell me, is it over between you two?"

Alma Rose dropped her head onto her palms and took a deep breath. "I don't know." Then she looked up at her father. "Do we have to talk about this right now?"

Jim leaned forward, set his elbows on his knees, and stared straight ahead. Then he turned to Alma Rose. "Not if you

211

don't want to. I think Acaraho gets the message. The next move is up to him."

Alma Rose glanced at her father. "It'll take us a while to reconcile."

Jim smiled. "So, there may be some hope to salvage what the two of you had?"

Alma Rose looked back at the ground. "Maybe…but I need to concentrate on my internship anyway."

Jim nodded. "So perhaps a separation not only benefits your relationship with Acaraho, but it'll also provide you with a clearer path as far as your career plans go."

Alma Rose stood up from the bench and started at her father. "I need some space this summer. After what happened in the house earlier this week, the woman I saw at the accident, the crime scene I visited, the missing women, and what I heard today is more than what I can deal with. I feel like I'm on a trestle a hundred feet in the air and just one step ahead of a runaway train."

Jim asked, "What happened today?"

Alma Rose took a deep breath and then exhaled. "I heard a voice in the evidence locker when the boxes in the Driver case were transferred from Mallory to Taylor."

"A voice?"

"Yes, it asked me to help Gary."

"Gary Driver?"

"I guess."

Jim stood up and faced Alma Rose. "I contacted Sarah Whispers and asked if Uncle Bobby and Great-grandfather Red Hawk can visit with us for a few days."

Alma Rose asked, "Why?"

Jim explained, "Great-grandfather remembers what your grandmother faced when she went through similar experiences when she was your age. He helped her and he can guide you."

Alma Rose shook her head. "What help can he give me?"

Jim took Alma Rose by the hand. "He can help you stay grounded. That way your soul won't become lost between our world and the spirit world."

·45·

Thursday morning Alma Rose was back in the evidence locker. She was busy logging the items inside the boxes related to the Janice Driver investigation with Sergeant Bonnie MacAskill by her side. They had cataloged nearly half of the forensic evidence taken from the Driver's home and Gary Driver's car when Bonnie's cellphone rang.

"MacAskill here." Bonnie then turned to Alma Rose. "It's Thea. I've got to take this call. I'll only be gone five minutes. Are you okay to continue while I'm gone?"

Alma Rose nodded. "I'm good here, take your time. I understand the cataloging protocol."

Bonnie exited the evidence locker and left Alma Rose alone inside. When Alma Rose opened the fourth box of evidence, she froze in place. There, alone in the box, in an enclosed plastic sleeve, was a Native American talking stick complete with red, blue, and yellow painted designs and a single fanned feather on one end.

She stared at it for a long moment. It was different than the Crow talking sticks that she had seen hanging in Red Hawk's cabin. Thinking back to the Indigenous Culture classes she attended at the reservation high school, she then recognized the fanned feather and realized this talking stick was of Blackfeet origin. Alma Rose knew that among their people, the Blackfeet referred to it as a speaker's staff.

Alma Rose reached into the box. Her fingers brushed against the talking stick, and even though the bag provided a barrier between Alma Rose and the talking stick, she felt an energy flow into her fingers.

Then a tinny sound accompanied a voice that called out to her, "Please help me."

213

Alma Rose looked toward her left where the voice came from and saw the shape of a young Native woman standing in the evidence locker. The woman didn't appear to be human as we would commonly know. Alma Rose could see the shelving against the far wall through the woman's partially transparent body which seemed to hover off the floor.

Alma Rose continued to hold the talking stick and kept her composure. "How can I help you?"

The woman stared at Alma Rose and said, "My husband is in danger."

"How so?" Alma Rose asked.

"He's blamed for what happened to me."

Alma Rose asked, "Is his name Gary Driver?"

"Yes."

"Have you tried to contact me before?"

"I have."

"At my father's house?"

"Yes and in your father's car."

"What can I do for you?" Alma Rose asked.

"Tell your father to bring Gary to Taylor right away. If not, he will die in Mallory."

Alma Rose asked, "How will he die?"

"A man who believes Gary killed me will seek revenge."

"Who killed you?"

"The man who…"

Alma Rose heard the door to the evidence locker open and dropped the bag with the talking stick into the evidence box. She glanced to her left and saw the vision of the woman fade away. Then Alma Rose noticed Bonnie step into the evidence locker with a smile that ran from ear to ear.

Bonnie said, "Thea wants to invite you to dinner at our place tonight."

Alma Rose felt a shortness of breath and then gasped, "Sure, all right."

"Are you okay?" Bonnie asked.

Alma Rose hesitated and then said, "Yeah, I'm all right."

"Please don't get sick on me again." Bonnie placed the back of her hand to Alma Rose's forehead. She flinched and then said, "Damn, you're warm…sweating too. It's not even sixty degrees in here." Then she reached for Alma Rose's hand. When she did, she withdrew it in an instant. "Ow, that hurts. Static electricity I guess." Bonnie then took Alma Rose's hand again and with concern on her face said, "Your hand is as cold as a corpse in a funeral home. Are you sure you're okay?"

Alma Rose placed the cover on the box containing the talking stick. "I'm fine." She looked back to the left where the image of the woman had been and upon seeing nothing, she then turned forward facing Bonnie. "Maybe I need a break."

Bonnie stared at her and then said, "Good idea, let's go upstairs. Coffee's on me."

·46·

Jim stood at the elevator doors as he waited to head upstairs to meet with Rocky. From Jim's point of view, a couple of issues needed clarification and he trusted Rocky to deliver. The doors opened and he came face to face with Alma Rose and Bonnie.

Jim tipped his Stetson. "Sergeant MacAskill...Deputy Two Elk, how's it going today?"

Bonnie spoke first, "Deputy Two Elk and I are taking a break and getting coffee in the cafeteria. Would you like to join us?"

Jim smiled. "Maybe another time...I'm heading upstairs to meet with Undersheriff Salentino." Then he stared at Alma Rose and remarked, "You seem a bit pale. Are you okay?"

Alma Rose flashed a brief smile and then said, "I'm all right. I just need to get something into my stomach." She turned to Bonnie. "I think orange juice and a muffin would be better than coffee."

Jim nodded. "Good choice, I'll see you tonight."

Alma rose piped up, "Sheriff Buchanan, I've accepted a dinner invitation for tonight from Sergeant MacAskill."

Jim hesitated before responding and then said, "That's great. Perhaps after you get home, we can discuss a few things before the evening is over."

Alma Rose nodded. "Yes sir."

As the two women stepped past Jim, the elevator door began to close. Jim reached out and buttressed his hand against the door causing it to slide back open. He stepped inside, the door closed, and he took a deep breath. Once the elevator reached the second floor, Jim stepped out and walked past the youth officer's office and Sergeant MacAskill's office.

Off to the right was the common office area populated by the deputies on duty and other staff personnel. Jim headed straight toward Rocky's corner office and knocked on the open door. Rocky lifted his head from a pile of paperwork scattered across his desk. Jim closed the door behind him.

Rocky grimaced and said, "Uh-oh, something's up."

Jim asked, "May I have a seat?"

Rocky replied, "Of course."

Jim sat facing Rocky and pulled the chair closer to the desk. Jim exhaled deeply and then said, "I need a favor to ask of you."

Rocky replied, "Sure."

Jim said, "Okay...number one, I know you live alone. I was wondering if you could put up Acaraho for at least a few weeks until I can find an apartment for him."

Rocky nodded. "Yeah, I'd love the company. You know I was looking for a roomie. The guest bedroom's never been used so anything that Acaraho has, he's welcome to bring along."

"That sounds great, Rocky. Are you sure it's not an inconvenience?"

"No, no. Maybe he would be willing to dog-sit for me on Friday nights? Linda and I go out to dinner and then a movie on Fridays."

Jim asked, "How's the dog? Olde English Bulldogge, right?"

Rocky smiled. "Yeah...he's no longer a puppy but he still can't stand to be alone. When we crate Butler, he destroys his bedding. He's already torn three blankets to shreds. The vet called it acute separation anxiety. My neighbor can only dog-sit Butler during the day so Acaraho could help me out on the evenings I work or go out. I'll pay him."

Jim nodded. "Sounds great."

Rocky asked, "What's the other thing?"

Jim pulled the chair closer until his knees were up against Rocky's desk. "Something came up and I'll be going to Glacier Park Lodge tomorrow to meet with Undercover FBI Agent Axe Killian. He worked on the Videl Tanas case."

"I recollect. What's up?"

Jim said, "Remember when I told you that Governor Ross' daughter went missing back in 1992?"

"You mean Peta Ross?"

218

"That's her," Jim said.

Rocky asked, "What about her?"

Jim replied, "Killian thinks he's located her living with that cult up in the Yaak Wilderness."

Rocky brought his right hand up to his face and rested his chin in his palm. Then he asked, "Do you think that cult has anything to do with any of the disappearances in Mallory and Spaulding?"

Jim shook his head. "No, I don't. There was no crime scene or any evidence when Peta Ross disappeared in '92. When you look at what happened in Mallory and Spaulding, there's no question that homicides occurred."

Rocky said, "I hope your meeting with Killian goes well. If you need backup or support, just contact me."

"I will. I'm not exactly sure what will be going on after I meet with him. Why don't you plan on handling things here at the office until you hear back from me?"

Rocky smiled. "Hopefully, all we'll have on our plate tomorrow is the 4th of July parade."

Then Jim asked, "Did you have a chance to look into any other disappearances in western Montana that have the same MOs as in Mallory and Spaulding?"

Rocky rolled back in his wheeled office chair, opened a desk drawer, and pulled out a notebook. "I did find something that seems similar to what we're looking at in Mallory."

"Tell me," Jim asked.

Rocky opened the notebook and read from his summary. "On July 10 1972 Sandra and Christa Sires, twin sisters from Billings, went missing. They were thirty-five, both were unmarried, and they jointly owned a little coffee shop. In the morning a regular customer stopped in and found the back door wide-open and blood everywhere but no bodies."

Jim asked, "What prompted the customer to check around back?"

Rocky replied, "It was a few minutes after they usually opened for the day and the front door was locked but the sign read open."

Jim tilted his head in confusion. "What did the police investigation show?"

Rocky shrugged his shoulders. "No signs of a struggle, no prints, no weapons, just a lot of blood."

Jim asked, "Any others?"

Rocky turned the page in his notebook. "In December of the same year there were two more women that went missing in Billings. On the 4th, Sara Martin a sixty-six-year-old retiree had her house broken into. They never found her body, but the kitchen was awash in blood. Again, there was no struggle, no prints, and no weapons."

Jim asked, "And the other woman who went missing?"

Rocky continued, "On Christmas Eve Sergeant Hattie Purcell, a Salvation Army bellringer leaves her post on North 27th Street to get a coffee for herself and one for her bellringer trainee, then never returns. They found her blood-soaked uniform in a secluded alleyway off 2nd Avenue North and pooled blood on the pavement."

Jim asked, "How did Billings reconcile the four women's disappearances in less than six months in nearly the same area."

Rocky replied, "They eventually hypothesized that it must have been a transient. They had trouble with homeless people sleeping overnight in the post office. After a couple of years the Billings Police cataloged the disappearances in their cold case files."

Jim shook his head. "Is that it?"

Rocky again turned the page. "No, it gets murkier. Now the location shifts to Mallory."

"Go on."

Rocky continued, "In 1988, sixteen years after the Sires twins go missing during the same day, we again have two disappearances during the same day but this time in Mallory. On September 30th, Beth Weatherwax went missing from her home. A trail of blood led from her bedroom out the back door."

Jim asked, "Same crime scene?"

"Some of it was the same, a lot of blood, no body, no weapon, no prints at the crime scene." Then Rocky continued, "Get this, Beth Weatherwax was Gary Driver's mother-in-law."

Jim's jaw dropped. "The same Gary Driver being held in Mallory for his wife's disappearance?"

Rocky nodded. "One and the same. But Gary Driver was only twelve years old when Beth Weatherwax disappeared and he hadn't yet met his future wife, Janice Weatherwax."

Jim asked, "Was Janice Weatherwax home when her mother disappeared?"

Rocky replied, "Yes, but she was too young to recall what happened. Her father disappeared from an alley outside a bar in Mallory a few years earlier...blood everywhere."

Jim said, "This is getting murky. You said there were two on the same day in Mallory."

Rocky once again turned the page. "Yes, a Cathy Dowd disappeared from her home. No body, just a lot of..."

Jim interrupted Rocky, "You needn't repeat the same crime scene to me, I get it. What did the Mallory Police do about these two people?"

Rocky replied, "Again, just like in Billings, after a few years with no leads they sent them to the cold case files."

Jim pushed his chair back and stood up. "Okay, see if you can summarize what you have there, leave a copy on my desk, and I'll follow-up with the authorities in those towns."

Jim turned to leave but Rocky stood up and said, "That's not all."

Jim looked back. "What else?"

"On July 4th 1992, there were two incidents In Mallory. The same day that Governor Ross' daughter disappeared at the 4th of July celebration in Troy, Kat Drew disappeared in Mallory. Blood everywhere again but this time we're sure she was murdered because her eyes were gouged from her face and left on her bedroom bureau."

Jim pondered. "That name, Drew sounds familiar to me."

Rocky explained, "That's because Kat Drew was Mac Drew's daughter."

Jim sat back down. "The Mac Drew who's in the Mallory jail with Gary Driver?"

"That's him?"

Jim asked, "What can you tell me about Mac Drew's daughter?"

"She was a prostitute. It may just be a coincidence but there's got to be something more to this. Gary Driver's wife, two other Weatherwax family members, Mac Drew, who's in jail with Driver, has his daughter missing. All four presumed dead in pretty much similar fashions all part of an extended family."

Jim stared at Rocky. "Do you know the connection?"

Rocky shook his head. "That's what's stumped me to no end. The more I look at this, the more questions I have."

Jim said, "Add Governor Ross' daughter, Peta to the club. Who else disappeared in Mallory on the 4th in 1992? You said there were two."

Rocky explained, "There was only one disappearance. I said there were two incidents on that day in Mallory. The other incident was an attempted kidnapping."

Jim asked, "Of who?"

Rocky said, "Althea Bond."

Jim stopped in his tracks. "Althea Bond...do you mean Thea Bond that works at Lucy's and shares a home with Sergeant MacAskill?"

Rocky nodded. "Yes sir. Our own police chief, John Peters stopped a sexual assault in progress."

Jim asked, "Why do you think that we've never heard of this before?"

Rocky surmised, "I think there was a lot of aftermath trauma and the victim chose to put it behind herself."

Jim said, "We'll have to see if Thea is willing to speak with us about it."

Rocky asked, "Regarding the Peta Ross disappearance in Troy on that same day."

Jim said, "Yes?"

Rocky blurted it out, "Because you know more about that case than I do, did they say if there was blood like the others?"

Jim shook his head. "No blood at all."

Rocky's eyes widened. "Then she may still be alive."

As Jim walked out of the room, he turned to Rocky and said with a parting shot, "When I meet up with Killian tomorrow, we'll know soon enough."

·47·

Alma Rose, a nineteen-year-old Native American woman, was caught between the sheltered traditional reservation life and the lure of newfound experiences in an uncertain white man's world. She knew her inherent fundamental Native values conflicted with the apparent negative stereotypes from people who knew absolutely nothing about her.

Alma Rose returned home from work and parked her pickup truck in the driveway. She unlocked the front door and raced into the kitchen to turn off the new security system's blaring alarm. Alma Rose then went upstairs into her bedroom. She first removed her boots and then her deputy's uniform. She pulled on a pair of stonewashed drainpipe jeans that she had recently purchased at the Salvation Army Thrift Store in Billings. Then she threw on a basic black tank top and a pair of white sneakers from the Walmart. She then walked toward the full-length mirror in the room. While focused on her image in the mirror, she turned her body to the left and then to the right.

Alma Rose then walked over to the bureau and stared into a tabletop vanity mirror. She attached her dangly silver earrings and again turned to her left and then to her right as she stared into the mirror. She approved of her new relaxed civilian look that was in direct contrast to the professional presence required by the Cedar County Sheriff's Office.

While she stared into the smaller mirror, Alma Rose realized that one more change needed to be made. She reached back over her head, took her rope-braided hair in her hands, and unraveled it. She then tossed her straight black hair aside so that it covered her earrings.

She waited in her bedroom until she heard Acaraho come home first, then Kate, and finally her father. When she

223

heard her father walk down the hallway and then close his bedroom door, Alma Rose threw on her flannel-lined denim jacket and stepped out of the bedroom. She went downstairs and sneaked toward the front door.

Alma Rose said to whoever would hear her, "Goodbye, I'm having dinner at Sergeant MacAskill and Thea's place."

She heard a fleeting remark from Kate preparing dinner in the kitchen. It sounded like Kate told her to have fun. That's exactly what Alma Rose planned to have. Just as Alma Rose stepped outside, she heard the distinct sound of Acaraho's boots hit the great room's hardwood floor. She closed the door behind her and hurried to her pickup truck.

Alma Rose looked back when she heard Acaraho call to her from the front porch.

"I need to speak with you."

Alma Rose said, "I'm going out for the night."

Acaraho pleaded as he ran to the truck, "This will only take a minute."

"We can talk tomorrow."

Alma Rose started the trunk's engine when she heard an unexpected comment from Acaraho.

"You look great tonight…in fact, beautiful."

Alma Rose held back a tear, swallowed hard, then looked at him and with a crack in her voice said, "I gotta go."

With that last response, she backed up the truck and then drove down the driveway. Alma Rose looked into the rearview mirror and noticed that Acaraho stood there and stared at her truck. She pulled onto U.S. 200 and headed west toward Route 56, also known as Bull River Road. Alma Rose turned off onto Bull River Extension and up to the clearing where a modest cabin stood. Alma Rose got out of her truck and spotted Bonnie and Thea waiting on the front porch.

Bonnie stood up. "I'm happy you made it."

Alma Rose walked up the porch steps, glanced at the scar on Thea's neck that ran from ear to ear, and extended her hand. "Hi, I'm Alma Rose."

Thea said, "It's nice to meet you. My name's Althea Bond but you can call me Thea, everyone does."

Alma Rose couldn't stop staring at the scar on Thea's neck and hesitated for a split second.

Thea then asked, "Is something wrong?"

Alma Rose shook her head. "No."

Thea asked, "Is it because I'm African-American?"

"Not really. I mean I don't know many African-Americans so I can't say that's why. It's just a feeling I have."

Thea laughed. "Well I for one don't know many Native Americans so it looks like we're at a stalemate. We'll have to start over. I'm Althea Bond but you can call me Thea, everyone does. It's nice to meet you." Thea offered her hand to Alma Rose.

While they shook hands, Bonnie said, "Shall we go inside? Appetizers are on the table."

The three women went into the house and settled in the kitchen. A full spread was on display at the kitchen table. There was an oversized lazy Susan consisting of a plate of cheese and crackers, a bowl of taco sauce and a companion bowl of salsa, a piled high platter of homemade nachos, with side cups of sour cream, guacamole, sliced olives, diced tomatoes and red onions, chopped lettuce, shredded cheddar cheese, ground bison, and jalapeno, cayenne, and habanero peppers. A cooler on the ground contained wine, beer, soda, juice, and water.

Alma Rose's eyes almost popped out of her head. "Oh my gosh, there's so much food. I don't think the grocery store on the Rez has this much food."

Thea laughed. "This is only the appetizer. Wait until you see the main course and then there's dessert."

Alma Rose laughed. "I'll have to pace myself or else I won't be able to drive home."

Bonnie smiled. "You're welcome to take leftovers home."

Alma Rose said, "You're both so kind. I'm totally amazed." When Thea glanced at Bonnie, Alma Rose took the chance to once again stare at the scar on Thea's neck.

Bonnie returned the glance from Thea and put her arm around her. "Thea worked so hard to put this altogether." Bonnie turned to look at Alma Rose and with a smile on her face said, "Isn't my sweetheart great?"

Thea faced Bonnie and shooed her with her hand. "Bonnie, you're always pumping me up." She turned to Alma Rose. "My boss, Lucy helped me with the recipes."

Alma Rose said, "I met Lucy Brown."

Bonnie changed the subject. "What are we waiting for? I'm hungry."

The three young women sat at the kitchen table and sampled a little bit of everything. An hour later, and after much casual conversation, the women cleared the appetizers off the kitchen table and then Thea brought out the main course. She scooped the contents from a crockpot into a large bowl and placed it onto the kitchen island.

"What's for dinner?" Alma Rose asked, taking one more opportunity to glance at Thea's scar.

Thea's smile ran from ear to ear. "Bison pot roast with carrots, celery, pearl onions, and potatoes, basted in Canadian pure maple syrup and porter beer from Blue Slide Brewery in Thompson Falls."

Bonnie handed out dinner plates and the women milled around the kitchen island and selected their food choices buffet style. They returned to the table, took their seats, and partook of their dinners. They ate mostly in silence, except for some small talk. When they were done with dinner, conversation continued for a few hours. Then dessert was served and after that, dishes were washed and then put away. More conversation occupied their evening, until around 11 p.m. As they sat around the living room, Alma Rose felt the inquisitive and penetrating nature of Thea's eyes.

Alma Rose looked up and caught Thea staring at her. "You can ask me," Alma Rose said.

"Ask you what?"

Alma Rose said in a matter-of-fact manner, "Ask me why I was staring at your scar."

Thea leaned back on the sofa. "How did you know?"

Alma Rose said, "I know."

Thea then asked, "All right, why ARE you staring at my scar?"

Alma Rose looked at Bonnie's furrowed brow and gaping mouth, then returned her gaze to Thea. "I want to find out if you think the people who almost killed you are responsible for the recent disappearances of women from this county."

"Alma Rose!" Bonnie said. Her voice grew louder. "Please don't ruin our evening by bringing up something that has no right being discussed here."

Thea raised her palm to Bonnie. "No let her speak. If that's such an important issue to her and if it eventually helps bring someone to justice...then by all means, let's discuss my scar."

Bonnie stood up. "I've already heard this damn story a hundred times. I don't need to hear it again."

226

Thea reached out for Bonnie's arm, but Bonnie pulled away and stepped out onto the front porch. Thea hung her head and then looked up to stare at Alma Rose.

Thea suggested, "Let's go on the back porch and talk."

Alma Rose nodded and followed Thea toward the back door. They went outside and Thea settled on a wrought iron chair while Alma Rose sat on a wrought iron bench.

Thea asked, "Do you mind if I smoke?"

Alma Rose said, "No, go right ahead."

Thea pulled out a pack of Marlboros and a lighter from her pocket. "I never smoked before they attacked me. Smoking keeps my nerves from going haywire. Are you sure you don't mind?"

"Not at all."

Thea stuck one cigarette between her lips, struck the lighter, and lit the cigarette. She took a deep drag, exhaled, and then said, "In 1992, I had just started working at Lucy's Luncheonette. Those days I was working the 4 p.m. to midnight shift. I served these two guys. They seemed okay at first, ate their meals, and then each guy ordered double servings of cheesecake with huckleberry topping and side orders of vanilla ice cream for dessert around 10ish." Thea laughed. "I thought it was funny these two burly guys ordering all those sweets so late at night." Thea laughed. "I kind of imagined they would have these belly aches all night. But I thought what the hell. They're allowed to order anything they want if it's on the menu."

Alma Rose asked, "Did they give you any indication that they were up to something?"

Thea took another drag, lifted her face to the starlit sky, exhaled, and returned Alma Rose's intent gaze. "Not really. They did give me a few odd smiles. But honey, when you're a waitress, you learn to ignore most of them."

"Then what happened?"

Thea continued, "They took turns using the men's room and that's when things got a little weird."

"What do you mean?"

Thea flicked away the ashes from her cigarette and then explained, "I could tell they were getting high. Then one of them says he'll marry me if I showed him where I lived."

Alma Rose leaned forward on the bench. "Oh no, what did you say?"

Thea took another drag and then exhaled. "At that point, I told Lucy about them. She moseyed on over to their table and introduced herself. She told them that she would be their new waitress. She said if they didn't like it they should haul their asses out of her place ASAP or else she would."

Alma Rose said, "I've met Lucy." Then she snickered. "I believe that she would do that."

Thea smiled. "Lucy has an intimidating way of getting people to put things into perspective."

Alma Rose nodded. "I guess. What happened next?"

Thea took another drag and then another exhale. "When my shift ended, some guy wearing one of them mechanic suits and what looked like a head cover that you sometimes see the military wearing, came up to me out back where I park my car. He asked if I could help him out. He didn't say a word and instead grabbed me. I fought like hell but he hit me on the head and I passed out. When I came around, about 6 a.m. these two other guys were raping me in the alley outside their hotel in Mallory."

"What did you do?"

"I thought it was a bad dream. I felt something wet on my head so I touched it and saw that I was bleeding. I started to scream and tried to struggle. That's when he put his hands around my neck and tried to choke me. When I tried to stop him, I felt cold metal against my neck and a whole lot of blood. I then realized that someone had slashed my neck. I don't know if the guy in the mask was one of the guys raping me and was going to finish me off, if there were three guys in on it, or if the two guys who raped me scared away the guy in the mask. All I know is that I can't tell who actually cut me, the guy with the mask or those two bozos who raped me but someone gave me this."

Thea lifted her head and gave Alma Rose a wide-angle view of her scar.

Tears flooded Alma Rose eyes and with her voice cracking, she said, "I'm so sorry."

Thea flicked the cigarette ashes once again and then continued, "Don't be. Hey, I survived. The police chief from Taylor happened to be in Mallory. He was going to present a training class to the local police. He heard screams, showed up in the alley, walked up with one helluva big shotgun, and arrested those men."

"Police Chief John Peters?"

"Yes, that's the man. Anyways, he brought me to the hospital. He requested assistance from the county sheriff's department cause it was a county matter when I told them the attack started in Taylor and that's when I met Bonnie. She looked in on me when I got home. We became friends and we've been together ever since."

Alma Rose asked, "What about that guy in the mechanic suit?"

Thea replied, "I have no idea. I'm not sure what he was doing there. There are a whole lot of gas meters behind the building so maybe he was working on some gas fittings? I'm just not sure."

Alma Rose then asked, "What happened to those men who raped you?"

Thea threw the cigarette to the ground and then stamped it out. She put her head in her hand and rubbed the tears from her eyes. "That was five years ago. It went to trial. They plead not guilty. There was no DNA testing taken. It was so new, not every police department knew how to collect it."

Alma Rose said, "I hope they were found guilty."

Thea grimaced with her eyes squeezed shut. Then she opened them and said, "They got ten-year sentences. One had his sentence reduced to three years and the other four years and three months."

"Then what happened?"

Thea wiped away another tear. "They took off, at least that's all we know. No one's heard from them since."

Alma Rose asked, "Do you know of anyone named Lester that may have been a customer at Lucy's and who may have known Janice Driver?"

Thea titled her head and in a contemplative voice said, "Let me think." After a brief moment she responded, "Come to think of it, yes. There was this English fellow named Lester. He was so hot-to-trot on Janice. He tried to pick her up many times."

Alma Rose said, "Lucy told me she only remembers him there once."

Thea laughed. "That's because Lucy's eyes are not always on the customers. Hell, she's got the kitchen, wait staff, and her food stock that keeps her busy." Then she continued, "I see all the customers. After what happened to me, I not only see all the customers, I listen in on all their conversations. I don't want to end up in a bad situation again so I make sure that I hear everything."

Alma Rose asked, "Did you ever see this Lester guy with Janice outside Lucy's?"

Thea replied, "I can't say that I have. I got the feeling that Janice knew that Lester was up to no good so she kept a safe distance."

"Do you know where I can find him?"

Thea lit another cigarette and then after taking a drag and exhaling she said, "You don't want to get involved."

Alma Rose asked, "Is there something that you're not telling me?"

Thea looked at the sky and then stared at Alma Rose. "Look, I don't want to get him in trouble and don't ever mention this to Bonnie. His name is Lester Throckmorton. He said he lives in Mallory but I don't know where. I kind of liked him because of his cockney accent. I haven't heard an accent like that since I left the east coast." Thea flicked the ashes from her cigarette. "Anyways one of the times that he was in Lucy's and Janice rejected him, I was his server. He apologized for how Janice reacted. Heck, I told him that she was married. He didn't know that and apparently Janice didn't tell him. Then he asks me if I was married and I said no. He asks me for a date and I tell him that I have a girlfriend. So he says all innocent and the like, can't we just share a drink or two. I'm new to this part of Montana and I don't know too many people. I'm just looking for conversation."

"Then what happened?"

"We drive to Billy's Bar in separate cars. We had a few drinks, and then he opens up to me. He asks me to see if I could fix him up with Janice. I tell him again that she's married and he says to me that marriage doesn't mean forever. Then later on he tells me that he was in prison."

"Prison?"

Thea nodded. "After a few minutes I excused myself. Then I headed for the door when he wasn't looking. I drove myself home and haven't seen him since."

Alma Rose asked, "Do you think he or those guys who attacked you are responsible for the missing women?"

Thea laughed, "I think it might be that Indian legend, the Moon Man."

Alma Rose said, "The Flathead call him *Saka'am Skaltamiax*."

Thea nodded. "Yeah, right." She then threw her cigarette to the ground, stomped on it and said, "Who knows? I doubt we'll ever find out unless they actually catch the goddamn motherfucker."

·48·

Friday arrived with a head-start bang as it always does on the 4th of July. The midnight sounds of M80s and Roman candles kept the Taylor Police patrols busy. A few minutes past 2 a.m. that Friday morning, things began to quiet down. Alma Rose, only an hour or so from her return from Bonnie and Thea's house, was fast asleep in her bedroom when a loud noise awakened her. She sat up in bed and stared straight ahead.

A voice emanated from the darkened room.

"Listen to me," it said.

Alma Rose's eyes searched for the source of the voice but saw nothing. Then she asked, "What do you want?"

The voice, a distinctly male voice responded from the darkness of the corner of her bedroom, "The talking stick."

"What about it?"

"Use it to find who killed the woman. Have them touch the talking stick."

"What'll happen when they do?" Alma Rose asked.

"They'll see her. And you'll be able to speak with them."

Alma Rose asked, "Who are you?" There was silence and then she asked again, "Tell me who you are."

"I'm sorry I did not get to know you. Someday you will know who I am, and we will spend the time I stole from you," the voice said.

"What can I do to help?" Alma Rose asked.

The voice said, "Be strong in your convictions. Don't allow people to control you. See through their intentions. Only you can control your own destiny. Follow what your people call the Red Road."

233

Alma Rose said, "I understand. Thank you." She rested her head on the pillow and contemplated what she had just heard. She knew it was a male voice and it seemed to her that it was not a Native spirit. She tried to think of who it might be. The fact was that she did not know many non-Native people.

The room was so quiet that Alma Rose heard the hum of the central air-conditioning system. She sat upright in bed for a moment and then heard the steps of bare feet down the hallway. A soft knock on the door, made Alma Rose jump out of bed. Then she heard someone whisper in the hallway.

"Alma Rose, it's me, Acaraho."

Alma Rose stepped toward the door, opened it, and pulled Acaraho inside. She looked down the hallway and saw that her father and Kate's bedroom door was closed. Alma Rose shut the door behind her and turned on the light.

She whispered, "What do you think you're doing?"

"*Shóotaachi*?" Acaraho said in a hushed voice.

Alma Rose whispered, "I know you didn't come in here to ask me how I am. And speak English. We're not on the Rez."

As they continued to converse in muted tones, Acaraho asked, "Well, are you okay?"

"Yes, I'm fine. Now what is it?"

Acaraho asked, "Can I sit?"

Alma Rose pointed with an upraised palm at the room's writing desk and chair. She offered Acaraho a seat. When Acaraho was settled, Alma Rose returned to her bed and pulled the comforter around herself.

She asked, "Why are you bothering me in the middle of the night?"

Acaraho rested his elbows on his thighs and covered his face with his hands. Then he stared at her. "First I want to tell you that I'm sorry for what happened this summer."

Alma Rose rolled her eyes. "I can't forgive you."

Acaraho stared at her and explained, "That girl was an FBI agent. She used me to get her and her fellow agent up on the Rimrocks to meet that biker gang."

Alma Rose shook her head. "You expect me to accept the fact that you had no feelings for her? What if she weren't an FBI agent, would you have stayed with her?"

Alma Rose noticed Acaraho look down at the floor, then raise his head and again stare at her. Then he said, "I apologize for that. You and I had just broken up. I was depressed and

Johntall was messing with my mind. He asked me to let him drive my brother's car. The excuse he used was that he was joining the Marines."

Alma Rose said, "Pfft...well, wasn't he?"

"Yeah, but I thought he was my friend. He stopped the car and it was his idea to give those two girls a ride. We only spent a couple of hours with them before that biker gang showed up."

Alma Rose said, "I met that girl at Jia Li's apartment."

"You did?"

Alma Rose nodded. "Yes, and I feel guilty about that because my dad told me that the biker gang followed me there. If I hadn't gone there Jia Li wouldn't be in the hospital and that police officer who was outside the apartment protecting that woman wouldn't have been murdered."

Acaraho shook his head. "You don't know how things would have turned out."

Alma Rose said, "What I do know is you can't convince me that what I did wasn't wrong."

Acaraho pleaded, "Don't beat yourself up."

Alma Rose asked, "Do you think she was pretty?"

"What?"

"Don't lie to me, I saw her."

Acaraho swallowed hard. "All right, she was pretty but not like you."

"What do you mean by that?" Alma Rose asked.

"She's not one of us. She's not *bíaitche* like you. She can never be *bíaitche*. Only Crow women are worthy of that beauty."

Alma Rose sat in silence for a moment and then said, "I accept your apology but that doesn't mean we're dating again."

Acaraho nodded repeatedly. "I know, I know." Then he stared at her and asked, "Are you closing the door on us?"

Alma Rose bit her bottom lip. "I'm not sure. I need some time and space." Then she said, "I need you to do me a favor."

Acaraho said, "Anything."

Alma Rose explained, "I can't do anything on my own without my dad either asking a bunch of questions or finding out where I am or what I'm doing from one of his friends. Can you go to Browning this weekend and buy a Blackfeet talking stick? I know you can find one in a souvenir store."

"Why?"

Alma Rose explained, "I'm going to switch one that's in evidence and I don't want anyone to know I have the real one. I need it for something very important."

"Alma Rose, can't you get arrested for that?" Then he left his mouth agape.

She said, "If I don't do this, more people will get killed."

Acaraho smirked. "It'll probably be from China."

Alma Rose said, "I don't really care as long as it looks real enough to fool everyone but my dad at the sheriff's office."

"But what if your dad finds out?"

Alma Rose said, "He won't until when I decide it's the right time to tell him." Then she climbed off the bed. "You better go now before my dad wakes up and finds you in here."

Acaraho nodded again and got up. "All right." Then he walked toward the door and turned to face her. "I have something else to tell you."

She asked, "What is it?"

"My boss, Easy is so nice. He's kind of like a surrogate father to me since I started working this week."

"And…"

"And he told me that him and his boss Lyndon Bell had an interview with a kid named Louis Miller."

Alma Rose rolled her eyes. "So what?"

"This Miller guy told him that he's dating you. Is that true?"

Alma Rose exhaled with a burst. "It's not a date-date. I'm only having dinner with him at Doctor Kelly's house tonight. That's all."

"Who's this Kelly guy?"

Alma Rose replied, "He's the chief medical examiner for western Montana."

Acaraho's voice grew above a whisper. "Why are you going with this Miller kid? I don't like what I've heard about him."

"Ssshhh, you'll wake my dad. What have you heard?"

"Mister Sheppard, I mean Easy…he says Miller's no good, a spoiled brat and that his parents are heathens."

Alma Rose cocked her head. "Why'd he say that?"

Acaraho backed himself against the bedroom wall. "Easy heard something from a contractor that was working on the Miller's house. The guy said that he saw a lot of stuff going on over there that shouldn't be going on."

"Like what?"

"Like three-way sex in the pool with Louis Miller's parents and a house guest."

Alma Rose replied, "That's their business, not anyone else's."

Acaraho took a step toward Alma Rose but she held her palm out front.

Acaraho pleaded, "I don't want to see you get hurt."

Alma Rose said, "I can take care of myself. Now go back to your room. I promise…I'll be fine."

Acaraho opened the door, stepped into the hallway, turned, and asked, "What about us?"

Alma Rose rested her cheek on the door. "We'll have time to discuss that this summer."

"So, there may be hope for us?"

Alma Rose smiled. "Maybe."

Acaraho returned the smile and walked down the hallway. Alma Rose shut the door, leaned her back against it, and took a deep breath.

·49·

Alma Rose climbed out of bed at 8:12 a.m. The 4th of July holiday gave her a respite from what had become a daily grind. The break permitted her to catch up on some badly needed sleep. She believed that her summer internship was going well. She had garnered so much valuable information, but the long hours and the mysterious illnesses took a toll on her stamina. The visitations from the spectral apparition affected her psyche and that disrupted her internal clock and her cognitive balance between the earthly plane and the spirit world. She recognized her weakened state and fully understood that in this specific time and place she was in a most vulnerable condition.

She showered and then dressed in causal jeans, a tank top, and sneakers. She grabbed a fringed leather purse with a long-braided leather strap and went downstairs. Kate sat alone at the kitchen table having her morning coffee while Angel and Shadow were by her side. When Alma Rose entered the room around 9 a.m., both dogs ran to greet her, and she knelt to pet them.

Alma Rose asked, "Where's my dad?"

Kate put down her coffee cup. "He had business in Troy. He said he hopes to be back later today. Would you like coffee and something to eat?"

Alma Rose stood up. "Coffee sounds good. Later, I think I'll have breakfast at Lucy's. I need to speak with someone who works there."

Kate got up from the table, grabbed a mug, and carried the coffee pot over to the table. She poured Alma Rose a coffee and then asked, "What are you doing later today?"

Alma Rose took a seat at the table. "After breakfast, I might stop at the office for a few minutes. I heard that both Rocky and Bonnie are working today, and I have some questions for them." Alma Rose looked around. "Is Acaraho up?"

"Rocky stopped by about a half-hour ago while you were in the shower to pick up Acaraho. Rocky's got a new roomie."

Alma Rose drank from her mug, put it down, and then asked, "Why'd they do that so soon?"

Kate explained, "Your father thought it best that Rocky put him up at his place until Acaraho gets his own apartment."

"I know but I didn't know it would happen today." Then Alma Rose asked, "Did my dad tell you that I was invited to have dinner tonight with Doctor Kelly and his wife?"

Kate took a sip from her coffee cup, placed it on the table, and then said, "He also told me that you're bringing that young man who caused that accident up on U.S. 228 to the Kelly's house."

Alma Rose took a last swallow from her coffee mug, stood up, and then placed the mug down onto the table. "I have my reasons why I invited him."

Kate stood up and said, "Alma Rose, I'm not telling you what you should or should not be doing. All I simply ask is that you consider how this will affect not only your internship at the sheriff's office and how it reflects on your father's job, but that boy may be facing criminal charges. From what your father has told me about Louis Miller, he doesn't seem like the kind of boy that your father would approve you associate with."

Alma Rose walked toward the back door, opened it, and then faced Kate. "And where was my father during all those years I lived on the Rez? If he chose not to be with me then, why should he have a say concerning whom I choose to be with now?"

Kate remained silent as Alma Rose stepped outside, shut the door, and walked to her pickup truck. She drove down the driveway and through the town of Taylor. She turned right onto Route 200, also known as Main Street. She headed west on Main until she reached a Taylor Police Officer in the middle of the street standing in front of a barricade.

She stuck her head out her truck's window and asked, "What's going on officer?"

The officer replied, "Sorry Ma'am, the road is closed for today's 4th of July Parade."

Alma Rose said, "I wanted to have breakfast at Lucy's."

The officer walked over to her truck. He looked at her and asked, "Are you Sheriff's Buchanan's daughter?"

"I am. How did you know?"

"Well ma'am, in one of our daily briefings, Chief Peters and Captain Stevens distributed a photo of you. They ordered us to provide any possible assistance you may request and then some. Ma'am, did you still want to go to the restaurant?"

Alma Rose said, "I do."

The officer pointed with his hand toward a side street. "Ma'am, you can hang a right over here and park in the restaurant's back lot. Then you can leave by way of Aspen Road."

Alma Rose thanked him and then drove down Blackfeet Avenue. She pulled her truck into the back lot and found a parking spot abutting Aspen Road. She got out of her truck, reached on the bench seat for her purse, and then slung it over her shoulder. As she walked down the sidewalk on Blackfeet Avenue and made the turn onto Main Street, she approached the front door of Tony L's Tobacco Emporium. Out of the corner of Alma Rose's right eye, she noticed movement from inside the store.

Once she was past the smoke shop, she heard a familiar voice call to her. "Hey, Alma...Alma."

She turned around and spotted Louis Miller standing on the sidewalk with a lit Padrón Anniversario cigar between his fingers.

Alma Rose asked, "Offering burnt cigar offerings to your God for the dead elk?"

"Very funny...I see you lost those braids and that uniform. I almost didn't recognize you. I said to myself, who's that hot-looking exotic babe." Louis smiled and nodded his head. "You're looking real good, Alma."

Alma Rose snapped back. "My name is Alma Rose."

Louis walked up to her. "Hey, where are you going...wanna go for a spin in my new car?"

"No." Alma Rose turned to walk away.

Louis reached out and grabbed Alma Rose's upper arm. "Hey hold on now. We're still going to that dinner tonight, right?"

Alma Rose turned back and whipped back her arm from Louis' grasp. She said, "We're supposed to. Do you want to back out?"

"No, but since we're both here right now, want to make it a full day together? We can hang out together at my parents' pool and relax in the hot tub and sauna."

Alma Rose shook her head. "You seem to let the world fly by and never grasp its beauty." She then turned around and headed toward Lucy's Luncheonette. She said as she walked away, "I'll call you when I'm ready to leave for the Kelly's house and then we'll meet there."

Louis asked, "Don't you want me to pick you up?"

Alma Rose opened the door to Lucy's, stared at Louis, said, "No," and then went inside.

Lucy was behind the counter as she poured coffee for her patrons. Five servers handled customers at fifteen of the twenty-five tables and booths in the building. Alma Rose noticed Thea nod toward a booth at the far corner of the room. Alma Rose walked to the booth and sat down.

Thea came over and asked, "How are you?"

Alma Rose replied, "I'm doing okay. I've had a few bumps in the road since last night. It's nothing I can't get over, and nothing I want to dwell on."

"So, what will you have?"

Alma Rose asked, "Can you sit and have coffee with me? I have questions I'd like to ask."

Thea said, "I have..." she turned and glanced at Lucy. Then she faced Alma Rose. "I'm working now, honey. Maybe when I get..."

"What're ya two hens cackling about?" Lucy said as she walked up to the booth with a towel in hand.

Alma Rose spoke up right away. "I asked Thea to have coffee with me. I have a couple of questions for her about what happened to her a few years ago."

Lucy nodded. "You're talking about those two men, aren't you?"

Alma Rose said, "Yes, I want to find out if they had anything to do with the women who have gone missing in Cedar County."

Lucy flipped her towel over her shoulder. "Why didn't you say that?" She turned to Thea. "Take a break. I'll handle your tables for twenty minutes." Lucy stared at Alma Rose. "If you're as good as your father like I think you are, then you'll solve what's been going on. Now, what'll you have for breakfast?"

Alma Rose placed her order and Lucy brought over two cups of coffee. When Lucy left, Alma Rose sat forward in her seat.

She asked, "What else can you tell me about those men?"

Thea said, "Last night I told you everything I know."

"Are you sure?"

Thea leaned forward and whispered, "I don't know if this has anything to do with what those two men did, but it still scares the living shit out of me. So, please don't repeat to anyone what I'm about to tell you. And don't ever say anything to Bonnie about this."

Alma Rose said, "I won't. Is it about that guy Lester?"

Thea nodded. "Yes, I think he's a bit weird but I don't think he's committing these murders."

"Then who is?"

Thea leaned even closer. "About a year ago, we started getting phone calls here at Lucy's."

"What kind of phone calls?"

Thea explained, "I usually answer the phone. About once a month, we get calls from someone asking for Lucy Brown. We hand the phone to Lucy and once she says hello, the guy asks, is this Lucy Brown. She says yes and then the guy said, watch your neck. Then he laughs and hangs up. The last time he calls, Lucy says to him, when I find out who you are..." Thea whispered, "I'll string you up by the balls. Then he hangs up."

Alma Rose asked, "What's happened since then?"

Thea sat back in the chair. "Nothing. We never heard back from the guy. I guess Lucy must have freaked him out."

Alma Rose looked around. "Do you have caller ID? Some folks in Billings have it."

"I understand they have it in Helena and Missoula too, but our local phone company here in Taylor doesn't offer it yet. Maybe we'll get it by nineteen-ninety-never," Thea said with a chuckle.

Lucy brought Alma Rose's order to the table. Thea pushed the chair away and stood up.

As Lucy placed Alma Rose's order on the table, she said, "Thea, now don't you leave on my account. I can handle your customers."

Alma Rose noticed Thea stare at her. Then Alma Rose glanced at Lucy and said, "We're all set here. I just had a few questions to ask Thea."

"Just like your dad," Lucy said.

Alma Rose asked, "What do you mean?"

Lucy laughed. "Your dad is relentless. I sense that same drive in you."

.

·50·

Alma Rose finished her breakfast, paid the bill, and left a tip. She went outside, climbed into her truck, and drove out of the parking lot onto Aspen Road. The parade had started on Main Street beginning near the dam on the Clark Fork River. Sirens blared from the fire trucks and emergency vehicles as the procession headed east along Main toward the town hall, police station, sheriff's office, state crime lab, and where it would finally end at Taylor Memorial Park for an open air brunch and an afternoon of music, softball, and vendors.

Alma Rose drove her truck down Aspen, turned right onto Cedar Street, and then hung a left onto Rimrocks Road. She took a left into the sheriff's office parking lot, got out of the truck, grabbed the large canvas bag on the passenger seat, and walked down the sidewalk toward the front of the building. She reached the corner of Cedar and Main and looked for a breach in the parade. She finally found one between the local Boy Scout troop and the Taylor High School Marching Band and hurried past the fluid crowd and toward the front of the building.

She hopped up the sheriff's office steps and waved to Martha at the dispatch desk. Alma Rose used her card key to enter the office and headed for the elevator. She took the elevator down to the upper basement and flashed her card key to the guard in the secure passage. She then used that same card key to gain entrance to the evidence locker and went directly to the boxes that were catalogued in the Gary Driver case.

Alma Rose took one of the boxes off the shelf and placed it on the table. She removed the lid and looked inside. She reached into the box and removed the plastic see-through evidence envelope that contained the talking stick. Alma Rose drew the talking stick from the bag, pulled it close to her chest, and then sat in one of the metal folding chairs in the room.

She held the stick in her hands and closed her eyes. She rubbed the rabbit's foot at one end of the stick. After a few minutes, a low whining noise invaded her senses along with the slight rustle of a breeze in the airtight room. The sound's pitch increased, and warmth enveloped the room. When Alma Rose opened her eyes, she noticed a green mist and the transparent silhouette of a young Native woman standing in front of her.

"Who are you?"

"I'm Janice Driver, who are you?"

"Alma Rose Two Elk."

"You're Native too?" Janice asked.

"Yes, I'm here to help you."

Janice asked, "Where am I? I don't recognize this place. I need to go. My husband will be home soon from the post office."

With a measured voice, Alma Rose said the words that she knew would hit the spirit of Janice Driver very hard, "You must go to the long day of quiet."

Janice dropped her head and began to whimper. "Why do you say that? You make me so afraid." Then Janice looked up and wiped away transparent tears from her cheeks. What evil tricks are you playing on me? Please tell me where I am and how to leave this place."

Alma Rose asked, "Do you know who the Holy Man of the Oglala Lakota was?"

Janice said, "Of course, everyone knows Black Elk."

Alma Rose continued, "Black Elk tells us that when we have faced the wind and walked the good road, then we must journey to the day of quiet."

Janice asked, "Why do you tell me these things? They are hurtful to me."

Alma Rose said, "I am my tribe's *Akbaalia.*"

Janice asked, "What tribe are you from? *Akbaalia* sounds *Siouan*. I am Salish, Bitterroot Salish. What are you?"

"*Apsáalooke.*"

"You are Crow?"

"Yes."

"What does *Akbaalia* mean?"

Alma Rose said, "It means healer."

"So you are a healer? Are you the spirit woman too, like the prophecy says will come from among the Plains Indians?"

"I don't think so."

"Well, I think you are but I don't understand. Why are you here and why would a spirit woman visit me?" Then Janice shrieked, "Am I dead?"

"Yes."

Janice wailed. "I can't be dead. There is so much to do. My little girl..."

"What little girl?" Alma Rose interrupted. She saw Janice star at her own stomach.

"The baby I carry."

"Gary told me about your baby"

"How is Gary, why hasn't he come home yet?"

Alma Rose said, "You'll see him soon."

Janice Driver asked, "But why isn't he here today, why am I so confused?"

Alma Rose said, "If you stay with me right here, I'll help you. I have to go now but I'll be back."

Janice Driver said, "All right...I trust you."

Then Alma Rose asked, "Do you know a man by the name of Lester Throckmorton?"

Janie Driver screamed and wailed. Alma Rose put down the talking stick next to the canvas bag and the vision of Janice Driver vanished.

·51·

Alma Rose left the evidence locker with the canvas bag and took the elevator to the second floor to find either Bonnie or Rocky, but their offices were empty. She then took the stairs down to the first floor and peeked in her father's first floor office. It was also empty. Alma Rose then walked over to the dispatch center and confronted Martha.

"Sergeant Wilson, I know my dad is...I mean Sheriff Buchanan is out of town but where are Sergeant MacAskill and Undersheriff Salentino?"

Martha responded, "They're out pulling duty for the parade."

"When will they be back?"

"After the parade they'll be at Taylor Memorial Park keeping the festivities under control." Martha then asked, "Can I help you?"

Alma Rose shook her head. "No." She started to walk away and then turned back to Martha. "If you see Rocky later today, tell him that I need to speak with him before Monday."

Martha smiled. "I sure will. Where are you off to?"

Alma Rose gritted her teeth and then said, "I'm going to Mallory. I need to speak with Detective Aronowitz about Gary Driver. Then I'm going back home. I need to apologize to my stepmom. Things were said in the heat of the moment this morning."

Martha nodded. "I understand. I had a stepmom once too. It never gets easy."

Alma Rose went outside, got into her truck, and put the canvas bag on the passenger seat. She drove on side streets until she got past the parade route and then headed west on U.S. 200. Just before the bridge that spanned the Clark Fork

River and east of the intersection with U.S. 228, Alma Rose heard knocking from under the hood of her truck. She threw the transmission into neutral and coasted toward the side of the road.

She grabbed a rag from the glove compartment, got out of the truck, and used the rag to lift the hood. Alma Rose looked inside and immediately spotted a glob of motor oil on the pavement under the engine. She slammed the hood down in anger, lowered the tailgate, and sat on it with her legs dangling off the edge. She thought to herself, someone will stop by and help. Her hopes were momentarily allied when she heard a car approach. Those hopes were dashed in an instant when she realized it was a canary yellow Corvette convertible.

Louis Miller pulled up alongside her truck. "Hey babe, what happened here?"

"My car broke down."

"Did you call AAA?"

Alma Rose said, "I don't have a cellphone, it was stolen."

"Then do you need a lift?"

Alma Rose looked up and saw that the sun was near its highest point in the sky. "No thank you. My dad's up in Troy today and he'll be coming by this way eventually."

"Oh come on babe, you can't sit in the hot sun all day."

Alma Rose spoke in anger, "I'm not a babe, so don't call me that."

Louis got out of his car. "No, you see that's where you're wrong. I don't mean any disrespect, but beauty is in the eye of the beholder."

Alma Rose felt Louis' eyes slowly undress her. After an uncomfortable few seconds, Louis' stare lingered a bit too long on Alma Rose's torso and she said, "I'm not an object."

"Did I say that you were?"

Alma Rose folded her arms. "When you refer to me as less than a human being, yes you do."

Louis stepped over to the truck bed and sat on the tailgate with Alma Rose. He gazed at her and said, "I'm sorry."

She stared at him and said, "I accept your apology on one condition."

"What's that?"

"That you treat me with respect."

Louis hung his head. "Like I told you, I can be a real jerk sometimes."

Alma Rose smiled at him and hit him hard on his thigh with her fist. "That's for being the jerk that you are."

Louis yelled, "Ow, that hurt. You don't even know your own strength, do you?"

Alma Rose laughed. "Then you better not get me mad or you'll face the full fury of my wrath."

Louis said, "Woah, I'll keep that in mind. Now do you need a lift?"

Alma Rose explained, "I was on my way to the police station in Mallory."

"Why?"

Alma Rose said, "I need to speak with a detective there."

Louis smiled. "I can give you a ride, hop in."

Alma Rose reached into the cab of her pickup truck and grabbed the canvas bag off the passenger seat. She climbed into Louis' Corvette hoping that she hadn't just made a grave mistake.

·52·

They continued west on U.S. 200, took a right onto U.S. 228, and drove east toward Mallory. Alma Rose stared out the passenger window and absorbed the landscape. She gazed long and hard at the gated ranches surrounded by forested mountain cliffs which were a far cry from the mostly barren high plains on the Crow Reservation.

They were closing in on where the accident took place earlier that week. As they approached the scene, Alma Rose spotted an elk cow that lumbered down from the forested highlands of the Kootenai National Forest on the left side of the highway. As the elk plodded onto the road, Alma Rose leaned forward in her seat.

"Watch out," she yelled to Louis.

Louis turned to look at her and asked, "Watch out for what?"

Alma Rose stared at the spirit of the elk. It glanced at her and then disappeared into thin air right before her eyes. "Nothing," she said and sat back in her seat. "I didn't get enough sleep last night. I'm a little on edge."

Louis touched Alma Rose on her arm. "It seems like your truck won't be fixed by tonight."

"My dad can drop me off."

Louis countered, "If you don't mind, I can pick you up."

Alma Rose said, "I'm not sure about that."

Louis again touched Alma Rose on her arm. "Come on, don't worry. We'll have fun tonight."

Alma Rose nodded. "Well, I guess you're right. I'll see if my dad can get the garage to bring in my truck. It does seem best for you to pick me up around five, if you don't mind."

Louis smiled. "Not at all, I don't mind one bit."

Alma Rose nodded. "Good, my eyes must be playing tricks on me."

When they got closer to Mallory, Alma Rose noticed the signpost for Howard Lake. As they passed the sign, she glanced to her left and stared at the road. She knew it was the same access road that Gary Driver would have taken if his story regarding spending most of the night with Mac Drew was accurate.

A few minutes later they entered the town of Mallory and after several city blocks, Louis parked his Corvette in front of the police station.

Alma Rose got out of the car and slung the canvas bag over her right shoulder. She turned to Louis. "Wait right here. I shouldn't be more than a half hour."

"Okay babe…I mean, all right Alma Rose."

Alma Rose smiled at him. "You're a bit slow but you're learning." She walked into the building and up to the front desk.

A sergeant asked her, "Can I help you?"

"I'd like to see Detective Aronowitz."

"What's this about?"

"It's about Gary Driver."

"What is it about ma'am?"

"I'm Deputy Two Elk from the Cedar County Sheriff's Office. Please, I need to speak with Detective Martin Aronowitz and Gary Driver."

The sergeant asked, "Credentials, ma'am. Do you have credentials?" When Alma Rose handed over her sheriff's department ID, the sergeant said, "I'm sorry ma'am, that's impossible."

"Why?"

"You have to make an appointment."

Alma Rose raised her voice, "Tell Detective Aronowitz that…"

"What's going on, Sergeant Cardwell?"

"Sir, this person says that she wishes to speak with you and Gary Driver."

Alma Rose spoke with a flash of authenticity. "Detective Aronowitz, with your permission I would like to try something that may prove Gary Driver's innocence or guilt."

Marty asked, "Are you sure?"

"Yes, may I see him with your help?"

Marty then asked, "Why are you out of uniform, Junior Deputy Two Elk?"

"I have the day off, sir."

Marty smiled. "Working on your day off? You are just like your father. Okay, I like that so let's go."

Alma Rose followed Marty through the building and into a room with a table and two chairs on either side. Two Mallory policemen entered the room. Marty grabbed a chair from the corner of the room and placed it at one end of the table.

Alma Rose hung her canvas bag onto the back of one of the chairs and asked, "How much time am I allowed to have with Mister Driver?"

Marty sat down and motioned to one of the guards in the room. "Bring Gary Driver here." He then turned to Alma Rose. "Will twenty minutes do?"

"Yes but I need to be alone with him."

Marty stood up. "I can't agree to that."

"Please sir, his life hangs in the balance. You can view us through the glass in the door but only he and I can be in the room together."

Marty took a deep breath. "All right, but I'll be right outside. If anything happens that I don't like, we're coming in."

Alma Rose said, "I'll agree to that but don't come inside unless you see either of us in danger. If you see anything that seems almost transparent, it's okay. Don't come inside because you will disturb who may be with us."

"What are you talking about?"

Alma Rose said, "Just trust me."

A few minutes later, the guard returned with Gary Driver restrained with handcuffs and a belly chain. The guard pushed Gary onto one of the chairs, secured him to the floor hooks, and then stepped outside with Marty and the other guard. They stood in the darkened hallway, faced the door, and stared into the room.

Inside, Gary asked, "What's going on?"

Alma Rose said, "I want you to close your eyes."

Gary closed his eyes. "Now what?"

Alma Rose reached into the canvas bag. She pulled out the talking stick that had been in the Cedar County Sheriff's Office evidence locker.

Alma Rose stood up, walked over to where Gary sat, and said, "Keep your eyes closed and hold this."

255

Gary reached out with his right hand and grabbed the talking stick. "I know what this is. It's Janice's."

Alma Rose said, "Be quiet and keep your eyes closed."

Gary asked, "What now?"

Alma Rose maneuvered his hand to the rabbit fur. "Now rub it." As Gary rubbed it, Alma Rose said to him, "Now open your eyes."

In front of Gary was the silhouette of a Native woman. Gary stared at the image, trembled, and then spoke one simple word, "Janice."

·53·

Detective Martin Aronowitz and the guard stood side-by-side in the hallway outside the interrogation room. As they stared through the door's window, they watched Alma Rose and Gary Driver seated inside. A blend of light green and yellow mist hovered and enveloped the room. It clouded the air just enough so that Marty couldn't make out what Alma Rose or Gary Driver were saying to one another.

"Can you tell what they're saying, and what is that fog?" Marty wiped the glass with his hand. "Is that moisture on the glass or is there something in the room?"

"Seems like it's in the room, sir," the guard said.

Marty squinted and asked, "Is there some kind of leak in there?"

"No sir."

Marty reached for the door handle and was about to open the door but then remembered what Alma Rose had said. He turned to the guard. "Get Sheriff Buchanan on the phone. I want to speak with him right now."

The guard pulled out his cellphone and exited the hallway. After a few minutes the guard returned and handed his cellphone to Marty.

The guard said, "Sir, he's in Troy investigating a robbery but he can speak with you for a few minutes."

Marty took the cellphone. "*Buchanan, we need to speak...it's about your daughter...well, right now she's meeting with Gary Driver and there's some weird stuff going on...like, stuff I've never seen before...yes, I can keep her here until you arrive...thanks, see you in about an hour.*" Marty handed the cellphone back to the guard and said to him, "*Call my friend in the governor's office. Tell him he's got about a half-hour to tell us everything he knows about Sheriff Buchanan's daughter. When you get that information, bring it to me.*"

After a few more minutes went by, Marty watched Alma Rose and Gary Driver stand up and step away from the table. He spotted Alma Rose tuck a Native talking stick deep into her canvas bag. Marty noticed that the green and yellow fog began to lift. Alma Rose waved to him just as he opened the door. Marty went inside and unhooked Gary Driver's belly chain from the hook in the floor.

He called another guard over. "Bring Mister Driver back to his cell." Once Gary Driver left the room, Marty turned to Alma Rose. "Please sit for a moment. I have a few questions for you."

Alma Rose sat down and asked, "What is it?"

The first guard knocked on the door and Marty waved him inside.

"I have what you requested." The guard handed a folder to Marty.

Marty took the folder and sat in one of the chairs. The guard left the room and stood outside the door. Marty thumbed through the folder's contents. He looked up every few seconds and glanced at Alma Rose as she continued to stare at him.

Alma Rose reminded him, "Detective Aronowitz, you said that you wanted to speak with me."

Marty could sense Alma Rose's impatience grow. Finally, he put the folder down. "Deputy Two Elk, I know the article that you have in your bag was evidence that was recovered in the Janice Driver case. Why did you remove it from the chain of evidence and bring it here?"

Alma Rose said, "I needed to show it to Gary Driver."

Marty raised his voice. "Miss Two Elk, do you realize that it's a felony to remove evidence without authorization? Just because your father is the county sheriff doesn't give you privilege to flaunt State of Montana law."

Alma Rose insisted, "Sir, I'm just doing my job."

Marty countered, "So tell me now, who authorized you to remove evidence?"

Alma Rose replied, "I uh, I'm sure that if you spoke with Doctor Kelly that he would provide that authorization."

Marty pressed forward. "Deputy Two Elk, is it true that you did not request that authorization from Doctor Kelly before you took the evidence?"

Alma Rose responded, "Detective Aronowitz, you are correct. I did not request authorization to remove that evidence."

Marty folded his arms and continued to scold Alma Rose. "So you went rogue. Perhaps you thought a summer intern has the right to decide for herself what is necessary in the eyes of the law?"

Alma Rose shook her head. "No sir, I only want to do what's right."

Marty pressed onward. "Miss Two Elk, your father will be here in about a half-hour. What do you think he'll have to say about all of this?"

·54·

Jim arrived outside the police station in Mallory. He was dressed in blue jeans, and a western-style red, short sleeve button shirt. A black Courtright Cowboy Hat and a red and blue paisley bandana around his neck completed his outfit. Jim parked his SUV on the street and got out. He noticed a familiar yellow Corvette convertible parked alongside the curb a few feet away. He walked over to the driver's side of the car and leaned his arms on the door just like he had done earlier in the week.

Jim said, "So we meet again."

Louis glanced up at Jim and did a double-take. "Oh shit. Hi, Sheriff Buchanan...nice day today, isn't it?"

Jim straightened up. "So what are you doing here?"

"I uh...I had to give someone a ride. They'll be out shortly and then we'll be leaving."

"That person you're talking about doesn't happen to be my daughter...does she?"

Louis took a deep breath, exhaled, and said, "Um...yes. But it's not what you think."

Jim leaned his arms back onto the driver's door. "And what are you up to with my daughter?"

Louis expunged the truth all in one long breath. "Um, her truck broke down on 200 and I stopped to see if she needed help. She said she was going to the Mallory police station so I asked her if she needed a ride. I'm giving her a lift to the Kelly's house tonight. She invited me to join her for dinner there." He coughed, then took in a deep breath, and then pleaded, "Please don't be angry with me, I'm only trying to help her."

Jim touched Louis on his left shoulder. "What time are you picking her up?"

261

"Uh…about 5."

"What time are you bringing her home?"

"Whenever she wants to."

Jim squeezed Louis' shoulder with a vice-like grip. "Wrong answer."

"Uh, eleven?"

Jim squeezed harder. "What time?"

"Uh, how about ten?"

Jim relaxed his grip. "Fine…you can go now. I'll take over from here. We'll expect to see you about five then."

Jim walked toward the police station's front door while Louis drove away. Jim glanced at his wristwatch and saw that it was nearly 2 p.m. He went up to the front desk and asked for Detective Martin Aronowitz. He was buzzed in and an officer led him to the interview room where Alma Rose and Marty waited.

Marty got up and reached for Jim's hand. "How are you sheriff?"

"I'm good. We had some trouble in Troy today. Sheriff Wallach of the Lincoln County Sheriff's Office is assisting the Troy police." Jim stared at Alma Rose who avoided eye contact with him. He turned to Marty. "What's going on here?"

Marty explained, "It's your daughter, Sheriff. She stole something from the evidence locker in your office. That's a potential felony charge of evidence tampering."

Jim turned to Alma Rose. "Is that true?"

Alma Rose rolled her eyes. "I'm only trying to help. Gary Driver is an innocent man and I can prove it."

Marty asked, "How can you prove it?"

Alma Rose said matter-of-factly, "Gary Driver and I just spoke with the spirit of his wife. She told us that a man wearing a mask slit her neck, stabbed her, threw her into a van, and drove her to a house."

Marty shook his head. "I can't believe what I'm hearing."

Jim turned to Marty. "Let's hear her side before we cast judgement." He then looked back at Alma Rose and asked, "Then what happened?"

Alma Rose continued, "She could only tell us what occurred while her soul lingered near her body. Once she transitioned to the spirit world, she was unable to see what happened next."

Marty shook his head. "Can you imagine what would happen if we brought this information to court? We'd be the laughingstock of the entire nation, the judicial system of a third world country. Your daughter works for you. If she is given a pass, then someone needs to be held accountable for the stolen evidence. Are you willing to take the hit for her?"

Jim turned again to Marty and glared at him. "Under my jurisdiction, I'll resume custody of the evidence and return it to the evidence locker at the sheriff's office."

Marty folded his arms. "Fine, you go ahead and do that. I'll speak with Doctor Kelly and inform him of this and see if the county prosecutor agrees with what I believe is a blatant and gross violation of evidence custody, handling, storage, and retention. We'll see if they believe the letter of the law was followed."

Jim took the canvas bag containing the talking stick, faced Marty, and said, "My daughter speaks of a historical tradition of the Plains Indians. Many of our ancestors have been visionaries. Some we call *Iláaxe-Bía*, Spirit Woman. They are privy to things that many of us can't see." Jim turned to Alma Rose. "Let's go." As Jim and Alma Rose walked past Marty, Jim threw a parting shot at him. "I believe in my daughter. She wouldn't lie to me and she wouldn't lie to you."

·55·

Jim and Alma Rose headed toward the sheriff's office in Taylor. On the way, they approached Alma Rose's pickup truck. Jim parked his SUV behind the truck, got out, and looked under the hood. After a few minutes, he returned to the SUV and climbed back into the driver's seat.

Alma Rose asked, "Is it bad?"

Jim stared at her. "You're right about the oil leak. You said that you threw it into neutral once you heard the knocking?"

"Yes."

"Well, I think you may have a seized engine because of the oil leak but by rolling to a stop, you may have saved the engine. I'll have it towed to the garage."

"Which garage?"

"The garage at the sheriff's office."

Alma Rose shook her head. "No, I want the truck towed to a private garage."

"Why?"

Alma Rose spoke in a blunt manner, "After what just happened in Mallory, I don't want anyone to accuse me of doing anything unethical."

Jim nodded. "Okay, I get it." He took out his cellphone and dialed Ernie's Garage. "Ernie, can you send a wrecker to U.S. 200 just south of Route 56? My daughter's pickup truck may have a blown engine...yeah, check it out for us and we'll hope for the best...oh, it's a red, 1956 Ford pickup truck..."

Alma Rose interrupted, "With a black driver's door, dad."

Jim pulled the phone away from his ear, glanced at Alma Rose, and then spoke into the phone. "And Ernie, you can't miss it. It's got a black driver's side door."

265

Jim ended the call and drove back onto the road. When they reached the sheriff's office, Alma Rose got out. Jim reached into the back seat and grabbed the canvas bag. He told Alma Rose to wait in the cafeteria and then went straight to the basement evidence locker.

When he opened the box, unzipped the plastic evidence bag, and dropped the talking stick into the bag, he thought he heard the faint sound of a wailing woman. Jim turned to look but saw no one. When Jim closed the lid of the box, the crying ceased.

Jim scanned the evidence locker and after he was sure that no one was inside the room, he left and went upstairs to the cafeteria.

He walked over to Alma Rose who was seated at a table in the corner. He stared at her and said, "I think I heard her."

"I knew you would."

Jim looked down at her. "Let's go home."

When they reached the house, they were greeted by Angel and Shadow. Jim went outside with them and gave the two dogs some needed exercise time. About a half-hour later he returned to the house and noticed Alma Rose in the great room.

"Dad, I'm going to take a nap. Around four I need to shower and change to go to the Kelly's. Louis is picking me up at five."

"Alma Rose, I have to say this. Louis Miller is a poor choice for a friend."

"Don't worry dad. I've got things under control." Alma Rose headed upstairs toward her bedroom as Angel and Shadow followed.

Jim went into the kitchen just as he heard Kate's Samba Bus head up the driveway. Kate walked into the house with two bags of groceries.

Jim walked over to her and said, "Let me help you."

Kate smiled. "I've got this, but you can help me put them in the fridge." She placed the groceries on the granite kitchen island. Then Kate asked, "What are we doing this weekend?"

As Jim restocked the refrigerator with care, he said, "I was thinking about us taking an early flight to Billings tomorrow and visiting my sister. Grandfather is having difficulty getting around so for us to travel there makes more sense. We can stay over until Monday morning and then fly back."

Kate hugged Jim from the back and said, "That sounds wonderful. Do you want to invite Alma Rose?"

Jim tuned around, faced Kate, and kissed her on the forehead. He replied, "That Louis Miller kid is picking her up at five and they're having dinner at Hank and Mary's tonight. I told him to bring her home by ten. I'll mention the flight to her then. I'm concerned that if I tell her now, she'll cancel the dinner invitation."

Kate asked, "What about Angel and Shadow?"

Jim replied, "I checked with Linda. She'll dog-sit and wanted to know if it would be all right if she slept here for the weekend."

"What did you say?"

"I told her that would be fine."

Kate then asked, "What about Acaraho?"

Jim replied, "I'm not inviting him. Acaraho's staying with Rocky until he finds his own apartment. It's best that Alma Rose and Acaraho take a break from their relationship. Too much has happened. They need to sort things out."

Kate asked, "Will this trip cause a problem with business at the sheriff's office?"

"I'm meeting with Dan on Monday afternoon. He should have information on what happened in Mallory and Spaulding."

"I know about the Native woman who disappeared. Are you now talking about that retired schoolteacher? I heard something on the news about it."

"That's the one."

Kate shivered. "Over in Missoula, the faculty is worried and the students on campus are frightened out of their minds."

Jim said, "I'm worried too, especially now that we had an apparent break-in."

Kate asked, "Was your meeting with the FBI agent in Troy to discuss the disappearance of that woman in Mallory?"

Jim sat at the kitchen table. "That meeting I had in Troy today was with a different agent, an undercover FBI agent who infiltrated that outlaw biker gang."

"The Screaming Skulls?"

"Yes."

"That name gives me the willies."

Jim replied, "Worse is that their leader's name is Videl Tanas. That's an anagram for the devil and Satan."

Kate responded without hesitation. "Who would name their child that?"

Jim shook his head. "Go figure, his parents were in a devil worshiper cult. Tanas is in the county jail awaiting trial in Helena."

Kate asked, "So what about that other FBI agent you were supposed to meet?"

"Paul Harris? When he heard that the undercover agent fled with the young girl that he was supposed to rescue, they reassigned him to find the agent and the girl, Peta Ross."

"Governor Ross' daughter?"

Jim nodded. "Yes, the cult she was in renamed her Eden Child."

Kate shook her head. "Oh dear."

Jim rubbed his weary eyes. "I guess the FBI figures that going after one of their own who defected and bringing back the governor's daughter is more important than finding a serial killer and preventing additional murders."

Kate asked, "Do you really think they would do that?"

"Well, why the hell not? It seems they prefer to let the locals deal with their own crap." Jim got up and pushed a kitchen chair clear across the floor. It hit the wooden kitchen wall and then toppled over. "Dammit, ever since we lost Jonathan it seems like the world has turned against us."

Kate rushed over to Jim and hugged him. "It's not our fault that our baby was stillborn."

Jim returned the hug and began to cry. "Doctor Donahue said you can't have children anymore. That hurts me so much. I wanted us to have our own family together."

Kate pulled Jim closer to her. "God just has a different plan for us. You still have Alma Rose."

Jim caressed Kate's head and let it rest on his chest. "I love Alma Rose. If anything were to happen to her I don't know what I'd do."

Kate looked up at Jim. "Don't say that. Someday you should bring her to visit with her mother. Alma Rose deserves to finally meet her."

Then Jim and Kate both looked toward the stairs when they head footsteps and then an upstairs bedroom door close.

·56·

It was a few minutes before 5 p.m. when Alma Rose got out of the shower and dried herself off. She pulled on a pair of black panties and threw on a tightfitting, black sleeveless tank mini-dress with a red print design and spaghetti straps with a mid-thigh hemline. Alma Rose completed her ensemble with a pair of sterling silver Navajo earrings and a matching necklace. She brushed back her silky black hair and let it fall over her shoulders. Then she took two strips of hair from either side of her head and pinned it back.

Alma Rose glanced toward the window when she heard a car pull up the driveway. She walked over and pushed aside the curtains. A yellow Corvette convertible pulled up to the front porch. Alma Rose slid into a pair of black high heels, stared into the mirror, winked, and then smiled.

The doorbell rang as she stepped outside the bedroom. As she stood silent in the upstairs hallway, Angel and Shadow ran past her and down to the front door barking the entire way. She heard her father open the door and command the dogs to sit. Then she heard Louis tell her father that he was here to escort Alma Rose to a dinner invitation at the Kelly's house.

When she heard her father call to her, she grabbed her pocketbook and closed her bedroom door. As she descended the staircase, Louis uttered a remark to Alma Rose that she was unaccustomed to hearing.

"Wow, you are unbelievably gorgeous," Louis said as he stood at the front door.

Jim cleared his throat and then asked, "Alma Rose, where did you get that outfit?"

"I bought it a few days ago at Cora's boutique on Main Street." Alma Rose noticed her father's raised eyebrows and

269

added, "Cora recommended it for evening wear. Her words were it's what all the young twentysomethings are wearing today."

Louis added, "I can verify that's a true statement."

Jim glanced at him and barked, "No one's speaking to you." Then he turned to Alma Rose. "You're not twenty yet. Is that appropriate for a teenager to wear for dinner at the Kelly's?"

Alma Rose stepped past her father, grabbed Louis by the hand, pulled him through the doorway, and said to her father, "We're going to find out."

Louis held the passenger door open for Alma Rose and she got in. Louis paused, took a deep breath, and then rushed over to the driver's side and climbed in.

Alma Rose could sense him gazing at her long legs. She turned to him and noticed that he seemed frozen with his fingers on the keys in the ignition.

"What?" she asked.

Louis took another deep breath and remarked, "I can't believe that you're the same girl that I first met at that accident scene."

Alma Rose turned to him. "Let's not go there."

Louis nodded. "Yeah, you're right. I won't go there." He fumbled with the keys and then started the engine. His right foot slipped off the accelerator pedal and revved the engine. "Oops, sorry."

"Can we leave...like now?" Alma Rose asked as she noticed her father staring through the living room window.

When they arrived at Hank and Mary Kelly's log home on Cottonwood Road, Louis parked behind Hank's Ford Crown Vic. Alma Rose and Louis got out of the Corvette, went up to the front door, and knocked. After a few seconds, the door opened, and Hank Kelly greeted them with a warm smile.

"Come in, come in. Right on time," Hank said.

Alma Rose and Louis stepped inside as Mary entered the great room wearing her apron.

"It's so nice to meet you my dear. Your father has told me so much about you." Mary then looked at Louis and asked, "And who is this handsome young man?"

"This is Louis Miller. He's my date for tonight."

Louis grinned from ear to ear and shook Mary's hand. "It's nice to meet you Mrs. Kelly."

Mary smiled. "He's so polite too, a real gentleman."

Mary gave Alma Rose a hug and that's when Alma Rose felt it. She heard a scream in her head and the room grew dark for just a split second. Alma Rose saw a vision of a disemboweled woman on a bed saturated in blood. When they ended their hug, Alma Rose noticed the room return to its normal illumination and the wailing sounds that dominated her thoughts ceased.

The two couples had dinner, dessert and sat around for an hour or so discussing the sheriff's office, Louis' goals in life, Hank's time as Chief Medical Examiner in New York City, and Alma's aspirations in law enforcement.

When they were done, Hank escorted Alma Rose into his study. They walked toward a large, 16th-century Italian credenza. When Hank opened the doors, articles, exhibits, and artifacts preserved under glass from Hank's long career in forensics were on full display. Louis spent time in the kitchen with Mary and discussed their mutual longing to return to New York City and its fast-paced life.

When it was a little after 8:30 p.m. Alma Rose said, "Louis, it's time to go." Louis was about to say something when Alma Rose continued, "Mr. and Mrs. Kelly, thank you for inviting us to share dinner with you. The food was great and the company even better. I enjoyed seeing your wonderful home, we had a fantastic time."

When Alma Rose got into the Corvette, Louis turned to her and said, "Wow, you are really good at saying all the right things, even though you're from the reservation and all...no offense. Where did you learn that etiquette?"

"On the Rez," Alma Rose said. "We are taught respect, kindness, and humility."

Louis said, "Uh, yeah, I guess so. Well, you don't have to be home for at least another hour. Did you want to go somewhere else?"

Alma Rose glanced at him. "Yes but don't get any ideas into that head of yours."

They drove downtown, and Alma Rose directed Louis to the sheriff's office. She pointed to a parking spot off Aspen Road and told him to wait in the car. Alma Rose walked up to the garage entrance, used her card key, and gained entrance to the office. She went downstairs into the upper basement level, into the Nautilus weight room, and then into the women's locker room. Alma Rose opened her locker, grabbed a towel, and then

271

used her key card to gain entrance to the evidence locker. Once inside, she opened the box labeled Gary Driver, removed the talking stick, and wrapped it inside the towel. Then she returned to the car.

Louis asked, "What do you have there?"

Alma Rose stared at him and with a hint of cunning in her voice said, "None of your beeswax."

·57·

Whe Alma Rose got home, she said goodbye to Louis who waved to her as he drove away. She carried the rolled-up towel under her arm with her pocketbook draped over it as she opened the front door. As soon as Alma Rose was inside, she was confronted by her father and Kate each sitting in club chairs inside the great room. Startled, Alma Rose nearly dropped the towel.

"What are you two still doing up?" she asked.

Jim spoke first, "It's only twenty minutes to ten. We were waiting up for you."

Kate said, "We didn't expect to see you until at least ten or even later."

Alma Rose yawned. "I decided to come home early. It was a long day and I'm tired."

Jim asked, "What's with the towel?"

Alma Rose looked down at it and then glanced at her father. "I didn't feel so well. You know, after such a long day. Mrs. Kelly soaked this towel in ice water to put on my forehead." Alma Rose took two steps up the staircase and then stopped when she heard her father's voice again.

"That looks like one of our towels from the gym."

Alma Rose replied, "It is. The day Rocky gave me that self-defense instruction I took a towel and some ice with me to prevent any swelling." Alma Rose laughed. "Rocky sure knows how to pack a punch."

Jim asked, "How did you end up with it tonight? I didn't see you leave the house with it and your pickup truck is in the repair shop."

Alma Rose had taken a few more steps and stopped again. "Later that same day I went with Doctor Kelly to Mallory.

273

He said I left the towel in his car." Alma Rose took a couple more steps up the staircase.

Jim got up from his chair and walked to the staircase. Alma Rose was now at the top of the steps.

Jim said, "Come back down, I'll take the towel. We have something important to discuss."

Alma Rose retreated down the staircase and saw that her father held out his hand.

"Dad, I'd rather not give you the towel."

"Why not? I'll bring it back to the office for you."

Alma Rose blushed. "I uh…after my headache, I soaked the towel in hot water, and I used it to relieve the cramping that I had. It's soiled and I'd be embarrassed to give it to you."

Kate said, "You can give it to me, I'll wash it for you."

Alma Rose replied, "I'd still be embarrassed. Besides I'm still a little crampy. I may need it tonight and tomorrow too. I don't want to dirty one of your towels."

Jim said, "That's too bad because I was going to ask you if you wanted to fly with us early tomorrow morning to Billings and we'd all stay at your mom's until Monday morning."

Alma Rose's mouth was agape. "Could I?"

Jim replied, "I'm not sure if you're up to it now. I don't want to force you to travel with us if you're not feeling well."

Alma Rose's words gushed from her lips. "I'll go. I'll be better by tomorrow. Yeah, I'll go."

"Are you sure?" Jim asked.

"Absolutely," Alma Rose said. "I'm going to bed right now so that I can get an early start in the morning." She ran up the stairs with Angel and Shadow at her heels as Jim and Kate stared at one another.

An hour later, when it was nearly 11 p.m., Alma Rose lay face up in bed staring at the ceiling and spoke these sincere words of forgiveness.

"Dear Creator, I know that lately I've strayed from the Red Road and I have deceived my father and Kate. Please forgive me. That's not who I am. I also know that I have been unfaithful to my vocation and have done things that are wrong like stealing evidence from the sheriff's office. I have also used another human being to help me get what I want. Louis isn't a bad person he just needs to grow up. I have made him think that I like him, and I…I don't. Well at least not yet. And Acaraho, my jury is still out on him. We haven't reached a verdict yet, we're still in recess. Please protect these people because I do love them all and wouldn't want anything bad to happen to any of them. Please protect all those people that I just mentioned, plus my mother Sara Whispers, and my real mother Shoshanna Pepper, then Hank and Mary Kelly, Rocky, Linda, Thea, Bonnie, and well, even mean old Detective Aronowitz because I really do love everyone."

Alma Rose heard two whimpers and felt a wet nose at her left hand. "And Creator please protect Angel and Shadow and that eagle who got hurt this week because I love them too. I think that sometimes they understand me more than people do."

Alma Rose felt the two dogs leap onto the bed and curl up next to her on either side of her legs. Shadow put his head on Alma Rose's right hip while Angel cuddled between Alma Rose's left arm and waist. Then she continued her prayer.

"And Creator, I know that you're real busy with other people, creatures, Turtle Island, and the whole of Mother Earth but please understand that I took the talking stick only because I know its power and I know what I must do with it. Please help me channel its energy into what has to be done. Thank you, good night."

·58·

It was late in the evening inside the Chuck Wagon Bar & Grill, an off-the-beaten-path dive on the edge of downtown Mallory. The bar was dark except for the neon-lit beer signs that adorned the barn-planked walls. The wall-mounted TV behind the bar was tuned to KTAY, Taylor's own TV station. The Channel 2 News was on and the station's news anchor announced that renowned news reporter Julie Franklin would be presenting a special weekend exposé regarding the recent disappearances in and around Mallory. Immediately, a heated discussion ensued among a few liquored-up male patrons and the bartender.

"I hope they find the bastard who did it. A friend of mine who works for the newspaper told me someone got killed. He was outside the apartment and saw a lot of blood," crewcut bartender and owner Chuck Black said as he poured a shot of whiskey for a customer seated at the bar. Chuck was a bit overweight but burly enough to toss an unruly customer out on his ear if necessary.

"How do you know it was a guy?" asked Walter Willison, a rail-thin man seated at a table near the bar. Walter topped out around five feet tall even with boots on. He wore blue jeans, a black western style shirt with stylized yoke on the front and a Stetson Bozeman black wool cowboy hat. "Maybe it was a broad?" Walter suggested.

Chuck laughed. "A woman wouldn't have the guts to rip the guts out of someone."

Walter choked on his beer as a few drips of suds ran from his nose. Then he nodded. "I like that play on words."

Chuck smiled. "I got a few more snappy jokes if you care to hear them."

Walter laughed and then said, "Yeah, let'er rip."

Chuck placed his towel on the bar and said, "That young lady who's missing answered her front door and a fella starts talking gibberish but she got the point."

Walter slapped his hand on his thigh and laughed so hard tears began to slide down his cheek. "Got another?" Walter asked.

Chuck put on a big smile and then said, "Her husband finds out she's cheating on him so she explains, 'But honey, I still love you and he tells her, I'm sure you do baby, but the knife cuts both ways."

Walter erupted in a sustained burst of laughter that echoed off the walls of the entire bar.

Another patron leaned over the bar and spoke in a surly manner with a cockney accent that grew louder the more he spoke. "Ter god's ears as I repent under the bloomin' bloody sound o' Bow Bells, it ain't no laughin' matter." He tossed his head back and knocked back a shot of Ballantine's Finest Blended Scotch Whisky, then dropped his head back down and slammed the shot glass on the bar.

He was middle-aged, tall, and muscular, with long curly brown hair and an odd black-ink tattoo on the left side of his neck. He wore green work pants, a green long-sleeved work shirt, and a green ballcap with the brim pulled down over his eyebrows. A logo, Howard Lake Brewery was prominently displayed on the front of the hat.

Walter swung his body around. He faced the back of the man and yelled, "Hey you, who the hell are you to say what we can and cannot laugh about?"

Without turning to face Walter, the man replied, "Bout time you got off yer plates. That Indian lassie's ole man did it. If yer find out sumfink else, call me back in a fortnight."

Chuck wiped the bar and asked the man, "What makes you think he did it?"

Before the man could respond, Walter butted into the conversation. "They said her husband had blood all over him and in his car but I still say a woman did it."

Chuck said, "I heard someone say that the husband accidently cut himself while filleting a trout."

Walter laughed. "Yeah, I don't believe that one."

The man said, "I knew that tart. If she accepted me offer she'd still be alive instead o' 'angin' on some trophy 'unter's wall.

'is trouble and strife were a real pretty lady, do wot Guvnor! I would 'ave treated 'er right. If yer find out who kidnapped 'er let me know. I'll do the bloomin' uncle Bob and kill the son o' a bitch for yer."

Chuck asked, "You knew her, when?"

The man waved Chuck closer and replied in a whisper, "Wen she were peddlin' 'er wares wiv 'er muvver. She were just a yorng lassie then and I wasn't copping any yornger, yer see Guvnor? I tried ter date 'er but she met 'er future ole man and then it were all over between us. I seen 'er a few times at the bleedin' local diner in Taylor but she rejected me offer ter leave 'er ole man. I even spoke ter 'er ole man about me feelings for 'er. I dropped in on 'im one day w 'e worked and asked 'im ter leave 'er, right? One finkbugger leads ter aunuvver and I popped 'im one. We then ended up in a tussle."

"Are you kidding me?" Chuck asked.

"Cor blimey guv, would I lie to you? I left 'im wiv a bloody nose before 'is boss chased me out o' there. I'm bloody well so upset that she didn't 'ave me. She'd still be alive today if she took me bloomin' offer."

Chuck straightened up. "I'm so sorry."

Walter raised his voice. "What are you two whispering about? I think a woman did it out of jealousy. Don't you see the rage? Who else would murder someone so violently that there'd be blood all over their own home? I say the husband was cheating on her and his lover did over the wife in a jealous rage. Don't you all agree?"

The man first slammed his balled fist onto the bar, then turned to face Walter and replied in a measured and melancholy manner, "I said…it were the bleedin' 'usband. That bastard son o' a bitch."

Chuck turned to the man, placed both palms down on the bar, and demanded, "Yeah, right...now how do you figure that one?"

The man slowly turned his head, stared at Chuck, and said with a sense of hardened rage in his voice, "The bleedin' bloke who killed that lass don't care about 'uman life. If 'e did 'e wouldn't 'ave ripped 'er body apart. The chuffin' lass and 'er ole man was both Indian. I don't trust them savages ter treat their bints wiv respect. Now as a proper English geezer, right, I would 'ave put 'er up on a pedestal and worshipped 'er till the chuffin' day I die, I would 'ave."

279

Walter lunged at the man and slammed his hand on the bar. "Were you screwing her? You English asshole, my wife's brother-in-law is Flathead. Take back what you just said."

The man cocked his head and without a word gave Walter a stare that could make a grizzly bear turn and run. He spoke in a deep growl, "Cop yor 'ands off the bleedin' bar if yer value yor life. I've done a bit o' bad finkbuggers in me life but cheatin' on aunuvver man's ole lady ain't one o' them. Now on yor bike, right, off wiv yer!"

Chuck intervened and said, "Walter get back to your seat or I'll kick your ass out of here so fast your head will spin."

Walter stared at Chuck for a split second, then at the man, and then back at Chuck. Walter hustled to his seat, then took a deep breath and said as if to clear the air, "I uh…I heard the wife was pregnant."

The man turned around to face Walter which prompted Walter to shift farther away in his seat. The man asked, "I didn't 'ear that on the bloomin' news."

Walter hesitated and then replied, "I…I heard it from a neighbor… a neighbor that said she knew the couple."

The man in the green ballcap asked, "So then 'er ole man killed two." He then turned, faced the bar, inhaled a deep breath, and then exhaled.

Chuck leaned his arms on the bar and asked the man, "Why, did you hear that he killed someone else?"

The man in the green ballcap stared at Chuck and said, "Yer daft bloke, now yor goin' on rubbish." He slugged down his drink, slammed the shot glass down on the bar, and then got up from his barstool. Walter flinched as the man walked away from the bar and stood next to his chair. The man stared at Walter and replied, "The bloody sonofabitch killed 'is trouble and strife and 'is unborn child." Then he turned to Chuck and left a parting shot. "I'll give yer one finkbugger, right, someone's tellin' porkies and it ain't me. Whoever killed the bleedin' trouble and strife ought ter cop 'is 'ead blown off and if no one is willin' ter do it, I'm yor man." The man then left the tavern and slammed the door behind him.

After a few seconds, Walter stared at Chuck and asked, "Who the hell was that?"

Chuck picked up the empty shot glass and then wiped down the bar. He first looked to the left and then to the right. He waved Walter toward him and whispered, "I know who he is. He moved to Mallory from Wolf Point a few years back. That's all I know."

"English, huh? What's his name?" Walter asked.

Chuck said, "I only know his first name...Lester."

"I never heard of him. Why's he all hyped up over that Indian lady's kidnapping?" Walter asked.

Chuck wiped the bar and shook his head. "Maybe he's still fighting his own wars." Then Chuck laughed and imitated Lester's cockney accent. "I guess you can say, 'is bloody wars."

Walter burst into a fit of hysterics.

·59·

Alma Rose's alarm clock went off at 5 a.m. She woke up, showered, and dressed in blue jeans and a red plaid long-sleeved shirt. Then she wrapped the talking stick in a roll of bubble wrap that she had brought home from the sheriff's office. She placed the package in her overnight bag and covered it with a pair of jeans, a couple of shirts, a sweatshirt, socks, and underwear.

Around 6:00 a.m., when Alma Rose opened the door to her bedroom, Angel and Shadow burst past her and ran down the staircase to the first floor. She heard them bark in the kitchen and her father call to them. Then she caught the sound of the back door open and the tap-tap-tap of eight paws on the kitchen tile and then the kitchen screen door slam shut.

Alma Rose carried her overnight bag down the stairs and plopped it onto a couch in the great room. Then she walked into the kitchen and saw her dad and Kate seated at the table as they ate their breakfast. They each wore jeans and button-down t-shirts but Jim sat upright in his black duty boots while under Kate's chair, her crossed legs sported a pair of unlaced white sneakers.

Alma Rose asked, "Dad, what time is the flight?"

"8:40 but we should leave soon. It'll take about a half hour to get to the airport and an hour to go through check-in. You should have something to eat."

Alma Rose looked about the kitchen. "Do you still have that oat granola cereal I've been eating?"

Kate said, "I bought a new box. It's in the cupboard."

"Thanks." Alma Rose fixed herself a bowl. The room was quiet as she finished her breakfast. Then she turned back to her dad and asked, "About our flight, I don't have checked baggage so that should save us some time, right?"

Jim nodded and Kate said, "We just have carry-ons too."

Alma Rose asked, "Where's Acaraho, isn't he coming?"

Jim explained, "I didn't tell him we were going."

Alma Rose's voice grew louder. "Why not?"

Jim said, "He's sorting out where to live. Rocky's helping him find an apartment this weekend. Plus Acaraho reports to work Monday morning at 7:00 a.m. and our flight doesn't return until late morning. Acaraho's boss, Easy is a real stickler for punctuality. It's bad enough that I have to rush after the flight to give Louis Miller a ride to work in the afternoon."

Alma Rose plopped herself onto a club chair. "Acaraho will be disappointed when he learns that we went to the Rez and didn't ask him if he wanted to go."

Jim said, "It's out of our hands. I told you that Acaraho has commitments." Then his voice grew louder and ended in a crescendo. "Now if you don't want to go with us and instead hang around with him then just tell me now so that I don't waste my precious time trying to accommodate you and your selfish ways."

"Jim!" Kate said.

Alma Rose turned her face away from her father, stifled a tear, and remained silent.

Then Jim said, "Alma Rose, I'm sorry I yelled at you. I've been on edge with what happened in the Yaak, what happened in Mallory, and now that FBI agent went AWOL in Troy. I'm just trying to keep my head above water."

Alma Rose glanced at her father. "I guess it goes with the territory."

Jim repeated, "I'm sorry."

"Yeah." Alma Rose stood up, grabbed her overnight bag, and walked toward the door. "I'll be outside in your car."

After nearly thirty minutes, Jim and Kate left the house. They arrived at Taylor International Airport a little after 7 a.m. Once they received their boarding passes, it was a wait of nearly forty-five minutes before gate #7 opened. They filed onto the tarmac with the twenty-eight other passengers, climbed aboard the Bombardier Dash 8 turboprop plane, and settled into their seats.

The morning fight of one hour and forty minutes was nearly unremarkable except for the plane's landing approach. A broad expanse of 300-foot-tall sandstone cliffs known as the Rimrocks, or just the Rims as they were affectionately referred to by the locals, sat at the beginning of the runway at Logan International Airport in Billings. Alma Rose became startled when she noticed the earth abruptly appear beneath their plane just prior to landing.

They deplaned and Jim secured the car rental. They packed their bags into the back of the brand-new, black Chevy Blazer and then climbed inside.

It was almost an hour's trip from Billings to Crow Agency via I-94 and then I-90. Jim then noticed the familiar road sign along the Interstate. It read, <u>WELCOME TO CROW COUNTRY</u>. Jim took Exit 509, drove down Makawasha Avenue, then onto Chief Plenty Coups Road, and finally parked in front of the Tribal Police Station. Jim, Kate, and Alma Rose climbed out of the SUV and went inside the old log building. A former western trading post, it was converted into a police station and jail. There was a large man in an olive green police chief's uniform seated behind one desk while one officer occupied a chair next to a long table.

Jim asked, "So how's my cousin doing these days?"

Crow Tribal Police Chief Preacher Running Wolf stood up from behind his desk and slid his chair away. He pushed his pony tail away from his shoulder and walked over to greet Kate and Alma Rose. He was nearly an inch shorter than Jim's 6'5" height and a few pounds lighter and softer than Jim's 240 pound athletic frame.

Preacher looked at Kate and said, "I'm honored to have the wife of *Issaxchí-Káata* here today." Preacher then turned to his niece. "Alma Rose, there is talk that you are not just our *Akbaalia* but that Creator has chosen you to be *Iláaxe-Bía*."

Jim knew that as is custom among the Crow, Alma Rose would not disrespect an elder. She nodded but kept silent.

When Jim extended his hand, Preacher said, "I give thanks to Creator for your company. I've still got saddle sores from riding that mustang up in the Yaak with you chasing that devil man." Then he asked, "Are you tired or thirsty? Have you eaten?" Preacher pointed to a pan that sat on a cast iron stove. "My wife broke out some *pimîhkân* and took your father's recipe for selkirk bannock and made a tray of both for us here at the station. I'd rather have *baaxawuatámmishe* but she says I don't need the extra grease. Would you like to share a meal with us?"

Jim shared a light and quick handshake with Preacher. "We'll have some, thank you." He turned to Kate. "*Pimîhkân* is bison and huckleberries and you know *baaxawuatámmishe* better as fry bread."

"Of course," Kate said and offered a smile for Preacher.

After they spent a considerable portion of their visit with Preacher it was time to travel to Sarah Whispers' home.

·60·

While Jim climbed into the driver's seat of the SUV, Kate buckled her passenger seatbelt and Alma Rose slid onto the rear bench seat. Jim drove back onto I-90 and then took exit 530. A series of turns, right onto Route 463, left onto Frontage Road, right down Old Grey Blanket Road, and a right onto George Street over the bridge that spanned Lodge Grass Creek. Then a right onto a dirt trail named Canster Road, and then onto an unnamed dirt road. Then Jim spotted the recognizable trailer amid the barren and dusty homestead.

Sarah Whispers Two Elk was fiercely possessive and protective of her residence and Jim knew it. The two-bedroom trailer still displayed its baby blue color where it hadn't rusted a drab brown. To Jim, it seemed odd not to see Alma Rose's red 1956 Ford pickup truck with its black driver's door, usually parked outside the trailer. Jim caught a mental image of it on the lift in Ernie's Garage back in Taylor.

Jim noticed that the familiar gas grill was gone as were its accompanying table and chair set. Since her liver transplant surgery and recuperation, Sarah Whisper's outdoor leisure time was limited. Jim assumed that Bobby had the grill, table, and chairs removed for good. The ripped window screen had been replaced but the familiar single electrical service wire still ran from the secondary power lines on the dirt path to a standpipe next to the trailer.

Jim always experienced a certain sense of guilt when he visited Sarah Whispers' home. Often he had asked her to allow him to buy her a new home, but she would have none of it.

Jim noticed the door to the trailer open and a woman step outside. It was Becca Running Wolf, Jim's cousin and Alma Rose's aunt.

"*Issaxchí-Káata, Iláaxe-Bía, Sapé-Bíawaaisee*," Becca screamed as she ran to greet them all.

Jim whispered to Kate, "She called me Little Hawk, Alma Rose is Spirit Woman, and you're Music Lady."

Kate smiled and nodded. "All right then. You can be my translator."

All four converged in the front yard and shared a group hug.

Becca turned to Alma Rose. "How's the summer job?"

Alma Rose rolled her eyes and smiled. "Hard work and very stressful but I love it."

Becca then placed her arms around Kate and kissed her on the cheek. "I love you *Sapé-Bíawaaisee*. I haven't seen you since you came home from the hospital two years ago. I pray for you every day."

Kate wiped the moisture from her eyes. "Thank you for the prayers. That's probably why I'm finally feeling well again."

Becca whispered to Kate, "Your husband told me though that you can no longer have children."

Kate nodded and wiped away a tear. "That's right."

Becca hugged her and asked, "Because of that doctor?"

Kate said, "Yes, Hamilton Jackson. But he's in jail now."

Becca pulled away and her face turned to anger. "That evil man, may he never find peace in this world and atone for his sins in the long day of quiet."

Kate reminded Becca. "He was responsible for procuring Sarah Whispers' liver transplant. He saved her life."

Becca pursed her lips and then said. "But how many people had to die so that he could take their organs? Does he think he is *Akbaatatdía*?"

"Who?" Kate asked.

Jim said, "Becca asked does he think he's God."

Alma Rose piped in, "Sometimes we act like we are God, sometimes we cry for God, and sometimes we curse God. The fact is that God is in all of us and God is all around us. We just have to open our eyes and look." Alma Rose took Kate by the hand and said, "Let's go in the house. My mother is waiting."

While Alma Rose and Kate walked ahead, Becca and Jim continued their conversation.

"How's Sarah Whispers doing?" Jim asked.

Becca took a step back. "Better but she still insists on doing the monthly books for her employer in Billings."

Jim asked, "The pharmacy on 1st Avenue North?"

Becca nodded. "Yes. The pharmacist knows Sarah Whispers needs the money and can't drive anymore. He comes to visit the first week of every month and has her do a balance sheet and income statement. Then every three months she does the quarterlies and prepares his taxes every spring for the past two years."

"And she likes doing that?" Jim asked.

Becca replied, "Like I said, she needs the money, but it saps the strength right out of her. Every month she needs a full day of rest to recuperate and the quarterlies keep her in bed for three days."

Jim asked, "What impact do the annual tax filings have on her?"

Becca took a deep breath. "She needs an entire week to recuperate. I'm worried it's too much. It's slowing her recovery."

"Did you tell her doctor?"

Becca replied, "Yes, but he doesn't see her when she's not well. And when she's well enough to go to the doctor's office, I tell him that I'm worried. Then she tells him that she enjoys doing the accounting work. So he tells us it's good that it keeps her mind and body active." Then Becca whispered to Jim, "I think the pharmacist likes her. He got divorced last year."

Jim said, "I'll speak with her."

Then Becca asked, "How's Willie? I heard he got hurt last month and your daughter convinced the Great Spirit to return him to us."

Jim said, "He's doing better. He's in a rehab facility learning to walk again."

Becca smiled. "If you see him, tell him I was thinking about him and that I will send smoke and prayers."

Jim and Becca caught up with Kate and Alma Rose as they approached the front door to the trailer.

Jim said, "Let's go inside and not keep Sarah Whispers waiting. I'm sure that she's peeking out her window."

Jim was the last one to step inside and he found Sarah Whispers leaning on a walker next to the kitchen window.

Little Hawk, you look well," Sarah Whispers said.

Jim responded, "So do you."

Sarah Whispers moved the walker and faced Jim. "Look at me. I'm forty-five years old and I feel as if I'm double that."

Alma Rose gave Sarah Whispers a hug. "Momma, it's only been a week, but I miss you so much."

Sarah Whispers waved her hand. "Go get settled. Jim and Kate will have Alma Rose's room. My daughter will sleep with me."

As Kate and Alma Rose went to put away their overnight bags in the bedrooms, Sarah Whispers called to Jim, "Come here, we need to speak."

"What is it?" Jim asked.

Once Kate and Alma Rose disappeared down the hallway and into the bedrooms, Sarah Whispers said to Jim, "Alma Rose's mother contacted me."

"Shoshanna?" Jim asked.

"Yes."

"Why, after all these years?"

"She heard through a friend that Alma Rose was going to attend college and she wants to help pay for school."

Jim titled his head, pursed his lips, and then said, "Alma Rose has a full scholarship but I'm paying for the rest of her expenses. She doesn't need money from Shoshanna."

Sarah Whispers explained to Jim, "Listen, Shoshanna and her husband are wealthy. He's a doctor and besides, she's her mother and wants to help."

Jim said, "You're Alma Rose's mother."

Sarah Whispers said, "I'm only her mother because the tribal council decided that you and Shoshanna were too young to raise a baby." Sarah Whispers stared at Jim. "You were sixteen and for god sakes, Shoshanna was only fourteen."

Jim sighed. "Must we go through this again?"

Sarah Whispers said, "Yes, our actions live with us for the rest of our lives. As you know, Shoshanna is coming to visit near the end of August. She wants to see Alma Rose."

"I know but why now?" Jim asked.

Sarah Whispers said with a sense of conviction in her voice, "Because you haven't brought your own daughter to see her real mother."

Jim changed the subject, "Do you need groceries?"

Sarah Whispers replied, "I can give you a list."

Jim said, "Good, it'll give me a chance to clear my head."

·61·

Sarah Whispers sat at the kitchen table next to Becca. She gazed at Alma Rose who stared through the screened upper window of the trailer's back door. Sarah Whispers then stood up and glanced out the kitchen window to discover what preoccupied Alma Rose's attention. She spotted Jim, with the grocery list in hand, climb into the rental SUV with Kate. Sarah Whispers watched the vehicle drive off and kick up dust along the dirt path that led away from the trailer.

When the SUV was out of view, Sarah Whispers noticed Alma Rose first turn away from the door and then hurry down the hallway.

"Alma Rose, why are you running?" Sarah Whispers asked.

"Momma, I have to get something from my bag." Alma Rose headed toward her mother's bedroom.

Less than a minute later, Sarah Whispers noticed Alma Rose come out of the bedroom with her overnight bag slung over her shoulder and then dip into her own bedroom where Jim and Kate planned to sleep.

When Alma Rose left the bedroom and headed back down the hallway, Sarah Whispers called to her, "Alma Rose, come here."

Alma Rose stopped in her tracks, placed the overnight bag onto the floor, turned around, and headed into the kitchen. She sat at the table next to Becca, focused on Sarah Whispers and asked, "What is it Momma?"

Sarah Whispers stared at Alma Rose with a quizzical look on her face and then asked, "What did you just put in your bedroom?"

"It's just something I brought with me from Taylor."

"What is it?" Sarah Whispers asked again.

"Momma, do we have to discuss this?"

"Yes we do."

Becca got up from her seat at the kitchen table, faced Sarah Whispers, and said, "Now that your brother and Kate are here, I think I'll go home. Call me if you need me, otherwise I'll be back on Monday."

Sarah Whispers replied, "Thank you Becca. You've been so kind to me. Have a good weekend." Once Becca left the trailer, Sarah Whispers turned her attention back to Alma Rose. "So tell me why did you bring your overnight bag into your bedroom?"

"Momma, there's a woman's talking stick in the bag."

"What woman?"

"She's from the Flathead Reservation."

Sarah Whispers asked, "Did you meet this woman while you were in Taylor?"

"Yes I did Momma."

Sarah Whispers continued her relentless interrogation. "What are you doing with her talking stick?"

Alma Rose replied, "I'm keeping it safe for her. I'll return it when we get back to Taylor."

Sarah Whispers said, "Come here child."

Alma Rose got up and walked over to Sarah Whispers. She leaned over, hugged Sarah Whispers, and received a hug in return.

Alma Rose brushed aside Sarah Whisper's long black hair and spoke softly in her ear, "Momma, I love you."

"I love you too child. I'm so glad you made a new friend. How often do you see this friend of yours?" Sarah Whispers asked.

Alma Rose stepped away from Sarah Whispers. "She comes to visit when she has free time."

"What's her name?"

Alma Rose sat down. "Janice."

"That's such a nice name. I hope I'll meet her someday."

Alma Rose smiled. "You will Momma. We all will."

·62·

Later in the afternoon, Jim and Kate arrived back at Sarah Whispers' trailer, climbed out of the SUV, and then carried the grocery bags inside. They prepared a meal according to the menu instructions from Sarah Whispers' doctor. No salt, no sugar, a small portion of meat, but plenty of vegetables. Jim created a bison stew with green beans, carrots, onions, potatoes and celery while Kate prepared a healthy salad.

Jim sat at the dinner table with Kate seated to his left and Sarah Whispers to his right. Alma Rose sat directly across the table from Jim. They each held hands with the person seated on either side while Jim offered a prayer to the Great Spirit.

He spoke deliberately, "Oh *Akbaatatdia*, the One Who Has Made Everything, we give You thanks for Your great blessings. Please keep us in good health so that we may live to honor You. As Your *wičháša wakȟáŋ*, *Heȟáka Sápa* once said, may we face the wind and walk the good road to the day of quiet."

Jim smiled and released his grip from the hands of Kate and Sarah Whispers. They began dinner with a serving of the Three Sisters soup, a delicious concoction of vegetable stock, yellow corn, kidney beans, chopped onion and celery, canned pumpkin, sage leaves, and curry powder. Once they finished the soup, the main course of bison stew and salad was offered. When dinner was over, Sarah Whispers began to prepare a special treat for dessert to satisfy their palates. She mixed together flour, baking powder, salt, and water. Then she kneaded it and divided the dough into four sections in an oversized skillet. When it was done, she served it warm with coffee.

293

"What is this?" Kate asked.

"*Ba xaawoo pau gua*," Sarah Whispers answered.

Jim turned to Kate and said, "Wheel bread. Better finish it before it gets cold." Jim then noticed Alma Rose's stare. He asked, "What is it?"

Alma Rose replied, "Why did you name me Alma Rose?"

Jim turned to look at Sarah Whispers who smirked and then said, "It's past time to tell her. We should be honest. She's been blinded for far too long."

Jim explained to Alma Rose, "I think you realize that you're named Rose because your grandmother liked roses. She was also gifted as you are."

Alma Rose nodded. "I know that. Grandma Jenny Night Star Two Elk was a medicine woman. But why did you name me Alma. No one else that I know on the Rez is named Alma, why me?"

Jim leaned back in his seat. "There is a woman. She's in her seventies by the name of Alma Hogan Snell. She doesn't live too far from here, on the Rez in Yellowtail."

Alma Rose said, "That's west from Momma's place, it's near the dam. I don't know the people that live there. I either drive to Hardin to shop or go to Crow Agency to visit Acaraho."

Jim noticed Alma Rose drop her head and her voice trail off for just a moment when she mentioned Acaraho Otaktay's name. Although Jim knew that Acaraho was basically a good boy, a few of his family relatives have had their run-ins with the law. However, Jim knew his daughter obviously still had strong feelings for the boy.

Jim continued, "Alma Hogan Snell's grandmother was Pretty Shield and she was a medicine woman. That's why you were named Alma Rose. You are named after two lineages of medicine women. You are our only hope for the future of the *Apsáalooke* culture. You must be true to *Akbaatatdia*. He chose you to receive this gift."

As Alma Rose withdrew a piece of wheel bread from her mouth, Jim noticed tears well up in her eyes. She placed the wheel bread on her dinner plate, got up, and said, "I didn't ask for these expectations. I can't take it anymore. Just leave me alone." Then she turned around, headed down the hallway, disappeared into Sarah Whispers' bedroom, and slammed the door shut.

Kate turned to Jim. "Well, that went over well."

Sarah Whispers said, "She'll get over it. If I only know one thing it's that she self-analyses herself. She'll apologize."

Jim flicked his napkin on his empty plate. "Maybe she's right. There's too many of us placing unusual demands on her. Sometimes I forget that she's only nineteen."

Sarah Whispers stared at Jim, shook her head, and said, "Do you still remember when you were just nineteen?"

Jim nodded. "I was a sophomore at Montana." He turned to Kate. "That's when Kate and I started dating."

Sarah Whispers said, "But no one placed demands on you when you were her age."

Jim countered. "I was a starter at defensive end on the football team. I dealt with prejudice from my teammates. Even the coaches didn't think I could succeed. Then when I was a senior, they awarded me the Outland Trophy as college football's best defensive lineman. Without the dedication and perseverance I wouldn't have attained that level of success."

Sarah Whispers slowly shook her head. "Oh my brother, my poor, foolish brother, how can you even compare playing football with what your daughter is going through?"

Jim grasped the sides of the table with both his hands. "I worked hard to achieve what I've accomplished."

Kate tilted her head slightly and then said, "Jim, Alma Rose has the weight of the world on her shoulders. When you were nineteen the only weight you had to worry about was how many plates were on the bench-press."

Jim was silent for a moment and then said, "Kate..." Then he got up and announced, "I'm going outside. I've got to clear my mind."

·63·

After dinner, Kate and Sarah Whispers sat in the living room as they waited for Jim to return from his walk. Alma Rose sequestered herself in her mother's bedroom and remained there even when Sarah Whispers got up, left the living room, and joined Alma Rose to retire for the evening.

Kate stood up and walked toward the living room's picture window. She observed Jim as he wandered around the property and then noticed him meander and disappear behind a grove of trees along Lodge Grass Creek. Kate knew it was pride that overrode Jim's common sense. She realized that for Jim, a father of a 19-year old and who had only been an active parent for just two years, this experience would become a practical lesson that he needed to experience.

After a few hours, Kate noticed that Jim headed back toward the trailer. She opened the front door and he stepped inside.

"Did you learn anything?" she asked. Kate closed the door behind him and then slipped her bare feet out of her sneakers.

Jim nodded. "I sat for a while on the bank of the crick. It gave me time to think and my thoughts spoke to me."

"And what did they tell you?"

Jim hung his head. "I've always tried to do exactly what others expect of me." Then he stared at Kate and said, "Somehow, I've forgotten that the only thing *Akbaatatdia* wants is for us to be true to ourselves."

Kate stood on her tiptoes to reach Jim's 6'5" height. She pulled down Jim's head, gave him a kiss on the cheek, and then stared into his eyes with a smile on her face. Tonight, Kate sensed something different about the energy in Sarah Whispers trailer. It was all about the here and now. There seemed to be a sense of urgency and a purpose to her thoughts and actions.

Kate reached up again, placed her arms around Jim's neck, and pulled his face down to hers. Kate next planted a kiss on Jim's lips and she felt him respond to her spontaneous act of affection. After a moment in each other's arms, Kate stepped back from him and then took him by the hand. She led Jim toward Alma Rose's empty bedroom and then ducked inside. When Jim walked past Kate she turned around, closed the door, and confronted him.

Kate whispered, "Take off your clothes."

Jim tilted his head, squinted, and then asked in a soft voice, "Did you say you wanted me to take off my clothes?"

Kate reiterated with a devilish smile, "Didn't you hear me sheriff? This is a strip search."

"Kate, what's going on?"

"It's time," she said.

She noticed a grin that began to grow across Jim's face. Kate then watched him sit on the bed and first pull off his boots and then his socks. While Jim stood up to remove his jeans, Kate pulled her shirt up over her head. She then removed her bra and jeans before Jim could finish pulling off his shirt. They each removed their underwear and fell onto the bed in an embrace. Kate felt the full weight of Jim's body press against her.

"Quiet," Kate said with a hush.

Jim nodded and planted a kiss on Kate's cheek. They then shared a long, drawn-out French kiss. Kate then pulled Jim closer to her and wrapped her legs around him.

It had been more than a year and a half, too long since she last felt the urge for intimacy. The loss of their stillborn baby left Kate both physically and emotionally damaged. But now there was a primal drive that overwhelmed her and filled her entire being with a desire to completely receive and experience Jim's full physical expression of love.

They repeatedly made love throughout the night and then as exhaustion set in, they fell asleep between 2 and 3 a.m. As they slept on Alma Rose's bed, with a thin sheet covering their bodies, Jim's head rested on Kate's bosom. His right arm was nestled across her waist and his right leg burrowed between her legs.

Around 6 a.m., Kate felt Jim stir and she opened her eyes. When he propped himself onto his knees, she reached up and wrapped her arms around his neck. She smiled at him and pulled his head down to hers.

"Where do you think you're going?" she asked.

Jim said, "I want to get an early start. Grandfather is visiting today."

She whispered into his ear, "Make love to me again."

Kate noticed a smile grow on Jim's face. They kissed and began another session of lovemaking.

About a half-hour later Kate heard a knock on the bedroom door.

"Who is it?" Jim asked.

"Dad, I need my clothes before I shower."

Kate stared at Jim and said, "Let's get moving."

"Alma Rose, we'll just be a minute," Jim said. He got up and threw on his clothes.

Kate pulled the sheet up to her neck. Jim unfolded the comforter at the foot of the bed and used it to cover Kate. She glanced toward the door as Jim opened it. Alma Rose stood in the doorway wearing a nightgown.

"Good morning," Jim said.

"Good morning dad." Alma Rose glanced over at the bed. "Good morning, Kate."

Kate pulled the covers closer to her neck and smiled. "Good morning, Alma Rose. How are you?"

"I'm okay." Alma Rose stepped inside and looked at her dad. "I need to get some things from my room."

Jim glanced at Kate and said, "We'll be out soon."

Alma Rose asked, "When? I need to shower right now and then make breakfast for my mom."

Jim said, "Kate and I can make breakfast for her. Give us a few minutes."

Alma Rose insisted, "Only Becca and I know the foods that my momma can eat and how she likes them prepared. I need to be careful that I shower before I prepare her breakfast. The drugs my momma takes compromises her immune system. I don't want to introduce germs into her food. I need to shower now."

Kate asked, "Alma Rose, can you give us five minutes? Then we'll be out of your way."

Alma Rose nodded and after she left the room, Jim shut the door. He opened his duffel bag and grabbed a towel. Kate got out of bed, slipped into her bathrobe, and slung her overnight bag onto her shoulder. They stepped into the hallway and while Jim headed for the bathroom, Kate went into the living room and sat in a chair.

When Kate gazed into the kitchen, she thought it odd that Sarah Whispers was not there. Based upon Alma Rose's comments, Kate expected to see Sarah Whispers seated at the table in anticipation of breakfast.

Then Kate turned and saw Alma Rose come out of the other bedroom and go into her bedroom with her canvas bag. After a few minutes, Kate noticed Alma Rose exit her bedroom with the canvas bag slung under her arm and then disappear into her mother's bedroom. Around 7 a.m., Jim joined Kate in the living room.

"I'm done in the bathroom," he said.

Kate nodded and got up. She walked down the hallway past the closed door of Sarah Whisper's bedroom, and into the bathroom.

When Kate was done, she walked down the hallway past Alma Rose's bedroom. Then she heard Sarah Whispers' bedroom door open. She looked back and spotted Alma Rose walk into the bathroom.

Kate stepped into the kitchen to find Jim seated at the table. She caught him with a mouthful of scrambled eggs and toast.

"Where are you off so early today?" she asked.

Jim lifted his index finger in the air and waited to speak. Then he said, "I'm driving into Hardin to pick up a copy of the Taylor Bulletin. I need to find out if they reported anything about what happened in Spaulding."

Kate asked, "Can't you give Rocky or Hank a call and find out?"

Jim explained, "I could, but once Hank and Leon were done at the crime scene because it occurred within the town limits, the Spaulding Police took charge of the investigation. They are a tight-lipped community and loath outsiders. Julie Franklin writes for the Taylor Bulletin and if anyone can extract information about that case it's her."

Kate said, "There's something up with Alma Rose."

"What do you mean?" Jim asked.

"I don't know but she seems to be secretive about something."

Jim finished his breakfast, got up and put on his Stetson. "I'm sure it has to do with taking care of Sarah Whispers. Alma Rose has done so much for her." He kissed Kate on her forehead.

Kate nodded. "Yeah, I guess you're right." Then she asked, "Where's Sarah Whispers?"

"She hasn't gotten up yet," Jim said as he adjusted his two-inch, concealed Colt Python revolver in his right boot.

"Don't you think it odd that Alma Rose said she needed to make her mother breakfast right away? Now it's a half-hour later and there's still no breakfast...and Sarah Whispers is still asleep?"

Jim smiled at Kate and said, "I'm sure that everything's all right. Just leave the investigating to me."

Kate grabbed Jim's arm as he started to walk toward the door. "I liked last night," she said.

Jim turned to her and smiled. "I did too. We should have more nights like that."

Kate caressed his hand and said, "We will."

·64·

An hour later Alma Rose finished serving breakfast to Sarah Whispers. Then she cleaned up the kitchen and assisted Sarah Whispers to the living room. Alma Rose then grabbed the laundry from the clothes dryer and folded them on a wooden bench. Then Kate entered the laundry room.

Alma Rose turned to her and asked, "Is my momma okay?"

Kate replied, "She's fine. She's on the couch reading the newspaper. Can I help with the laundry?"

Without looking up, Alma Rose replied, "No thank you, I've got this." After a brief and uncomfortable moment passed, she continued, "Me and my momma are one of the few families on the Rez who have their own washer and dryer. I bought them for her."

"I know you did. Your father told me."

Alma Rose waved her hand in the air. "This room used to be my closet." She placed a pair of folded sweat pants onto the pile and then stared at Kate. "What else does my father tell you about me?"

Kate turned and closed the door to the laundry room. Then she turned and stepped up behind Alma Rose. "Your father told me that he loves you."

Alma Rose caught her breath, turned, and faced Kate. "He said that?"

Kate placed her hands on Alma Rose's shoulders. "Your father would do anything for you."

Alma Rose stepped back and Kate's hands slipped off her shoulders. Then Alma Rose whispered, "Where has my father been since I was a little girl? I was lied to. I thought Sarah

Whispers was my mother and then I found out that she's really my aunt."

"Oh Alma Rose, that was a long time ago. No one told you because you were too young to understand."

Alma Rose raised her voice. "Everyone told me that my father left the reservation. When I asked who my father was they told me I would find out when I was older. Did everyone think I couldn't deal with the truth?"

Kate said, "They wanted to protect you."

Alma Rose shook her head. "No, I grew up calling my father Uncle Jim. Was that right?" A tear ran down Alma Rose's cheek.

Kate reached out and wiped away Alma Rose's tear. "He always loved you...he still loves you. He wants you to meet your real mother someday."

"When?" Alma Rose asked.

"Soon."

"When will that be?" Alma Rose noticed Kate take a deep breath. Then she asked again, "How soon?"

Kate said, "I'll speak with your father today."

Alma Rose stared at Kate upon hearing those last few words. Then she reached out, hugged Kate, and rested her head on Kate's shoulder.

There was a knock on the door. Kate turned and opened it. Sarah Whispers stood in the hallway.

"Is something wrong? I heard yelling," Sarah Whispers said.

Alma Rose replied, "No momma. Everything is all right."

·65·

Hardin was a typical Montana town, a jumping-off place along I-90. Gas stations, a truck stop, pickup trucks, one-floor single-family homes, mobile homes, a few bars with slot machines, liquor stores within close proximity of the Crow Reservation, the occasional Bureau of Indian Affairs patrol car, and dust everywhere kicked up by the springtime winds off the high plains.

Jim parked in front of Custer's Supermarket and went inside. He surveyed the expansive newspaper rack and found what he was looking for. He paid the cashier and returned to his rental SUV to read the Taylor Bulletin.

The front page screamed to Jim: Moon Man Returns.

As expected, Julie Franklin had written an article not just about the mysterious disappearance of Janice Driver but she linked Janice's unknown whereabouts to the apparent murder of Louise Leonard.

Jim read on.

"Take a sharp instrument, vulnerable women, mix in the dead of night, along with a dash of déjà vu and you've got the recipe for what happened in the towns of Mallory and Spaulding last week. Within just twenty-four hours, two innocent women suffered horrific deaths in their own homes as they faced off against pure evil."

Jim couldn't read anymore and threw the paper down on the passenger front seat. He rubbed his eyes and then grabbed his cellphone and dialed a familiar number. He placed the phone on speaker.

"Kelly speaking."

"Hank, did you read Franklin's piece in the Bulletin?"

"Sure did, but I made the mistake of reading it over breakfast."

"Hank, what information are you able to tell me about what happened to Louise Leonard?"

"Well Jim, I can say that it was the most violent one yet. The crime scene tells me that we're not dealing with a murderer, this is a monster. Louise Leonard's body was missing but most of her organs were strewn about the room. It was as if someone literally ripped her apart."

Jim asked, "Any chance Gary Driver killed Louise Leonard?"

"Well Jim, we know that Driver is still in the Mallory jail and by the condition of the organs, I place Leonard's death sometime early Tuesday morning. Gary Driver could not have killed Louise Leonard. He was sitting in jail in Mallory."

"How about Mac Drew?" Jim asked.

"Not likely. They brought Mac Drew in for questioning on Monday evening and held him under lock and key until they released him for lack of evidence on Friday morning. A relative drove him straight to rehab. He's been there ever since."

Jim exhaled. "Any other leads?"

Hank replied, "Dan McCoy's been assisting but we have no suspects in either case."

"Okay, then do what you have to do and fill me in when I get back. I'll be on the first flight from Billings tomorrow."

Jim hung up his phone and threw it on the seat next to the newspaper.

"Dammit."

·66·

When Jim returned to Sarah Whispers' trailer he recognized the 1964 red Chevy Impala sedan parked outside and knew who was visiting. The car was more than thirty years old but the lacquer finish was in near mint condition and the white leather interior was impeccably spotless.

Jim stepped inside the trailer and first spotted Kate and Alma Rose seated at the kitchen table. At one end of the living room couch he saw the owner of the Chevy Impala, his half-brother, Bobby Rides in Clouds Two Elk. Bobby was nearly six-feet tall and lean, with waist-length black hair dressed in bones, feathers, and beads. He wore a green tank top that exposed his muscular shoulders, jeans, and moccasins.

Bobby was forty-eight years old, three years older than Sarah Whispers who sat next to him. At the far end of the couch was the family patriarch, Grandfather Red Hawk. Known to his family as Cecil Gordon Two Elk, his Native name Red Hawk, or spoken in the Crow language as *Chilaxchíipshiile*, referred to the bird that white men simply referred to as a Red-tailed Hawk.

The accumulation of eighty-four years was plainly illustrated on Red Hawk's face. Summer days spent under the hot Montana sun and those long, cold winters endured on the windblown high plains had long ago plastered leathery wrinkles on Red Hawk's neck, lips, nose, cheeks, eyes, and forehead. He wore a pair of baggy blue work pants and a red, long-sleeved checkerboard flannel shirt.

Bobby got up from the couch and spoke first. "Brother Jim how are you?"

"I'm fine, how's grandfather?"

Red Hawk shifted his position on the couch and gazed upwards at Jim. After a brief pause, he spoke in the *Apsáalooke* language, "*Chilinníate xaalíakaashe*."

Bobby said, "He says he feels very old."

Kate got up from the kitchen table and walked over to Jim's side. She looped her arm around Jim's waist. "I'm so happy to see your family together." She called to Alma Rose, "Come here with us."

Alma Rose got up from the table and walked over to Jim's side across from Kate.

Red Hawk began to tremble. Then with a shaking hand, he raised it to his face and wiped away tears from both his eyes. He then glanced at Bobby and spoke in *Apsáalooke*, "*Baapéesh bíihe Báakkaammaaschiile...Issaxchí-Káata*."

Jim gazed at Bobby with a question written on his face.

Bobby explained, "Grandfather said today is an honor from God. He wants to spend the rest of the evening speaking with you."

Jim asked, "I know God as *Akbaatatdía*. I never heard the word, *Báakkaammaaschiile* before. What does it mean?"

Bobby explained, "Grandfather speaks of the Old Age when our people lived by the Great Water. The white man now calls it Lake Erie. When we lived there our people were visited by the God of the Sky World. He visited all the different chiefs of our *Apsáalooke* Nation and He told them of the Death Journey that our souls must cross the day we die. It's the ancient passageway from Cygnus to Orion. When we each complete that journey then we return to our people's origins."

Jim asked, "Do you mean the Path of Souls? The white man describes that as the tunnel they encounter in near-death experiences."

"Yes, that's what it is. *Báakkaammaaschiile* is the old name our people gave to Him, our God. Our chiefs from the Old Age gave *Báakkaammaaschiile* a place of honor to stay with them in their tipis. *Báakkaammaaschiile's* name has been in our *Apsáalooke* culture since before there were horses, and before the white man stepped foot on our land. Grandfather believes that today, because we are all together as a family in Sarah Whispers' tipi, we have reciprocated our ancestors' gift to *Báakkaammaaschiile*. It's a special message from Him and He tells us not to forget about Him."

A cold shiver ran up Jim's spine as he pulled up a chair. Jim and Red Hawk spoke for hours. They touched on Jim's youth, his time on the Crow Reservation until he was sixteen, and then when he abruptly left to live with his birth father, Angus Buchanan. Jim and Red Hawk then discussed Jim's mother Jenny Nightstar Two Elk and her sacred calling as the tribe's spirit woman.

Then Red Hawk compared the blessed gifts of Jenny Nightstar and Jim's daughter Alma Rose. He spoke of how these *Apsáalooke* spiritual blessings skipped a generation. Red Hawk reminded Jim that Alma Rose needs to visit with her birth mother, Shoshanna. Jim agreed and said that would happen soon.

Red Hawk touched on Jim's relationship with his half-siblings, Sarah Whispers and Bobby Rides in Clouds. Then Jim felt disarmed when Red Hawk asked him what he has done with his life since he left the reservation. It was a reckoning that Jim was utterly unprepared for.

Jim said, "I went to college, played football, and won the Outland Trophy in my senior year. I played in the NFL for three years and was MVP in the Super Bowl. I served four years in the United States Air Force as an MP. I was a Montana highway patrolman for two years, and then was elected sheriff of Cedar County."

Red Hawk smiled and in a burst of English said, "A lot of accomplishments for one so young. Isn't it?"

Jim replied, "I always gave it my best effort."

Red Hawk grew a stern look on his face and then stared at Jim. He pointed to his heart with his index finger and asked Jim, "But what have you done here?" Red Hawk then moved his finger to his temple. "And what have you learned here? We do not move forward in this world until we empty our hearts and minds of hate, envy, and pride and fill our hearts with love and our minds with compassion. Only then will we discover what the Great Spirit has in store for us."

Red Hawk saved a portion of their meeting to discuss Jim's relationship with Kate and the loss of their stillborn baby, Jonathan a year and a half ago. Red Hawk told Jim that he was sure that Jonathan was looking down at them from the stars. Red Hawk said that he believed Jonathan knew it was not the time for him to enter into this world and that a time would come someday when he would return.

It was late into the evening when Bobby interrupted their conversation to bring things back down to earth. "Little Hawk, grandfather is getting very tired. I need to bring him back to my house and I have to get up early for work tomorrow."

Jim said, "I have to get up early too. We have a flight from Billings to Taylor that leaves at 8:45 in the morning so we need to get up a few hours earlier than that." Jim touched Bobby's left forearm with his right hand. "I'm pleased that you took in grandfather."

Bobby nodded. "Thank you. He no longer can live alone. During the day, Rita sees to his needs."

"How is your wife?" Jim asked.

"Rita is fine. Next month will be our thirtieth wedding anniversary."

Jim asked, "How are the kids?"

Bobby smiled. "They're all grown up. Both married and moved away but we stay in touch. You should see them."

Jim then spoke with clarity in his voice. "This is my last year as sheriff. I need to spend more time with my family."

·67·

Jim, Kate, and Alma Rose took the morning flight from Billings and arrived at Taylor International Airport just before 10 a.m. As they drove up the driveway to Jim and Kate's house, Alma Rose noticed that her pickup truck was parked facing the garage doors.

Jim said, "I got a call from Ernie's Garage over the weekend. They fixed your truck."

Alma Rose asked, "What was wrong with it?"

Jim replied, "The bearing in your water pump wore out. You're lucky the engine didn't seize. They replaced your water pump and I had them look at and take care of a few other things that needed fixing. Your truck's as good as new."

"Thanks Dad. How much do I owe you?"

"It's on me."

"No dad, tell me how much I owe."

Jim reiterated, "I took care of it."

Kate turned to look at Jim. "If she wants to pay for the repairs herself, let her."

"Dad, Kate's right. I'm a grownup so treat me like one."

"Okay, with the sheriff's department discount, it came to $550."

Alma Rose nodded. "Okay, I'll write you a check tonight."

They got out of the SUV and Alma Rose headed toward the truck. She opened the driver's side door and dropped her overnight bag inside. Then she heard her father call to her.

"Alma Rose, you can do your laundry in the house."

"Dad, I'm going to test the truck. I'll be back in a couple of hours. Will you be home?"

Jim said, "Today is Louis Miller's first day of work at the highway department in Mallory and I'm giving him a ride."

Alma Rose said, "He told me about the job. Thanks for doing that."

Jim added, "His boss, Easy is a stickler for promptness and I've already gone out of my way to convince him to move up Louis' reporting time to noon."

Alma Rose asked, "You'll be back in Taylor after that?"

Jim replied, "First, I'm picking up Angel and Shadow. Then, after I'm done at the highway department, I'm heading to the police station to coordinate the transfer of Gary Driver from the Mallory Police to the Cedar County Sheriff's Office. I'm taking custody of Mister Driver from Detective Aronowitz at one o'clock and transporting him to the county jail. Then we have to process him, file the required paperwork, and evaluate and classify his protective status. Would you like to attend later this afternoon? I think it would be beneficial for your internship requirements."

Alma Rose winced. "Gary Driver doesn't deserve to be arraigned. He's innocent."

Jim replied, "That may be true but it's up to the court to decide."

Alma Rose spoke with conviction in her voice, "Dad, Gary Driver's case will not make it to court."

·68·

Jim changed into his sheriff's uniform and then drove to the Taylor Police Station. He went inside, up to Captain Linda Stevens' office, and spotted Angel and Shadow as they lie quietly behind her desk. Jim thanked Linda for dog-sitting Angel and Shadow during the weekend while he was visiting his sister. Jim brought his two dogs outside the police station and secured them inside his SUV.

Then he drove to the Miller's home and spotted Louis as he stood outside. Jim nodded to him and Miller climbed into the passenger side of Jim's SUV.

Louis Miller looked into the back of the SUV and noticed Angel and Shadow. "Who called in the hounds?"

Jim said, "They're my dogs."

Louis laughed. "Oh, pets then?"

"Yes and no. They're faithful companions at home but they're also trained service dogs."

Louis nodded. "Trained for what?"

Jim replied, "Shadow, the German Shepherd is a single-purpose dog. He's used for backup, personal protection, and tracking."

Louis turned to Jim and then asked, "What about the other dog? I never saw a dog like that with all those spots."

Jim laughed. "Angel's a German Shorthaired Pointer. Those spots are called ticking. She's had a lot more experience than Shadow. Angel is a true dual-purpose dog. She can do everything that Shadow can do but she's also trained to detect either explosives or narcotics. She's also trained in search and rescue."

"Can they capture criminals?" Louis asked.

Jim winked at Louis. "Apprehension and attack dogs."

313

Louis visibly shuddered and then he faced forward in his seat. "Promise me one thing, sheriff."

"What's that?" Jim asked.

Louis replied, "If you decide to stop somewhere on our way to Mallory, please don't leave me alone with them."

Jim said with a straight face, "As long as you don't move a muscle, they won't tear you limb from limb." Jim noticed Louis' blank stare. Jim's tongue-in-cheek posture slowly evaporated and then he said, "I'm only kidding."

Louis breathed a sigh of relief. "Okay. I get it." He smiled at Jim. "Sheriff, you're a cool dude. Alma Rose is lucky to have you as her dad."

Jim replied, "And I'm lucky to have her as my daughter."

They shared a smile and then Jim drove off. When they reached the town of Mallory, Jim parked outside the public works building and left the SUV windows open for Angel and Shadow. Jim walked up the building's front steps and went inside with Louis a stride or two behind. Jim located Lyndon Bell behind his desk in the back corner of the office.

Jim called aloud, "Bell, thanks for accommodating us."

Lyndon Bell got up from his desk and offered his hand to Jim. "Sheriff, I'm so glad to see you again. Is this our new employee, the rich kid from back east that needs to learn a lesson or two?" Lyndon smiled at Louis.

Jim said, "Yes, he's ready to get started."

"Good. Right this way young fella. I'll introduce you to your new boss."

Jim and Louis followed Lyndon through a door that led to a back office. Lyndon said, "Easy, here's your new trainee."

Louis stood next to Jim with a grin from ear to ear. He said, "Mister Sheppard, when do I start?"

"Hey kid, call me Easy, everyone does." Easy got up from his desk and smiled.

When Jim saw that Louis was about to respond he whispered to him, "Keep your mouth shut."

Easy walked past a half dozen other employee desks and made his way toward the front of the back office to greet Jim and Louis. He then asked, "What's your name kid?"

"Louis Miller."

Easy paused and his eyes widened. "Really now, you don't say?" Easy chuckled and then continued, "Well, Louis is just a little bit sissified for Montana. We'll call you Louie."

Louis' voice crackled. "My name is Louis, not Louie."

Easy laughed. "Listen here kid, quit your bellyaching. A good-lookin' fella like you gotta go by Louie, not Louis." Easy then turned to the other employees. "Hey, this here's Louie Miller and he's going to be working with us the rest of the summer." Then Easy addressed Jim, "Leave him here with me. I'll give him a tour and then Lyndon said that he'd have him back in Taylor by the end of the day. That okay with you Jim?"

Jim nodded. "It is." He glanced down at Louis. "Are you all right with that?"

Louis said, "Do I have a choice, sheriff?"

Easy laughed and then responded, "As much of a choice as a drunken sailor has a chance of walking a straight line." Then he added, "Don't worry, with all the hard-earned cash you'll be earning from the overtime this summer, the babe's will be coming out of the woodwork, sneaking around the corner, searching for you."

Jim said, "Okay Louis, I guess you're good to go."

Louis turned to Easy, "Can I speak with the sheriff before he leaves?"

Easy glanced at Jim. "Is that all right with you, sheriff?"

"Sure."

"Good then I'll leave you two to together. You can talk in there." Easy pointed to the conference room at the far end of the office.

Once Jim closed the door to the conference room, he turned to Louis and asked, "What's up?"

Louis faced Jim and said, "I apologize for everything that's happened, the accident and my wise-ass remarks."

Jim asked, "Is that all?"

Louis stared at Jim. "Is there anything else?"

Jim replied, "My daughter, Alma Rose."

"What about her?" Louis asked.

Jim pressed on. "What're your intentions? I don't want you to break her heart. She has her whole life ahead of her."

Louis shook his head and smiled. "Sheriff Buchanan, your daughter is a remarkable young woman. I know she's way out of my league. She's going to do a lot of good in this world. I'm just a playboy gearhead. Someday when I'm in my forties, I'll decide to settle down and marry someone. In the meantime I would never harm Alma Rose and she's smart enough to know that I'm not the guy for her."

"Why the sudden change of heart?" Jim asked.

"I took your daughter's suggestion to see a therapist. I had my first appointment on Saturday. I've got a lot of work to do but I now know where and when I went off the rails. I now realize what I have to do. It's something I've thought about. Something that I've always wanted to tell a special girl but never had the courage to do so before. I'm going to tell her soon."

Jim nodded. "Then good luck and thank-you." He shook hands with Louis and left.

·69·

Jim drove to and pulled into the parking lot of the Mallory Police Station. He brought Angel and Shadow inside with him. Jim strode up to the front desk, and asked for Detective Martin Aronowitz. He was told to wait and sat on a bench seat across from the front door. Angel sat beside Jim and Shadow sat next to her. Jim noticed Attorney Jeremy Bowers in an arm chair at one end of the lobby. Bowers got up, lifted a briefcase off the floor, and made his way to the bench.

He offered his hand to Jim. "Sheriff Buchanan, are you here to escort Mister Driver to the county jail?"

Jim stood up and shook his hand. Then he took a step back. "Attorney Bowers, yes I have a court order to transfer the prisoner to the Cedar County Jail. With only two jail cells, the Mallory Police Station was never meant for long-term incarceration. Mister Driver's arraignment is scheduled for this afternoon."

"Well Sheriff Buchanan, I have a pending writ of Habeas Corpus. Gary Driver was detained without probable cause and without evidence that he was in the area when and where Janice Driver disappeared."

Jim said, "We have a very high degree of suspicion that Janice Driver is dead."

Bowers nodded. "Unfortunately I have to agree with you but I am also positive that Mister Driver had nothing to do with her demise. Municipal Court Judge Adam Steele is reviewing my petition right now and I'm hoping that he will issue a court order before Mister Driver's arraignment. My only intent is that as an innocent man, Mister Driver not be subjected to the indignity of facing a false charge that he was responsible for his own wife's death."

317

After they spoke for a few minutes, Detective Martin Aronowitz and two police officers entered the lobby alongside Cedar County Chief Prosecutor Emily Cronin. Marty and Emily greeted Jim as Angel and Shadow sat and waited for Jim's next command.

Jim nodded to Emily. "Attorney Cronin, it's been a while. How are you?"

She responded, "I'm fine." Then she turned to Attorney Bowers. "Well, are you ready to get sent to the cleaners in court?"

Bowers responded, "With all due respect, Ms. Cronin, I believe that my client is innocent."

"Innocent?" Emily laughed. "Gary Driver was arrested at the crime scene with the town drunk as his alibi."

Marty added, "That town drunk has a name."

Emily spoke with sarcasm in her voice, "I'm so sorry Detective Aronowitz. Did I hit a nerve?"

Marty responded, "We released Mac Drew on Friday morning. We couldn't hold him. We determined that he didn't have anything to do with Janice Driver's disappearance. And as a far as your opinion of his weakness for alcohol, I'll have you know that his nephew picked him up and checked him into a rehab facility."

Emily stared at Jim and then said, "Well, that makes my case that much easier to prove. No one will believe anything Mister Drew has to say even if he's deemed fit to appear in court."

Bowers repeated, "Again, with all due respect Ms. Cronin, my client was merely returning to his home and his wife went missing while he was away."

Emily smirked and then said, "Oh but you have so much to learn, Mister Bowers. Janice Driver was a blood donor and on her donor card inside her pocketbook was her blood type, A+ the same blood type that was on her husband's clothes and in the car that he was driving."

Attorney Bowers took a deep breath, pursed his lips, and then said, "Ms. Cronin, I did the leg work and researched their marriage license application which apparently you didn't. Both Janice and Gary Driver have the same blood type, A+."

Attorney Cronin looked away and snapped, "We'll meet in court." She turned to Jim and Marty. "Goodbye gentlemen, I have a murder case to prepare for."

Once she left through the front door Marty turned to Jim. "Sheriff Buchanan, you're early."

Jim shook Marty's hand and said, "I want to ensure that we safely transfer Mister Driver."

"You don't have to worry about that," Marty said. He stared at Attorney Bowers. "Well, if you're here to speak with the prisoner, he's unavailable."

Attorney Bowers said, "No sir, I'm not here to speak with my client. I planned to meet Sheriff Buchanan in Taylor and be present for Mister Driver's arraignment."

Marty replied, "Good, you do that."

With that last comment, Attorney Bowers said goodbye to both men. After Bowers left the building Jim gazed through the front windows and spotted Bowers climb into his car. Jim heard Marty's voice crackle.

"Hey wake up. Are you daydreaming?" Marty asked.

"What, what did you say?" Jim asked.

"I said, you can back up your SUV to the rear parking lot and we'll escort Driver out of the building. Didn't you hear me?"

Jim said, "I was watching Bowers get into his car."

Marty replied, "That's clearly obvious. Please try and stay attentive escorting the prisoner."

Jim said, "I notice that you don't have a sally port."

In a fit of sarcasm, Marty said, "Not many of us can make a boast that Governor Ross has our back."

Jim challenged him. "And what do you mean by that?"

"Come on Jim, he built a state of the art law enforcement facility for the county. What favors did you do for him?"

Jim said, "I had nothing to do with that. Ross allocated money from the capital projects fund. You know that a committee reviews the proposed capital projects for the state. Cedar County was due for construction of a major capital facilities project."

Marty raised his arms in the air. "Well when will the town of Mallory be due for some of those so-called capital improvement projects?" He then returned his hands to his side.

Jim replied, "I can't answer that. You might want to ask the governor when he plans to invest in the town of Mallory?"

Marty shook his head. "I can sure as hell tell you that when he does, that's when you'll see a goddamn sally port in my building. Until then we don't have any money in the budget."

Jim said, "I'll tell you that a sally port makes transferring a prisoner that much easier and safer. Almost two weeks ago when the FBI captured and transported Videl Tanas to our county jail, they brought him to Taylor in an armored vehicle. We opened the sally port doors and they drove right in. We had no problem getting him from the sally port into the building where we then processed him and locked him up."

Marty responded, "Well then, I got to get me one of them there Sally Porters. I'll call the governor tomorrow and demand that the Mallory Police Station needs one. Now let's see about transferring Mister Driver the goddamned old-fashioned way."

Marty opened the door to the officer proper and invited Jim to follow. They headed toward Gary Driver's jail cell. Angel and Shadow followed Jim as he held their leashes in his left hand.

Jim asked, "I'm very concerned about what I've heard regarding Julie Franklin, the news reporter for KTAY in Taylor. She seems to be privy to confidential information regarding the recent disappearances."

Marty said, "I know what you mean. Last evening she spoke about the disappearances and..."

Jim interrupted Marty, "On the Channel 2 News at six p.m.?"

Marty corrected Jim. "No, she hosted an exposé, as she called it, during prime time regarding the disappearances. She said it was the first in a series of reports called *Crime in our Own Backyard*."

Jim asked, "She used those exact words?"

Marty said, "Do you know what else she said about Gary Driver? Franklin also found out from the Driver's family doctor that Janice was pregnant and mentioned it on the air."

Jim shook his head. "Now she's playing with fire."

Marty asked, "What do you mean?"

Jim continued, "Anything that appears in the news cycle influences people by changing their minds or reinforcing their prejudices. Today it may only affect the conversations people have in their homes or cars but tomorrow a person may decide to act upon their fears and hurt someone."

Marty stood silent for a moment and then said, "Nothing like that is going to happen here. Go get your car and move it around back. I'll meet you there with the prisoner."

Jim headed toward the front of the building with Angel and Shadow in tow. He opened the front door and ran down the granite steps. He secured Angel and Shadow in the back of his SUV, then removed his Stetson in his left hand, and wiped the perspiration from his brow with the sleeve of his uniform. As the warmth of the sun beat down upon his head, his cellphone rang.

"Buchanan here, who is it…yeah Dan, I know we were supposed to talk today. I have a lot going on. I'm in Mallory right now…what did you learn in Spaulding about the disappearance of Louise Leonard…really, that's interesting. She used to live in Mallory back in the 80s…what did you say…WHAT, are you sure…hold on, I have to sit down."

Jim took a seat on the wall in front of the police station. Then he resumed his call.

"Dan, are you sure about what you're telling me…it can't be…are you sure…I can't believe it…well, if it's true then we're, we're looking for a real monster…do you have time to drop by my house tonight and share that information with me…yes, all of it…Agent Harris and Hank will be there too, why…okay, I can't wait to hear what they have to say, see you later."

Jim ended the call, ran to his SUV, climbed inside, and slammed the door shut. Jim placed his forearms on the steering wheel and then rested his head on his arms. He thought about Gary Driver, the missing women, and his decision to not run for sheriff in the fall. But mostly he thought about what Dan had just told him on the phone.

Jim drove around to the back of the building and parked next to the rear door alongside a loading dock. Jim got out of his SUV and waited. After a few minutes, the rear door opened and Gary Driver, wearing leg irons, handcuffs, and a belly chain, was led outside by Detective Aronowitz.

Jim opened the rear door of his SUV and called out, "Mister Driver, please this way."

As Gary Driver shuffled toward the SUV, Jim heard a distinct high-pitched sonic crack fly past his head. A sudden impact into Gary Driver's chest knocked him off his feet. Jim felt the immediate splash of blood spatters plaster his face and uniform. In an instant, Jim dropped to the ground, slid next to Gary Driver and propped himself over Gary's body to shelter him from further gunshots. Jim drew his Colt Python revolver and then looked down to see the life slip away from Gary Driver's eyes. With Detective Aronowitz also on the ground and on the lookout for an active shooter, the two law enforcement officers slid behind Jim's SUV for cover. Inside the SUV, Angel and Shadow paced in the back.

·70·

Alma Rose met Acaraho for lunch at Lucy's. When they were done, they tailgated at their vehicles in the back parking lot. Acaraho handed her a rolled up paper bag. Alma Rose placed it in her canvas bag and then set the canvas bag in her truck with care. Then they left the parking lot separately.

Alma Rose drove her pickup truck to the rear of the Cedar County Sheriff's Office. She then rode the elevator to the upper basement. When the doors opened she stepped outside with the canvas bag over her shoulder and headed toward the evidence locker.

She ran her card key through the reader, waited for the buzzer to sound, and then entered the evidence locker. Alma Rose placed the canvas bag on the locker room desk and zipped it open. When she lifted the talking stick from inside the bag, she heard a weeping sound emanate from the depths of the evidence locker.

Alma Rose turned and stared into the corner of the room. She noticed a green and yellow mist that evolved into the hunched-over shape of a Native woman covering her face with her hands.

"Janice Driver?" Alma Rose asked.

She saw the shape of the woman drop her hands to her side, and then turn and stare at her.

"Why do you call me?" the spirit of Janice Driver asked.

Alma Rose replied, "I'm worried about you. Why are you crying?"

"A tragedy occurred that should never have happened."

Alma Rose asked, "What tragedy?"

"My husband has left this world and soon I'll meet him."

323

"Gary Driver is dead?"

The spirit of Janice Driver said, "Yes."

"That's not possible," Alma Rose said.

"It happened."

"How?"

The spirit of Janice Driver responded. "He was killed."

Alma Rose said, "So you will see him. In a way that's good, right?"

The spirit of Janice Driver screamed, "No, he had more to accomplish on this Earth."

"I'm sorry," Alma Rose said. "What can I do?"

The spirit of Janice Driver asked, "Do you know Psalm 91?"

Alma Rose said, "It starts with, *Whoever dwells in the shelter of the Most High will rest in the shadow of the Almighty.* I know it by heart. Preacher Running Wolf taught it to me in Sunday School."

The spirit of Janice Driver said, "Please pray that psalm for my dear husband. Make sure that your father captures the right person who has done this."

"Do you know who killed Gary Driver?" Alma Rose asked.

The spirit of Janice Driver said, "A man who has killed before."

Alma Rose asked, "And who is that?"

The woman said, "I must go now. Gary is waiting and I must help him find his place in our new world."

With that last comment, the woman began to fade from view and then was gone.

Alma Rose put the talking stick down on the table in the evidence room and reached back into the bag. She pulled out the rolled up paper bag and removed the facsimile Blackfeet talking stick that Acaraho had purchased in Browning over the weekend. She placed it in the evidence box and then took Janice Driver's talking stick and placed it in the paper bag and then in the canvas bag. Alma Rose left the evidence locker, went back to her pickup truck, and secured the canvas bag under her seat and locked her truck.

·71·

Jim stood up as all chaos broke out. Two officers ran from the police station to the parking lot. They secured and then attended to Gary Driver's corpse. With no other gunshots emanating from the building across the street, Detective Martin Aronowitz bolted from the parking lot and toward that building. Jim sped after him. They ran past four dark-colored vans that served as Howard Lake Brewery's delivery trucks for shipments to local bars and package stores. Jim reached the building just as Marty stood at the entrance. Marty gazed at the upper floors, drew back his sport jacket, and pulled his snub-nosed revolver from his shoulder holster.

Jim asked, "What did you see?"

Marty replied, "I spotted a muzzle flash from a third floor open window. I don't see anyone up there now but I believe the shooter is still there."

"What is this building?" Jim asked.

"It used to be the Mallory Daily Register. When the newspaper went out of business, they repurposed the building into the Howard Lake Brewery. The upper floors were tuned into office and warehouse space."

Just then, four additional Mallory Police officers arrived from across the street.

Marty turned to them. "Paul, stay here and guard the front entrance. Roger, go around back and post up at the rear entrance and keep an eye on the fire escape. Ed and Steve, you two come with the sheriff and me. We're going inside."

When the law enforcement officers entered the building, the brewery workers stopped and huddled against the walls. One of the employees reached up with his hand and hit a large red button which shut down the noisy conveyor belt system.

Once the glass bottles on the conveyor belt stopped clanking against one another, the entire building went silent.

Marty ordered, "Steve, check these men out and make sure that none of them are the suspect we're looking for. Ed, stand guard at the elevator. If anyone opens that door, greet them with the barrel of your service revolver."

Marty and Jim ran up the steps. When they reached the second floor landing, they huddled against the wall near the door to the second floor.

Jim suggested, "We should sweep the second floor before we go upstairs. We'll need more officers."

"Stay here," Marty ordered. "We don't have time to call in more officers. I'm going upstairs. I know the landscape. Keep an eye on the stairwell in case the shooter escapes from the third floor. If you hear a gunshot and the shooter comes down these stairs, then you better be ready to pop 'em one."

Jim watched Marty run upstairs, heard the door to the third floor open and then close. Jim turned his attention to the stairwell and looked upward toward the third floor.

"Dammit," Jim said. He shook his head, led with his revolver, and opened the second floor door just a crack. He spotted the open doors of the freight elevator and its birdcage-like enclosure.

When Jim swung the second floor door wide open, a gunshot sailed past his head and chipped away part of the plywood-covered wall. Jim ran inside and the door swung closed behind him. He returned fire and engaged the suspect. Jim spotted someone dart in and among the many pallets of beer kegs and beer crates. As the exchange of gunfire continued, rifle bullets exploded into multiple beer kegs. Torrents of beer and suds gushed from the kegs and flooded the warehouse floor.

The door behind Jim swung open. He swiveled his head to see who it was and saw Detective Aronowitz run up to him, his gun cocked.

Jim's peripheral vision caught the shooter dash toward an adjacent room in the warehouse. Marty fired at the fleeing suspect but missed. Jim and Marty ran toward the suspect but Marty slipped on the beer laced floor and fell flat on his back banging his head on the concrete floor. Jim ran toward the door but just as he entered the adjacent room, he spotted the butt of a 30-06 Springfield bolt action rifle.

Jim ducked at the last minute but still caught the full force of the weapon against his right cheek. He fell facedown onto the floor and felt the warm blood surge down his face and onto his lips.

From his prone position, Jim spotted a lanky man in black work boots and a green workwear outfit leap over him and run toward the doorway. Jim lifted his head and saw the suspect leap over a dazed Marty, then slip on the beer suds and fall. Jim pushed himself up and pursued the suspect who got up and ran toward the stairwell. Jim sprinted toward the door, reached out, grabbed at the suspect's shoulder at the top of the stairway, and pulled him down.

The suspect fell onto his back as the rifle tumbled from his grasp, plummeted down the stairs, and ended on the first floor landing. Jim fell to the side of the suspect, then got up on his knees, aimed his revolver at the man, and noticed the man's green ballcap with the logo that read, Howard Lake Brewery.

"You're under arrest for the murder of Gary Driver. You have the right to remain..."

The suspect interrupted Jim and in a labored cockney accent said, "You daft cow, I need a doctor."

The man held onto his left arm. Blood oozed between his fingers and Jim realized that one of his bullets hit its mark.

When the suspect got onto his knees, he reached for his bleeding bicep. "I'm shot."

Jim pulled back the hammer of his revolver and yelled, "Get on your belly."

"Well that's blooming marvelous. Yer just shot me in me bloody arm."

Jim replied, "If you don't cooperate, I'll shoot again."

The man said, "Go ahead, nick me again. I'll be glad ter explain why Gary Driver deserved ter die."

Jim barked an order, "Get on your stomach, right now."

Jim was distracted by the hurried footsteps up the stairs from two officers from the first floor and looked down the stairwell. The commotion was enough for the man to slide his right arm off his left bicep and reach inside his waistband. He pulled out a Colt model Junior and just before he fired a .22 Short bullet, Jim turned to look at the man. Jim realized he was caught in the Killing Zone.

Jim instinctively stood up, raised his left hand to his face, and squeezed the hammer on his Colt Python. The .357

Magnum round sliced into the man's chest and drove him back onto the floor. The man's .22 caliber bullet entered Jim's raised hand at the third joint of his little finger, slid along the bony contour of the side of his palm, exited at the base of his wrist, and embedded itself in the wall.

Jim screamed in pain. He lost muscle control of his left hand and it dropped to his side. He glanced down and noticed his hand drenched in blood. Jim touched his face again and ran his right hand down his neck. He felt a trail of wetness down his neck and under his shirt.

It was then that he heard Marty stagger up behind him as the two police officers arrived from the first floor. Jim dropped to his knees and the revolver slipped from his hand. Then he fell off to one side and slipped into unconsciousness. The two officers passed the suspect's lifeless body on the landing and ran to Jim's aid.

·72·

An ambulance arrived at Howard Lake Brewery in a matter of minutes to transport Jim and Marty to Cedar County Hospital. On the way there Jim lapsed in and out of consciousness. The ER doctor treated Jim's bullet wound and gave him a tetanus shot, an antibiotic injection, and a script for an antibiotic. Marty was treated for a superficial head wound but fortunate for him, he had no concussion. Dan McCoy, ever his ear to the scanner, heard of Jim's injury in the line of duty, then contacted Kate and Alma Rose and drove them to the hospital. Rocky and a deputy arrived in Mallory to return Jim's SUV to Taylor along with Angel and Shadow.

Later in the afternoon, as soon as the suspect's body was secured, Hank and Leon arrived on scene and took custody of Gary Driver's corpse. Once Jim was discharged from the ER, Dan drove Jim, Kate, and Alma Rose to the crime scene. While Kate and Alma Rose sat in Dan's car, Jim and Dan stood outside the van marked with the insignia of the Cedar County Office of the State Crime Lab. Jim's left hand was dressed in gauze and wrapped in an Ace bandage. His injured right cheek was covered by a sterile dressing. Hank walked up to them.

"Dan, I'm glad you're here to support Jim," Hank said.

Dan smiled. "I couldn't let Montana's best county sheriff be out of commission. He's got an election in a few months."

Jim shook his head. "Dan, I'm not running."

Dan scoffed. "Like hell you're not."

Jim said, "Anyway, I'm on administrative leave due to the shooting and won't be allowed back until I pass a psych exam. I was isolated, gave my statement, and Rocky verified that my emotional and physical wellbeing are intact. That is, except for this." Jim raised his bandaged left hand.

Hank took the conversation into another direction and demanded, "Jim, tell me what occurred here. Aronowitz filled me in on some of it but I want your account of what happened."

Jim responded, "We were preparing Mister Driver for transport to Taylor when he was struck by a bullet fired from the third floor window of the brewery across the street."

Hank asked, "What happened next?"

"Detective Aronowitz, a few of his officers, and I ran toward the building. We assessed the situation, secured the perimeter of the building, and its first floor. Detective Aronowitz and I went up to the second floor. He was sure that the shooter was still on the third floor so he tasked me to guard the hallway and he went up the stairs to investigate. I then realized that the suspect was likely on the second floor. I went in and was pinned down by gunfire. Aronowitz joined me and the suspect caught me in the face with the butt of his rifle."

Hank said, "Yeah, I see that bloody gauze against your cheek. Let me see what it really looks like." When Jim lifted a corner of the gauze bandage from his face, Hank continued, "What a nasty looking cut and bruise on your cheek. What happened to your hand?" Hank asked.

"I tackled the suspect and had my gun trained on him. I was distracted by the officers in the stairwell when the suspect drew a small caliber handgun from, I dunno, his pocket or waistband and shot me. We exchanged point blank fire. He probably died instantly."

Hank said, "I would say that seems correct. The body's still upstairs. The Mallory Police are examining the scene. When they're done then Leon and I get our turn up there."

Dan offered, "Sounds like the guy wanted to end it right there."

Hank said, "Leave the forensics to me. Detective Aronowitz said the suspect's name is Lester Throckmorton."

"What can you tell me about him?" Jim asked.

Hank shook his head. "He's a delivery driver for Howard Lake Brewery but get this. Detective Aronowitz said that back in the day the man was a physician serving on the HMS Ledbury."

"A doctor?" Dan asked.

Hank turned to Dan and continued, "Yeah. While his ship was in port after the Falklands War in '82, he came under suspicion for raping a local Argentinean woman. There was no proof and the woman didn't want to get involved but upon mutual agreement he was dismissed from the Royal Marines with disgrace."

"Damn fool," Dan said.

Jim asked, "Tell me how he surfaced in Montana?"

Hank turned to Jim and replied, "He left England and headed for California. After a couple of years he settled in Montana. He moved to Mallory a few years ago. Additional research turned up that he was a convicted felon."

"A felon?" Dan asked. "Of all the bad news that flushes downstream from Mallory, I hadn't heard about this guy."

Hank replied, "I was told the community leaders wanted it hushed up. With all the rumors of missing women their intent was to limit the fallout. If more people knew Throckmorton was living in their midst that would have been the last straw. He was a model citizen since he moved here, that is, before this."

"What was this suspect in jail for?" Jim asked.

Hank said, "Before he moved to Mallory, he lived in Great Falls. They say back then he attacked a sixteen year-old at knifepoint when she was home babysitting her infant brother."

Jim shook his head. "That's troubling."

Hank continued, "They say she put up a good fight but he cut her up pretty bad. There was blood in the living room and in the bedroom where he raped her. Then he kidnapped her and took her to his place and kept her in the basement for almost two months before she was able to escape. The state tried to convict him of kidnapping and rape but the girl refused to testify. She said she fell in love with him after he took care of her medical wounds and that they had continuous consensual sex. They could only convict him of the lesser charges of aggravated assault in the third degree, a Class C felony, and risk of injury for the infant he left behind. He spent four years in Deer Lodge where they gave him the nickname, Lester the Molester. He was released in 1992 and moved to Wolf Point before arriving in Mallory. We'll be performing autopsies on both Gary Driver and Mister Throckmorton in the coming weeks."

Jim shook his head. "I don't know...I don't think this dead suspect is responsible for the missing women. He likely killed Gary Driver and shot at me but until someone proves to me that this suspect kidnapped and harmed Janice Driver and Louise Leonard, I'm not buying it."

331

Hank nodded. "Jim, I understand how you feel. But we do have motive. Your daughter heard of Gary Driver's murder and called my office. She told me of a conversation she had with an anonymous source that Throckmorton knew Janice Driver, had a romantic interest in her, but was continuously rebuffed by her."

"Who's this anonymous source?" Jim asked as he gazed back at Alma Rose in Dan's SUV.

Hank continued, "The intent of the source is to remain anonymous. But let's put two and two together. I suspect that Throckmorton killed Janice Driver because if he couldn't have her then no one could. If we make that assumption, then we can take another leap and say that Throckmorton may have been convinced Janice Driver told her husband about him. If so, then Throckmorton may have believed the best way to keep the Mallory Police from considering him the suspect in Janice Driver's disappearance, even if he was an innocent party, was to eliminate Gary Driver as a witness."

Jim glared at Hank. "That's a lot of assumptions."

Hank replied, "Until we perform additional investigating, this is simply a starting point."

"What about Louise Leonard?" Jim asked.

Hank replied, "We'll look at the cases of both women. If there's a connection we'll find it. For now we'll simply assume that at the least, Throckmorton had something to do with the Janice Driver case."

"What do you think Dan?" Jim asked. "You've been sheriff in these parts a lot longer than I have. What do you sense is going on here? Is Throckmorton the lone suspect in these kidnappings or did he have an accomplice or is there someone else that we should be looking at altogether?"

Dan clenched his teeth, shook his head, and then said, "It's hard to tell. Throckmorton could be our suspect. The evidence seems to fit but we need to finish the investigation. One thing I will tell you is that the suspect in Louise Leonard's murder..."

"Not murder, a disappearance," Hank said.

Dan replied, "The suspect in the...uh, disappearance used titanium spikes embedded at an angle in a heavy metal bar to disable the patrol car. Officer Nilsen had no chance. The second his car ran over the spikes, the tires were in pieces and his car ran off the road."

"Do we have any information on where the suspect purchased that stop stick?" Jim asked.

Dan replied, "Not a purchase, it was a homemade stop stick. Hell, even though it was blacker than the inside of a cow that night, Officer Nilsen found it on the dirt road right in front of Louise Leonard's driveway."

"What's the point?" Hank asked.

Dan said, "We might be looking at someone who's a welder or has access to a machine shop."

"Any prints?" Hank asked.

Dan said, "The stop stick is with the Spaulding PD. They said it was clean."

Jim's peripheral vision caught Alma Rose's stare through the driver's side backseat window of Dan's SUV. Dan and Hank spoke to Jim but their voices seemed subdued and their fleeting words appeared to float on the warm summer breeze in Mallory.

But Alma Rose's thoughts were almost plain as day to Jim. He sensed her apology for using Janice Driver's talking stick but he also knew of something else. Jim felt the duality of Alma Rose's heartfelt expression of love and her dark apprehension of what was still to come. He heard her thoughts speak to him, "Dad it's not over."

Then Jim awoke from his reverie to the touch of Hank's hand on his right arm.

"Jim are you okay? Did you hear anything I said?" Hank asked.

Jim nodded and said, "Yes but I'm holding off on my assumptions until I gather all the evidence."

Hank replied. "Jim, let it go. Lester Throckmorton's dead. We've got our man. It's over."

·73·

It was Monday, August 18th when Jim convinced Kate to see her doctor. Kate hadn't been feeling well for more than a week and Jim attributed it to worry over his safety. Jim also knew that an upcoming meeting with Alma Rose's birth mother, Shoshanna Pepper Johnson preyed on Kate's mind. Jim was also concerned of the possibility that Kate may be on the verge of a sudden relapse of the heart ailment that Alma Rose miraculously cured Kate of a few years ago.

Jim was still on administrative leave and drove Kate to Missoula for an appointment with Doctor Donnelly at the University of Montana's Health Unit. Jim followed Kate inside the doctor's office.

After the usual blood pressure checks and examination of Kate's lung functions were measured, Doctor Donnelly asked Kate, "Everything seems normal. I'll order a blood panel."

Kate spoke first, "Doctor, could this be a recurrence of my previous illness?"

"No," Doctor Donnelly said. Then he turned to Jim. "Can you wait outside while I give Kate a thorough exam?"

Despite Jim's puzzled look on his face, he said to Kate, "I'll be in the waiting room. If you need me, just ask."

Jim sat for what seemed like hours. He remembered the downward spiral that Kate suffered at the hands of Mayor Hamilton Jackson whose actions almost killed Kate. Thoughts of strangling Hamilton always seemed to creep into Jim's mind, especially in his dreams. Then the door to the interior offices opened and Doctor Donnelly stepped out.

Jim first noticed Doctor Donnelly stare at him. Then he heard the dreaded question, "Jim, can you come here please?"

Jim got up from his seat. He followed the doctor into the examination room and sat in a chair next to Kate.

"What's this all about?" Jim asked. "Is Kate all right?"

Doctor Donnelly glanced at Kate. "Tell him."

Jim braced himself for unfortunate news. Then he heard the fleeting words he thought he would never hear again.

Kate said, "I'm pregnant."

To Jim, the room seemed to expand to an infinite height and depth. He felt time stop. There was not a sound in the room except for the buzz from the florescent lights. Jim stared at Doctor Donnelly and then at Kate. "How?" he asked.

Doctor Donnelly shrugged his shoulders and then smiled. "I have no idea. It's beyond my medical knowledge how Kate miscarried and suffered extensive damage to her internal organs a few years back but is now in fact pregnant."

Jim hugged Kate and kissed her. As he embraced her and with a measure of caution, Jim turned to Doctor Donnelly and asked, "Can you ensure that everything will be all right?"

Doctor Donnelly nodded. "Because of Kate's medical history we'll monitor her very closely. I'll provide a strict diet that I want her to follow and supplements that will keep her body in balance. I will do everything I can to ensure that all goes well. We will not lose these babies."

Jim gave Kate another kiss and then turned to stare at Doctor Donnelly. "I'm sorry. I thought I heard you say…babies?"

Doctor Donnelly smiled. "Yes, Kate is carrying twins."

Jim wiped away Kate's tears as he hugged her. He then remembered that 4th of July weekend at his sister's trailer on the Rez and how secretive Alma Rose was with her towel and canvas bag. Jim saw firsthand the extensive powers of Janice Driver's talking stick. He surmised that with Alma Rose's help, or better yet due to her compassion, something special happened. But perhaps the spirit of Janice Driver, who suffered the loss of her only mortal child, was in a blessing mood and by giving back twofold, a miracle of the talking stick had occurred.

But something else gnawed away at Jim's soul, something unresolved, something much older than the recent missing persons. It was pure evil and Jim knew it would affect him and his family. He felt the compelling urge to wipe his sweaty hands, to rid it of a malevolent filth. Something or someone he recently came into contact with was perched and waiting to strike again.

·74·

Later that same day on the Crow Reservation, Sarah Whispers Two Elk had been feeling much better. Cousin Becca just left for the day and Sarah Whispers was preparing her dinner. The TV was on in anticipation of the 6 p.m. news when Sarah Whispers heard a vehicle drive up to her trailer on her rural and remote homesite. It took her some time to maneuver the walker over to the kitchen window. She looked outside and stared at a dark van that was parked out front.

"Now who can that be?" she asked herself.

Sarah Whispers let go of the walker and used the kitchen countertop to steady herself over to the kitchen door. She opened the door only an inch and felt the full force of the door shoved into her face. She fell backwards and onto the floor. When she looked up, she noticed a person dressed all in black, mechanic coveralls, gloves, booties, and a balaclava over his head. He held a large Bowie knife in his right hand.

Sarah Whispers asked, "What do you want?"

The man grabbed her telephone. Sarah expected the man to rip it out of the wall, but instead he rifled through her contact list, and speed dialed a certain number.

When the party on the other end answered, the man put the phone on speaker.

"Sarah Whispers, it's Jim. What's up?"

"Jim," Sarah Whispers screamed.

The man placed the back of his hand over his mouth and spoke in a loud, deep voice, "Buchanan, you piece of shit. Stay out of my work."

"Who is this?" Jim asked.

"You know who this is. I got rid of Janice Driver, Louise Leonard, and quite a few others."

"Are you at my sister's house?"

"Yeah, you want me to put her on?" The man handed the pone to Sarah Whispers who was still lying on the kitchen floor.

Jim asked, "Sarah Whispers, are you all right?"

She screamed into the phone, "Little Hawk, help me, please call Preacher."

The man ripped the phone from Sarah Whispers' hand and said to Jim, "If you're thinking of placing a call with another phone or if you already did, I'm going to make this quick. I want you and your nosey little daughter to stop interfering with my business."

"I won't call anyone if you just leave my sister alone," Jim pleaded.

The man laughed and then said, "I'm going to leave your sister with a souvenir just like the one I gave Althea Bond a few years back. If you decide to do anything stupid, I'll track down your daughter and do the same to her. You got that or do you want me to repeat it?"

There was hesitation on the other end and then Jim spoke, "I understand but if you cut my sister, I'll hunt you down."

The man screamed, "Wrong fuckin' answer."

"All right, do you want money? Jim asked. "I can get you money."

"I don't want no money, I got all the fuckin' money I need." The man waved the knife at the phone. "I told you, I got a job to do and there ain't nothing you can do to stop me. So stay the fuck out of my way. Call the police after I hang up."

Sarah Whispers huddled on the floor between the table and kitchen cabinets while she stared at the man as he hung up the phone.

She used her elbows to push herself further back into the kitchen. "Leave me alone," she screamed.

When the man approached her, Sarah Whispers kicked at him.

"So we're going to play that game, are we?" the man asked.

He stepped around the table and approached Sarah Whispers from behind. She tried to drag herself away but he caught her by the back of her collar. He wrapped his arm around her neck and yanked her toward him. He dropped his arm around her chest, took the knife and sliced it across her throat. Not a deep cut but enough of a slash that it drew blood from ear to ear.

When Sarah Whispers reached for her neck with both hands, the man reared back and slugged her in her face. Sarah Whispers fell into unconsciousness.

The man grabbed the phone in his gloved hand and dialed 911. "Sarah Whispers trailer on the Crow Reservation. Nonfatal but serious knife wound, possible concussion. Send EMTs right away, she's alone, the front door will be open." The man hung up the phone.

He grabbed a pillow from the living room and placed it under Sarah Whispers' head. Then he stepped outside, climbed into his van, placed the bloody Bowie knife on the floor near the passenger seat, and drove off.

*** END ***

Made in the USA
Middletown, DE
10 August 2021